Praise for *Behind the Red Door*

"Harrowing... Collins plays her cards carefully to maximize suspense."
—*Publishers Weekly*

"*Behind the Red Door* isn't just a gripping, finely tuned thriller; it's a masterful meditation on fear. I was hooked from the first page."
—Mindy Mejia, author of *Strike Me Down*

"Megan Collins is the master of emotionally resonant, deeply personal suspense fiction, where the small details are just as chilling as the dramatic turns. *Behind the Red Door* is gripping and gorgeously written, and, like her stellar debut, *The Winter Sister*, I'm certain this book will haunt me for years to come."

—Layne Fargo, author of *Temper*

"An absorbing psychological thriller."

—*Booklist*

"Taut, provocative, disturbing—Megan Collins's sophomore novel is more than a thriller; it's a dark and deeply compelling examination of the knife's edge between trust and fear. With muscular prose and richly wrought characters, *Behind the Red Door* grabbed me, startled me, and didn't let go until I'd torn through every chilling word."
—Andrea Bartz, author of *The Lost Night*
and *The Herd*

"Haunting and compelling."

—*The Strand*

behind
the red door

Also by Megan Collins

The Winter Sister

behind
the red door

A Novel

MEGAN COLLINS

ATRIA PAPERBACK

New York London Toronto Sydney New Delhi

An Imprint of Simon & Schuster, Inc.
1230 Avenue of the Americas
New York, NY 10020

First Atria Paperback edition May 2021

ATRIA PAPERBACK and colophon are trademarks of Simon & Schuster, Inc.

For information about special discounts for bulk purchases, please contact Simon & Schuster Special Sales at 1-866-506-1949 or business@simonandschuster.com.

The Simon & Schuster Speakers Bureau can bring authors to your live event. For more information or to book an event, contact the Simon & Schuster Speakers Bureau at 1-866-248-3049 or visit our website at www.simonspeakers.com.

Interior design by A. Kathryn Barrett

Manufactured in the United States of America

1 3 5 7 9 10 8 6 4 2

Library of Congress Cataloging-in-Publication Data
Names: Collins, Megan, 1984- author.
Title: Behind the red door / Megan Collins.
Description: First Atria Books hardcover edition. | New York : Atria Books, 2020.
Identifiers: LCCN 2019043818 (print) | LCCN 2019043819 (ebook) | ISBN 9781982130398 (hardcover) | ISBN 9781982130404 (trade paperback) | ISBN 9781982130411 (ebook)
Subjects: LCSH: Missing persons—Fiction. | GSAFD: Suspense fiction.
Classification: LCC PS3603.O454463 B44 2020 (print) | LCC PS3603.O454463 (ebook) | DDC 813/.6—dc23
LC record available at https://lccn.loc.gov/2019043818
LC ebook record available at https://lccn.loc.gov/2019043819

ISBN 978-1-9821-3039-8
ISBN 978-1-9821-3040-4 (pbk)
ISBN 978-1-9821-3041-1 (ebook)

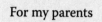
For my parents

behind
the red door

one

Now that it's summer, it's not my job to protect the children. I have finished the follow-ups on the girl who submitted a suicide note for her English essay. I have closed the file on the boy who came to school with rope burns on his neck. The suicide note was written with pink Magic Marker. The burns were from a jump rope that the teenage stepbrother wrapped around the boy like a scarf, just before he squeezed.

The children don't stop needing protection, but every job has a contract, and mine stipulates that from June to September, I am to forget everything I've witnessed, to not think of what else that girl might be writing, how else that boy might be marked. I am to relax on the couch in our Kendall Square loft and sip the chardonnay that Eric has handed me. I am to scroll through my phone while my husband cooks our dinner and the news drones on in the background.

I should be doing my homework. Fresh off an appointment with Dr. Lockwood, I've been told to make a list of anxiety triggers. She thinks if I get them down on paper, I'll get them out of my head. But on paper, the words growl at me, take on body and breath. *Our upstairs neighbors' footsteps. My recurring nightmare. The guy on the T who coughed without covering his mouth.* I filled up a third of the page before I had to throw the list away, my throat tight.

I don't think my new prescription is working.

"Do you want tomatoes in this?" Eric asks, but I'm looking at a Facebook post from one of my colleagues, the other social worker with whom I share an office. She's smiling on the beach, her skin glowing, and I'm wincing at the burn I'm sure she'll get.

"Fern?" Eric says. "Tomatoes?"

I look up. He's wearing the stethoscope apron I bought him. It was supposed to be cute and stupid and funny, but from here, it looks like a snake is slithering along his chest.

"Whatever you want," I answer.

"No, whatever *you* want. This could be your last real meal for days. With Ted, it'll just be takeout and frozen dinners."

"I think I saw him cook some rice once."

"Was it instant?"

"Might've been."

Eric pinches his lips together, then nods. "We'll do tomatoes."

He's always like this. Indignant about my parents. When you have a mother and father like he does—who leaned across the dinner table to kiss each other, who took Eric and his four siblings to Disney World every summer, who treated each of their kids' birthdays like a national holiday—it's hard to feel warm toward parents like Ted and Mara.

He doesn't think I should go to New Hampshire tomorrow. Ever since Ted called me last week asking for my help in packing up the house, Eric's been in a mood. He thinks I'm too kind to my father, too "How high?" when he says "Jump"—and he's sometimes right. But when it comes to Ted, there are certain things I can't say no to.

After a few minutes, Eric turns off the stove, plates our meals, and brings over two steaming dishes of pasta. During the school year, we eat at the table so I can shovel food into my mouth while writing case reports on my laptop. But it's summer now and I'm not allowed to bring my work home with me anymore, so we eat in front of the TV, perched on the edge of the couch.

Eric loves to watch the news, so we're watching the local news. It's our trade-off for him doing the cooking. When I cook, we watch game shows. I find the rhythm of them soothing. The rules are laid out right at the beginning. Somebody always wins. When Eric cooks, I play it cool so he can have what he wants, but truthfully, I prefer to avoid the news. I don't need more things to add to my list. *E. coli outbreak. Carjackings. A rare disease that killed a woman my age.* If I tell Eric I'm convinced I'll develop this same disease, I know what he'll say: *You will not. It's extremely rare.* As a doctor, the word *rare* means something different to him than it does to me. To me, it means "possible."

"Oh, this is crazy. Have you heard about this?" Eric increases the volume on the TV. I look up from my pasta to see a picture of a woman on the screen. Next they show footage of a house on an unpaved road, followed by a shot of police officers traipsing through a forest with German shepherds. I scratch an itch on my wrist.

"Sullivan was first reported missing ten days ago by her wife, Rita Diaz," the reporter says in a voiceover. "Diaz told police that Sullivan left for her usual morning walk around five thirty a.m. on June seventh and did not return."

"Where's this?" I ask. The area looks heavily wooded, not like you'd find around here.

"Maine," Eric says.

"Maine? Why are they talking about it in Boston?"

He glances at me. "It's Astrid Sullivan."

"Who?"

The reporter continues: "The timing of Sullivan's disappearance— almost exactly twenty years since her abduction from a small New Hampshire town on June 24, 2000—has residents of Ridgeway concerned that this is the work of Sullivan's original abductor, who was never caught."

I scratch my wrist again as a new photo appears on the screen. It's the same woman as before, evident by her mane of curly red hair, only she's much younger. A teenager. I set my plate on the coffee table and lean forward. There's something about the freckles sprayed like splatter paint across the girl's nose that makes me squint at the TV.

"Hold on." I reach for the remote and press pause. The screen freezes right as the picture enlarges to fill the frame. The girl has a wide face with high cheekbones, a closed-lipped smile that borders on a smirk. Her freckles fan out onto her cheeks, and there's a rogue one below the arch of her left eyebrow that's darker than the rest.

"I think I know her," I say.

Eric looks at me as his mouth closes around his fork. "Well yeah," he says, chewing. "It's Astrid Sullivan."

"You keep saying that. But who is she?"

His brow furrows. "Are you serious? She's that girl who was kidnapped twenty years ago."

"They said that. But why would I know who she is?"

"Everyone knows her. It was national news."

"Why?"

Eric shakes his head a little. "You really don't remember?"

"Twenty years ago, I was only twelve," I remind him.

"And I was thirteen," he says, "but I still remember."

"Well, I didn't have TV growing up. You know Ted and Mara."

He shrugs. "Still. It happened in your state. Down in Virginia, everyone was talking about it, so I can't imagine that Cedar somehow missed the story."

I stare at the girl's face, trying to remember where I've seen her before. It feels like trying to remember a dream. "What *is* the story?" I ask.

Eric sets his plate beside mine. As he speaks, he kneads my back with his knuckles. It's a gesture I usually love, but the itch on my wrist demands so much attention, I can hardly feel his hand.

"She was missing for weeks," he says. "She was fourteen, I think, and she disappeared during some party her parents were having. The front yard was supposedly packed with people—but nobody saw what happened to her. And then, like a month later, they found her on the side of the road a couple blocks from her house. She was blindfolded and drugged and said she'd been kept in a basement that whole time by some guy in a mask."

Girls who disappear. Kidnappers. Masks.

My scratching reminds me of the crickets in Cedar. Growing up, I would listen to them through my window screen at night, marveling at how their rhythm was the same as Ted's when he clawed at his psoriasis. I have not inherited my father's skin condition, but sometimes I itch.

"And this happened in New Hampshire?" I ask.

"Yeah, hang on." Eric grabs his phone, opens an app, and types. "This says it was Foster, New Hampshire, which is . . ." He pulls up a map and zooms in. "Maybe forty-five miles from Cedar?"

Astrid's eyes stare out at me from the TV. They're green like the oak leaves that hem in my childhood home, and the longer I look at them, the more I feel the need to look away.

"I've never heard about any of this," I say, "but I really think I know her from somewhere."

Eric pulls his plate back onto his lap, takes a bite of tomato and feta. "Her face was all over the newspapers. There's no way you could have missed it. Everyone was obsessed with the story since her reappearance was so weird. Oh—also . . ." He eats another forkful before continuing. "She just had a memoir come out, so she's been doing a bunch of publicity for it. I think she was on *Good Morning America* recently."

I don't remind him that, until a couple days ago, I was still Mrs. Douglas, school social worker at Stuart Halloway Middle School, juggling meetings and home visits and paperwork. This is the first news of any kind I've watched in weeks.

I press Play on the remote, but Astrid's picture stays frozen. If the reporter wasn't speaking, I'd think the TV was still on pause.

"Oh, see?" Eric says after a moment, and the sound of his fork clanging against his plate makes me jump.

He gestures toward the screen, which has filled with a picture of Astrid's book. *Behind the Red Door: A Memoir.* On the cover, a bare bulb illuminates a door the color of rashes, of sunburns, of things that must be scratched. The reporter mentions the book's recent spike in sales, how it's zoomed up all the bestseller lists since news first broke about Astrid's disappearance.

"Some readers of the memoir are speculating that it was the book's publication that drew Sullivan's original kidnapper out of hiding. Some even say he might have used the memoir to track her down and take her for a second time. Those close to Sullivan, however, say these theories are unhelpful distractions."

The shot switches to a woman with dark hair speaking to a microphone held in front of her face. *Rita Diaz, wife of Astrid Sullivan*, reads a bar across the bottom of the screen.

"I appreciate that people have taken an interest in my wife's book," Rita says, her forehead creased, her hair in a messy bun. "But right now, these conspiracy theories aren't helping us find her. I know, to many people, the *why* of her disappearance is important, but honestly, all I care about is the *where*. And the *when* she will return. So if you have any information to share that might help us find her, please—don't go on Reddit or Twitter or Facebook; go to the police."

Right before the news moves on to the next story, the station shows a phone number for police in Ridgeway, Maine, along with another recent picture of Astrid. There are lines around her eyes that weren't in her photo as a teenager. Her freckles aren't as vivid, but I can still see the one beneath the arch of her eyebrow that sits like a stray punctuation mark. Staring at it, I feel a pinch in my throat, as if, for some reason, this single freckle belongs on my list of triggers. It makes me certain—with a level of conviction I can't explain—that I know her. And not just know her. Not just seen her picture in a newspaper. I've *met* her. But when? But where?

"Hey, what's this?" Eric asks. "What happened?"

I look down to where he's pointing. My wrist is slashed with thick stripes of pink. I've scratched so hard that I'm bleeding, the beads of red perforating my skin.

———

The sheets scrape against my Band-Aid as we get into bed. The bleeding stopped hours ago, but Eric did such a good job patching me up that I'm reluctant to peel off his handiwork. The bandage is clean and smooth and perfectly square. Looking at it soothes me.

Eric reaches for me before I've even shut off the bedside lamp. His hand rests on my hip, then inches upward, his fingers spidering along my ribs. I turn to him, nuzzle my face against his neck.

"You're insatiable," I say.

"Can't help it, Bird."

I kiss his Adam's apple. It's been six years, and I still love that nickname. He's been calling me Bird since the night we met, when he misheard my name at a noisy Harvard Square bar. It stuck because it suits me: sparrow-brown hair, a slightly hooked nose, bony and petite (so small, in fact, that from behind, I sometimes get confused for students at school). But what I love most about *Bird* is how, every time he says it, I'm reminded why I decided to go out with him in the first place. The reason I thought, like I never had about anyone before, *I could marry this guy*.

I'd been standing with him at the bar, the two of us talking so long I didn't notice my friend getting sick at one of the tables. When she stumbled past us, puking, I lurched forward to help her toward the door. Eric grabbed a napkin off the bar and followed. When we got outside, he wiped at the vomit in her hair. Never mind that she was a stranger to him. Never mind that the puke was clotted with chunks of olive from her martini. He stepped right in, a hero with a bar napkin. Afterward, when I thanked him, he said, *Of course, Bird*, shrugging it off like it was nothing. But it was the kindest thing I'd ever seen.

"Do you want to try one more time before you go?" he asks now.

I stiffen, and he pulls me closer, reading the tension in my body as desire. "I'm not even ovulating anymore," I tell him.

When those circled days passed on my calendar this month, I let out a breath that took a long time to exhale.

"We can only have sex when you're ovulating?" He's kissing me as he says it, slowly and teasingly, his words fluttering against my mouth. "It can't be because I'm going to miss you?"

I arch my neck as he slides his lips toward my collarbone. "Of course not," I breathe. "You just said 'try,' so."

I've been off the pill for three months now. I want to make my husband happy. He spends his days caring for other people's children—same as me, I guess—and when his patients' parents ask if he has kids of his own, I know it hurts when he has to say no. That's where we're not the same. When I do home visits, and the parents get defensive, ask me if I know from personal experience how hard it is to raise a child, I feel momentarily weightless as I get to shake my head no.

I like kids. I do. Sometimes, I even get that primal, womb-stirring feeling when I see a baby. But I've witnessed so many ways that a parent can fail a child, and it seems so easy to do. Easier than being good. And then there's everything else, every little threat that hisses in the air or coils into genetic code, waiting to strike. I can't imagine how much I'll have to add to my list if I ever become pregnant. *SIDS, heart defects, car seats improperly installed. Girls who disappear. Kidnappers who catch and release, then catch again.* My hands grow slick on Eric's skin just thinking about it.

I keep hoping I'll get infected by his enthusiasm, come down with baby fever. But so far, I still react to my period each month as if it's a miracle.

"Hey," Eric says. "Bird." He moves back a little to meet my eyes. "If you're not into this, we don't have to do it."

For a moment, I think he's talking about having a baby. Then he takes his hand off my breast.

"No, I am," I say. "I'm just a little distracted."

"Yeah? What's going on?"

I want to make my husband happy. I don't like to burden him with the lists that scroll through my mind. I know he'd be sweet, talk me through each anxiety until he's sure his logic has tamed it. But I'd still feel it clawing inside me, still hear its nails skittering across my skull, and even Eric has a limit to his patience.

I could throw him off the scent, say that I'm dreading my trip to New Hampshire. He'd appreciate that. But the truth is, I'm looking forward to going home. Ted is retired now, and sometimes, I find myself mouthing that word—*retired*—because it feels as good as it does impossible. I had to stalk the Psychology Department's Facebook page, scour the pictures labeled "Professor Brierley's Farewell Reception," to believe it was true. He finished up his final semester last month, and without the pressure to publish or perish—"jump through hoops or jump into the grave," he always says—things might actually be different. That's why I agreed to help him, even though Eric keeps saying he doesn't deserve it. When Ted called last week to tell me he's moving to Florida, he said, "Now that I'm free from the tyranny of academia, I want to be equally free from the tyranny of snow." Then he said, "I need you, Fern."

I had to ask him to repeat it. And when he did, I tried to savor it. Ted has never needed me, not outside the context of his Experiments, anyway, so it seems his retirement has already changed him, made him think twice about his daughter, see that she can offer him something his work cannot. Without Ted's compulsive need to compete with the superstars of his field, this time won't be like all the others. This time, he won't keep typing his ideas as I clutch my stomach, suffering from what turns out to be appendicitis. He won't retreat to his office as soon as I return from the hospital, wearing a bandage I'll struggle to change on my own. He won't imply that I'm wasting his time simply by wanting his care.

To Eric, stories like these are enough to warrant me never going home again. He calls what I went through child neglect. But I've seen true neglect, gone to fly-infested houses where parents are passed out with needles in their arms, a diapered five-year-old eating cat food while his sister cries in the nurse's office at school. Whatever I endured with Ted and Mara—it's miles away from that. No one from Cedar Public Schools or child services ever came to our house.

"Wow, you really *are* distracted," Eric says now. "Is everything okay?"

I have to say something, but everything's a minefield. I look at the Band-Aid on my wrist, and it's as if I can hear my wound whispering beneath it. After Eric patched me up, I read the Wikipedia page for

Astrid Sullivan. It did nothing to clarify where I've met her before, but I've added *sedatives* and *blindfolds* to my list.

"I keep thinking about that woman," I finally say. "Astrid."

Eric stretches out his arm so I can burrow into him. "Yeah, it's crazy," he says. "But I'm sure they'll find her soon."

"You don't know that."

"No. I don't. But they found her last time."

Only because whoever took her brought her back. Dragged her from the basement where he'd kept her. Tied a black sash around her eyes, plunged a syringe into her veins, left her on the side of the road like trash. I shiver against Eric, and he rubs the goose bumps flecking my arm.

"There weren't any witnesses, right?" I ask. "Twenty years ago?"

"To her kidnapping? No. That was the whole problem."

"And no one saw who brought her back?"

"No. She just—reappeared," he says.

I shake my head against his chest. "I feel like . . ."

He tucks my hair behind my ear, then massages my scalp. "Feel like what?"

"Like I've seen her before. In person. Like I actually *knew* her."

Eric's hand goes still. "She lived almost fifty miles away, Bird. Have you ever even been to Foster?"

"I don't know," I say. "Maybe. But—"

"Don't you think you'd remember if someone you knew was kidnapped?"

"Not if I didn't *know* she got kidnapped." When Eric doesn't respond right away, I keep going. "I told you, I have no memory of that story. So if I knew her but didn't—or even if I did—hear about the kidnapping, maybe it . . . I've had students who—you know, there's some trauma or they find out about something—and they can't even—"

"Fern." He uses my real name because he wants to make sure I'm paying attention.

"What?"

"You're spiraling."

This is what he says whenever my thoughts get away from me. I picture a marble shooting through an endlessly curving slide, corkscrewing down and down along a tube so smooth there isn't any friction to stop it. Dr. Lockwood has offered me another metaphor. "Think of your brain as a record," she's said. "Sometimes the needle gets stuck, and the record begins to skip. It keeps coming back to this one little nanosecond of a song, plays it over and over again. That, right there, is your anxiety. It's telling you that you *have* to stay on this thought. But it's a lie. You can actually train yourself to move the needle, set it on top of another thought altogether and keep on going."

Sometimes these images help. Sometimes I can picture myself plucking the marble from the slide, the needle from the record, and I can carry on, calmer than before. Other times, like right now, my nerves still feel like wires buzzing with electricity.

"You're right," I say to Eric. It's our last night together for at least a week. I don't want to ruin it by spiraling. "I'm sorry."

"You don't have to be sorry. I know the news kind of freaked you out. But like I said, her picture's been everywhere. You must have seen it at some point."

I tilt my face toward his, kiss his bottom lip. "I know. You're right," I say again. *Girls who disappear. Girls who can't remember.* "Let's get back to what we were doing before, okay?"

"Yeah?" He smiles a little, his fingers skimming my skin. "How much before?"

I put my hand on his cheek, feel the dark stubble he'll shave off in the morning. Then I cup the back of his neck and pull him so close that, as we kiss, our bodies are practically seamless. I'm certain that if I leave even an inch of space, the woman from the news will slip between us.

———

The girl has no face.

Where her eyes and nose and mouth should be, there is only skin. A flat plane of flesh stretched tight as a mask.

Bent at the waist at a forty-five-degree angle, her body looks crooked. Not wholly human. Her head is tilted down, toward my feet. She stretches out her arms. Lurches and lurches toward me.

Her fingers twitch as she reaches out, trying to grab or scratch or gouge me. She's so close, I can almost feel her nails piercing my skin.

But now, hunched over, she stops. Lifts her head—slowly, agonizingly—toward mine. And as I stare at her, bracing myself for that grotesque mask of skin, I open my mouth to scream.

I shoot upward in bed, gulping for air in the dark. My hair is stuck to my neck, my lips trembling, the sheets bunched in my fists.

The nightmare is back. The same one I've been having since I was a kid, once every few months.

I look over at Eric, who hasn't stirred. Sometimes he sleeps right through it, especially when the whir of the AC drowns out the sharpest of my gasps.

My heart knocks hard, and I slip out of bed, head to the bathroom. I've learned how to drag myself from the powerful suction of that dream: splash water on my face, stand beneath the light, stare into the sink until reality clicks into place.

But something is different this time. Water drips from my chin, I see it swirl away, but my heart is still pounding.

What is it? What is it?

I go against instinct, allow myself to reel the nightmare back in. I play it again, starting at the tips of her fingers as they come so close. Her hands are the same, trying to grasp me. Her arms are the same, extending with urgency. Her body is bent as it always is. But now as the face tilts up—I have to cover my mouth so I don't cry out.

Where there was skin, there are eyes, green as summer leaves. A nose dotted with freckles. A mouth forming words I can't hear. And her hair, always dim and unremarkable, is suddenly bright as fire.

Moments pass. Maybe minutes. After the initial shock of it, I relax. I'm only dreaming of Astrid Sullivan because I saw her on TV, because my thoughts were tangled up with her right before bed. That's what Eric would say. Dr. Lockwood, too.

But I look at my fingers. They're gripping the lip of the sink, knuckles white. My arm is taut, the bandage on my wrist peeled back. As if I've been scratching in my sleep. As if my body knows something my mind hasn't caught up to yet.

I force myself to picture it again. And again and again, until I'm sure of what I'm seeing. Those hands—empty. Beseeching. Open as wide as a mouth gasping for air. That face—Astrid's. And with her features filled in, I see her actions differently, too. She wasn't trying to hurt me, like I've always thought. She was asking—no, begging—for help. Because as I play back the images in my head, recall her moon-wide eyes, I see it so clearly: the girl isn't terrifying; she's terrified.

My jaw falls slack. The itch on my wrist flares.

I watch the questions solidify on my face, reflected in the mirror in front of me. The nightmare that's haunted me for so many years—what if it hasn't been a nightmare at all? Hasn't even been a dream?

What if, all this time, all these nights, it's actually been a memory?

Excerpt from Prologue of
Behind the Red Door: A Memoir **by Astrid Sullivan**

You think you know the story. You've seen the news cover-
age, the magazine articles, the true crime episodes dedicated
to the Astrid Sullivan Case. You've read about the man in
the mask, the weeks I spent locked in a basement—gray and
dim but for its bright red door. You've heard about the curb
I was left on, two blocks from my family's home in Foster,
New Hampshire.

There are many things you don't know, details the
police didn't release and urged me not to speak of. "We
always withhold some key information," they explained.
Something about it being easier to find and interrogate sus-
pects. Something about maintaining the integrity of the investigation. For a long time, I played by those rules, trusting
what they told me, that justice is slow but inevitable.

But now, it's been two decades, more than half my life.
I've stopped believing that the man who took me will ever
be caught. In a way, I've stopped believing in the police altogether. So this is my story now, the way it always should
have been.

Here are some things you don't know: the type of mask
he wore, his clothes, the words we spoke. I know these
things matter to you. Reporters have been asking me about
them for years. But here's what matters to me: what I did
to make myself vulnerable; what I did in that basement to

survive; what I still want to say to the girl who saw the man who took me.

Because, yes, there was such a girl. I know the police have told you there weren't any witnesses. But there was one. She was ten, maybe eleven years old.

When the police came to question me, I begged them to find her, search every house in America if that's what it took. She knew what happened. She saw a feature of the man that I never did. But they returned a few days later shaking their heads. They claimed there was no one who'd come forward fitting the description I gave them.

Not long after, I began seeing a therapist, who ended our first session by suggesting that I had imagined the girl, that I'd invented her as a way to cope with the trauma, a way to find some hope to hold on to while I endured my basement nightmare.

When I pleaded with my parents to take me seriously, to help me look for her, to help me get the answers that only she could provide, they stared at me, a skeptical sadness in their eyes that still hurts to remember.

The police wouldn't let me talk about her. "If she's real," they said, "it could jeopardize the investigation to let this go public. Think of all the crazies who would crawl out of the woodwork, claiming this girl is their daughter."

I didn't buy their reasons. *If she's real* told me everything I needed to know.

But she was there. I'd bet my life on it. My future children's lives.

She was not a coping strategy. She was not a dream. She was real: the girl who saw everything but never said a word.

Only sometimes, in my darkest hours, do I momentarily doubt this. Only sometimes, for a sliver of a second, do I think she might have been someone else the whole time—me. A ghost of my former self. A girl I still believed should be spared.

two

In the daylight, things are different. They always are.

Now that it's morning, I'm less convinced that the dream was really a memory, that it wasn't just the news story laid like a transparency over my usual nightmare, fanning the flames of my anxieties. I don't even tell Eric about it when I say good-bye to him, hugging him especially tightly before he leaves for the hospital. I already know how it will sound. I can picture him struggling to think of a word that's one step up from *spiraling*.

Even so, it's like I've walked into a spiderweb I can't wipe off, the silk of that dream sticking to my skin. As soon as Eric's gone, I curl up on the couch, stare at my suitcase by the door, allow Astrid's face and bent body and outstretched arms to muddle the space between me and the way back home to Cedar.

Sinking deeper into the cushions, I want to dismiss my thoughts as absurd. I want to believe that I can shrug them off to Dr. Lockwood at my next appointment. But my heart bangs in my chest, and suddenly I can't stop thinking about one of my students—Jackson Price—the day his little sister was taken.

The two of them had been walking home from school together when Jackson heard a loud noise—"a gigantic explosion," he claimed.

He fell to the ground at the sound, and when he got back up, his sister was gone. Vanished. As if the noise had triggered her evaporation.

That's the way he tells it, anyway. What really happened was that the kids' ex-stepfather had jumped out from between two buildings and snatched the little girl. Jackson never remembered seeing him. He only remembered a thunderous noise, powerful and loud enough to bring him to his knees.

I didn't need the police report to tell me there wasn't an explosion. When I met with Jackson, twice a week for a month after that, it was obvious: the sound was a story his mind made up, remapping the memory of that day. Our brains can do that. Especially when we're kids. They can scrub out whole people, whole experiences, leaving only a tiny trace of the truth.

So, that sticky web. That silk spun straight from a spider.

For a few minutes, I consider postponing my trip to Ted's. I can't imagine going down to my car right now, buckling my seat belt, releasing the emergency brake. *Astrid's hands finally reaching me. Astrid's hands forcing mine to turn the wheel.* But the second I think of Ted's *I need you* on the phone last week, I find I can move again. I actually jump off the couch as if its leather has burned me. I grab my keys, grab my bag. Open our loft door and let it shut behind me. Focusing on Ted's voice, the low gravelly timbre of it, I will the red-haired girl away.

All things considered, I should have outgrown my craving for Ted's attention. Dr. Lockwood and I have talked about the ways he made me ache—his gestures of dismissal, his Experiments, his obsession with other people's success, which kept him type-type-typing in his study all hours of the day. I've told her I can't hear the clack of typewriter keys without feeling nauseated, but Dr. Lockwood thinks that Ted's work methods actually have a lot to do with my "attachment" to him. She says his praise and attention during our post-Experiment interviews was so effusive that he basically trained me to excuse his long stretches of neglect. (She, too, uses this word, even though I always balk at it. I've told her about the cat-food-eating children.)

"He taught you that your reward for enduring his absence, for playing along with his Experiments, was attention," she said. "And the way he spoke to you during those interviews validated the idea that his attention was something worth wanting."

I hate to think this way—that Ted's *I need you* provoked a kind of Pavlovian response in me. But Dr. Lockwood is right about the way I felt during our interviews, how Ted's enthusiasm and encouragement flushed my body with warmth, even as something like dread prickled the back of my neck.

That prickle interested Ted, too. Dread, after all, is closely related to fear.

"Did it scare you," Dr. Lockwood once asked, "living with your father?"

My answer came quickly. "No."

"But the subject of his research was fear," she pushed. "His Experiments were all about making you feel scared."

"No. They weren't. His Experiments were about the fear *response*. He studied its triggers, its duration, things like that."

"I'm afraid I don't see the difference."

"It's— He doesn't . . . There *is* a difference, but it's hard to explain."

I wasn't lying to Dr. Lockwood. It really didn't scare me to live with Ted, not even after the worst of his Experiments, that August night I can still feel in my body whenever I recall it. Before then, Ted's Experiments had been mostly benign—driving home from a store without me, only coming back to pick me up after an hour or two had passed;

gluing a jar of garden spiders to my bedside table, despite (or because of) my arachnophobia; screaming in the kitchen with a red-soaked rag clutched to his arm, finally revealing after my seconds of panic that the red was paint, his body was woundless, the only marks on his skin were the scales of his psoriasis.

I was ten when the worst Experiment happened. Ted and Mara left one night for a rare dinner out, and the note I found in the kitchen told me they'd be back in an hour. (This is where I should have known. Ted and Mara never leave notes.) When the sun set and they hadn't returned, I stood vigil by the window, watching for their headlights. When the driveway stayed dark and carless, I thought of *collisions, murders, explosions.* I wrapped myself in an afghan and crouched under the coffee table. I piled books on the edges of the blanket to keep it firmly in place. *Shootings. Sinkholes. Choking on chicken bones.* I stared at the phone, wanting to call the police, but believing that if I did, I would doom my parents further, make real the possibilities swarming my mind. This is "magical thinking," Dr. Lockwood often reminds me.

At six the next morning, I finally gave in. *Caskets. Funerals. Orphans.* Ted and Mara never spent so long away from home. Mara stayed close to her art studio, as if leaving it was the same as abandoning a newborn, and the only time Ted ever left was to run an errand or teach his classes at Wicker.

It was definite, then: something horrible and irreversible had happened to them.

I extracted myself from my hiding spot. My hands shook as I reached for the phone, and it was then that the door burst open, Ted leaping into the house with Mara trailing behind him. Before I could react, Ted picked me up and twirled me around, his laughter thundering against my ear. I closed my eyes, savored the tightness of his grip, let the relief fill me up and up, my body buoyant as a balloon. When he set me down, I was smiling, because I still didn't get it. I actually asked, "Where were you guys?"

"We were outside!" Ted answered.

"No, I mean—where did you go after dinner?"

"Dinner? There wasn't any dinner. We were outside, Fern. Watching you!"

I tried to speak through the lump hardening in my throat. "You were here?" I asked. "The whole time?" My voice was squeaky and small.

"Of course!"

"So you were gonna . . . leave me alone, in the house . . . forever?"

"Forever?" he repeats. "No, no, an Experiment is never forever. You know I always reveal what I've been doing, always let you know what's real and what isn't. I do that for you, Fern. Because I value your participation in my work. So, come on now, let's get upstairs. I've got so many excellent notes that I need to transcribe. So many questions, too. That thing with the coffee table and the blanket? It's like you were *paralyzed*. This is wonderful, Fern. Truly sensational. We're going to have a very productive interview. Let's go!"

But I didn't follow him the way I usually did. Instead, I opened my mouth and wailed. Closed my eyes and shoved out tears. Dropped to the floor and rocked.

"Fern," Ted said. "What is this?"

I sobbed out my answer in thick gasps of words. "I thought . . . you were . . . dead!"

He smiled then. Pleased with himself. With me. "But we're not dead, Fern. Not yet. Look, we're standing right in front of you. You can reach out and touch us." He held out his hand to me. I stared at the empty palm that waited for mine. "Let's start the interview, okay? You'll feel better once we do."

For the first and only time in my life, I screamed at him. "No! I won't do it! No more interviews—ever!"

Ted opened his mouth to protest, but Mara stepped forward. "Ted," she said. I jumped at the sound of her voice; I'd forgotten she was there. "Perhaps you've gone too far this time."

Her arms were crossed over her cotton floor-length dress, one of the many she always wore. I was surprised by what she'd said—she was usually quick to defend Ted's research, having work of her own that kept her occupied for days at a time—but then again, her Break Room was evidence that she, too, needed an outlet.

Chuckling dismissively, Ted looked at her. He looked at me. He crouched down on the floor and, as tears kept spilling down my cheeks, he caught one on his finger, swallowing down his laughter as he examined the drop like a slide under a microscope. Then his face became serious.

"Mara's right," he said. "I'm sorry, Fern. You know how I get—so wrapped up in the science of it all. Sometimes I forget that you . . . well. Know that I won't take it that far again."

And he didn't. In the years that followed, his Experiments were startling and intrusive, but never again as cruel. Maybe that, more than anything, is the reason I'm so quick to return to him: he realized he crossed a line, and he gradually backed away from it. It's a difficult thing, admitting you were wrong. I've seen parents exhale excuses as easily as air. But Ted showed me that day that he loved me enough to see me as more than a research subject. That incredible truth— that a man so devoted to data could love me, when love is messy and immeasurable, impossible to pin down—made me feel powerful and electric.

Dr. Lockwood would probably say that, ever since, I've been yearning to feel that way again.

The drive from Boston to Cedar is always excruciating. The highway only takes you so far. Then it's twenty miles of back roads: gaping potholes, deer crossing signs, speed limits that shoot up and down. There are no sidewalks, either, so if someone's walking along the road, you have to give them plenty of room. You move to the opposite lane, watch the oncoming traffic get so close you glimpse the drivers' faces before veering back to your own side. *Hitting a pedestrian. Hitting a car to avoid a pedestrian. Hitting a pothole or deer.*

Today, the drive is even worse. My fingers are tight on the steering wheel, and no matter what I pass—vegetable stands, sugar shacks, shuttered restaurants—all I see is Astrid. She's there, in the middle of the road, reaching out to me like she did in my dream. Her mouth is shaping words I can't make out, and I have to grip the wheel even harder to control my instinct to swerve.

But ten minutes from Cedar, another figure appears. I squint to make out the young girl up ahead, and when I see a man—her father, I hope—following behind her, I'm relieved to find that they're real. Not residue from a dream.

They're in my lane, walking against traffic. Steering to the left, I give them the space they require. They do their part, too. Edge closer to the grass, even while I'm still a good distance away. But the girl stares at my car, does not notice the ditch she's veering toward. I want to warn her—*twisted ankles, big falls for small girls*—but all I have is the blare of my horn, and I don't want to startle her into slipping.

Her father sees the danger. In an instant of instinct, he wraps his arm around her waist and jerks her back to safety. Her body nearly folds in half at the force of his grasp. She's bent at the waist. Exactly like—

I swerve. Jolted by what I'm seeing, I steer right toward them. I catch their horrified looks just in time to slam the wheel the other way, back toward the opposite lane. I overcompensate, push to the left too hard, and end up braking on the strip of dirt that lines the road.

I struggle to catch my breath. That girl—she became Astrid. That man's arm—it became someone else's. I don't have time to make sense of this image before the man, holding his daughter's hand, peers into my passenger window. He gestures for me to open it, and I do.

"What happened?" he asks. "Are you okay?"

I nod.

"Are you sure?" He sweeps his eyes over me, runs them along the interior of my car. Then he lowers his voice. Leans in closer. "Are you high or something?"

"No, I . . ." I try to think of a way to explain it but can only come up with a lie. "There was a spider in the car, and I freaked out."

I try a sheepish smile, but the man is not amused. "Well, watch it, huh?" he says as he guides his daughter back to the road. "You could have killed us, you know."

I stare at them until they're two dots in the distance. I watch cars go by, their drivers glaring at me with narrowed eyes. My hands are at ten and two on the wheel, but I can't remember how to pull back into my lane. *An arm around Astrid's waist. An arm yanking her back.* That's what made me swerve. A single burst of an image.

My mind jerks back to the nightmare I've had a hundred times. The girl is always bent at the waist. Even last night, when it was Astrid in the dream, the angle of her body made it harder for her to reach me. But now I see it differently: she isn't bending over, exactly; she's stretching forward while someone pulls her back, their arm unyielding as a hook.

I know what Eric would say. That I've been influenced by the news.

That I'm superimposing the images of a kidnapping over a dream of a featureless girl, whose face has always been ripe for filling in.

But still. My pulse pounds with the certainty of it: Astrid's face means something to me. And it's clear that, until I find out why, she will not let me go.

———

When my phone rings a few minutes later, I'm still on the wrong side of the road. I suspect it's Eric, calling to check in, but it would be a bad idea to pick up. My breathing remains raspy, uneven. My heart is hurting my chest.

But it isn't Eric. It's Mara. I answer so fast my hand is a blur.

"Mara."

"Hello, dear." She always calls me *dear*, even though I don't believe I've ever been that to her. "I only have a minute, but I'm calling to—"

"Did I know Astrid Sullivan?"

I don't care why Mara called. She hardly ever does, but right now, her timing is perfect.

There's a pause before a rush of laughter. "What?"

"Did I know Astrid Sullivan?" I repeat.

Another pause. "Who's Astrid Sullivan?"

"You've never heard of her?"

"No, I haven't," she says. "Is she a celebrity or something? You know I don't care much for—"

"She's not a celebrity," I cut in. "Well, she's famous, I guess, but I'd never heard of her either. Or at least I thought I hadn't. She's this girl who was kidnapped twenty years ago. When she was fourteen. She had red hair, and she was from New Hamp—"

"Fern, what's going on? Is this a joke?"

"No, I'm—it's serious. I saw her on the news, and I've been having these dreams and I just had a flash that . . ." I trail off. Try to start over. "She had red hair. A couple years older than me. Are you sure you don't remember me knowing a girl like that?"

Mara sighs, long and slow against my ear. "I can't speak to every person you knew, dear, but as far as I know, the only girl you hung around with was Kyla Kelley. Of course, I was very busy when you were a child. How am I supposed to know who you spent your time with?"

In the pause stretching out between us, I almost chuckle. Why did I bother asking her at all? Mara was never the type of mother to take an interest in her daughter's acquaintances. Or even her whereabouts.

"You seem very agitated," Mara says. "Have you been taking your meds?"

"Yes, I—" I have a brief moment of alarm where I can't remember if I packed my pills this morning, but then I pick up my purse from the passenger seat, hear them rattling inside.

"Yes," I repeat. "My doctor put me on a new prescription, though. My old one wasn't working."

Mara chuckles. "Sounds like this one's not doing too great, either."

I'm about to shrug the comment aside, but then I stop. Could that be what this is, a side effect of my change in medication? Is my brain just mixing its signals, firing off incorrect messages as it adjusts to the new chemicals? My panic softens at the thought. In a few moments, my breath comes more gently. Because, if I'm honest, my brain has always done this. It's the reason I went on medication in the first place. I'm always leaping from ordinary sights to sinister assumptions. I see a construction worker descending through a manhole and I'm sure there'll be an explosion that traps him underground. I see a woman pedaling in the bike lane and I'm positive a bus will hit her.

Eric says I'm an unreliable narrator, especially when it comes to my own life. I get a mosquito bite, and I'm convinced I have West Nile. I cough two times and I'm certain it's bronchitis. I spiral. I get stuck in all the wrong grooves. I see something as innocent as a father pulling his daughter toward safety, and I flash to a disembodied arm snatching a girl away.

"So is it my turn now?" Mara asks. "Can I get to the reason I called?"

"Uh, yeah. Sure. Sorry."

I check my mirrors and pull back onto the road. I don't see Astrid anywhere.

"Ted tells me you're headed there to help him pack," Mara says. "Because apparently he's become a cliché overnight. Moving to Florida . . . How conventional."

She groans, and in the background, I hear someone announce that a Bikram yoga class will start in ten minutes.

"Are you on one of your cruises?" I ask.

Mara's been obsessed with spiritual cruises for years. She and Ted separated when I was in high school, and ever since, she's been tetherless. Where once she couldn't stand leaving her studio for more than a few hours at a time, now she hops from ship to ship, living off a steady diet of qigong exercises, psychic readings, and daily Reiki.

"Yes, I have my yoga soon, so I have to hurry this along," Mara says. "I need you to do me a favor."

"Okay . . ."

"As it turns out, Ted's being a bit of a copycat with his move. My spiritual adviser has been urging me to make a move myself. Find a different studio space. 'A steadier place to land,' she calls it. And when I told Ted about my decision last week, he called me back two hours later to announce he was selling the house."

"Wow," I say. "So you won't be following Ted to Florida then?"

"Me in Florida?" Mara's laughter thunders in my ear. "Never."

"Yeah, I can't really picture you there," I concede. "Or Ted, for that matter. But I guess I assumed you'd set up shop wherever he goes."

Separated but never actually divorced, Ted and Mara still share a house, though in the last decade, I've only seen Mara there a handful of times. She mostly uses it as her home base between cruises, spending a few nights on a cot in her studio before setting sail again. But Ted insisted on the phone last week that she would "find her own way" once he sold the property. I guess he was right.

"Our living arrangement has long been a measure of convenience," she says. "And now Ted is insisting that you pack up my studio right away. He's annoyed with me, I think, for being the first of us to make a permanent change. My spiritual adviser says his pride must be bruised, so he needs to act as if he doesn't care—hence, selling the house, emptying out my studio. So do me a favor and don't let him touch my art. He knows he's not allowed in there, but maybe he thinks the rules have changed because we're moving. But no. They haven't. He'll only bungle the whole thing up. You're much more careful than he is, so pack up the pottery and prints, won't you, dear? Leave the Break Room for me, though. I'll have to figure out what to do with all that. Who knows—maybe I'll leave it as is. Drive up the value of the house."

As she laughs, I picture her Break Room, the place in her studio where the cracks in her marriage first started to show. It was named for the broken pieces of pottery Mara glued to the ground. I wonder if the floor still looks too sharp to walk on. If my feet would come away with cuts like they did when I was young.

"Anyway, can you do that, dear? I'd say it could wait until I'm back—our ship docks at the end of the week—but you know how Ted is when he gets something in his head. He was actually nagging me to fly home from our next stop. I swear, that man . . ."

"Yes, that's fine. I'll take care of it."

"Oh, that's lovely, thank you. And remember . . . gallery pieces . . . because the . . . has to go on top of . . . but I think there are extras."

"Mara? You're breaking up. I'm getting too close to the house."

". . . hear me . . . the gallery pieces? You have to—"

The line goes dead, and I'm not surprised. The cell reception in Cedar has always been terrible. The only tower that reaches us isn't even in town; it's across the border in Duxbury. This is just one way that going back to Cedar always feels like going back in time. In Boston, no one I know has a landline, but here, it's still a necessity.

I want to think about Astrid, reconcile the vividness of those reaching hands, that flash of an arm around her waist, with the tricks I've learned my anxiety plays. I want to return to Mara's quip about my meds, let it keep convincing me that the dream is just a dream. The wrong synapses firing. But I'm nearly to Ted's house now. I pass the antiques store with the metal pig out front, the fire department with its sign for a spaghetti dinner. I pass the llama farm and feel the familiar catch of breath in my throat. The woods are just ahead. If I walked straight into them, I could walk for fifteen miles. Never pass another person or house. Get lost, maybe. Never find my way out.

These woods have always rattled me. They darken the road, obstructing the sun with their trees. They make my stomach churn, and even now, I feel a swirl of nausea. Once, when I was thirteen, I asked Ted as we drove by them, "Did someone die in there?"

He looked at me. His eyes held something eerie in them. "You feel it?" he asked.

"Feel what?"

"Here. Let's stop for a minute. I'll tell you the story."

He pulled over and got out of the car, heading straight into the woods. I didn't want to follow him through those dense leaves and thick branches, stepping on twigs that snap at your feet, but I wanted even less to be left alone. I hurried after him, careful not to brush against the poison ivy that I knew must be everywhere.

"It's over here," Ted said. He pointed to something, but all I saw were trees. It was early afternoon, a sunny day, but I would have believed it was dusk.

"Now, this may be difficult to hear," he started.

And then he told me anyway. The story of a couple that got lost while hiking. As soon as it got dark, they grew ravenously hungry. It hit them out of nowhere, like a curse whispered by the wind. Their stomachs, the husband later told police, felt like bottomless wells. Their bones shone through their skin in the moonlight.

"See this tree?" Ted said, pointing to one with an engraving in it: *J + L.* "They came in this way. Same as we did. Ordinary people like you and me. Except—these woods . . . they change you."

"Change you?" I echoed, wrapping my arms around myself. "What do you mean?"

His eyes glinted, twin sparks igniting. "Shh-shh-shh," he said. "Listen."

The husband was convinced they wouldn't make it through the night unless they found something to sufficiently fill their stomachs. But not a single animal scurried by. Leaves did nothing. Berries were no better than air. The wife, weakened by her hunger, eventually passed out, leaving the husband to search for sustenance on his own. Hours went by, and still there was nothing. The husband became desperate and deranged, his body feverish with starvation.

"But the wife, you see," Ted said, "was six months pregnant. And the husband had a knife."

I dropped to the mossy ground. Closed my eyes and covered my ears. I screamed so I couldn't hear the ending, even though I'd already guessed what it was. *Hunger that makes you a monster. Parents and weapons.* I screamed until my throat felt ripped to shreds.

Then Ted's hand was on my shoulders. He shook me until I opened my eyes and looked up at him, towering over me like just another tree.

"That was an Experiment, Fern. Now come on, let's get back to the house so I can interview you while the fear is still fresh."

As he walked away from me, I was momentarily soothed. The story wasn't real. Of course it wasn't. Hunger curses, fathers that carve their child right out of the womb—how could I have believed it?

"So nobody died in here?" I called after Ted, brushing the dirt off my legs as I stood.

He turned. Walked backward toward the car so he could see me as he spoke. "I'm sure lots of people have died in here," he said.

The woods stop at the edge of Ted's property. Or rather, Ted's property is an acre-deep notch set into the woods. The trees keep going for another couple miles, with other houses perched on open lots along the way, and if I were to keep driving, I'd eventually get to The Diner, to Rusty's, to the tiny high school from which I graduated in a class of fifty. But I've reached Ted's driveway now, that steep dirt slope, and I have to make the turn.

As I drive up, I see him sitting on the porch swing, a book in his hands. My heart kicks for a second. He's been waiting for me; things are already different. When Eric and I visit, we usually have to let ourselves in, wait around in the dim, dusty living room until Ted comes down the stairs, announcing that he'd forgotten we were coming.

But now, he waves without looking up as I park. His eyes linger on a page before he turns it, folds the corner down, and stands. I'm gathering up my purse when I notice him scratching hard at his wrist.

Same as I did last night. Ted's fingers rake over his skin, but unlike me, his itching has a physical cause: the red patches of psoriasis snaking along his arms.

I glance at my own wrist, at my faint pink scratches, and the dream from last night replays. The images are sharper now, as if brought into focus by the flash I had on the road.

Astrid's hands were reaching. Astrid's waist was grabbed by a too-tight arm. Astrid's wide, terrified eyes were begging for help.

The nausea surges up, even stronger than before, and I open the car door just in time to lean over and puke onto the dirt.

"Well," Ted says from the porch. "Okay then. Welcome home."

three

Ted doesn't give me a chance to unpack, or even brush my teeth after throwing up. I keep flicking my tongue against the roof of my mouth, trying to scrape off the sick, but it isn't working. I need toothpaste. Mouthwash. I need time to process these images of Astrid, which made me lose my breakfast in the first place.

But Ted can't be stopped. As soon as I drop my bag at the bottom of the stairs, he hooks his hand around my wrist and pulls me out toward his car, the same green Subaru he's been driving since I left home for college.

"We're going to Rusty's," he explains.

He plops me into the passenger seat and shuts the door, then walks toward the driver's side with a particular jaunt I know too well. He's excited about something. Worked up. Inspired.

"I need typewriter ribbon," he announces as he lurches down the driveway. "And you need packing supplies."

"Typewriter ribbon?" I say. "You're—working? What about retirement?"

He waves his hand as if swatting away a fly. "That's just from Wicker. But I'm still *working*, of course. It's amazing how productive the mind can be when it's not shackled by the arbitrary edicts of academia. My brain is fizzing, Fern. Like a can of soda that's been shaken up. I would have gotten the ribbon this morning, but I waited for you, you're welcome very much. Figured you'd want to go as soon as you got here, for boxes and all that."

I shake my head, trying to catch up. A wave of nausea crests in my stomach once again. "You haven't bought boxes yet?"

"No. Of course not."

"Then what have you been packing with?"

Ted looks at me as he brakes at a stop sign. His eyes narrow. "Nothing," he says. "I haven't been packing at all. That's why I need you. You're always so good at that organizational stuff. Plus, I told you, my mind is a live wire! Packing would waste all that brainpower."

He's about to step on the gas again, but I jerk my arm out to stop him. There's a mother goose, followed by six goslings, beginning to cross the road. They're oblivious to the dangers of traffic. Of tires. Of impatient men behind the wheel. The only awareness the goslings have is of their mother, the animal that will teach them how to move through this world.

Ted sighs as we wait, and I allow myself to feel the impact of what he just said. He used that phrase again—*I need you*—only this time, it's clear that the need is merely a practicality. My stomach roils at how stupid I was to believe it was something else—an expression of love, a desire for connection. *Of course it wasn't*, Eric would say. *It's Ted we're talking about here.*

As soon as the geese edge past our car, Ted zooms ahead. I tug on my seat belt, make sure it's tight. I hate how quickly he drives down Cedar streets. You never know what will dart from the woods, what family of animals you could crush in an instant.

I run my tongue along my teeth, feel the film that's stuck there. "Your semester only ended a month ago. Maybe you should take a break for a while. Come back to your work once you've had a chance to recharge. We could pack things up together. We could—"

"A *break*?" He spits out the word as if it's poison. "You know who's not taking a break? Brennan Llewellyn. I'm sure you've seen his new book—*The Desolation of Fear*." He says the title with a mocking high-pitched tone.

"It's complete garbage, of course. I was reading it when you pulled in. Five hundred pages of mind-numbing research and case studies that make the same argument as all his other books. But the critics don't care. Nor the consumers. It debuted at number nine." He scoffs. "Everyone's a brain-dead lemming."

I lean my head against the window, watch the oak trees whiz by. I'm too weary for one of Ted's rants about Brennan Llewellyn, his old grad school classmate who went on to enjoy the success that Ted always wanted. Bestselling books. Spots on morning talk shows. The reverence of the entire psychology community. Brennan is Ted's "friemesis," a term Ted uses without irony. Whenever Brennan's in town, the two of them have a meal together, laugh about whichever former classmate is currently embroiled in some university scandal, raise a glass to old professors who've recently passed away. But even as they clink their drinks, as they chuckle about the public humiliations of people they used to know, Ted's teeth are always clenched.

Brennan didn't start as Ted's friemesis. In grad school, they were close, bonded by their shared specialization in fear. Ted says they used to have the same bold ideas, the same impulsive methods (which he swears is not an oxymoron). For a couple years, they thought of each other as research partners, both on a mission to break the field of psychology out of its rigid traditions, shake up the whole community. One night, Brennan got an idea for an experiment in which they would follow women home from the campus library. He showed Ted how to make his body hunched and menacing, and then, together, they crept along sidewalks, matching their pace with that of their subjects. It was only once the women began to run that they caught up to them, laughing, and tried to interview them about the experience.

But then Brennan betrayed him, Ted claims, by selling out. Brennan's adviser encouraged him to submit a paper he'd written for class to scientific journals, even though it was virtually unheard of for a student so early in his graduate studies to be published. But when a prestigious journal actually accepted his paper, Brennan became intoxicated by his morsel of success. Abandoning his work with Ted, he dedicated himself to more generically academic methods—case studies, meta-analyses, experiments with controls—and Ted said that, from then on, the fear research Brennan conducted wouldn't scare a baby.

After graduating, Brennan landed a position at Stanford, but none of the Ivy League schools would have Ted. His work wasn't sterile enough—his words, not theirs. They couldn't afford to be associated with such wild-card research—their words, not his—and they wanted someone like Brennan Llewellyn instead. Someone whose methods were rigorous but inoffensive. They wanted research like Corn Flakes, Ted said.

So he got stuck at Wicker, a school he deemed to be second-rate, and there, he published papers with the frequency required to keep his job. But the papers, by necessity, were always on topics that bored him—anxiety disorders, run-of-the-mill phobias, the startle reflex—because even second-rate schools, he claims, insist on playing it safe.

When it came to the *real* work, the *real* research, he had to do it on his own time.

The real work, of course, was his Experiments. But nobody would fund them. No journals accepted the articles he wrote about them.

Nobody saw them as anything legitimate. "These 'experiments' you do," Eric once said to Ted, "you know they're not real science, right? They're really just . . . pranks."

The comment made me wince, but Ted actually laughed.

"Not real science?" he echoed. "Maybe they're not the kind of science you're accustomed to, Dr. Eric. After all, it's not like you can smear the human mind onto a slide and discover its secrets under a microscope. Psychological studies are much more of an art." Eric rolled his eyes, but Ted kept going. "Brennan pretends to disagree, and that's why his work remains embarrassingly unimaginative. He took our subject and neutered it—to the point where no one can comprehend the brilliance of what I'm doing. But someday—soon, I suspect—the world will finally see Brennan for the fair-weather, suit-and-tie fraud he is."

But Ted's "embarrassingly unimaginative" is the psychology community's "scientific." In Brennan's first book, *The Legacy of Fear* (a required text for my social work degree), he included countless case studies of people who had witnessed something traumatic as children—domestic abuse, familial murder/suicide—and studied the impact those experiences had in different facets of their life: academic performance, mental health, success in romantic relationships. To replicate the effects of fear in a safe, controlled environment, he performed the now-famous Exam Experiment, in which undergraduates volunteered to take a written test. In one group, students completed the test with no interruptions. In another, a student who had been planted in the front row let out a choreographed scream, ran up the stairs of the lecture hall, and burst out the door in the back of the room. The startled students were then told not to worry and to continue on with the test, the results of which were compared against months of identically run experiments.

To Ted, the Exam Experiment is the funniest joke he's ever heard. There's a world of difference, he says, between witnessing a murder and hearing a scream. And what a waste of time—a yearslong project with hardly anything to show for it: "Just research as thin as the paper it was printed on. Just jump scares, Fern! *Jump scares.* For God's sake, he used to have *ideas*; he used to stalk people on the streets!"

Now, Ted turns the car sharply onto Main Street, and I put my hand against the door to brace myself. A stretch of buildings comes into view—the old Victorian repurposed as a post office; the two-room brick library, with an "Under Reconstruction" sign that's been posted out front since I was seventeen; The Diner, which serves the best corned beef sandwiches; and, finally, Rusty's Got Everything.

Ted whips into a space in front of the store, parallel parking with a confidence I can't imagine having. When he taps the bumper of the car in front of him, he huffs "Serves 'em right" before reversing a couple inches and cutting the engine. He runs a hand through his wispy gray hair, messing it up rather than smoothing it out. Ted loves to look frazzled and unkempt, as if you've interrupted him during the middle of a work binge.

When I step out of the car, I'm blasted with a heat so potent it feels like a sauna. I didn't register how hot it was when I first got to Ted's; I probably thought the sweat that sprang to my forehead was from the woods, the vomit, the flashes of Astrid. Inside the store, it isn't much better. Rusty's got five giant fans going, one at the end of each aisle, but the air feels like bathwater. All these years and he's never invested in AC. Nothing in Cedar ever changes.

"Hey, Ted," Rusty calls from the counter. "Perfect timing. Your order came in this morning. I shelved it only ten minutes ago." His eyes widen when he notices me lurking at the door. "Hey, kiddo. Good to see ya. How're things in the big city these days?"

"Don't distract her," Ted barks. "She's on a mission. Here to help me pack."

"Ah," Rusty says. "Sorry about that." He mimes zipping his lips and smiles at me. I smile back weakly and shrug.

Ted turns down the second aisle, where there are phone chargers, boxes of toner, ink cartridges for ancient printer models, and the typewriter ribbon that Rusty stocks just for him. I head to the back of the store, marked "Hardware, Storage, and Books," and I grab all the flattened boxes I can tuck beneath my arms. Reaching for the rolls of packing tape, I slip them around my wrists like shackles.

In a minute, I make my way toward the register, ready to catch up with Rusty out of Ted's earshot, but at the end of the aisle, I stop so quickly that one of my boxes drops to the floor.

Astrid is staring at me.

Her red hair flames out from her face. Her green eyes bore into mine. The freckle beneath her eyebrow hooks my gaze and I look at it until it blurs.

Blinking a few times, I wait for my vision to clear. Then I glance at my hand, find it white knuckled, clutching a shelf. I loosen my grip. Steady myself.

Astrid isn't staring at me. She's glossy and two-dimensional on a promotional poster taped beside copies of her memoir. The books have been squeezed in to fit among the airport mysteries, shiny romances, and various new releases that Rusty keeps in stock—Brennan Llewellyn's latest among them. I set the rest of my boxes down, pick up one of Astrid's hardcovers, run my finger along the slightly raised font of its title: *Behind the Red Door*. The spine cracks as I open it.

When Astrid Sullivan was fourteen years old, the bolded words on the inside cover read, *she went missing for almost a month. Ever since, the truth of what happened to her has been missing, too—until now.*

It's a little heavy-handed, but it chills me all the same, even in this stifling heat. I skim the rest of the book jacket, eyes leaping from phrase to phrase—*raised in a strict Catholic household, vacillated between guilt and rebellion*—but when I land on one sentence in particular, my heart hammers so hard I can almost hear it.

For the first time, it says, *Astrid writes about details and memories previously undisclosed, including the startling revelation that there was a witness to what happened, a young girl who never came forward.*

Something jolts in my brain. It's a jerking sensation I know very well, one that Dr. Lockwood tells me I can't actually feel, but I do. I do.

Girls who see girls disappear. Girls who never speak up.

I grab my boxes in a daze, tuck them under my arms along with the book, and stumble toward the counter, where Rusty leans, turning the page in a magazine.

"Hi again," he says as I plunk my purchases down. I'm breathing hard, but he doesn't seem to notice. "It's good to see ya, Fern. How ya been?"

"Okay." My pulse whirs. My wrist itches.

"Yeah?" He scans the boxes and packing tape—*beep, beep, beep.* I flinch at every sound. "Nice of you to help Ted with his move. Me, I still can't believe he's going to Florida. Cedar without Ted Brierley? Uh-uh, can't picture it. Last week, I was telling him how . . ." He trails off, staring at me. "Hey. Are you okay?"

My phone chirps with a text in the back pocket of my shorts. I pull it out and read. Eric. *How's it going there, Bird? On a scale of one to Ted, how Ted is Ted today?*

"Fern?"

Rusty rubs his hand along his beard. I wince at the scrape of it: coarse skin against coarse hair. I try to concentrate on the round, red-cheeked face of this man I've known since I was a kid. He used to give me candy and stickers every time I came into the store.

"I'm just hot," I finally say. I wipe my arm against my forehead for effect. Smile a little, though my lips feel like rubber.

Rusty nods. He reaches for Astrid's book without looking at it, then pulls the trigger on the scanner gun to ring it up. "Make sure you're drinking plenty of water. They say eight glasses a day, but when it's this humid, I shoot for ten."

He glances down at the hardcover in his hand and frowns. "Poor girl," he says. "Or—poor woman. She's all grown up now."

"You know her?" I take a step forward and my toes crush against the bottom of the counter.

"Sure," Rusty says. "I mean—not personally. Just the way everyone knows her." He shakes his head. "It's terrible. As if she didn't go through enough as a kid. But it looks like the same thing's happening all over again. More than a week and no real leads. Exactly like before. How can that be?"

I swallow, and it's as if a concrete ball drops into my stomach. I've been so caught up with Astrid's original disappearance that I almost forgot about her current one. Right in this very moment, she's missing for the second time, while I stand at Rusty's, sweaty and itchy but safe.

Astrid would be thirty-four now. Surely much stronger than she was at fourteen. Surely capable of fighting back. But drugs. But blindfolds. But basements. There are so many ways to make someone vulnerable. And anyway—trauma doesn't care how old you are; it makes children of us all.

"The jacket says there's . . ." My voice shakes. Rusty looks up from the book. "This girl?" I try to continue. "I guess she was there when Astrid . . ." His gaze is gentle but feels like a light shined right in my eyes. "And she never came forward?"

"Right," Rusty says, nodding. "Lily."

"Who?" I try to take another step forward, but I'm as close to the counter as I can get.

Rusty bags the book and packing tape. "The other girl," he says. "Lily. Astrid writes about her in the book, and how— Well, I won't spoil it for you." He taps a couple buttons on the register, then looks at me expectantly. "How d'ya wanna pay today, kiddo?"

He has to repeat the question two more times before I finally hand him my credit card.

I'm waiting for Ted outside, my purchases at my feet. The sun beats down, and I'm light-headed and disoriented. Practically panting from all the pivots my brain has made today.

Taking out my phone, I type out a text to Eric: *I'm spiraling.*

Sometimes it's enough simply to tell him this. It steadies me to admit it. Slows the marble enough that, on a good day, I can pluck it from the slide.

His response comes quickly, and I imagine him in the hospital break room, having just distracted a sniffling child from shots or pain or fear.

Oh no! he writes. *About what?*

I can almost picture it: being on a street in Foster, New Hampshire, all lush lawns and tree-lined roads, no cars except one—a gray van, maybe, into which a masked man pulls a fourteen-year-old girl.

I keep feeling like I know something about Astrid Sullivan's kidnapping. Her memoir talks about there being a witness, and I thought for a sec that maybe it was me. But I was wrong, I guess.

It's a few minutes before his response comes in. I stare at the phone the entire time.

You GUESS? he finally asks. *Do you want me to call you? I've got an appointment in five, but I can try to talk you down first.*

My fingers skitter across the keys. *No, I'm fine now. I just panicked because the memoir says the witness was a girl and I had this dream and I've been seeing a man's arm around Astrid's waist. It turns out the witness was someone named Lily, though, so I guess the dream was just a dream and the man's arm is . . . part of the spiral.*

I reread the last two sentences, and even I can see how ridiculous they sound. I press the backspace button, send only *No, I'm fine now.* Then I add, *Let's talk later. Love you!*

When the door to Rusty's jingles behind me, I turn around expecting to see Ted, but it's somebody else. I spin back to face the street, but a hand touches my arm. I stiffen against it, right as the person says my maiden name.

"Brierley?"

I look at the man beside me and take an instinctive step back.

"Cooper," I say. Cooper Kelley. The brother of my childhood best friend, Kyla.

He's bulked up since the last time I saw him, five years ago at Kyla's wedding. His biceps stretch the sleeves of his T-shirt, and I can see the outline of his chest beneath the cotton. But the tattoo on his forearm—that hasn't changed at all.

Cooper leans forward to hug me, a move I couldn't have predicted, and I stand taut in his embrace, arms pinned to my sides, heart already racing. My knees go rubbery, instantly unstable, and I can't catch my breath in his constricting grip. When he finally releases me, his grin crinkles the skin around his eyes.

"Wow, it's good to see you, Brierley."

I can't bring myself to meet his gaze, so I look at his teeth instead. The bottom ones are still crooked, pointing toward and away from each other like old gravestones in a cemetery. They're yellow, too, and his voice is raspier than I remember. He's still a smoker.

"It's Douglas now," I correct him.

He cocks his head for a moment, then nods. "Right," he says. "Kyla told me you got married. Congrats."

"Thanks." I shrug. "It's been a few years, but—"

"Have you seen Kyla's kids lately? Thomas is only two months, so he's still, like, a sack of potatoes. But Leland? The three-year-old? She's fuckin' reading already." He takes a pack of cigarettes out of his back pocket, taps it against his palm. "But you probably know all that. I'm sure you visit all the time."

I nod, even though he's wrong. I've seen pictures of Leland, but that's it. I only know about Thomas through Facebook. Kyla told me she was pregnant with Leland at my wedding, and I tried so hard to give her the reaction she deserved—a squeal of delight, a promise to visit her in Maine for baby clothes shopping—but panic shot through me. Kyla and Jeff had only been married for a year. Would I, too, be expected to start having babies so soon? I wanted to pull her aside, yell over the DJ's music to ask if she knew what she was doing. I wanted to tell her how fragile children are, how easily broken and bruised. I wanted to crouch down on the floor in my wedding dress, rocking back and forth like a kid myself.

That's why I've distanced myself from Kyla, whose childhood home I used to sleep at more often than my own. I haven't trusted myself to be as warm about her new family as I should be. I don't want to seem indifferent to the children she loves more than anyone. Mostly, though, I've been afraid of the anxiety that swirls in my stomach whenever I see photos of her kids. Last week, right after sex with Eric, I unfollowed her on Facebook. I muted her stories on Instagram.

Cooper lights his cigarette and blows the smoke away from my face. I'm grateful for this. When Kyla and I were kids, he'd exhale so close to us that our throats often burned—*secondhand smoke, lung cancer that lurks in cells and bides its time*—and when he drove us around in the summer, he'd ash on our bare legs. He was always trying to torture us. Me, especially. He locked me in a linen closet once. He slipped a dead snake into my backpack. He messed with the brakes on my bike. In a lot of ways, I was an easy target. Ted had taught me to wear my fear like perfume, and Cooper was an animal who could pick up a scent.

One time, when Cooper was eighteen, Kyla and I ten, he was supposed to be watching us at the Kelleys' house while their parents were out. Instead, he drove us to a tattoo parlor, had us sit beside him and watch as a needle pricked him over and over. When it was done, he presented his forearm to us as if it were a masterpiece in a museum.

A section of honeycomb, looking like holes in his skin.

Bees crawling around, seeming almost 3-D.

And then the stingers: exaggerated, talon-sharp, big as syringes.

Cooper smelled my reaction right away. It didn't matter that I covered my arms, concealing the goose bumps that swelled there in an instant. He knew. And for years after that, he used his tattoo as a weapon. How many times did he wrestle me to the ground, pressing the bees, the honeycomb, the stingers against my screaming mouth? I lost count after the seventh attack. Every time he held me down, the bees on his skin squirming as he flexed with anticipation, his arm shoving my lips so far apart my jaw ached, he laughed hysterically. Kyla would always try to yank him off, and his parents, whose house he still lived in well into his twenties, would threaten to take his car keys. But it didn't matter. Even as a teenager, I could never enter my best friend's house without my eyes peeled for her brother, my heart knocking against my ribs.

"I saw Ted," he says now.

I wrench my eyes away from his tattoo, and he smiles. He knows I was looking.

"Yeah, I'm waiting for him," I say, careful to keep my voice steady. "He's been inside for a while." I click my phone, look at the time. "A long while," I mumble.

Cooper taps his cigarette, ashes on the sidewalk next to my feet. I look at my shoes—flip-flops. Such a vulnerable choice.

"No," he says, "I mean I saw him leaving when I got here."

"Just now?"

Cooper nods. "A few minutes ago. I tried to say hi, but he had that look in his eye. You know the one I'm talking about. Then he peeled on out of here."

I look at the space where Ted had parked. It holds a tan Prius—not a green Subaru. My heart clenches with a familiar pain. He left me at the store again. When I was a kid, he sometimes abandoned me in unfamiliar places as Experiments. Worse, there were other times when he flat-out forgot about me. For a moment, I wonder which it is now. Then I remember his voice full of fervor, his live-wire mind, his need for the typewriter ribbon the second I arrived, and I know it's the latter. He was in and out at Rusty's while I was still grabbing boxes or staring at Astrid's face. And now he's back in his office, without a single thought of me, type-type-typing away.

Through a new surge of nausea, I call the house phone. I wait twelve rings before I finally hang up. I can feel Cooper's eyes on me the entire time.

"You want a ride home?" he asks. He stamps out his cigarette with a paint-streaked boot.

"No. Thanks."

"You sure? It's pretty brutal out here. And last I checked, your house was a couple miles away."

I look down at my phone, the black screen a void where Ted's name won't appear. Cooper's right, and I hate that. The heat feels like a sweaty sleeping bag. My flip-flops have a tiny hole in the sole, and the road back home is full of gravel.

"Fine," I say.

When he leads me to his red pickup and opens the passenger door for me, I try to forget the weight of his body, the taste of his arm as it pushed against my tongue.

———

Cooper flips houses now. This is all he talks about as he drives me to Ted's. He points out past projects as we pass them—the red colonial on Walnut, the blue ranch on Pine—and I try to act impressed. He tells me how he practically lives at Rusty's for all the materials he has him stock for him there, and he waxes poetic about how renovating houses is a metaphor for the work he's done on himself.

"Seriously, I've matured so much," he says, "in the last six years especially."

That was when he first witnessed the power of transforming something shabby into something where a person can make a life.

"Oh, check this out," he says, and as he slows, I look out the window, ready to nod at the next house he shows me. But he's gesturing ahead, pointing to a man walking on the side of the road, dressed in black pants, black boots, and a black raincoat, the hood pulled up even though it's sun, not rain, that gushes. Looking at him makes a trickle of sweat run down my leg.

"Have you met our drifter?" Cooper asks. He's driving so slowly a squirrel could outpace us.

"Drifter?" I echo. "No."

He points again, his finger arrow-stiff. "This guy. He showed up a few weeks ago. No one knows who he is, but he walks around all day, dressed like that. And watch, if you try to talk to him . . ." Cooper leans his head out the window. "Hey!" he shouts. "Who are you? What the hell are you doing here?"

The man darts into the woods like a startled deer. By the time we pass him, I can't even see him through the trees.

"Maybe he's homeless and you should leave him alone," I say, but my pulse feels like somebody's plucking it.

"Nah," Cooper says, "he's not homeless. I asked Peg at The Diner—because she helps out at the soup kitchen, you know? And she said no one there's ever seen him come in. So . . ." He takes a left onto Ted's road. "He's got to have a story. All he does is walk back and forth along the edge of the woods all day." He glances at me out of the corner of his eye. "You better watch out, Brierley. Lord knows there's plenty of woods on your street. Hey—in fact . . ."

He slams his foot on the gas and we whoosh by Ted's driveway, zoom on down the road. My heart's in my throat as I grab the door handle. I see a flash of Astrid, wonder if I'm about to share her fate. Was she taken like this the second time? Did someone offer her a ride home, only to speed her away?

"What are you doing?" I manage.

He doesn't answer. Just drives another few hundred yards before turning the wheel sharply and barreling straight toward the woods. My hand leaps to the ceiling of his truck. My foot slams against the floor, instinctively searching for the brake. He's not stopping. He isn't going to stop. I clench my teeth and squeeze my eyes shut. Wait for the impact that will break my legs, my spine.

The pickup jerks over uneven ground, but it doesn't hit anything. Branches scrape against the truck. I open one eye, then the other, and I see that we're driving along a path. A narrow lane has been carved out between the trees, bumpy and overgrown, but a passageway none-theless. I can't speak yet; my lungs are still heaving too hard. I can only watch as we slice through the woods, nothing but green forest ahead of us until we crest over a tiny hill, pull around a bend, and suddenly there's a house.

"Here we are," Cooper says. He lurches to a stop and turns off the engine.

Did Astrid scratch and claw? Did she kick and punch and push and bite? Or did her body betray her? Did she forget how to scream? How to fight?

"What do you think?" Cooper asks. "It's my dream flip."

I look at him. He's gazing at the house through the windshield, a smile pulling at the corner of his lips. He sighs as he shakes his head, his face full of awe.

I relax my shoulders. Let out my breath.

The house is a small, two-story cabin. Its front porch sags in the middle, its windows are boarded up and shutterless, and the roof is blanketed with moss. The wood siding is covered in mold spores—and I know, even without seeing them, that the floorboards inside are damp and rotted.

"It's owned by the town," Cooper says, soft and reverent. "Hardly anyone knows it's back here. I bet you didn't either, did you?"

I shake my head.

"Exactly," he says, "and you lived right down the street."

But I stayed away from the woods. Even when I walked down our driveway, which skirts along the trees, I kept as far away as I could manage, turning my back to them at times, striding sideways if I had to.

I'm itchy again. It's as if the mold spores have jumped from the cabin and latched on to my skin.

"Seems like most people who do know it's here just think of it as ruins," Cooper continues. "But you clear out a few of these trees, and you put in some bone-hard work—new roof, new siding, new porch, new floors—it'd be an incredible property. Some people would probably raze it and start from scratch. Build a twenty-first-century cottage in its place. Give it gas fireplaces and central air. But not me. I would respect the house's history."

"Which is what?" I ask. I put my hands beneath my legs to keep from scratching.

"Well, for one thing, it was built in the 1800s. For a while, it stayed within this one family—the McEwans—who passed it down from generation to generation. But according to town records, the last time anyone lived here was in the seventies. Since then it's been empty. Waiting for me to get my act together and love it into shape."

My fingers twitch. Something about the house feels familiar.

"Did you take me here before?" I ask. "Me and Kyla? When we were kids?"

The front door used to be blue. It's gray right now, but I would bet my life that it used to be blue. That when it swings open, it gives a discordant, three-noted creak.

"No," Cooper says. "Not that I remember. But it's familiar, isn't it?"

I nod. "I think I've been here before."

Cooper shrugs. "Maybe. But you probably saw it in *Cutthroat Cabin 2*."

I rip my eyes from the house to squint at him. "Huh?"

"*Cutthroat Cabin 2*? The movie? They filmed the exterior shots here."

"When?"

"I dunno. Early 2000s? You must've seen it. I'd pull up the poster on my phone, but—you know how the reception is here."

The name of the movie doesn't ring a bell, and I can't imagine I saw it. I've always hated horror.

"It's the one with the woman who just got divorced," Cooper says, "so she goes to the cabin to get away from it all, and pretty soon the walls start bleeding. She was bald for some reason, remember? So every day she put on a different wig, until the last day, when the blood starts coming from her scalp. She tries to put on a wig to stop it, but it seeps through and starts pouring out, and she's screaming and screaming and . . ."

I stop hearing him. I remember the movie now. A bleeding head is hard to forget.

I was in ninth grade at the time, and it must have been May because Ted's semester had recently ended. He called me out of school that day, telling the principal's secretary that I wouldn't be in again "until you drop the Earth Science requirement in favor of something far more useful. Freud! Jung! Piaget! Asch!" I laughed as he shouted names into Mrs. Keller's ear.

We ate leftover Chinese food for breakfast that morning, Ted educating me about all the psychologists that Cedar High was too much of a "spineless giraffe" to teach. Then we microwaved slices of bread, covered them with mayo, and called it lunch. Even as he quizzed me about the scientists he'd just taught me, telling me I was "a brilliant girl" with "an unprecedented mind" every time I answered correctly, I was afraid to speak above a whisper, to laugh louder than a chuckle. I thought that if I did, Ted would realize he was wasting his day by spending it in the kitchen with me, instead of with the books and papers in his office.

"I have a thrilling idea!" Ted said as we ate. "Let's go to the movies!"

I nearly choked on my crust. Ted didn't go to the movies. Ted thought the movies were "colorful excrement." But I didn't question him as he pushed open the screen door and headed to his car.

In the refrigerated darkness of the theater, Ted laughed at all the previews—the gorier they were, the harder he guffawed. Twenty minutes into the movie, my excitement over our impromptu outing drained from me like blood from a face. The cabin on the screen was veiled in a weblike fog. Its blue door opened with the creaky sound of a witch's voice. When the walls welled with red, when the woman's head did, too, I shook in my seat until I couldn't take it anymore. I covered my eyes with my arm and waited through the woman's screams and the audience's gasps until, finally, the theater flooded with light.

In the car on the way home, Ted said, "That movie really scared you, huh?"

I pulled at the bottom of my T-shirt, feeling myself blush. "I don't like horror movies," I said.

"I thought it was hilarious. Come on, Fern. You know blood doesn't really look like that. And the floating ax? You could see the wires!" He paused, put a finger to his chin. "But it's noteworthy that it scared you so much. Do you think we should do an interview?"

I snapped my head toward him. Didn't say a word.

"I know I told you I'm taking the day off," he added. Then he paused again. Longer this time. "But I could make an exception for this."

Cooper's voice breaks through the memory. "Hey, whatcha got there, a bug bite?"

I follow his gaze to the back of my hand. I've been scratching. My skin is flaking off beneath my nails. The trees form an awning against the sun, but I'm still sweating hard.

"Can we go now?" I ask.

"Sure," Cooper says. "Thanks for indulging me." The truck growls as he turns it on. "I'll get you home in two secs."

Not home, I almost correct him. *Ted's.*

There are parts of my story I can only tell now that my parents are dead.

Like how my knees grew sore every Sunday, the wooden pew kneelers leaving half-moon marks that were always too slow to fade. Hymns often scraped instead of sang in my throat. All the lacy collars itched. And each week, beneath my virginal dress, I wore an Ani DiFranco shirt. Sometimes, before I put it on, I even stroked Ani's face, ran my tongue along her lips.

Now that I've lost my father to a heart attack, my mother to an aneurysm, I can say that the eight p.m. curfews humiliated me to the point of nearly hating my parents. (I once poured my mom a glass of orange juice and turned my back to spit in it before I handed it to her. She smiled at me and sipped; I smiled at her and watched.) I can also call the broken lock on my bedroom door what it actually was: a betrayal. A vow that they would not trust me, no matter how well I projected my prayers so they could hear them through the walls.

My parents were not bad people. They simply believed in God and guilt, and they wanted me to believe the same. (And no, it isn't lost on me that they devoted their hearts and brains to God, and those were the organs that failed them.) When I was little, I pictured God as a jovial white man, Santa Claus in a cream-colored robe, just like the ones that Father Murphy wore. But when I grew older, and my mom explained my period to me as a punishment I must endure for the sin of a woman I'd never met, I imagined God as a scowling black-clad judge, raising his gavel, ready to slam it down on my head.

My parents were not bad people. But I can't unsee the horror on my mother's face when she found me with Bridget in the basement, our breath hot between our lips, our hands roaming each other's bodies. My parents said *how could you*. They said *filth*. They said *unholy* and *abomination*. But Bridget's tongue in my mouth felt like the communion I'd been waiting my entire life to taste. Body of Christ or body of Bridget—I'd choose Bridget every time.

And anyway, I met her at CCD (Catholic City Dump, we all used to call it). So if God really condemned our union, then why did he bring us together at all—in his place of worship, no less? During Confirmation rehearsals, I sat in the pews and imagined Bridget and I making out right on top of the altar. I saw myself peel back her yellow cardigan, lift up the white T-shirt beneath. I saw my fingers inch toward the bra that I knew would have a tight little bow in its center.

Before we got caught, we'd been talking on the phone every night for weeks. After my parents went to sleep, I huddled under my blankets and kept my voice low and soft. I wanted the vibration of my whisper to feel like breath against her ear. I wanted to tell her about my altar fantasy, to confess that when our teacher asked if I was feeling okay, noting the flush in my cheeks, I'd only been thinking of her. But I didn't tell her these things. And for her part, she didn't divulge her feelings either. But we knew.

All these years later, I still remember this about Bridget: she ate the outsides of Oreos first, nibbling at the chocolate cookies until there was nothing left, until the stiff circle of cream crumbled in her fingers. And I remember this, too: she was embarrassed to love Top 40, especially when she saw my secret stash of Ani and Fiona and Tori. She tucked her hair behind her ear, and she asked me to play her a song. I picked "Shy," and I hoped she heard within it the hymn I would have written for her if Ani hadn't gotten there first.

That day in the basement was the first time I'd ever kissed a girl. Until then, I'd had only fumbling, dry-lipped kisses with boys at Youth Group. But Bridget's lips were soft. It's a cliché, I know, for a girl to be softer than a boy, but what do you expect? Women have been taught so well to be pliant.

When my mother came downstairs with a laundry basket in her arms, Bridget and I broke apart like a wishbone snapping in half. Too late, it turned out. The basket fell to the floor, all the carefully sorted whites spilling out. Then the screaming began. Words like *wicked* and *immoral*, words that had nothing to do with love.

Here's the thing, though. In CCD they taught us that the very first woman sucked the juice from a forbidden fruit, so is it any wonder that the juice remains on our lips? That even now, we get all kinds of hunger we're not supposed to have?

After Bridget left, my parents removed my doorknob, leaving a fist-sized hole that could always be seen through. The invitation list for my Confirmation party doubled in size. They wanted as many witnesses as they could get.

And yet, when it mattered most, none of them saw a thing.

four

The arm around her waist won't budge. It's dark and bodiless and tight as a belt on the very last hole.

She looks at me. A glance at first. Then a double take. Now she lurches forward. Her arms stretch, her fingers twitch, her hands grasp for me but only close on air.

I take a step back. She tries to shuffle forward. Her freckles are spots of dirt on her porcelain face. The one beneath her brow is darker. A fleck of mud. I want to wipe it off, but then I'd have to touch her. And to touch her, I'd have to get close. And if I get close, I can get grabbed.

Her mouth opens and shuts. There's a sound—a muffled, underwater sound—that surges and crescendos until it finally becomes clear. It's her voice. Thick but a little raspy.

"—going to—please!"

She freezes. Something snaps. Time bounces back. Unfreezes.

"Please. He's going to—please!"

She freezes. Something snaps. Time bounces back. Unfreezes.

"Please. He's going to—please!"

I'm a record needle stuck in a groove. Time snaps. Bounces back.

"Please. He's going to—"

"Please!" I shout, shooting upward.

Fistfuls of scratchy cotton. A rasp. A snap. Rectangle of light.

An ancient rotating fan struggles to move the air. Wheezes as it turns its head. Snaps as it spins back. The clock beside my bed says it's 1:32 a.m.

"You were talking in your sleep."

I gasp as I look toward the door. Ted's leaning against its frame, holding something in his hand. He stares at me as I try to catch my breath. I squint to make out his expression, but he's backlit by the hall-way. His face is all shadow.

I open my mouth to say something, but only a squeak comes out. It doesn't matter. He's not waiting for me to respond. He nods once and disappears. His feet clomp across the hardwood to his office at the end of the hall. His door shuts.

Flicking on the lamp beside my bed, I watch the room fill with beige, sickly light. The bulb is old. Barely even illuminates the book be-neath it. *Behind the Red Door*. When I opened the back cover tonight, stared at Astrid's author photo, that freckle near her brow was like a tiny black hole sucking me in. The crest of her cheekbones, which I felt I could trace even with my eyes shut tight, insisted I was part of her story.

I read the prologue right before I went to bed, and at the first mention of "a witness," I sat up straighter. My knees locked in place. I waited to see the name Lily, like Rusty had said. Waited for today's spiral to be proven wrong in print. But as it turned out, the prologue never mentioned a Lily. Just a "girl who saw the man who took me." A girl who knew what happened but never said a word.

My heart thumped when I read that. My stomach roiled. I had to set the book aside, curl into myself, wrap my arms around my knees. At some point, I must have drifted off to sleep—only to have Astrid's voice follow me into dreams.

Now, I rip off my sheets, reach for my cell phone, and try without Wi-Fi to search for "Astrid Sullivan witness" and "Astrid Sullivan Lily." But the webpages are slow to load and incomplete when they do, offering me only ad banners. I shake my phone as if it will help. When it doesn't, I grab the memoir, flip through its pages, and blink as my vision blurs, my head spins. I clutch the bedpost, dizzy and sweat drenched.

I haven't been drinking enough water. I'm used to our loft's clinical cool. This muggy heat, this house with poor insulation, this revision of such an old dream—it's boiling me up inside.

Stumbling out of my bedroom, I steady myself against the wall. I'm almost to the bathroom where I'll slurp down water straight from the tap, but the light beneath Ted's door catches my eye, and I head toward it. I pad barefoot across the grainy hardwood, and I open his door without a knock.

His fingers stall on the typewriter keys, but he doesn't turn around. "Yes?"

His study is the same as it ever was: book cramped, paper crowded, lit slightly green from a banker's lamp. The ceiling is sloped, making it difficult to stand in places, and there's only one window. It's pushed wide open, but the room feels airless as a coffin.

"What was I saying in my sleep?" I ask.

Ted swivels his chair to face me. "I don't know. I was on my way back from grabbing some dinner downstairs"—he gestures to a box of Nilla Wafers on his desk—"and I heard you mumbling. You sounded agitated. Couldn't make out exactly what you were saying, though."

I stare at his meal. The yellow box. The crumbs on a stack of papers. When I packed for Cedar, I assumed we'd go to The Diner on my first night back. I actually salivated over the thought of Peg's corned beef sandwiches. But here we are. Nilla Wafers. I, on the other hand, ordered Thai, which I ate alone in the kitchen—huge forkfuls of drunken noodles—until the spice of it gave me heartburn.

"You left me today," I say.

"Left you?" He cocks an eyebrow.

"At Rusty's."

"I didn't *leave* you. Cooper Kelley was there. I figured you'd get a ride back with him."

"You could've told me you were leaving at least."

"Actually, I couldn't have."

"Why not?"

His eyes twinkle, and right away I know what he's going to say. "Ted, don't," I preempt.

But his hands go up, stiffening into claws. "It was the witch . . ."

"Stop it."

"She cut off my tongue. Put a curse on me. And do you know what she said?"

I make a show of rolling my eyes. "That you're ridiculous?"

He stands up and takes three shuffling steps toward me, dragging one ankle behind him as if it were broken. When he speaks, the syllables come out as elongated croaks. "She said . . . 'I'm the witch from Forest Near. Now I'll do the thing you fear.'" He leans his head back, throat exposed, and cackles. Then he grabs me by the arms and shakes me.

I bite my lip, try to suppress my smile, but the laughter bubbles out anyway. "You *are* ridiculous," I say when he lets me go.

"The Witch from Forest Near" was the only fairy tale I was ever told. It starred Ted as both protagonist and villain. He invented the witch and, through the crackling cadence of his voice, instantly became her. His long wisps of hair, which were gray even when I was a child, transformed into her moon-silver locks. His hands turned convincingly gnarled.

I think he created her to scare me—and so, to study me—but unlike his other tactics, the fear never took. Even at five or six, I always giggled when he said his rhyme, laughed when he latched on to my arms and shook. It was like a hug. And though Eric says the witch is weird, I've always loved her. Loved how Ted still brought her out in my teens, my twenties, even on my wedding day. He's a man of science, after all. Has no time for playing. So the witch from Forest Near is special. She's someone Ted becomes to make me laugh, to show he cares. And right now, she's an apology.

"But to be serious," he says, sitting back in his chair, just a man again, nothing magical about him. "I couldn't tell you I was leaving because when the ideas are swelling, I can't *speak*. It would be like puncturing a balloon!"

My smile wilts, but there's still a bit of laughter in my voice as I humor him. "Okay, Ted. But a few words don't make too big of a hole."

He shakes his head emphatically. "I can't expect you to understand. Maybe you would if you'd chosen psychology over"—he grimaces like some cheesy B-movie actor—"social work."

I stiffen. Ted's pulling out all his favorites tonight. The witch from Forest Near. A crack about my profession, which he believes is basically slumming it.

"And I was right, wasn't I?" he adds. "Cooper gave you a ride."

"Cooper creeps me out. You know that."

Ted reaches into the Nilla Wafers box, pops one into his mouth, and talks while he chews. "What, that business with his tattoo?" A spray of crumbs shoots out. "Really, Fern, I would have thought you'd outgrown that by now. No?"

Ted was always fascinated by this particular fear of mine. Once, I came home crying about Cooper's latest attack, how I'd practically been able to taste the honeycomb on his arm as he shoved it against my tongue, and Ted immediately steered me into his study. He made me sit in the corner—the chair is still here, the rickety interview chair with a missing spindle in its back; my body aches just glancing at it— while he pummeled me with questions to pinpoint the exact source of my fear. But I already knew the source. It was Cooper. His cruelty and one-sided games.

Now a thought slides into me, sharp and sudden as a blade.

"Wait," I say. "Was leaving me with Cooper some sort of Experiment?"

Ted chuckles. "No, Fern."

"But you're all fired up," I insist. "You're excited about a new project. You're *working*, Ted." When he doesn't say anything—only stares at me, unblinking and interested—I continue. "You better not be doing Experiments on me while I'm here. I'll leave tomorrow, I swear."

I don't know where this threat comes from. It isn't one I've ever made before, and even as I say it, I hear how hollow it sounds, as if the center of each word were scooped out.

"I'm not doing Experiments," Ted says. "My new ideas don't require them." He swivels back and forth. His chair squeaks. "I recently had an epiphany about some past projects—a brilliant way to tie them together—so that's what I'm doing. I'm connecting all these threads I thought were totally separate. It's exhilarating. Groundbreaking! Brennan Llewellyn can eat his five-hundred-page doorstop for breakfast. And yes, I'm dipping into the notes from Experiments I've done with you and Mara in the past, but I don't need to perform any new ones yet."

Yet. My skin prickles with fresh sweat. The room reels.

"Are you telling the truth?" I ask.

"Fern." He stamps my name into the air. "Can't you see how busy I am?"

As he turns back toward his typewriter, he scratches his psoriasis. There are patches on the back of his neck, right at the hairline, but the one on his arm is particularly bad, the skin so red I wince. He refuses to use creams or lotions or to see a doctor with any regularity ("The itch is an affliction of the mind," he used to say). So instead, he scratches. The sound grates against my ears, like it always has, and as I watch him scrape the scales that sprawl along the inside of his wrist, it makes my own skin itch.

I look at the inside of my arm. It would be so easy to dig my nails into last night's marks. Keep troubling the skin without treating the cause.

"Did you ever take me to Foster?" I blurt.

Ted's already typing. Even after decades, he still uses his pointer fingers to punch out words on his old Underwood.

"Foster?" he repeats. His voice is dim with distraction, even as he pauses, hands hovering over the keys. "Foster, New Hampshire, you mean?"

"Yes."

Clack. Clack. Clack-clack. "No," he says. "We never went to Foster." *Clack.*

The sound knocks against my brain. A steel fist. I'm about to leave when Ted adds, "But didn't you go there with Kyla Kelley?"

"With Kyla?" I have no idea what he's talking about. He clacks through my confusion. And then, suddenly, I see it: her family's vacation rental, that summer on Edgewood Lake. Not in Foster, but—what town was that? The name eludes me for a second, until I remember a line from the Wikipedia page I read last night. Something like: *Sullivan first gained national attention at fourteen when she was abducted from her neighborhood in Foster, New Hampshire, a small town right outside Fall View.* That's where Edgewood Lake is, I remember now, but the name didn't even faze me yesterday. Edgewood Lake is such a popular vacation spot that I never really think of it as belonging to a town.

"Why are you bringing up Foster?" Ted asks.

But I'm too embedded in the memory to answer.

It was the first family vacation I'd ever been on—even if the family wasn't my own—and I remember watching someone's fireworks from the deck of the house Kyla's parents had rented for the week. The fireworks were early, well before the Fourth. "It's only June goddamn twenty-second!" an elderly neighbor complained, and for the rest of that week, Kyla and I echoed the woman's indignant, high-pitched protest, laughing until we had to wipe our eyes. But that night, my laughter dried up quickly when I noticed Cooper lurking in the corner of the deck. I edged closer to Kyla, burying my face in her abundant blond hair. Right then, it was the longest it had ever been, all the way down to her hips. I remember we measured it before she got it cut, on that very vacation.

Later, Kyla entered eighth grade with hair that was short and spunky, which means—I inhale sharply—I was at Edgewood Lake, in Fall View, right next to Foster, when I was twelve. The same summer, the same *week* ("June goddamn twenty-second") when Astrid was kidnapped on the twenty-fourth.

Something squeezes my stomach, wrings it out like a wet cloth, and I lurch out of the study, toward the bathroom, my Thai food pushing up my esophagus until—I reach the toilet just in time, vomit hard into its bowl. I heave again. And again. And again. And then, forehead sweaty, abs sore, I lean against the wall. Pant on the floor.

Ted slips around the corner to stand in the doorway. He looks me over, rumpled hair and dirty toes, knobby knees and the hollows of my collarbones. "That's the second time today," he says, chuckling. "What are you, pregnant?"

I can feel my eyes bulge, almost cartoonish. But I recover, quickly, as Ted watches me. Somehow, I stand up, even though my legs feel boneless. I flush the toilet and wash my hands. Rinse out my mouth. Splash water onto my face. As I brush past him, I don't look at him, just toss a "No, I'm not" over my shoulder before entering my room and closing the door.

I crawl into bed, get under sheets that are damp with my sweat, and burrow as far as I can. Despite the heat that feels like a wool sweater. Despite the loud, clunking fan that does nothing. I try to focus on Astrid: Astrid, who might be back in a basement she thought she escaped; Astrid, whose therapist claimed the witness was a "coping mechanism" that gave her hope; Astrid, who I definitely had the opportunity to meet, to know.

That's what this is. I'm sure of it. I'm only sick because of everything whirling inside me. The confusion. The dredged-up memories.

The memories I've yet to find.

───────

I wake with nausea so strong I start retching in bed. I make it to the trash can in the corner of the room, see that it's lined with crumpled papers, and now it's lined with my puke. My mouth tastes like sour Thai, the air smells like rancid molasses, and I will never eat drunken noodles again.

The blue light coming through the window tells me it must be dawn. The clock on my nightstand confirms it. I rest my head against a bookshelf filled with *Little House on the Prairie* and *Anne of Green Gables*. I inherited those books from Kyla when she outgrew each series. Me, I was never too old for comfort.

I heave again, rock toward the trash can, and only bile comes out. My hand shakes as I reach for my purse hanging from the bedpost, and I root around for my tin of Altoids. I'm too tired to make it to my toothbrush, the sink. The bathroom is a thousand miles away.

As my fingers wrap around the cool metal of the mints' case, they bump against something smooth and plasticky too. A long thin box. I pull it out and hold it close to my face to read it in the weak morning light. *First Response Pregnancy.* And then, remembering, I groan.

Eric urged me to pack it. He looked at my calendar and said it was possible I'd be able to know while I was at Ted's. *It would be a little early*, he said, *but tests are so good these days. See, look—"Get results six days sooner."* I smiled at him and joked that he would have me pack a crystal ball if he had one. He smiled back and said, *If I can find one online with good reviews, I'll pay the one-day shipping.* I kissed him, inhaled the clean scent of his skin, and felt him reach toward my purse on the bed, stuff the test inside. We laughed about it then, but now I'm close to crying.

The bathroom tiles are warm against my feet when I stagger onto them. *I'm only puking because of Astrid*, I remind myself, even as I'm ripping open the box. *I'm sick from regurgitating memories*—yet I pee on the stick, click on the cap. Place the test on the sink, sit on the toilet, and wait.

This is not the first pregnancy test I've taken. Two months ago, Eric guided me to the bathroom after I'd complained of feeling woozy all afternoon. When I emerged with the test in my hand, he was waiting for me on the other side of the door, his face nervous but hopeful. I showed him the digital reader, *Not Pregnant*, watched his features droop, and pretended to be as disappointed as he was.

It'll happen, I told him. *We haven't been trying very long.*

I want to make my husband happy. He's a good man who could have had anyone, but he chose me. I want him to believe I'm worthy. As it turned out, though, my wooziness was from the expired creamer

I'd used in my coffee that morning. And hours later, when we went to bed, side by side and hand in hand, I slept better than I had in weeks.

Now, it's been three minutes. Maybe five. Either way, enough. Too many. Not enough. As I pull the test toward me, squinting, I can't read the gray letters with precision, but I see that there's only one word.

I toss the test across the room, hear it clatter against the tile. I'm sucking in air but can't seem to push it back out. I'm inhaling and inhaling and growing bigger by the second, my body all breath and womb. *Grasping hands. Gaping mouths. Someone who needs help from me that I won't give.* My anxiety is not a broken record, it's a train that's chugging off the track. *Someone reaching for me. Someone expecting me to keep them safe. Someone I forget, as if they're a dream.*

Clack. Clack-clack-clack. Clack-clack.

Ted's awake. He's connecting old threads of fear. All those times I screamed? All those times I cried out? I want to scream now, too, open my mouth and release a wail, but this pregnancy test is no Experiment. No prank. I wish like hell it was.

I scramble for the door, the hall, my room, only to scurry back to the bathroom when I remember the test is still on the floor. The plastic cap is broken. The tiles are hot. The test is still marked by only one word, which I cover with my fist as I grab it.

When I'm back on my bed, I remember Eric's instructions: "If it happens—you have to call me right away. I don't care if it's one thirty in the morning, Bird. I don't care if it's during the day and I'm with a patient. Call the hospital and tell them it's an emergency."

I tried to tease him then. Asked, "What if I want to surprise you with the news? Bake you a cake with a rattle inside?" My throat tightened as I eked out the questions.

"Eh, you know me," Eric said. "I hate surprises. And I definitely hate cakes with rattles in them. They're so loud."

I look at the clock. Eric will be eating breakfast, an egg white omelet with two strips of turkey bacon and half a grapefruit.

I could call him, see if his excitement and joy are strong enough to clamp down my fear. But then I'd have to speak the word that, so far, has only appeared in steely letters on a screen. I'd have to taste it on my tongue. Hear its buzz in the air.

Clack-clack. Clack-clack-clack-clack. Clack-clack-clack.

Ted's fingers are picking up the pace. He's onto something and I have to get out of here. Get away. Even if just for an hour.

The cover of Astrid's book glares at me from the nightstand—that naked bulb; that bright red door. The longer I look at it, the more solid the door seems. Like if I touched it, I would feel the rough grain of real wood.

Is Astrid behind that door again? Did her abductor drag her all the way back to Foster? Is she in a dark corner, hunched up and hopeless, because—this time—nobody saw her?

I bang the heel of my hand against my head. It's all in there somewhere, tightly and agonizingly entombed—how, exactly, my path crossed with Astrid's; why I can't stop seeing her with that arm around her waist.

I consider the origins of what I've remembered. Astrid's photo on the news is what triggered my truer dream. The father saving his daughter is what led me to the arm. So I need something else. Something tangible I can stare at until I remember. Something identical—or at least very close—to something I've seen before. And now, shoving the pregnancy test deep into my bedside drawer, I know exactly where I'm going to go.

five

The coffeehouse is rooster themed. I find it on the road that runs through the center of Foster. The parking lot is gravel and the roosters are everywhere—metal ones whose rear feathers are pinwheels; ceramic ones lining the ramp to the entrance; a rooster wreath that crows when I open the door; and inside, roosters on mugs and walls and napkins and aprons, all printed above the café's name: Cock-a-doodle Coffee.

Small-town New Hampshire loves a good theme, especially when the town is so close to a tourist destination like Edgewood Lake, but this one is a little much. Waiting in line, I jolt as the door opens and the rooster wreath crows again. I think about leaving, getting back in my car, and driving until I find what I'm looking for, but I left Ted's in such a rush that I need a moment to stop. Get my bearings. Get a coffee and a plan.

When I reach the front of the line, I'm about to order a latte, but a lingering wave of nausea freezes me midsentence. Are pregnant women allowed to have caffeine? I don't know the rules. I don't know the first thing about carrying a baby. About being a hospitable home to something that is, right now, probably smaller than a coffee bean itself. Behind the counter, someone turns on the coffee grinder and my stomach clenches. I order a bottle of water and a plain croissant.

There's an open table by the window, where the sun floods in so hot that I begin to sweat as soon as I sit down. I pull out my phone, log in to the café's Wi-Fi—password "FowlPlay," according to the sign on the wall—and do a search for "Astrid Sullivan Foster New Hampshire." I came to Foster for one reason only: to trigger memories. The problem is—other than crossing the town border, I have no idea where to start. The whole drive over, I kept telling myself that if I can recover more images—or put the ones I have into context—I can make better sense of what I might have seen. Then maybe I can help the police find who's taken Astrid now.

I'm scrolling through search results—the Wikipedia page I've already read, the Amazon listing for her book—when the name I'm reading over and over is suddenly spoken aloud. Looking up, I register the TV mounted to the wall, and my lips part as Astrid's face fills the screen. The freckle beneath her eyebrow is faint beneath the sun's glare, but it's there. It's there.

"Hey, Chelsea, can you turn that up?" A woman standing near my table gestures to the TV and the barista picks up a remote. The volume crescendos and the customers fall into a hush as they angle their heads toward the screen.

". . . that it'll be soon, but police say their tip line is still open to anyone who can help them locate Sullivan. Earlier today, Eyewitness News 8 spoke to Rita Diaz, Sullivan's wife, at her home in Ridgeway, Maine. Diaz says she's trying to remain hopeful, even as days continue to pass with no new leads."

When the shot changes, Rita is sitting on a couch, a painting of a ballerina hanging a little off-kilter on the wall behind her. Her dark hair is pushed back into a ponytail, but flyaways frizz around her face. Her eyes look puffy and sleepless.

"If it's true," she says, "what everyone's speculating—that she was taken by the same man who took her twenty years ago—then she'll be back. I know she will. He brought her home last time, and aside from the . . . aftereffects of the trauma, she was fine."

Rita squints with conviction at someone off camera. "So I have to . . . I have to believe she'll be fine this time, too. It's the only thing keeping me together. But Astrid—" She pivots to look straight into the camera. Her dark eyes soften. "If you're seeing this somehow . . . I love you, okay? I'm waiting for you, baby."

A lump grows in my throat. I sip my water to try to swallow it down.

"What a fucking travesty."

I tear my eyes from the TV and look at the woman still standing next to my table. She's glaring at the screen, shaking her head, arms crossed tight. "I mean, Jesus, Astrid," she mutters. "What are the chances?"

The news moves on, and the barista turns the volume back down. Conversations resume, though something somber hangs in the air, heavy as the humidity outside. A few moments pass, but the woman beside me doesn't move. She's still staring at the TV as if the reporter will interrupt herself to break the news that Astrid has been found.

"Excuse me," I say, and I'm not surprised to hear my Social Worker Voice come out. Usually, it's the only way I can speak to strangers. Social Worker Voice is a little lower than my regular voice. Gentler, too, as if I can't think of a single reason to be anxious. It's something I've been crafting since my internship days, and it's how I let students and parents know that I'm on their side, that we're going to work together until everything's okay.

"Do you know her?" I ask the woman. "Astrid Sullivan?"

She glances at me, then locks her eyes back onto the screen. "She was my neighbor."

My breath hitches. I set down my phone on the table. "Oh wow," I say, careful to stay steady, as Social Worker Voice demands. I struggle for something to add. Come up with only: "Were you close?"

She shrugs. "Not really. She was a couple years older than me. But we carpooled to St. Cecilia's for CCD."

"CCD?" I say the letters slowly. They mean nothing to me.

When she looks at me this time, she meets my gaze with narrowed eyes. "Catechism classes? Don't you remember the CCD stuff in her book?"

"I haven't read past the prologue," I admit.

Her brows pinch together. "I'm sorry—who are you?"

Social Worker Smile—easy, soft, a glimpse of gritless teeth. "I'm Fern. I don't live here or anything, I'm . . . passing through."

She nods slowly. "Uh-huh."

The café door opens and a rooster crows. I do my best not to flinch. Instead, I press: "You said you were neighbors. What street was that exactly?"

Now she rolls her eyes, instantly exasperated. "Oh god, you're one of the rubberneckers, aren't you?"

"Um . . . I don't think so? I'm—"

"Because it was bad enough the first time. All those people showing up, standing vigil on her parents' front lawn. But now, I cut through Bleeker yesterday to take my daughter to ballet, and there's a line of cars, right in front of the house, everyone gaping." She puts her palms on the table and leans toward me. I press my back against the chair. "She doesn't live there anymore—her parents are dead! She wasn't even taken from Foster this time!"

She straightens up and crosses her arms again. Shakes her head as she looks out the window.

"I'm not a rubbernecker," I assure her.

I use GPS to navigate to Bleeker, and once I turn onto the street, it isn't hard to find Astrid's old house. Just like the woman said, there's a line of cars—three, I count, plus one news van—parked along the side of the road. The properties are spaced out enough that it's easy to tell which is the one the rubberneckers are here for. The house is quintessential suburbia—big and white, gray shuttered and picket fenced—but stabbed into the front lawn is a For Sale sign, its corners rounded and chipped, as if it's weathered several seasons.

I pull up behind the van—*WKRZ, News Without the Snooze*—and roll my window down. The heat barrels into my car. There's a cameraman and a reporter standing in front of the Sullivans' house. As the reporter fidgets with her hair, then counts down from five to one, I lean closer to the window so I can hear her better.

"Thanks, Mark," she says. "I'm standing outside the front lawn in Foster where, twenty years ago, Astrid Sullivan was last seen before she disappeared. The kidnapping, on the afternoon of June 24, 2000, occurred during a party celebrating her Confirmation at St. Cecilia's Catholic Church. At the time, Sullivan's father, Jacob Sullivan, told WKRZ, quote, 'She was right there at the party, until suddenly she wasn't,' words that became a warning to parents everywhere that, even in seemingly safe communities like this one, danger can be as close as your own front yard."

She gestures to the lawn behind her. Its parched yellow grass is a stark contrast to the lawns on adjacent properties. Those have unnaturally green blades that look sharp enough to slice through leather soles.

"But in Astrid Sullivan's recent memoir," the reporter continues, "which reached number five on the *New York Times* bestseller list this week, she reveals that it was only when she snuck away from that party that her abductor was able to apprehend her. Some Foster residents, especially those who attended the party that day, have been critical of this fact, claiming that Sullivan made herself a target by leaving the safety of her family and friends. Now, some of those same people wonder if she recently made another, quote, 'reckless and immature decision' that led to her disappearance in Ridgeway, Maine, twelve days ago."

In a moment, the reporter relaxes and fluffs her hair again. Stuck on this side of the camera, I can only assume that WKRZ is playing footage of an interview, but—reckless and immature decision? Made herself a target? At school, one of the first things I do when working with a student is assure them that, whatever bad thing has happened to them, it's not their fault. They'll try to tell me how they cried too loudly when their mother was sick, so she died to keep from hearing them. Or they knew their stepdad didn't want them in his room, but they snuck in anyway. They'll be clutching arms with bruises, pulling down their sleeves to cover scratches, and still, they'll find any way possible to take the blame.

I wonder what my child will blame itself for.

Milk that doesn't come. Clothes that aren't warm enough. Turning around for one second in which a man comes along and— No. Not now. I'm here for Astrid right now. Astrid who might have left her own party but did not ask to be snatched. Did not ask to be kept in a basement, terrified and alone. And definitely did not ask to be freed for twenty years only to be taken a second time. It's chilling—how her town would turn against her.

I squint at the house that looms behind the reporter. I don't recognize it at all. I'm wasting my time parked along this curb. There's another car behind me now, and I pull out of the space they've wedged me into.

Driving through the neighborhood, I look for something that will snag a memory. I see houses so indistinguishable from one another that I wonder if I'm going in circles. I see swing sets so large they belong at parks. I see children playing at the edges of yards and dogs sniffing at the edges of fences. But I don't see Astrid. I don't see a man, masked or otherwise, who grabs her by the waist and drags her away.

Eventually, one of the streets in this labyrinthine neighborhood spits me back onto the road where Cock-a-doodle Coffee was. There are quaint little storefronts lined on either side of me: Gifts & Gardens, Books & Birds, Tom's Tackle. Foster loves alliteration, apparently, but even with these memorable names, none of it is familiar.

I pass a town green with a gazebo in its center. There's a sign for an upcoming art fair, and there are kids doing cartwheels, adults with their noses in books. I scour the grass for anyone who looks sinister, but the worst I see is a little boy chasing a girl—and she is laughing as she runs.

Driving on, the stores thin out—Foster Flowers, Cuts by Christy—and now to the right there's an ample parking lot and a sign with gilded letters: "St. Cecilia's Roman Catholic Church."

I lurch to a stop. I've heard this church's name twice already today. It's where Astrid and her family went.

Cars honk and veer around me as I stare at the building. Brown brick and white trim, ornate windows and stone steps. But none of that is what holds my attention. It's the door—painted a vivid, almost violent red, like the one on the cover of Astrid's book.

I know it's not the same one. Astrid's led to a basement—not a large, open room where people worship and pray. But a red door on a place where Astrid spent so much time? Maybe it's a sign. Maybe it's leading me somewhere I wouldn't have thought to go on my own. And right now, as I pull into the driveway and ease into a spot, "maybe" is still the only lead that I've got.

———

The church is not air-conditioned. There's no relief from the heat as I enter. The temperature of the dim vestibule behind the red door is indistinguishable from outside. As I move into the main church, the air cools slightly, aided by the fans whirring noisily on the altar, but my forehead still beads with sweat.

It's a weekday, so there's hardly anyone here. Only a few elderly women dot the wooden benches, hands clasped in prayer, as I make my way down the aisle, and I realize that this might be the first church aisle I've ever walked down at all. Eric and I weren't married in a church; we had our ceremony in the same room as our reception— a hotel banquet hall in Boston. I didn't loop my arm through Ted's that day. Didn't walk with him down a path sprinkled with petals. The wedding coordinator had insisted I could, that it'd be easy to rearrange the tables to create an aisle. But I told her no. I didn't want to risk Ted telling me that the tradition of a father giving away his daughter is antiquated and unnecessary, all "dog and jackass show." He'd have been right, I think. But I couldn't bear to hear him say it.

The carpeted aisle at St. Cecilia's is the same shade of red as the door. And now I see crimson touches everywhere: in the panes of stained glass that line the walls, in the floral arrangements at the front, in the books that are tucked into the back of each bench. This aisle is a bright red tongue stretching toward the altar, and when I reach the tip of it, I stop. Stare at the wooden lectern, the thronelike chair where I imagine the priest sits, and—in the center of it all—the huge marble table that looks like a tomb.

One of the bench women is looking at me. She has a long beaded necklace braided between arthritic fingers, and her squint is full of suspicion. Noticing an open doorway off to the right, I ignore her stare to keep on searching—for what, I still don't know.

The doorway leads to a windowless hall. It's dark and narrow. Soupy with heat. The walls are lined with wood paneling, and I run my fingers along it as I shuffle forward. My nails catch in the grooves between boards, and a drop of sweat slithers down my back.

Then I see it. Even through the shadows. At the end of the hallway is another red door.

My feet fumble toward it, and I grab the knob, listen to it click as I turn it. It's locked, clearly, but I keep on twisting as if my wrist were strong enough to break through any bolt.

"Can I help you?"

I whirl around to see a man about Ted's age. He's wearing all black—button-down shirt, pants, belt—except for his white collar. It's difficult to tell in the dim hallway, but I imagine his bald head is shiny with sweat.

"Is there something I can do for you?" he tries again when I don't respond. "I'm Father Murphy."

I clear my throat. Croak out, "What's—what's behind the red door?" Then I wince at the words, how I've parroted Astrid's title, not a single trace of Social Worker Voice left inside me.

Father Murphy cocks his head to the side. "It's our basement," he says, and my eyes widen. "We hold Youth Group and CCD classes down there. But it's summer, so it's mostly unused right now."

The heat presses against me. I feel myself getting lost inside it. *Red doors. Locked doors. Spaces that go unused in summer.* But surely a CCD teacher or youth pastor would have a key to the basement if they taught down there. Anyone who works at the church could have a key. An office assistant. A janitor. Didn't I hear of a case at school once, predating my time there, where a student began to feel creeped out by the custodian at her temple? Didn't her parents call the school to warn them in case he showed up? I glance back at the red door behind me.

"Can I go down there?" I ask.

Father Murphy tilts his head again, skeptical, but he smiles a little, and even in the shadows, I can see that his eyes look kind. "Are you a parishioner? I don't believe I've seen you before."

"No, I'm not," I admit. "Is that okay? I'm here because of Astrid Sullivan. I'm . . . I knew her. When we were kids."

His face instantly changes. His mouth tightens and his smile, small as it is, goes sharp. "Ah, Astrid," he says. "Tragic, what I've been hearing about her these days. You were a friend of hers?"

"Um. No. Not friends exactly."

He blinks at me.

"I lived on her street," I add. "On Bleeker."

I cringe at the lie, but Father Murphy doesn't see. He's just removed a handkerchief from his pocket and is running it along his forehead. "I see," he says. He folds the cloth into a tiny square before putting it back. "And what brought you to St. Cecilia's today?"

An arm around a waist. A girl who reaches and pleads.

"I'm worried about her," I say. "Being missing again. And I, um, moved away—before her first kidnapping. I know she went here and everything, for church, and classes, so—" I struggle to keep connecting the dots I've created, but I don't know how to explain my presence with anything but the truth. I let out a breath. "I'm just looking for answers about what happened to her."

Father Murphy scrutinizes me. My posture stiffens as his eyes linger on my face. "That's understandable," he finally says. "I'm sure a lot of people are looking for answers. From God, from the police. In a way, it's a blessing that her parents aren't here to endure this all over again. What they went through last time . . ." He shakes his head. "I was there the day she went missing. At the Confirmation party."

My pulse thumps in my neck, but I lean against the wall. Cross my arms. Try to look casual. "Wow," I say. Then I inhale. Exhale. Load my Social Worker Voice back into my throat. "Can you tell me about it? That day, I mean."

He shrugs, and his white collar scrapes against his neck. "What would you like to know?"

I shrug too. Casual. "Whatever you remember."

"Oh, I don't know," he says, "it's been such a long time." But when he continues, it doesn't seem like he's forgotten much at all. It seems like he's told this story again and again.

"I remember it was a lovely party. A lot of parishioners were there. I think the Sullivans—God bless them—invited the entire church. They were clearly very proud of her. Confirmation is an important sacrament, you know."

I nod, but I don't know. As a child, the closest I ever came to praying was when I blew the puffy head off a dandelion stem and wished for Ted to open his door.

"I remember speaking to Astrid for a bit," Father Murphy adds, smiling slightly. "She had some questions for me. About God and faith. I was happy to hear she was continuing to think about these things. It's no secret that some people only get confirmed because their parents push them into it—and then I never see them on Sundays again. It's supposed to be the opposite, of course. It's supposed to be a strengthening of the grace received at Baptism, a deeper commitment to the Church, willingly made, so that you may be sealed with the gifts of the Holy Spirit. But I'm not naïve. I've been doing this for a very long time."

"Right," I say when he doesn't continue. "I, um—I remember Astrid being . . . pretty religious?"

I mean to sound confident, but it comes out as a question. I'm trying to picture this dim hallway, this cavernous echoing church, as a sanctuary for her. But all I can think is *sanctuaries that become prisons* and I imagine the red door behind me throbbing like a heart.

"She was devoted," Father Murphy says, "to the Word of God. And she pulled me aside that day in hopes of gaining a deeper understanding of it. I greatly respect her for that. She was fourteen, you know. Many girls her age would have been more concerned with the pile of gifts on the table."

I narrow my eyes at the blatant sexism.

"Actually, the gifts," he adds, a crease in his brow. "That's when we noticed she was gone."

I pull away from the wall. Stand pillar straight. "What do you mean?"

"Well, her mother announced that it was time to open the presents. But when we looked around for her, she wasn't there. Not ten minutes before that she and I had been having a conversation, and then she was—gone."

He stops speaking—lost, it seems, in the memory.

"That must have been terrifying," I prompt.

Father Murphy shoves his hands in his pockets, and for a moment, he looks like one of my middle schoolers, nervous and guilty about something.

"Not at first," he says. He takes out his handkerchief again, wipes his brow. "Jacob and Ruth—they thought that maybe Astrid had gone inside. But when they didn't find her there, they called someone. A friend of hers. Another parishioner—one of the only ones who wasn't at the party. But the friend's parents assured Ruth that their daughter was upstairs, alone. The two girls weren't allowed to see each other— they'd gotten into some kind of trouble together—but the parents said they'd call if Astrid showed up."

He stuffs his handkerchief back into his pocket. "Anyway, it was another half hour or so before people gave up and started to go home. But I waited there, at the Sullivans' request. Ruth was certain that Astrid had gone to see the friend, and that the parents would call them back any minute. She wanted me to be there, when Astrid got back, to counsel her about disobeying one's parents, how doing so leads you away from God. But I . . ."

He swallows. His Adam's apple bobs against his collar.

"What's wrong?" I ask.

His smile looks like a wince. "Oh, just old regrets," he says. "But it's been twenty years. I've made my peace with them, through the help of our Heavenly Father." He takes a breath, his shoulders rising and falling. "I do wonder, though, how much time we might have wasted, waiting to hear from the friend's parents. Because I didn't say it at the time, but I didn't believe she went there. As I said, Astrid and I had just had a very good conversation. And in that conversation, I got the sense that she cared—deeply—about obeying her parents. She wanted to be a good child to them, as well as a good child of God."

He sighs, and I feel his breath cross the distance between us. "But I'm a priest. Not a parent. And as such, I let them handle her disappearance from the party the way they saw best. I stayed with them until dusk, waiting."

"So it wasn't until . . . several hours later that her parents called the police?"

At first, he doesn't answer. Only stares at me. Blinks once, twice. Which is answer enough. But then he says, solemnly, "It wasn't until the next morning."

The air hisses in my throat as I suck it in. *Parents who get it all wrong. Parents who see threats in something innocent, then miss the real monsters, let them get away.*

"I do regret that we didn't know sooner," Father Murphy finally replies. "As I said, almost the entire parish was at the party. We could have driven around, gone looking for her." He shrugs. "Maybe it wouldn't have mattered. I guess we'll never know . . ."

As he trails off, I glance at the red door behind me. Almost the entire parish was at the party, he said. *Almost.* That word feels like a clue meant only for me.

"She isn't down there," Father Murphy says.

A chill shoots down my spine. "Excuse me?"

"The red door," he answers, gesturing toward it. Then he tilts his head, considers me for a moment. "You didn't really know her, did you?"

My throat goes dry in an instant. "Yes, I did," I say. "I even saw—I think I saw—"

"It's okay." He stops me with a hand in the air. "You're not the first person to read the memoir and come here."

"But I haven't—"

"It's okay," he repeats, looking at me like I'm a child who's been caught. Like his forgiveness will be my salvation. "I understand that people are eager to find her. Who wouldn't be? I pray every day for her safe return."

"But that's not—" I start. Then I squint through the shadows. "Why did you tell me about the party then? If you think I'm some rubbernecker?"

The handkerchief comes out again. He wipes it across his brow. "Oh, it's a type of penance, I suppose."

"Penance?"

"Not in the official sense, of course. That involves confession and prayer—though I have always believed righteous action to be a form of praying. And perhaps telling this story can help others who are equally troubled."

I shake my head. "I don't understand."

"God forgives us," he continues. "So easily, it seems. But forgiving ourselves is sometimes a greater challenge. I thought I'd forgiven myself. I told you I've worked through my regrets, but that's not completely true. Twenty years ago, when she was returned, I thought I had, because she was home. She was safe. But here she is, she's missing again, as you well know. And I wonder. If I'd done things differently that day, would any of this have happened at all?"

"If you'd done what differently? Told her parents you didn't think she went to the friend's house?"

His eyes become distant. It's not until he focuses on me that I realize he was staring over my shoulder. Straight at the red door.

He takes a few steps backward, then puts a hand on a slightly ajar door to his right. As he opens it wider, I see a desk. A bookshelf. Jesus on the cross.

"St. Cecilia's is an open place of worship," Father Murphy says, his voice cold. "But if you're not here to pray, or for spiritual guidance, then I think you should go."

Excerpt from Chapter Two of
Behind the Red Door: A Memoir **by Astrid Sullivan**

I have tried to forget the part I played in my abduction. I have tried to remember how I wore the dress my mother laid out for me, I kissed the guests on the cheek, I laid the linen napkin on my lap. The dress was tea-length and white, ballooning out as it reached my calves. It had scalloped edges and lace embroidery and could not avoid comparisons to a bridal gown—as if my Confirmation had been a wedding to God.

I suppose, in a way, it was. Only I was terrible at keeping my promises. I broke my vows as easily as fingernails.

But I tried to be good that day. The day of the party. I kept on parting my lips for the spoonfuls of guilt my mother emptied into my throat. I let that bitter medicine numb my tongue, erase the taste of Bridget's skin. I did not call her, did not run to her house, even though I overflowed with longing. Even though my mouth was a chalice from which I needed her to sip.

I almost kissed her at the Confirmation service, three days before my party. I almost cheated on God, my groom, to pledge myself to her lips. We looked at each other as we waited in line for the bishop to anoint us, and I was so close to latching my fingers to her wrist, pulling her to me, marrying my mouth to hers with the entire church as our witness.

What stopped me, though, was Bridget herself. She broke our gaze to look at the floor, and the shame that flamed in her cheeks was as bright as the scarlet aisle beneath our feet. In that moment, I saw it clearly: she believed that what we'd done, what we felt, was wrong. More than that, it hurt her. I saw the pain in the pinch of her eyes. I practically heard the hiss of *sin, sin, sin,* said by some serpent into her ear.

It was then that my mother's medicine flooded back onto my tongue. It pooled in the insides of my cheeks. It threatened to drown me if I didn't swallow it down.

I watched Bridget offer her forehead to the bishop's thumb. He touched the oil to her flesh and made the sign of the cross. Her "Amen" was her "I do" to God. And I was next in line to be his bride. So I, too, tipped my head toward the bishop. I said my vow. I walked back to my pew and prayed.

By the day of the party, my legs had a perpetual bend in them, as if always about to kneel.

My parents had filled our front yard with round tables and white cloths, but the guest list was so enormous that there weren't enough chairs for everyone who came. My mother brought out blankets for people to sit on, laying them on the perfectly manicured lawn.

For an hour that afternoon, I wove through tables, thanked everyone for coming, showed the tag of my dress when ladies from church asked about the designer. "It's darling," one said. "You look like an angel." My mother heard the comment and smiled.

I was taking a break from all that, finally filling a plate with salmon puffs and sticks of chicken satay, when Father Murphy looped his fingers around my arm and pulled me aside. His grip was light, his pull gentle and slow, but I still looked at his hand like it was a hook. My narrowed eyes flicked from his fingers to his face and back to his fingers, but he didn't seem to get my pointed gaze.

"Astrid," he said. By now, we were on the side of the house, hidden behind the lilac bushes. "I'd like to speak to you for a moment."

"About what?"

"About your recent impropriety."

I'd had a salmon puff halfway to my mouth, but now I dropped it. "My what?"

"I heard about what happened," he said, "with you and Bridget Matthews."

I squeezed the rim of my paper plate. Her name sounded ugly in his mouth. Like a cough instead of a song.

"We're friends," I said.

"Ah, but friends do not engage in the kind of activity your mother told me about. You've upset her, you know. She came to me, shortly after it happened. She was shaking, Astrid. I thought someone in the family had died."

Father Murphy had medicine, too, I saw, and every word he spoke felt like another spoon thrust onto my tongue.

"Then there's God," he added. "Do you know what the Bible says about what you did?"

"That it's really fun?"

I couldn't help the response. My body was rejecting the treatment.

His lips pressed together, a flat unbroken line. "That it's sinful. That you should ask God for forgiveness, which I know he will grant if you come to him with an open heart."

My chest burned. I plucked up a salmon puff and popped it into my mouth. I spoke through my chewing. "So you mean, like, any old heart that I cut open? Or specifically mine? Because if he's not too picky, there's this raccoon in the neighborhood that—"

"Do you think this is a joke?"

I swallowed the fishy pastry.

"I did," I said. "But now that I see you're not laughing, I understand I was wrong."

"Your salvation is at stake here, Astrid." He said *salvation* like it meant the same as *life*.

"I was confirmed, wasn't I? I'm pretty sure that me and God are, like, together now, so."

A part of me wanted to stop, submit, shake my head in apology. But I'd been good all day. I'd been good for several days. I didn't deserve this reminder of the girl I couldn't have. My kitten heels were still on my feet, weren't they? My pantyhose still felt like a new skin that didn't fit.

Anger flashed in Father Murphy's eyes. But then he closed them, inhaled deeply, and when he looked at me again, his expression was closer to pity.

"You're not taking this seriously. What you did with Bridget . . . it's a sin."

There was that word again, still sounding like a hiss.

"Why?" I asked.

Father Murphy tilted his head. "Why what?"

"Why is it a sin? I *like* her. And I can't control that fact any more than you can control the fact that you love God. So how can it be wrong to feel something like that?"

"Ah," he said. "It's the act that's the sin. Not the feeling. You must understand that to engage in . . . improper activity . . . with another girl—" He slipped a finger between his collar and neck, as if his shirt were too tight. "That's the problem. That's what you must turn away from so you can be back in the grace of God."

I stuck another puff into my mouth and took a long time chewing it. When I finally swallowed, I said, "So I can like Bridget. Romantically. But I can't act on that feeling. I have to find some guy to make out with instead. Which means I have to lie to the guy, lie to everyone who thinks I'm into the guy, lie to my parents. Only—lying's a sin too, right? 'Thou shalt not bear false witness' and all that?"

The corner of his mouth twitched. "Perhaps, in time," he said, "it will no longer be a lie."

I shook my head. "I don't believe that."

"You don't need to. You need only believe in God. In his unfailing goodness and light. Believe that if you repent for your sins, you will receive the healing power of his forgiveness, and everything else will fall into place. But don't wait too long, Astrid."

He dragged his eyes down the length of my body like a tailor appraising the fit of a garment. His gaze lingered on my lacy hem as he said, "Hell is no place for a girl."

I laughed at him then. It gurgled out from between my lips and I did not place a hand over my mouth to stop it. "If hell is where the lesbians are," I said, "then I think I'd like to burn."

Despite everything that happened afterward, I'm really proud of that.

But thirty minutes later, back among the chaste and

chatting guests, I regretted it. If Father Murphy relayed the details of our conversation to my parents, who knew what they'd take from me next. They'd already taken Bridget, and my doorknob. Maybe next would be the door itself. Or perhaps they'd try a different tactic and lock me in instead, reinforce the wood with steel bars, keep the key on the same chain as the cross that hung from my mother's neck.

I looked for Father Murphy. I planned to pull him aside, the way he'd pulled me, and put on a meek and mortified face. I planned to stammer and apologize and promise to come to confession the following week. But I couldn't find him anywhere. Not on the front lawn. Not at the food table. Not even in the house. I asked one of the old ladies if she'd seen him, and she said, "No, dear, not for a while. Oh, but twirl for us, won't you?" I did, and I smiled, and I excused myself.

Had I offended him so much that he'd left? I stood on the curb, peered up and down the line of vehicles, searching for the Lincoln that Father Murphy drove. The cars stretched down the block farther than I could make out, so I walked down the street until I could see them all, until the laughter from the party began to fade. Then, even when I found his car and confirmed he wasn't inside it, I kept on walking. Just a few steps at first. Just to see how far I could get without my mother calling me back. But I didn't hear my name. So I didn't stop. And it was like the air became easier to breathe, like the band of my pantyhose no longer pinched my waist.

Nobody noticed, I said to myself, rounding a corner. *Nobody noticed, nobody noticed.*

At an intersection, I turned left, onto another street altogether, and I moved forward and forward and forward. It was completely quiet now—no kids in any yards, no dogs that yipped or barked—and when I reached the stretch of the road, Kimble Lane, that was a few acres of trees, I inhaled and inhaled and walked and walked. I didn't even pause when I heard a car driving slowly behind me. Every step between me and that party, my parents, that priest, was a step I took unchained, and suddenly I could not stop for anyone.

The car rolled to a crawl. Then its brakes squeaked. But I didn't turn my head. I figured it was someone from the party, there to bring me back. I didn't look at the driver, not even when I heard the door open, the footsteps clomping behind me. I never saw a face, only a hand, as it was placed over my mouth to usher me into the dark.

six

The inside of my car feels like a greenhouse. I haven't turned it on yet to get the AC flowing. I'm punishing myself, I think. For coming all this way just to end up in a church parking lot, no closer to remembering anything than when I first arrived. I'm leaning against the headrest and my eyes are closed, but burning on the back of my lids is the red door that Father Murphy didn't allow me to open.

I could have tried harder. I could have knocked on his office door and pleaded with him to hand over the keys. But what could I say to convince him? *I think someone who worked at, or went to, your church might have kept Astrid down there?* No. I'd need evidence before making an accusation like that—and all I have is a paint color.

Is this spiraling? Or desperation? I don't know. The only thing I'm certain of is this: every minute in which I can't remember anything useful is another minute in which Astrid's life is in danger. So whatever I saw during that vacation with Kyla is—

Kyla.

I actually smack my head at how stupid I've been. Then I turn on my car, crank the air-conditioning, and pull up her name on my phone. As it rings, my heart beats faster. It's been over two years since I last heard her voice, when I called her on her thirtieth birthday. Since then it's been sporadic texts, Facebook likes, and Instagram comments only, and there's a part of me that wonders if she'll see my name on her caller ID and send it to voice mail. I haven't acted like a real friend to her in a long time.

"Fern!"

I jolt as I hear the excitement in her voice. I clear my throat and try to match her tone.

"Kyla, hey!"

"Hi! This is so weird. I was just thinking about you this morning."

"Really?"

"Yeah! Brennan Llewellyn was on *The Today Show*, and I was picturing Ted watching the interview with his fists shaking, and his face getting all red, and steam coming out of his ears. I was, like, *giggling* at the image." She laughs before pausing. "I also might watch too many cartoons."

I force myself to chuckle. "Well, if he had TV or internet, I'm sure he'd have done that. Guess you'll have to picture him shaking his fist at Brennan's book instead."

"Oh god, that's even better."

A shrill cry pierces my ear, and I have to hold the phone away from my face.

"Is this a bad time?" I ask.

"No, not at all." Kyla's voice shakes like she's bouncing up and down. I picture a child clamped against her hip and it's as if I can feel the weight of him, or her, pressing on my own body. The cry continues for a few moments. Then it's a scream.

"Sorry, it's just Thomas," Kyla says, but her voice barely reaches me. The line is clogged with this cry for help. I will hear it tonight in my dreams. "He's really sick."

"Oh no! Should you take him to the hospital?"

"The hospital? No, he's— Jeff, can you take him for a minute? It's Fern." The wailing remains megaphone loud for another moment, and then it grows distant, fading into white noise. "Sorry about that. No, he's okay. He just caught Leland's cold."

"Are you sure?" I ask. "Aren't colds supposed to be dangerous for babies? I can let you go if you need to call the doctor or—"

"Fern, it's fine," she says. "He's okay," and it's as if we're kids again: me panicking about something—bugs, boys, her brother—and Kyla shushing me, soothing me, telling me that everything's all right. Sometimes it felt like the only mothering I got was from my best friend.

"Okay," I concede. "Good. Um. So I know we haven't talked in a—"

"Leland! What did I say? The brush goes in the paint, not your mouth . . ."

My eyes widen. *Poisonous chemicals. Colors that look like candy. A tongue too young to know the taste of toxins.*

"This kid, I swear," Kyla continues. "She would try to eat the refrigerator if I told her not to. Yesterday, she actually—no! Leland, no. Not on the floor. On your—yes, good. Goooood. Isn't that fun?" I hear her breathe deeply before coming back to me. "Sorry, what were you saying?"

I laugh, in spite of myself. In spite of the prickly feeling crawling along my arms.

"How do you do that?" I ask.

Another cry in the background. It's high but robust. Hell-bent on being heard.

"Do what?"

"Do . . . motherhood, I guess. Stay calm while your baby is sick. While your kid is . . . eating paint, it sounds like?"

There's a rush of air against the phone, and I know that Kyla is blowing her bangs out of her eyes.

"It's not as bad as it seems," she says. "The paint is kids' stuff. She probably *could* eat it and be fine, but obviously I—wait."

"What?"

"What's with this interest in my kids all of a sudden?" Her tone is light. Playful, even. But the question still jabs me. I've never seen either of her children in person, and she only lives in Maine. I could have made the trip there and back in a single day. If I'd wanted to.

"Nothing," I say, "I just—"

"Fern."

"What?"

"Are you pregnant? Is that why you're calling?"

Her voice rises. In volume. In pitch. And I know that if I answer her truthfully, the next sound she'll make is a squeal. When we were little, Kyla always used to talk about us raising kids together. She designed matching outfits for our children to wear, planned out their birthday parties from appetizers to gifts. We practiced being hostesses, setting up a circle of stuffed animal guests, using her dolls as makeshift babies. "Excellent crumpets, Fern," she'd say to me, "I simply *must* get this recipe." And I'd respond with "Oh there's no recipe, Kyla. I just threw some things together!"

It was easy enough to play along—the future was so far away back then—but even still, whenever she thrust a doll at me, said "This is Fern Jr., isn't she adorable," I'd fidget on the pink carpet in her bedroom. I'd take the doll from her hands with no idea how to hold it.

"No," I say now. "I'm not pregnant." Then I hurry along, before she has time to consider how my voice flattens with the lie. "I'm actually calling because—do you know about Astrid Sullivan?"

"Like, how she's missing again?"

"Yeah. And remember that time I went with your family to Edgewood Lake?"

"Uh-huuuh . . ."

"Okay. So do you remember meeting, or maybe just seeing, Astrid Sullivan on that trip?"

Silence. I can't even hear Thomas crying in the background anymore. I play with one of the air vents, flicking its knob back and forth, waiting for Kyla to respond.

"Do I remember meeting Astrid Sullivan?" she repeats.

"Yeah," I say. "She had red hair, and freckles, and—"

"No, I know what she looks like, but—where the hexagon is this coming from?"

My fingers pause on the vent. "Hexagon?"

"Oh . . . sorry. Autopilot. Leland's starting to repeat everything we say now, so Jeff and I are replacing bad words with bigger ones."

Even words can be dangerous? Ted and Mara never said too much, so I didn't have many curses to parrot. The worst four-letter word I knew was *fear*.

"Question still stands, though," Kyla says. "Where is this coming from?"

I move my hand to the steering wheel. Grip it hard. Then I tell her everything—about my nightmares that feel more and more like memories, about Astrid's face jolted loose inside me—and I finish with the most chilling fact of all: we were at Edgewood Lake, right on the border of Astrid's town, during the time she went missing. When I'm done, I hear a clatter in the background, like a cup falling to the floor.

"Leland," Kyla says limply. Then, to me: "I remember your nightmares."

"Right," I say. "So do you remember seeing her, too? Or-or maybe you don't remember seeing *her* exactly, because I didn't. Not until recently. But maybe you remember something weird happening. Something off. Something that maybe you haven't thought much about, until now."

Her sigh sounds like static. "Are you okay, Fern?"

"Yes, I'm fine, just . . . please. Did you see anything unusual? Anything at all."

There's a flash of red through my windshield. I peer through the glass to see the church door opening. An old woman hobbles out. The same one who eyed me from the bench as she prayed.

"No," Kyla says. "I'm sorry, I didn't. Which means you probably didn't either. We were joined at the hip that week, never out of each other's sight. Except—oh god—remember that *awful* haircut I got that week?"

I pause at her abrupt change of subject. "Huh?"

The woman uses the railing to make her way down the cement steps. She keeps her eyes on her feet.

"You know," Kyla says, "that pixie cut I was obsessed with getting."

It had been such a big deal. Something Kyla had planned for weeks, scouring through magazines, cutting out glossy photos, making an album of options. We were doing it in secret, too. Kyla's mother loved her blond hair, so long it sometimes caught inside the back of her jeans. But Kyla was eager for the breeze on her neck.

"Of course," I say. "But what about it?"

"That was the only time we were apart."

"Your haircut? No, I was with you for that."

"Yeah, at first," she says. "But remember? We went to some place in Foster to get it done, and—"

"Foster?" My heart kicks. "That's where Astrid lived."

I don't mention that I'm there right now, in the parking lot of Astrid's church, eyes on an old woman as she shuffles toward her car. But my pulse thrums. I scratch my wrist. Because it's confirmation: I wasn't just close to where Astrid lived. It's not a theory anymore that I might have ended up in her town. I was here.

"Okay," Kyla says. "But anyway, there was a long wait at the salon, and I was starting to have second thoughts. So you went with Cooper to get me some candy so I'd stop freaking—"

"Cooper?" I say it loud and fast. As if the name burns my tongue and needs to be spit out. "Why was he there?"

"He drove us," Kyla says. "And he was heading to the gas station to get some cigarettes, so I asked you to go with him to get me some Nerds Ropes."

I remember that now. The request had seemed so unfair. Kyla knew what Cooper did to me. How sitting in the same car as him made me feel like I was in a cage. I remember being mad at her for even asking such a thing—but I went anyway.

"I vaguely remember leaving with him," I say. "But I can't really remember anything after that. What day was this?"

"You actually expect me to remember something like that?"

I wait for her to consider, because I do. Kyla's always had an impeccable memory—what shirt she wore to a party ten years ago, what she got for Christmas in 1999; she could probably even tell me the exact date of the last time I called her—and right now, I need that precision. I know the fireworks we watched were on "June goddamn twenty-second." I know Astrid was taken on June 24. But when was I in Foster?

"Saturday, I guess?" Kyla says. "Yeah, Saturday. Because our Edgewood Lake rental was always Sunday to Sunday, and I got the haircut on our last full day. But why does that matter?"

"Hold on," I say, and I pull the phone from my ear to look up what day of the week June 24, 2000 was. When the answer appears, my heart lurches. My breath sputters.

Saturday.

"How long were we gone?" I almost shout. "Cooper and me."

There's a beat of silence before she answers. "A *long* time, actually.

My haircut was done by the time you guys came back. I remember waiting out front like a loser for, like, twenty minutes. I'm *still* waiting on my Nerds Ropes, by the way."

She laughs, but my abs have all tightened. My mouth feels incredibly dry. "So I could have seen something," I say. "While I was gone. With Cooper."

Kyla's laughter cuts off. "I mean . . . I *guess*? But then Cooper would have seen it, too, and he's never mentioned anything weird happening."

That's because he's Cooper, I want to say. *He was sadistic. He probably could have seen someone get dragged away and think it was just a game.*

"Can I have his number?" I ask.

"Who—Cooper?"

"Yeah."

She hesitates. "I can give it to you, yes. But I wouldn't bother talking to him, Fern."

"Why not?"

"I don't think there's anything he could say to help you. I don't think you really—" Her sentence cuts off with a crash. "Oh, shit. I mean shish kabob!" A wail starts up, siren-sharp in my ear.

"Kyla? Are you okay?"

"Yes, I'm— Jeff! Can you— Look what she did!" Voices tangle together. A cacophony of cries. "I don't know, I turned around for a— Fern? I gotta go. I'll text you my brother's number."

"Okay, but what—" Then there's nothing in my ear but the sound of air.

I close my eyes, rest my forehead against the steering wheel. My nerves are sizzling. My skin is still slick. Cooper, of all people, knows something. But will he tell me what it is?

A knock at my window startles me. I snap my head up and squint at the old woman squinting back at me. Her gray hair puffs out like a cloud. Her hands are so arthritic that her knuckles, still pressed against the glass, look like tiny fists.

I roll down the window. But only a crack.

"Can I help you?" I ask.

"I heard you in there." She points to the church with a finger that won't stay straight. "Talking to Father Murphy."

I look at the church door. Red like a firetruck. Like the cross on an ambulance. Red like an open wound.

"Yes," I say, "I—"

"Your plates say Massachusetts."

I stare at her. Nod once. "They do."

"You need to stay away from all this," she croaks.

"All this?"

She leans closer. I can smell her breath through the gap in the window. Cough drops and lipstick. "What happens to that girl," she says, "it's in God's hands now."

I open my mouth. Close it again. Her eyes, murky as they are, drill into mine. Finally, I manage, "I'm trying to help."

She straightens up. Takes a step back. "You can't," she says. "What's done is done. The rest is up to God."

My heart is in my throat as she clicks a key fob. A car two spots away from us beeps. She heads toward it, her feet moving as if through sludge.

"What's done?" I call out to her. She puts a hand in the air, a halting gesture, but doesn't look back.

"What's done?" Almost a yell this time. But she's opening her car door. Settling down with a *humph* inside. Her seat belt goes on and the car rumbles to life.

My phone chirps with a text. I rip my eyes from the woman. *Here's Cooper's number. Let's talk more soon.* When I look at the car again, it's pulling out of the space. I watch, unmoving, pulse throbbing, as it lurches through the parking lot. Jerks to a stop at the sign. Takes a blinkerless right.

My gaze sinks back to my phone, where Cooper's number stares up at me. I press it with a shaking thumb until the option to text him appears.

Hi Cooper, it's Fern, I write. My fingers stumble over the letters. My entire body shivers. *Can we meet up?*

seven

When I get to The Diner, Cooper's already there, eating in a bright orange booth. Like Rusty's and the rest of Cedar, The Diner never changes. Same chalkboard with decades-old "specials." Same place-mat menus with the misspelled "choclate." Same salty smell greeting me at the door. I inhale it like the scent of home.

I watch Cooper before approaching. His face is filthy, streaked with dirt and flecked with something blue. His big hands are clutching a hamburger, and when he bites into it, he closes his eyes. Even from here, I can see it: the juice from the dead animal slithers down his chin.

"Hi," I say, sliding into the seat opposite him. He wipes his mouth and grins, meat between his teeth.

"I had to order without you," he says. "I'm always starving after work."

I'm about to tell him it's fine when someone grasps me from behind. Envelops my upper body, pins my arms to my sides. Air catches in my throat and my heart skips. Someone is squeezing me. Cooper looks at whoever it is. Chews his burger slowly. Completely unconcerned.

"My little Ferny," the person says, and my muscles loosen. My breath whooshes out.

"Peg."

I twist around to hug her, and it's like hugging Mrs. Claus. Her white hair is pulled back into a bun. Her chest is a cushion for my head. When we separate, I notice her cheeks are pink and shiny. Just as they've always been.

"Ted mentioned you were back," she says. "So nice of you to help him with the move."

"Oh. I'm doing what I can."

Peg's eyes well up a little. "This'll be one of the last times you're here then, huh?"

"What do you mean?"

"Well, once Ted heads to Florida . . . Cedar'll always be home, of course, but—there'll be no house for you to come back to. It'll belong to somebody else."

I gape at her, watch the tears collect in her eyelashes. (Peg always vacillates between smiling and crying—"chronically emotional," Ted calls her.) I hadn't thought about Ted's move like that. But she's right. Soon, someone else will live in Ted's house. A whole family, probably. They'll walk up the creaky staircase and have no idea how often I sat there, elbows on knees, chin in the palm of my hands, waiting for Ted to notice me. They'll fill his study with—what, exactly? Craft supplies? A rocking chair and cradle? It's impossible to imagine. Impossible to think that Ted himself won't be there. A ghost behind a closed door.

"Oh, Ferny, I'm sorry," Peg says. "Don't look so worried, okay? We'll make sure you still come back plenty, won't we?" She elbows Cooper, who swallows a bite of burger and nods. "And you can always stay upstairs with me. I've got one of those sleep-sofa things. My nephew says it's comfier than a cloud."

I chuckle in acknowledgment, even though she was right the first time. Once Ted's gone, I'll have no reason to come back. Not even Rusty or Peg will be enough, though they spoiled me as a kid with stickers and milkshakes and smiles. Just like that, Cedar will be erased from the map of my life. No town with spotty reception. No woods that darken the road to home. No Cooper, either. I look at him now. There's ketchup in the corner of his lips. He stares up at Peg, chewing with his mouth wide open.

"Hey, why Florida, by the way?" Peg asks. "Of all the places for Ted to go."

I have no answer. Ted among tourists? Ted among all those "senile shuffleboard addicts," those "hip-replacement hippies"? Ted has no shortage of epithets for people who move to Florida.

"I don't know," I tell Peg. "Mara told him she wanted to find a new studio space, and I guess he took the opportunity to make a change."

"But it's still weird, right?" she asks. "Florida?"

"Yeah," I say. "It's really weird."

"Hmm." She stares into the distance, then shakes her head. Taps the table twice. "Corned beef sandwich coming right up."

As she walks away, I fidget with my fingers in my lap.

"So," I begin, but Cooper cuts me off.

"You're probably wondering why I asked you here," he says.

I meet his eyes. They're stony and serious. "Huh?" I mutter. Then he breaks into a smile. Shoves a fry into his mouth.

"I'm kidding," he says. "What's up, Brierley? Why'd you wanna meet? You sick of Ted already?"

"No, I . . ."

To be sick of him, I'd have to spend time with him.

"My name's Douglas now," I remind him.

"Yeah, I know," he says. He closes his hand into a fist, nudges my chin with it. "But you'll always be Brierley to me."

I lean back until my shoulder blades touch the booth. Something flickers in his eyes and he laughs through his nose.

"Out with it," he insists.

There's a wad of potato bobbing on his tongue. I keep my gaze focused on his eyes. "Do you remember that summer I went with you guys to Edgewood Lake?"

"I think so, yeah."

"And you drove Kyla and me to a hair salon? But then she wanted us to get her some candy from the gas station?"

"Okay . . ."

"What happened after that?" I ask. "When we went to get the candy. I can't remember."

He stops chewing. His jaw freezes at a strange angle. I hold my breath.

"You wanted to meet up so you could ask me about a trip to the gas station . . . from twenty years ago?"

I nod. How quickly he recalled that it was exactly twenty years.

He picks up a fry, stabs at the ketchup on his plate. "Brierley, I have no idea. But I'm gonna go out on a limb here and guess that . . . we got candy?"

I shake my head. Fast and hard. "Kyla said no. She said we were gone a really long time. Way longer than it would take to pick up cigarettes and Nerds Ropes. So something must have gone wrong somehow. You must've . . ." I trail off.

"Are you talking about what happened when we were kids?" he asks.

My jaw clenches. It's a moment before I can respond. "What do you mean?"

He snips a fry in half with his teeth. "How I used to, you know, mess with you and stuff."

Mess with me? When we were kids? He was eighteen the first time he shoved his arm into my mouth. I look at his tattoo and I swear I can feel that honeycomb on my tongue.

"Because I've grown up a lot since then," he continues. "I mean, obviously." He flexes his arm muscles. The bees convulse. "So if this is about confronting me or something—for maybe freaking you out that day, or whatever—there's no need. I'm a completely different person now. It wouldn't even make sense for me to apologize, you know? Because I'd be apologizing for something that someone else did."

I stare at him. Gape, really. I'm still struggling for a response when Peg slaps a sandwich and milkshake in front of me. I jump a little.

"That was fast," I say.

She winks at me. "I poached it from table seven. Shirley Schmidt can wait a minute."

She spins around, heads to another table, and I rip the paper off a straw. Plunk it into my shake. I'm about to suck some of it up when I feel a ripple of nausea. I look at the corned beef fringing the bread on my plate. Usually just the sight of it makes my mouth water. Now, I can't help but see it as the pile of flesh I know it is.

"Listen," I say, "I'm not talking about what you did to me when I was a kid. I'm talking about that day in particular, when we went to the gas station. Can you think of any reason why it would have taken us so long to get back?"

He shoves the last bite of burger into his mouth. His cheek bulges with the meat as he considers. After a moment, his eyes brighten.

"I know what you're talking about now," he says. "Christy Miller."

"Christy? No—Astrid."

"Who?"

"Astrid Sullivan. Did we see her that day?"

He's slurping his soda but stops when he hears her name. "The missing chick?"

I nod. Watch him turn his head a little, look at me out the side of his eyes.

"Uh, I don't know who you did or didn't see, Brierley. But there's only one girl I remember seeing that day."

"Who? Did she have red hair and freckles?"

"No, she had blond hair and incredible tits."

"What?"

"Christy Miller. She was this girl whose family always went to the lake the same time ours did. Shit, she was, like, supermodel hot. You should've seen her in a bikini."

I'm trying to process what he's saying. Find some connection between Christy and Astrid. But I'm struck by how young he sounds. Forty years old and still talking like he's half that.

"Anyway." He picks up his glass, jabs at the ice with his straw. "We finally hooked up that summer, and then I saw her at the gas station." He shrugs. "I must've told you to scram and that's why you don't remember her."

"But where did I go?"

Another shrug. "Fuck if I know. I was pretty preoccupied."

I lean forward. Put my hand on the table. "Well, how long was I gone?"

Cooper smirks. "A while," he says. "Definitely a while." His eyes go hazy. "Christy Miller, man. I wonder if she's on Facebook."

"So you have no idea where I went?"

He focuses on me again. "No, Brierley. I wasn't your babysitter." His gaze narrows. "What's this even about? Why were you asking about Astrid Sullivan?"

I slump back against the booth. Cooper's another dead end. Like Foster. Like all the roads in my mind that stop right when the memory should start. All he's done is confirm that I had time and opportunity to see Astrid. Maybe I should take that as a victory. But I was already sure of that.

"Where did we meet back up?" I ask, ignoring his question. Now that I know he didn't see anything, I don't want to tell him more than I have to. Don't want him to glimpse the source of my anxiety so he can gnaw on it like a bone.

"Who knows," he says. "I left so me and Christy could—you know." He bites his lip, closes his eyes, bobs his head. I wait through the gesture. "So I guess I would have gone looking for your skinny ass afterward. And then we went back to Christy's."

I wrinkle my brow. "You took me back to your girlfriend's place?"

He chuckles—a single slap of sound. "Christy Miller was not my girlfriend. But no, I mean the haircut place. It had Christy in the name. I remember that because, well . . . I thought it was funny that my sister and I were both getting blown by someone named Christy that day."

I squint at his crudeness. He picks up three fries and crams them into his mouth. Then he looks at his hand, flecked with the same blue paint that freckles his face.

"Oh—before I forget," he says. "I wanted to thank you."

His lips shine with grease. I have to concentrate on my breathing. Between Cooper's eating habits and the smell of corned beef, I'm close to losing what little I've gotten down today.

"What do you mean?" I ask.

He picks up his napkin, wipes his hands. Smiles like he's got a secret. "You inspired me."

"Inspired you."

"Mm-hmm. The way you reacted to the cabin yesterday. My dream flip. It gave me the push I needed."

"The way I reacted?"

All I can remember is my body stiffening as Cooper plunged his truck through the woods.

Cooper nods. "I saw the way you looked at it. So serious. And so . . . awed. I could tell you felt the same as me about it. That it's special. That little house tucked into the woods. Peace and privacy for miles. A person could get lost there."

His tongue cradles the word *lost* like it's something precious. Something desired.

"I'm not following," I say.

He smiles again. A twitch of his lips. "I went to Town Hall today. Started the process of buying the property. I even took my folks to see it this morning. They think it's a fool's errand. Too much work, my dad says. No way I'll turn a profit. But, man, I'm telling you . . . sometimes you just *know* something, you know? And yeah, the property's gonna cost me a lot, but I'm fine with that. Because when you're that certain of something, when you feel it in your *gut*"—he clutches his stomach, gives it a shake—"you have to see it through to the end."

He leans back, grinning at me. He crosses his arms over his chest. "You know what I'm saying?"

Astrid could be in a cabin. One that's like Cooper's—somewhere overlooked, underloved. Right now, she could be locked in a basement, her red hair the only bright thing in all the darkness, and every day, every moment that goes by, the walls could be crumbling a little bit more. Is she worried she'll run out of time? That they'll collapse altogether, bury her in a tomb of wood and rot? Is she waiting for the witness, still, to tell someone what she saw?

"You get me, right, Brierley?" Cooper continues. "How when you know, you know?"

All these dead ends, but I'm certain—I *know*—that if I keep looking, I'll find the road that leads me back to her.

"I do," I tell Cooper. "I know exactly what you mean."

It's not until I'm driving back to Ted's that I put it together.

Christy. Cuts by Christy.

That was the name of a place I saw in Foster today. One of the businesses made memorable by the alliteration on its sign. It was a few turns from Astrid's neighborhood. A very short drive. A perfectly reasonable walk.

So there it is, then—more confirmation. I was close. I was there. And today, I drove down the same streets I traveled two decades ago.

I should feel validated. Or buzzing with the promise of this new puzzle piece. But I don't. When I saw those businesses, those houses, those roads, I recognized nothing. Every sign might as well have been blank, every building empty and shuttered.

I can go back there, though. I can read the memoir. Find out more details about where she was taken, what the witness saw. If her words on the page don't trigger a memory, they'll at least give me a map.

My hands grip the steering wheel tighter. I step on the gas a little bit harder. My headlights slice through the purple dusk, the road ahead the color of a bruise that will take a while to heal. The houses are starting to space out, growing woodsy in between. A figure appears in the distance. Dark and difficult to distinguish from the backdrop of night.

I slow down. Let my lights creep up his body. Black boots. Black pants. Black raincoat. I check the temperature gauge on my dashboard—eighty-two degrees. I bet his body's burning. Mine flushes just from looking at him.

Cooper called this guy a drifter, acted as if he was a suspicious intrusion to our town. But he has to be headed somewhere. And maybe his clothing is protection from mosquitoes, which in New Hampshire can seem as big as birds. I glance at my own uncovered skin. All of it so prickable. So close to the blood beneath—which suddenly flows faster.

He's walking in the direction I'm driving, but now, bathed in my headlights, he stops. Turns slowly. As if he's a knob that's screwed too tight. My foot squeezes the brake. My car crawls.

In a few moments, he's facing me. We're the only two on this road and then—one second, two seconds, three—neither of us are moving. Why don't I pass him? Why do I feel like there's something about him I need to see? Ten yards, I think—that's all that lies between us—but I can't make out his face at all. His hood is so big, so dark, that it conceals his head completely. Falls over him like a mask.

Like a hard mask.

The kind that protects the eyes and nose and mouth.

The kind a welder might wear.

My pulse kicks and kicks. I blink, and he's still frozen. His hood is just a hood again. His hands are the only skin I can see.

But there were gloves, once. Long, dark gloves. They went halfway to somebody's elbows.

I lean over the wheel. My heart pounds against it. He's a guy in a raincoat, a hood, black jeans. But he's someone else, too. Dark gloves. A welder's mask. And—overalls?

No. Waders.

A welder's mask. Gloves. Waders.

I gasp a mouthful of air and instantly scream it out. The sound shoves the drifter out of his stillness. Sends him shooting away. I stomp my foot on the gas, but he's through the trees before I reach him. An inky streak in a smudge of woods. I skid to a stop. Jerk forward, back. Reverse. Do half a K-turn until my lights splash against the trees. I don't see him anywhere. He's animal-fast. He's gone. And I'm panting. Panting. Clutching my chest as I breathe.

I remember him now. The man who grabbed Astrid's waist. My flashes have been of a bodiless arm, but now I remember the rest of him—or at least what he wore: welder's mask, gloves, waders. Black on black on black.

eight

D r. Lockwood would write this off, tell me I've internalized a description of Astrid's kidnapper, regurgitated it as an image indistinguishable from memory. Eric would say I read it online. But they'd both be wrong. Wikipedia only said the man wore a mask. Not what kind. And Astrid's prologue said she hadn't been allowed to share that detail until now. She promised it would appear in a later chapter, one I've yet to read.

Still. I have to be sure.

Stray pebbles pop under my tires as I climb Ted's driveway. I picture the man again—waders, welder's mask, gloves—and there it is, the pounding in my chest that makes me believe in this image as memory. As fact. But as I close my car door, as I enter Ted's house, I still need to see it in Astrid's memoir—printed, published, permanent. Because wherever she is, Astrid might be counting on that witness from twenty years ago, and I can't waste the time she has left by being wrong.

I'm halfway up the stairs when Ted calls out to me from the first floor. "Fern?"

And just like that, I stop. My foot hovers in midair.

"Come here," he says.

My body obeys. My flip-flops clunk down the staircase. Even with all the adrenaline pumping through my veins, even with how fiercely Astrid might need me, I still feel a whoosh of warmth in my chest.

Ted's asking for me. I can spare a minute for that.

I find him in the kitchen. He's putting a plate into the microwave, then setting the timer. The microwave whirs into action.

"Hi," I say.

He turns around, leans against the counter, crosses one foot over the other. "I noticed the boxes you bought yesterday are still in the living room," he says.

I glance at the gray stubble along his jaw. He must have been working the entire day. For all his untucked shirts and misaligned buttons and wild wisps of hair, he likes to keep an impeccable face. Each follicle sliced away before it has a chance to grow.

"Yeah, sorry," I say. "I've been busy."

"Busy," he repeats. "With what?" He narrows his eyes. Studies me for several seconds. "Where have you been all day?"

"Oh. Well, actually . . ."

I'm about to answer him, unburden myself of all I suspect, but his gaze is relentless. Sharp and focused as it ever was, every time I sat in the interview chair. He'd pounce on me if I told him. *You think you witnessed a kidnapping? You must have been terrified. We have to explore this, Fern, come on.* He'd drag me up the stairs, straight into his office. My stomach churns with the image. I can practically feel the tug of his hand on my wrist.

"I've just been out," I tell him.

"Out," he repeats, his voice spiky with suspicion. "But you came here to be *in*. To pack. And look—" He nods toward the living room. "Rusty brought over newspaper for wrapping things up. You haven't even touched them yet."

The microwave goes off—too soon, it seems, to have heated up his meal. But he spins toward it, anyway, opens the door, and takes out his plate without closing it again. He grabs a fork from the drawer and stabs it into the food. No steam rises from the noodles—my noodles, I realize, as he twirls them up and thrusts them into his mouth.

"Those are my leftovers," I say.

He chews slowly. Takes his time.

"Oh," he says once he swallows. "You want a bite?"

The smell wafts over to me. Nausea surges up. I press my lips together and breathe until it passes.

"No," I say. "It's just—you know, polite—to ask someone before eating their leftovers."

He chomps on another forkful. "We're family," he replies. "We don't need to be polite."

The warmth in my chest is rapidly cooling. I cross my arms. Try to look impenetrable. "Eric's my family. And he would ask before eating my leftovers."

Ted's laugh is a snort. "Eric does a lot of superfluous things."

I straighten for a second, open my mouth to respond. Then I stop, force myself to relax. This is not the time to entertain Ted's digs at Eric. I need to get up to my room, back to Astrid's book.

I start to turn away from him but then pause. "Ted?" I say. "Do you know anything about that guy who keeps walking around town, dressed in all black?"

Ted sucks up more of my noodles. Chews them as he thinks. "Can't say I know what you're talking about."

"He seems to stay on roads that run along the woods. And if you go anywhere near him or try to talk to him, he darts away. Takes off into the forest."

Ted's eyes flicker with recognition. He sets his plate on the counter.

Takes a step toward me. "Maybe he's . . ." he starts. Then his hands go up, curl into claws.

"No, I'm serious," I say. But Ted can't be stopped.

". . . The witch from Forest Near," he continues, words slow, almost melodic, "here to do the thing you fear."

He shuffles. He shakes me. He cackles. I bite my lip, even though the urge to smile is weak at best.

"Ted."

He backs up. Backs off. He can hear that I'm in no mood for our only game. His brow furrows as he reaches for his plate again.

"So are you going to start tonight?" he asks.

"Start what?"

He pushes the noodles around with his fork. "Packing."

I look at the clock on the microwave, feel Astrid's book pulling me toward it, the pages eager to turn. "It's getting late," I say.

"Late! I've been working all day and I'm just getting started!"

"Well, that's great. For you. But—you know, I thought we were going to be doing this together. That's why I came."

His fork clinks against the plate. "You're mad," he says.

"No, I'm just—"

"You are." He shakes his head, his eyelids drooping with disappointment. "Fern, you know how important the work is."

"I do, but—"

"And you know that for me to stop would endanger the whole thing. Projects like these are very fragile in their early stages."

"I know. I'm sorry. All I meant was . . . I thought we'd have a chance to spend some time together. Before you move a thousand miles away."

Ted chuckles. "What, like father-daughter bonding? That's not really our thing."

A lump hardens in my throat. I think of all the times Eric and I have visited his parents in Virginia. His mom sets the table with their wedding china. She makes appetizers and salad and a main course for dinner. There's always a choice of two desserts.

"I didn't mean we'd hold hands and skip down the street," I say. My tone is sarcastic, but my voice wavers. "I just thought—since you're retired now, you would"—I shrug—"have a little more time for me? But instead you're still always working."

Ted's eyes narrow. Then he steps on the foot of the trash can, scrapes the rest of my noodles—still half a plate full—into it.

"You act like my work is such a terrible thing," he says, his voice all steel. "That you've been so deprived. But my work is who I am. And for a long time, you *were* the work. Helping me with my Experiments. Donating yourself to the cause. What better bonding is there than that? We've had *interviews*, Fern."

I take a deep breath, register for the first time how exhausted I feel. "I just thought we could talk."

"We're talking right now."

"Share a meal together," I continue. "Discuss what's in Florida in the first place. Something."

Ted tosses his plate into the sink. I'm surprised to hear it only clatters instead of breaks. "Something, huh," he says. "I never laid a hand on you, you know."

To most people, it would be a non sequitur. But as soon as he says it, I understand what I've triggered.

"I know that," I say.

"I never pretended to be one person out there"—he points toward the front door—"and another in here." He jabs his finger against the counter. "You never had to wear sweaters to school in May so the teachers wouldn't see."

"You're right. I didn't."

And this is why I don't blame Ted for the father that he is. How could I, when his blueprint for parenting is so faintly drawn?

His father was abusive. His mother practically mute. Ted says the only words he ever heard her say were *Yes, dear, I'll do that, dear*, even while her husband was beating their son with a cutting board. I never met Ted's parents—he cut off contact with them as soon as he left for college—and now they're both dead. His mom passed away when I was in high school. Cause of death: falling down the stairs. But Ted believes she was pushed. He said so, with no horror in his voice. Said it as if it were a fact he was reading in her obituary: *Lydia Brierley is survived by her son, Edward, and her husband, Saul, who shoved her down the stairs.* We didn't go to the funeral.

A few years later, when a neighbor of Ted's parents contacted Ted to tell him Saul had died, I was home from college for winter break. Ted didn't say much after he got the call. Just drank half a bottle of whiskey, even though he never really drinks at all. Then, when he was good and hammered, he stood in my bedroom doorway. Stared at me as he slurred, "Whatever I've done to you, Fern. My Experiments. Whatever fear I've made you feel. I never hurt you. Never laid a hand on you. You never have to worry about that from me."

I remember lying in my bed, sheets pulled to my chin like a child. I stared at him with wide, admiring eyes. Besides the time he left me alone overnight, let me spiral into thoughts of being orphaned—it was the closest he'd come to acknowledging that his Experiments weren't always to be revered. It felt like hearing *I love you*.

I know I shouldn't psychoanalyze my own father, but it's difficult not to do. According to his obituary, Saul Brierley was deeply respected. He was known around town as a good, dependable man who helped out his neighbors and worked his fingers to the bone to provide for his family. But behind closed doors, he was someone else entirely. Mara says that Saul was a red-faced electrician who believed that the measure of a man was in what he did with his hands. He called Ted a "faggot" for doing well in school, for nearly acing the SATs. Ted's always acted as if it didn't bother him—*A faggot's a bundle of sticks*, he said to me once, as he emerged from his office after seventeen hours of loud, frenetic typing, *and do you know what sticks do, Fern? They burn*—but why else would he latch on to the success of Brennan Llewellyn, the top of their class in grad school, as the benchmark he must meet and surpass? If he can be on talk shows, too, if he can publish a bestseller every other year, if he can hear an audience's applause, see all the starred reviews flood in, he'll know for sure that his father was wrong. That his mind made him more of a man than his hands ever did. That he didn't need to hurt anyone else to know he was strong.

So I don't blame him for the way he is. If anything, I admire him. Ted is a man who saw the truth about his father—how toxic he was—and got the hell out. A lot of people wouldn't have the strength to leave someone behind so completely.

And honestly, he's done okay. He never called me names. Never hit me or punched me or twisted my arm so far back the bone actually snapped. It's not like he even wanted me in the first place. Ted and Mara never planned to have kids. They had no ovulation tests, no calendars with circled dates. But it happened anyway and they did the best they could.

Still, when I think of my childhood, most of what I remember is a persistent ache. Like a fist pressed against my ribs. Like legs that cramp after sitting in the same position for too long. So was their best enough?

Will mine be?

I know that Eric will be great. As a father, he'll know the lyrics to every lullaby. He'll know details of fairy tales that are still fuzzy to me. I know there's one about a girl who gets eaten by a wolf disguised as her grandmother. But I have no idea how she arrives at that moment. How she doesn't even see that the woman is really a beast.

And why are these the stories we tell to children? How do we tuck them in afterward and expect them to sleep? I wonder if it's really so different—the fear Ted provoked and prodded, and the telling of tales where kids are devoured. Maybe we scare our children to prepare them for the world. *Men in welder's masks. Witnesses who see but don't help. Basements that double as dungeons.* But if my world is soon to be that of a parent, I'm not prepared for it at all. My own blueprint is blurry at best.

I shake my head. Try to shake these thoughts out, too. I can't think about the baby right now. The baby is nine months away—the length of an entire school year—and there's someone who, this very moment, needs me even more than the life inside me does. Her book still waits for me. Upstairs on my nightstand. Away from this kitchen and Ted.

"I'm sorry I upset you," I say. "I'll start packing in the morning."

"Good. Because I'm finished with this conversation."

And there it is—that ache again. That fist against my ribs. I rub my side as Ted heads toward the stairs, disappears out of view. In a few moments, the landline rings and Ted groans.

"Yeah," he says in the hallway upstairs—his standard greeting when answering the phone.

"Oh, of course, Dr. Eric," he says a second later. He hardly addresses Eric in any other way. He hits the middle consonants hard in "Doctor." The condescension drips from his voice like saliva from a fang. "Won't you hold on a moment, please?"

I'm about to climb the stairs to take the phone, but my foot freezes above the second step. This is the first time I'll be talking to Eric since

I took the pregnancy test this morning. I'll have to tell him—there's no way around it; he'll hear it in my voice and ask—but I haven't practiced my enthusiasm yet. He'll know right away that I'm terrified, and my fear will be the pinprick in his ballooning joy.

I love my husband. I want to make him happy. But I don't have it in me to do that right now.

"Tell him I'm sleeping," I hiss to Ted.

There's a moment of hesitation before Ted walks to the top of the staircase. He puts his palm over the mouthpiece of the phone and gazes down at me.

"Please," I whisper.

Even from the bottom of the stairs, I see the twitch at the corner of his lips. He knows I'm scared of something. Last night, he said he wouldn't do any Experiments on me while I'm in Cedar, but it's obvious: his brain is still hardwired to my fear.

He removes his hand from the phone, lifts it to his face. "Sorry, Doctor," he says. "She's passed out in her room." He stares straight into my eyes when he says the next part. "Been so busy packing, she must've worn herself out. I'll have her call you tomorrow."

He doesn't wait for an answer before he ends the call.

"Thank you," I say. "I just didn't—"

He puts a hand in the air to stop me. "I don't need to know," he says with a smirk. "I need to get back to work."

———

Astrid's parents were the exact opposite of mine.

Where Ted and Mara were distracted, eyes barely skimming me on their way to separate spaces, the Sullivans were hyperfocused, eyes probably sore from squinting at their daughter so hard.

For Ted and Mara, doors were the things they shut to stay closer to their work. For the Sullivans, doors were dangerous. Keepers of secrets. Barriers that must be weakened.

Astrid's life was bound by rules and expectations. Mine was without any bounds at all. I could come and go whenever I wanted, and no one cared to ask me where I was headed or when I'd be back.

Astrid hated her parents' relentless attention. I was starved for a scrap from mine.

I'm turning pages, imagining the whisper of them as Astrid's voice beside me in my room. I fly through the first chapter, sink into the second. These differences between us should make her feel foreign. But instead I feel closer to her. As if we're long-lost sisters with two distinct upbringings, but the same central need: to be seen as we actually are. Not as an Experiment. Not as a pillar of purity and piety.

When Father Murphy steps onto the page in chapter two, pulling Astrid aside at her Confirmation party, my heart thumps. Here is someone I know. Someone I spoke to hours earlier. I try to imagine him as he would have been twenty years ago—more hair probably, but maybe the same sweat he wiped off his forehead today, the heat of a June sun similar to that of the airless hallway we stood in at the church.

My eyes speed ahead. Soon, the kidnapper will enter the story. But first, this conversation with the priest, just like Father Murphy relayed to me today. Except—something is wrong with this scene. Already the details are off. Nothing at all like the portrait he painted earlier.

She was devoted to the Word of God, he told me in that dim, narrow hallway. *And she pulled me aside that day in hopes of gaining a deeper understanding of it.*

But in Astrid's memoir, Father Murphy initiated the conversation. Astrid looked at his hand on her arm as he guided her away from the party and eyed it with annoyance and suspicion. More important, she was angry at him for portraying her relationship with Bridget as some dirty, sinful mistake. She was hardly the curious, wide-eyed in-nocent he described. As I read her final line to him—"If hell is where the lesbians are, then I think I'd like to burn"—I can't help but laugh. Can't help but love her for saying exactly what she feels—and being unafraid of the consequences.

Why would Father Murphy lie to me? I know that memory dis-torts, rewrites. I know that the truth usually lies between the different stories we hear. But the discrepancies here are as unsettling to me as Ted's clacking, which punches through the walls as I read. They make me wish I'd fought harder to see behind that red door at the church. Make me think of the priest's sweating in a whole different light.

I don't have time to follow this thought. The scene in the book is shifting, and Astrid is leaving the party. She's walking the same streets I drove down today, and my heart knocks. There's a car now. She hears it slowing behind her. She doesn't look. Doesn't know to record the color or model or license plate in her mind. I want to reach into the pages and pull her out of them. Rescue her before this horror story can start—but the chapter is ending. He's about to "usher [her] into the dark," a phrase too delicate for the evil thing I know has occurred.

As I flip the page to begin the next chapter, dread and anticipation weigh me down. This is where she'll describe the man who took her. This is where I'll know if I can trust my own mind.

Except—what's going on? She's already in the basement. There's no scene where she thrashes away from her captor and begs a girl to help her. The story, like my heart, has skipped a couple beats.

Astrid wakes to find a chain attached to her foot, a mattress in the corner of a dim, cement room. I read on, barely taking in the details, searching only for a mention of the witness. My eyes race across the page—then skid to a stop.

I saw his boots first, Astrid writes, *black like the rest of what he wore. Then his pants, which revealed themselves to be waders, and his rubber gloves, which stretched up his forearms. And finally, instead of a face, instead of something human and identifiable, he wore a welding mask.*

My stomach feels like I've crested a hill on a roller coaster, and now I'm whooshing down. I read the description again to be sure, but it's all here, every detail I remembered about the man.

No, not the man. The abductor.

I pull in a breath so sharply it feels like it cuts my lungs. Ever since I came back to Cedar, I've been circling around the truth. I've been saying *if*. Saying *maybe*. Saying *might have*. But it's clear to me now that, all this time, I was only searching for confirmation of what I already knew.

Because here it seems to be, validated in black and white: I was the witness. The girl who saw everything.

Eric could tell me I'm spiraling. Dr. Lockwood could say I've been stuck in a groove. But I would know that I'm not. My nightmares and flashes, my time alone in Foster, this description in the memoir—it's telling me it was all real, a memory and not a dream.

I do have a whisper of doubt, though. A tiny one. So insignificant I can barely hear it. It's just—I flip back to the beginning of the book. Skim the prologue until I find the sentence I'm looking for. Place my finger beneath it.

She saw a feature of the man that I never did, Astrid wrote about the witness. But in my memory of the man, I can't see his face at all. The mask is a shield.

Because the memory—it's still only a flash. A single moment without scenery or context. In the next moment, if only I could recall it, the man might grapple with Astrid. His mask might slip as he holds her back, giving me a glimpse of his face.

But why didn't she describe that struggle, the man's arm around her waist? Why didn't she mention me at all?

Maybe she'll portray it as a flashback. Render that day a nonlinear tale. I return to chapter three, sweep my eyes all over the pages, look for the word *grabbed*, the word *witness*, the word *waist*. Because I know I saw it happen. I was in the same place at the same time, I remembered exactly what the man wore, and I—

Here's the name Lily. The name Rusty said belonged to the witness. *I ended up calling her Lily*, Astrid writes, *once I understood what she meant to me*.

I puzzle over the sentence until it dawns on me: if she only saw me glimpse the man snatching her from the street, only knew me as a scrap of hope to hold on to in the basement, she wouldn't have known me as Fern. She would have had to invent me, the witness, nearly from scratch. And though it's not my name, I see the letters of *Lily* like a stamp that proves my existence. For the tiniest of moments, I relax. Let out a ragged breath. But then I focus on the words themselves. The sentences that conclude the chapter, that want to captivate the reader so completely they don't even think before they turn the page.

Only I can't keep going. I'm frozen.

I don't know how much time passes. I don't know how many keys I hear Ted press. At some point, I blink. Shake my head. Snap the book shut. Toss it away from me, only for it to bounce against the foot of my bed and splay back open like an invitation to continue. But I can't keep reading it. I won't even look at those words again. To do so would be to admit the possibility that what Astrid wrote is true.

And it's not. It can't be. It simply isn't possible.

I know that memory distorts, rewrites. That entire experiences can be repressed. But the thing she said really happened—I know she's wrong. She has to be. Because that's something I could never forget.

Excerpt from Chapter Three of
Behind the Red Door: A Memoir **by Astrid Sullivan**

When I opened my eyes, there was darkness.

It was a kind of darkness I'd never known before, one so thorough I had to touch my face to make sure my eyes weren't actually closed.

My tongue was fuzzy. My head throbbed. It felt as if someone was trapped inside my skull, banging their hands against bone, desperate to find a way out. I tried to prop myself up, but my arms shook so badly they struggled to bear my weight. When they collapsed beneath me, I fell back onto a surface that was firm but forgiving.

I closed my eyes again, though it made no difference. I could have slept with them open.

———

When I awoke for the second time, there was light. And a staircase. And a bright red door. The light was from a bulb at the top of the stairs, and it was almost obscene the way it hung from the ceiling, large and round and naked like a breast that could blind. It wasn't enough to illuminate the entire room, but it showed me what mattered: I was in a basement, on an air mattress, with a chain attached to my ankle, long enough for me to walk around but not escape. There was a window, too—a rectangle of grimy, cobwebbed glass too high for me to reach. It was boarded up, from the outside, with a piece of wood that looked so solid, I didn't even bother to scream.

Not at first, anyway. The screaming came a few minutes later, after he stomped down the stairs to bring me food. I saw his boots first—black like the rest of what he wore. Then his pants, which were waders, then rubber gloves, which stretched up his forearms. And finally, instead of a face, instead of something human and identifiable, he wore a welding mask, which made him look more ridiculous than menacing.

I could gauge nothing from his height or build. He seemed relatively thin, but it was difficult to tell beneath the waders that were bulky on his torso. I later told the police that he was between five ten and six feet tall, but even that might not have been true. I've never been good at guessing heights or weights. I never knew I'd have to be.

He offered me a can of Sprite and a plastic-wrapped sandwich, like the kind you'd buy at a gas station. I didn't take them. I kept my arms around my legs, which were pulled in toward my chest, and I made my gaze as sharp as a blade.

"Who are you?" I demanded.

He leaned down to set the meal on the mattress, and I scooted back as his fingers got close to my foot. I registered then that I was still wearing the kitten heels I'd put on for the party. My dress had a smear of dirt on the hem, but otherwise it was white as a christening gown. I'd been too stunned to put up a fight as he covered my mouth and injected me with a drug, so the delicate lace remained unsnagged. When he came for me, scouring my quiet neighborhood—looking, I'm sure, for someone as stupid and careless as me—I flopped into his arms like a swooning damsel. He was probably disappointed at how easy it all had been.

"Who are you?" I asked again, but he straightened up, looked down at me through the tinted screen of the mask, and he didn't answer.

"What are you going to do with me?" I tried.

When he spoke, his voice was not one I recognized—but then again, it was muffled by plastic.

"I don't know yet," he said. "But definitely something."

And that's when I screamed. Not because I was scared of him, exactly, but because I was deeply and consumingly angry. And yes, terrified. Of course I was terrified. I was fourteen years old, chained to a metal ring on a concrete floor, wearing a dress that would take almost nothing to tear. I thought about torture and rape. I thought about all the girls I'd ever heard of who had disappeared, only to be found, years later, as bones in a makeshift grave.

Mostly, though, I screamed because I was burning with a red-hot rage that would set me on fire if I didn't get it out. I screamed because I hadn't screamed when I'd heard the car pull up behind me. I screamed because I'd done this to myself, and the anger I felt—in that moment at least—was for me alone. I had left the party, even knowing that to do so would horrify and humiliate my parents. I had wanted to horrify them. I had wanted them to stammer and shrug to their friends as they tried to explain where I had gone. I'd wanted to sully the perfect sheen of their massive spectacle, the Confirmation party that was more for them than it ever was for me.

My throat became raw with screaming, but the discomfort was something I believed I deserved. I had made my promises to God. I had committed myself to his teachings and commandments. But I did not honor my mother and father. And he had seen fit to punish me. I was Eve eating the forbidden apple, only to discover that I was naked and vulnerable. I was banished from Paradise, given a dirty basement instead of a big house with walls that would protect me.

The man was not moved by the noise I made. He watched me for a while, head tilted, and I thought that maybe, at some point, I even heard him laugh. Then, apparently bored with me, he turned around and climbed the stairs, closed the door at the top, and bolted a lock.

I stopped screaming. And then slowly I shut my eyes. And then, yes, I'll admit it, I'll say it here in black and white: I curled into a ball and I cried.

———

Despite all the TV interviews and *Dateline* specials, all the bloggers who still publish anniversary stories about my case, there isn't a lot to say about the time I spent alone in that basement.

The masked man came twice a day. The bolt clicked, the red door opened, a flash of daylight flooded the stairs. He always brought me a sandwich and Sprite—which, after that initial offering, I couldn't help but devour—and at the end of each day, a change of clothes: sweatpants, a T-shirt, a zip-up hoodie. He took my waste bucket and promptly returned it.

Most of the time, he never said a word, not even when I yelled at him to tell me who he was, why he'd chosen me. The second question was a pointless one. I knew why he had chosen me. It was because I'd walked away from the safety of my home, from all those witnesses who would have guarded me. It was because I'd been an easy target.

If only I'd been the pious girl my parents had wanted.

A week into my captivity, I stopped eating the food he brought me, stopped sucking down the too-sweet soda. I tried to make myself holy with fasting. The man seemed perturbed by this. He held the sandwiches closer to me. Then he let them pile up, as if convinced I would decide one day to eat them all at once. When the meat began to rot, I threw them in my waste bucket and he had no choice but to take them away. Still, every day another can of soda I opened only for a few survival sips; every day another sandwich I left untouched. My stomach hurt with hunger. It growled and then it roared. But I needed to atone, to finally deny my body its basest desires.

And on the seventh day of my second week, things finally changed. Instead of a sandwich, the man brought me a girl. I ended up calling her Lily, once I understood what she meant to me—but on that day, when he brought her down the stairs, she was still nameless. She had ropes tied tightly around her wrists. She had hair the color of toffee. She was small and fragile as a bird. And suddenly, for the first time, when I looked at the top of the stairs, the red door appeared to shine like light through stained glass.

nine

Something stabs me. A little pinch of pain. I look at my finger and find a bead of blood on the tip.

I'm in Mara's studio, packing it up like she asked me to, and there's a broken bowl on the counter that lines one wall of the main room. She might have been saving the pieces for a project, but she's not here to tell me that, so I'm throwing them away. I thought I was being careful, but one of the smaller shards must have pricked me.

The cut is tiny, barely a cut at all, and I won't go back into the house to wash it out—because in the house is Astrid's book. I don't want to see it, or read it. I'll pack up pottery and tools and stacks of photographs, and I will not think about what I read last night. Or how, each time I fell back asleep, I dreamed of Astrid—only this time, I dreamed her in a concrete room. A room I, too, was in, with ropes around my wrists.

But those dreams have to have been a lie. They were just my anxiety making the terrible things that happen to other people feel like real possibilities for my own life. How many times have I heard of someone's rare disease and been convinced I had it? How many times have I seen an accident on the news and been sure that Eric was in it?

The girl named Lily could not have been me. Because there's no way that a person can forget being abducted, being locked for days in a basement, or even a red door as bright as the one on the memoir's cover. So I had to have been wrong last night when I was certain I was the witness. And my nightmares—they were always just nightmares. Just synapses firing. Just a vague and meaningless image only recently contorted by a face I saw on the news.

And yes, I was in Foster at the time of Astrid's kidnapping. But so were thousands of people.

And yes, I remembered the kidnapper's clothes. But Dr. Lockwood's voice in my head had been right; I must have read about them somewhere.

Early this morning, I huddled over my phone, slogged through the agonizingly slow and stuttering service to reread Astrid's Wikipedia page. And there it was. *The kidnapper wore all black: boots, rubber gloves, waders, and a welding mask.*

It's a quick detail, only one sentence. I must have skimmed the line the first time around, then promptly forgotten it for the story's greater horror: how he injected her with a drug to steal her more easily, how he locked her beneath the ground.

Then there was this other paragraph in the Wikipedia page: *Sullivan writes in her memoir,* Behind the Red Door, *that she was kept in the basement with another girl, whom she called Lily, a witness to Astrid's captivity and a victim in her own right. However, authorities were unable to find any evidence to corroborate this claim, as no young girls with Lily's description had been reported missing. Sullivan's therapist later proposed that Lily was a figment of Sullivan's imagination, a coping mechanism to help her survive in the basement.*

That paragraph must have been added after I last read the article. If it had been there all along, I would've known right away that I wasn't the witness. When I read Astrid's prologue, I assumed that the girl she referenced was someone who saw the moments of abduction. But now I know: it was a girl who saw what happened in the basement. Because she was there, too. Because she was a victim herself—something I have never been.

I forgot to take my meds last night. Might not have taken them the night before, either. Missing a couple pills won't do much damage—but it's a new medication. My body and brain are still adjusting to its effects. So the arm I believed I remembered was just a trap in my mind, a needle stuck on a record. I told Ted I'd help him pack for his move, but instead, my anxiety sent me running off to Foster, spending time with Cooper—*Cooper*—at The Diner. Ted was right to be annoyed last night. And it was unfair of me to expect much more from him than what he's given in the past. Ted is a creature of habit. We all are. And Ted's habit, retired or not, is work.

I swaddle a clay bowl in newspaper, set it down in a box, move on to the next. Mara's art is all around me, but it doesn't make me miss her. Which is why I'm starting here. Packing Mara's studio is the perfect activity to soothe this week's anxiety spike. It's neutral and mindless. I feel almost nothing as I handle the plates and vases, the mugs from her lipstick series, where each piece has a painted groove at the rim fit for a bottom lip. I will lose myself in this process. Let the panic of the last few days slip off me like sweat.

Dr. Lockwood and I have talked at length about why I feel so little attachment to my mother. We once spent session after session crafting a metaphor that helped me define our relationship: Mara treated me, for most of my life, as a houseguest. She was always polite to me. But polite was cool. Polite was giving me money each August to buy new school clothes, but only after I reminded her I'd outgrown the ones from the year before. Polite was glancing at my report cards, saying *That's wonderful, dear*, even in eighth grade when I got all Cs. In the

metaphor, Mara is the hands-off host who always seemed to be waiting for me to leave. At night, we'd bump into each other in the hallway,
and sometimes, the look on her face would be one of surprise and
disbelief: *You're still here?* it seemed to ask.

For many years, I assumed this was the way all mothers behaved.
By the time I understood that Kyla's mom was not an anomaly, that
most mothers actually were the curfew-setting, prom-paparazzi type,
it was too late for me to miss what I'd never had with Mara. Our roles
had been cemented. Houseguest and host.

Now, the studio door whips open and bangs against the wall. I drop
the mug I'm holding. Watch it smash onto the concrete floor, split into
three large chunks. I turn to the doorway, where Ted leans over, but
doesn't cross, the threshold. He knows that, even when she isn't here,
this space is sacred, protected by Mara's only rule: Ted is not allowed.

He looks at the damaged pottery and chuckles. "Mara will be
thrilled," he says. "More material for her Break Room."

My voice is flat when I answer, but my pulse is thumping. "That's
not how the Break Room works."

He shrugs, then steps inside.

"Hey, you're not supposed to—" I start. But he stoops down to pick
up the mug's pieces, tosses them into the trash. Then he grabs a bowl,
wraps it in a sheet of newspaper, and puts it in the box. Grabs another
and does it again.

"What are you doing?" I ask.

"I'm packing," he says. "Isn't that what you were going on about
last night? You wanted us to do this together? Well." He gestures to the
walls around us. "Here I am."

The studio, already stuffy and hot, floods with a new rush of
warmth. It feels like Ted has pulled the sun right into the space. Like if
I stay too long, I might burn.

"What about your work?" I ask.

He scratches his arm, the skin red and blistered. "It can wait."

My spine goes straight. Stiff as a tree in the woods. "It can?"

He clamps his lips together, breathing out through his nose. "Do you want the help or not? Mara's hell-bent on moving on with her life, no matter the years we spent here, no matter the *history* we . . ." His forehead creases as he trails off. "But if you don't want me to—"

"I do. Thanks."

Mara doesn't have to know. Her No-Ted Rule is petty. A jab at him in the wake of their separation. *He has his space, and I have mine*, she told me back in high school, a nonanswer to my question of why they were separating in the first place.

"Do you know when she's getting back?" I ask Ted. I have a fleeting concern that Mara will march into the studio, see that I've let Ted inside, and yell at me for not doing as she asked. But the image is all wrong. Mara hardly ever cares enough to yell.

"Eh, I forget," Ted says, sealing up a box. He's clumsy with the tape dispenser, clearly unaccustomed to its simple machinery. "In a few days, I think. She'll be in and out. You know how it is."

But I don't. I've never understood their arrangement at all, or why it's only now that Mara's decided to find a "home base" somewhere else. When I was still in high school, I thought it was because of me. Some last-ditch maternal instinct, scraped up from deep inside her. But even after I left Cedar, she stuck around—when she wasn't on her cruises, that is. She claims she's devoted to her spiritual health now. That solidifying the connection between her mind and body is the highest form of art. These days, it's only in the time between cruises that she ever gets back to work, creating enough pieces to place in galleries and stores. Then she collects her money, funnels it into her Cruise Fund, and the cycle starts all over again. It would be fine—I wouldn't even question this vocation of hers—except that it's so un-Mara.

Her studio was always more home to her than the house. In my memories, she's either heading out the door to get to work, or she's coming inside after hours away, only to scavenge for food before leaving again. When she did eat, often standing at the sink, her fingers were caked with dried clay. There was sometimes paint or glaze on her arms, and the kitchen would fill with the sharp scent of the chemicals she used in her tiny darkroom. Mara was always drenched and encrusted with her art. Even before the separation, she sometimes slept on the cot in her studio, so she could snap back to work if inspiration struck.

But people change, I guess. Look at Ted. He's here. With me. Stacking plates in boxes. I can't wait to tell Eric, even though he'll tell me I shouldn't get my hopes up, that Ted probably wants something from me.

He doesn't, though. We work in silence for fifteen minutes. No Experiments. No interviews. Just Ted handing me wrapped pieces of pottery. Just me receiving each one like it's a gift, then placing it in a box. It goes quicker with the two of us, and it isn't long before Ted moves to the island counter, opens drawers to pack up sculpting tools.

The point chisels chill me, exactly as they always did. Some look flat and harmless, but even those have a sharpness to them. I leave Ted to it, turn my attention to the closed door in the back that leads to Mara's Break Room. She said she'd take care of it—by which I assume she meant dismantle it—but I'd like to see it one more time. Its glorified rage. Its dazzling grief.

I'm halfway to the door when Ted's voice booms out, "It's locked." His back is to me, his hands on the island.

I try the knob anyway. He's right; it doesn't budge. "Do you have the key?" I ask.

Ted turns to look at me. "No." He rolls his eyes. "Only Mara has the key. But there's nothing to pack in there. You know what the Break Room is."

A haunted place. An angry place. An achingly gorgeous place.

It used to be only storage. A space for half-finished projects and pieces that didn't sell. Until the day that Ted came into the kitchen with a suitcase and confessed to Mara that he'd slept with the Psych Department secretary at Wicker. That she was pregnant now. That he was leaving us both. I was young at the time, only on the cusp of double digits, and what shocked me most was not that he was leaving—Ted always felt temporary to me; the unpredictable bursts of his attention had trained me to see him that way—but that he said the phrase "slept with." I only knew what it meant because Cooper tossed it around whenever I hung out with Kyla. *I slept with Jenny Musgraves last night*, he once bragged. Then he looked sharply at us, and we stared wide-eyed up at him, the pieces to some board game clenched in our hands. *That means sex, you prudes.*

It shocked me, then, to hear one of Cooper's phrases come out of Ted's mouth. Ted, who chose his words as precisely as numbers on a lottery ticket. Ted who loathed euphemisms—"language dressing and word curtains," he hypocritically called them. Mara was equally shocked, though for very different reasons.

Her eyes were stormy. Lightning hot and turbulent. She looked at Ted, and then at me, as if I'd somehow betrayed her, too, and she spun around, stomped to the front door, and slapped the screen open. Ted followed her, carrying his suitcase, and I followed Ted. We marched behind Mara as she marched to her studio. Then she bolted for the door to what was about to become her Break Room. There, she picked up the nearest piece of pottery—a bowl with an eggshell glaze—and hurled it at the wall. It shattered. The shards plinked onto the floor like hail.

After that, a few moments of stillness. Nobody moved. Nobody seemed to breathe. The second hand on Ted's watch ticked and ticked, and I thought we might stay in that room forever. Surrounded by broken pieces. But then Mara grabbed a mug. She thundered out a shout and she smashed it. Picked up a plate. Shouted and smashed it, too. This went on for so long that the concrete floor, once only gray, began to resemble a mosaic.

I looked at Ted. He looked at me. And he laughed. First in his throat. Then in his mouth. Finally, out into the air, where the sound squeezed us tight.

"You think this is funny?" Mara demanded.

Ted sobered then. He closed his mouth and seemed to consider her question before answering. "No, not funny. Perfect."

Mara's nostrils flared. "Excuse me?"

"Don't you see what fear does to you? It makes you believe almost anything! Why would I sleep with *Rebecca*? And even if I did, why would I pack up my life to be a father to her child? This was wonderful, though. Really. The smashing. The screaming." He circled his fingers around her wrist. "Let's go to my office. We need to begin the interview while all this is fresh."

He tried to tug her toward the door, but Mara didn't budge. Her feet seemed glued to the ground. "This was an Experiment," she said. Not a question. A realized-too-late fact.

"Yes, of course," Ted said. "Was my reveal not clear?" He continued without her answer. "What a shame. Revealing the Experiment is my favorite part." He tugged her wrist again. "Let's go. You know this can't wait."

"No."

"Mara, we don't—"

"No, Ted." She almost yelled it. But still, there was an eerie calmness to the sentence that made Ted and I stare. She took in all the pieces of pottery at our feet, her eyes glittering as she absorbed the brokenness. Then she walked into the studio, rummaged in a drawer for a moment, and returned with a tube.

Mara knelt onto the floor. Picked up a piece of what had once been a plate.

"What are you doing?" Ted asked.

She squirted something onto the back and pressed it into place, exactly where it had landed.

"I'm gluing," she said. She picked up the shards, added adhesive, and stuck them to the floor. "You might as well leave. Both of you. I have work to do now."

"But—so do I," Ted said.

"I respect that," Mara said. A small square of cobalt sat in her hand. "I've always respected your work. And you've always respected mine. And as you can see, I'm working right now."

For a few moments, Ted sputtered, indignant and confused. Then he snatched up his suitcase and walked away. I was close on his heels, my stomach fizzing like freshly poured soda. I had that slightly sick feeling I got whenever an Experiment went on, but I was giddy, too. Ted would not be leaving.

"You can interview me if you want," I chirped from behind him. "I saw the whole thing."

He turned to look at me right before we reached the door of the house. Our house.

"Hmm," he considered. "That's not what I wanted, but—I suppose that might work. Tell me, Fern, were you scared? When I said I was leaving? When Mara threw the pottery?"

I took stock of my feelings for the first time since he made his suitcase confession. The specific things he mentioned—they hadn't surprised me. Ted was temporary. Mara had a flare for the dramatic ("Artists!" Ted always complained). But if I peeled back my lack of surprise, looked under its calm veneer, did I see something dark and swirling? Maybe. Maybe. Yes. If Ted left, there'd be no one to notice me anymore. I'd slip unseen into the fabric of the house. Become only wallpaper or furniture. Something that Mara forgot was there until she bumped right into it. *Oh. Excuse me, dear. I didn't see you.*

When Ted spoke to me, when he asked me question after question, typing up my answers with his long, jabbing fingers, I knew I was real. The spindles of the interview chair hurt my back, left vertical impressions on my skin, but the pain did what pain does: it let me know I was alive.

"Yes," I told him. "I was so scared."

Ted's eyes glittered. Like Mara's had as she looked at her pottery on the floor. "Excellent," he said. "You're a very good girl. You know that, Fern?"

I smiled up at him. Shrugged.

I was a good girl. Not furniture. Not wallpaper. But girl.

I've only been packing up Mara's photographs for a minute when I pause to flip through them. They're all a part of the same series: *Exquisite Fragments*. The end result of Mara's Break Room rage.

After that first time, she retreated into her Break Room whenever Ted made her angry. She smashed up some of her pottery. Glued down pieces where they landed. Even the tiny shards. Then she photographed the room from different angles, focusing on the scattered patterns, the random mix of colors, always finding new ways to explore and exploit the brokenness all around her.

The photos turned out beautiful. In the one I'm holding, there are fragments glued onto other fragments. A close-up of glossy cobalt over a deep matte red. The concrete beneath is barely visible, and there's a splotch of something on the shining blue that looks like dried blood. I'm not surprised to see it. Mara always worked barefoot. The floor became jagged and sharp.

The series received just local attention at first. But then a man from a New York gallery saw the photos while on a "quaint New Hampshire vacation" and he signed her on for two shows in the city, in back-to-back seasons. He told her what he was offering her was unheard of, but that what she'd created was *extraordinary*. He raised a fist in the air to emphasize the word. He wore an orange suit. "Artists," Ted grumbled.

The New York shows didn't catapult Mara to stardom, but they did enough to sell her work and guarantee her a spot, in perpetuity, in any New Hampshire gallery—which is all she wanted in the first place.

"What are those?" Ted asks. He's just come out of Mara's closet-sized darkroom, carrying a box. He juts his chin toward the photographs.

"*Exquisite Fragments*," I say.

"Oh. Did you want a trash bag for those?"

I ignore the comment. Ted hates that Mara channeled her emotions into smashing and gluing. Hates that she closed the Break Room door and kept her explosions private. *I could have worked with that*, I heard him tell her once. *Think of the research you've deprived me of. Just beneath anger is fear, Mara. You know this. Beneath every single feeling is fear!*

"Hey, look," he says to me. "Now these I liked."

He's opened a drawer beneath the work counter and is holding a yellow bowl. I recognize it instantly. Part of a pottery series in which all the pieces could be used as instruments. Mara rimmed each one with bronze, and when you struck it, a distinctive sound rang out, halfway between a ping and a clang.

"Mara said she never got the tone the way she wanted it," Ted says. He grabs a spoon from the drawer and leans against the counter. "But I always found it to be pleasant."

He strikes the bowl, and the sound bounces into my ears. *Pling!* Something in my brain jolts. It's that feeling that Dr. Lockwood tells me isn't real, but I know it is. He strikes it again—*pling!*—and my breath quickens. *Pling!*—and my knees go rubbery.

I hear a voice in my head. Throaty and half startled. It's Mara's. *Well, hello there.*

Pling!

Well, hello there.

Pling!

I'm on the verge of a memory. I can feel it just out of frame. Mara— she stood at the counter. Struck a bowl or plate. *Well, hello there*, she said. I place my hand on the wall and squeeze my eyes shut. *Well, hello there. You've certainly been gone for a while.*

Pling! Pling!

The room is tilting. Ted is playing. I feel like I'm going to be sick.

But why? The words I'm remembering are benign. An example of Mara snapping out of the world inside her own head, surprised all of a sudden to see me.

Pling!

I was out of breath. Mara was at the counter and I had my hands on my knees and I was sucking in air like I'd never tasted it before. There were tears in my eyes. Mara was blurry.

Pling!

Well, hello there. You've certainly been gone for a while.

"Fern?" Ted says.

I shake my head. Put my hand in the air to shush him. There's something in this memory. Something horrible and heavy. I'm doubled over with it.

Pling!

I was running. Something was scratching at my face. Branches. Twigs. I was darting through trees. The woods. A rush of green and brown and green. I couldn't breathe. I couldn't breathe.

I'm gasping now. As if I'm back in those woods. My legs are as weak as if I've sprinted three miles.

Pling! Pling!

I sprang out of the trees. Onto the edge of our property. That plinging sound sang out. Mara's studio was just ahead, the door and windows all open—and I burst inside. Put my hands on my knees. Panted as tears pooled in my eyes. *Well, hello there*, she said. *You've certainly been gone for a while.*

Relief swelled inside me. I was safe now. I was somewhere familiar. I was finally with someone I knew. Unlike—what? Where had I come from? Who was I running from? I'm trying so hard—eyes pinched, fists clenched—but I can't rewind the memory any further back.

"Fern?" Ted says again. He's put down the bowl. The spoon. He isn't playing anymore.

"Shh," I say. "I . . ."

But I can't continue. Because I think I know. I think a part of me has known since last night, when I read how Lily was not really a witness at all, but a victim. I've been distracting myself with boxes and pottery and memories of Mara. I've been telling myself I had it all wrong, I never met Astrid at all. But last night I dreamed that my wrists were tied together, that I was standing with Astrid in a concrete room. And now I'm remembering a sprint into Mara's studio, the relief I felt so potent only because of the terror that preceded it.

"Fern," Ted says, "perhaps you should sit down. You look very pale."

I ignore him. Because I'm thinking of Astrid's story. Not the memoir, but the one that everyone knows. She was taken from her neighborhood, and weeks later, she was returned. Left on a curb two streets from her house.

What if I, too, was returned? To a place very close to Ted's. The woods. The acres of trees that have always haunted me.

"Ted."

I'm surprised by how steady my voice is. It comes out as clear as the sound of spoon against bowl.

"Yes. What's happening to you?" he replies.

"Did I disappear when I was a kid?"

He's going to laugh. He's going to tell me it's my meds, like Mara did when I asked if I knew Astrid Sullivan.

Except he doesn't laugh. He sighs.

Then he lowers his head, eyes dipping into his crossed arms before he lifts his gaze to look at me. There's something on his face I've never seen before. Sadness? Confliction? I don't know. But it makes my skin crawl. My mouth dry.

"Oh, Fern," he says. His voice is gentler than I've ever heard it. "What do you remember?"

ten

I stumble toward the pottery wheel. Reach for the stool. Feel it shudder beneath me as I sit down hard. I press my feet against the floor.

"What?" I ask. It's the only word I'm capable of.

Ted sighs again, but there's something theatrical about it. And now, behind the sadness or confliction, or whatever it is that's in his eyes—there's something else. A spark.

"You seemed to forget all of that so thoroughly. But you must have remembered something, to ask me that question. So how much do you recall?"

I stutter through my response. Like a person whose teeth are chattering. Only mine feel hot. My tongue a flame. "Nothing, I-I-I remember a girl. And a-a man in a . . ."

"I can tell you the truth," Ted interjects. "If you think you're ready to know. I should warn you, though. Your mind would have blocked it for a reason. And telling you the pieces I know could make it all come flooding back. So are you sure?"

I nod.

"Okay," Ted says. He rubs the side of his face, hand pressed hard to his cheek, as if struggling for where to begin. "You were twelve, I think."

Twenty years ago. My pulse feels electric.

"And during that summer, there was a period of time when you weren't at home."

"My vacation with Kyla."

"No," Ted says. "A couple weeks after that, I think. You left one day and didn't come home. We assumed you were staying at Kyla's. You were always doing that. Going off for days at a time. Always happier there than here."

I shake my head. Not true. I was not happier there than here. Even though *there* was lasagna around the table—strings of cheese stretching between pan and plate, looking like they could keep on stretching for miles—and *here* was chips for dinner, straight from the bag, knuckles greasy the rest of the night. *There* was TV shows that made us laugh until our stomachs hurt, and *here* was blank walls, clacking keys. But *there* did not have Ted. So *there* was lonely in ways that here never was.

"It was for the best," Ted continues. "Mara and I were both in the midst of important projects. We figured it was better for you to be with a friend. And perhaps we . . ."

He hesitates. His face pinches with something. On anyone else, I'd call it guilt.

"Well, we might have lost track of time for a bit."

"How much time?"

Ted looks past me, through the window screen.

"How long was I gone, Ted?"

His gaze comes back. Clicks onto mine.

"About a week," he says, and I buckle.

There was a mother who called us in when we were playing in the yard past dark.

There was a father who made us recite his phone number, forward and back, before he'd let us ride scooters down sunny streets.

There was a brother who held me down, dug his arm into my mouth, but still warned me and Kyla about the potholes on Maple Lane.

And *here* was a woman in her studio. A man in his office. Neither of them noticing their daughter was gone.

"When you *did* come home," he says, "it was like you materialized right out of the woods. Mara says you burst in here hysterically. Dirt on your face. Leaves in your hair. Crying about a basement. Some red-haired girl. A man in a mask."

My body is still. Hard as Mara's pottery fresh from the kiln. This room is a kiln.

"We gave you some sleeping pills," Ted says.

"Sleeping pills?" My voice sounds far away. Someone else must be speaking and I'm just mouthing along.

"Yes," he says. "You weren't making any sense. Mara had some pills, so we gave you a couple. Just to try to calm you down. But then you slept for nearly twenty-four hours. It was . . . fascinating, actually."

Fascinating. Part of me knows to store that word in my head for later. I cannot linger on it now.

"I don't—I don't remember this."

Ted scratches the back of his neck. "When you woke up, it was as if nothing had happened. We asked about the things you'd said, of course, but that only confused you. Made you agitated. Otherwise, you went on as if everything was normal. So we figured it was. Until we saw the newspaper."

I wait for him to continue. He doesn't. He's looking at me and I can tell there's a part of him—probably a large part—that is relishing this moment. That, perhaps, he has looked forward to it for a very long time. "What was in the newspaper?" I ask.

He responds with a question of his own. "Does the name Astrid Sullivan mean anything to you?"

My breath hitches. My skin burns from the inside out.

"Yes."

"Noteworthy," he says. He stands a little straighter. "When we said the name to you back then, you acted as if you didn't even hear us. It was the most . . ." His eyes go soft. Unseeing. Then he focuses again. "Anyway. I was at Rusty's, and people were buzzing all over the stack of newspapers."

He grunts his disapproval. Ted doesn't care for anyone who cares about the news. He calls all media "the enemy of the mind."

"I saw the headline. Inadvertently, mind you. It said that a girl who had been missing for weeks had suddenly turned up in her hometown. She was left only yards away from her own house."

He clears his throat. In discomfort or anticipation, I can't be sure. "She had red hair," he says. "And according to the article—which, I'll admit, I then read—she'd been kept in a basement. By a man in a mask."

"Just like I told you."

"Yes," he says. "And that's when we knew that something actually *had* happened to you, but you were experiencing a sort of dissociative amnesia." I squint at him. "Memory repression," he clarifies, "as those who know nothing about it tend to call it."

My muscles tighten. My stomach clenches. I imagine the life inside me recoiling from Ted's confession. *Children so wounded they can't remember why. Children so haunted they become their own ghost.*

Parents with horrifying secrets.

"But I talked to Mara," I say. "On my way up to Cedar. I mentioned Astrid Sullivan and she acted like she'd never even heard of her."

Ted tilts his head. Looks almost hurt. "You asked Mara? Why didn't you ask me?"

"Because I—that's not . . . Why didn't you ever tell me about this?"

"Because you didn't want to know. Aren't you listening? When we tried to talk to you about it, you went completely still. Catatonic. And then a minute would go by, and you'd be normal again. So we took your lead—which was Mara's idea, *not* mine—and we stopped bringing it up. I imagine that's why Mara said what she did on the phone. She must not have wanted to upset you."

I chuckle, despite the subject. "I don't think Mara cares that much about my emotional well-being."

"Oh, believe me, she does." The words are cryptic. Heavy with resentment. But I don't have time to figure out why. I'm already gasping with a new thought.

"You didn't tell the police?" I nearly shout. Then I put my hands on my knees—*steady, steady*—and find them slippery with sweat. "You just acted like nothing happened, without ever trying to find out who took me? That is—completely outrageous, Ted. Even for you."

"Even for me? What is that supposed to mean?" He doesn't wait for me to answer. "We *did* call the police."

"When?"

"Right after that Astrid Sullivan business. We filed a report, and they came out to question you, but you wouldn't answer them. Like I said: catatonia."

"And so they just gave up?"

"More or less. They gave us a card for some bogus therapist, did whatever passes for an investigation at the Cedar PD, and said they didn't have enough to go off of. Apparently all sorts of people were claiming to know something about the Sullivan girl. And all we had was our word about what you'd said in Mara's studio. One of them even hypothesized, and I quote, 'Maybe she had a nightmare. The mind is very powerful, you know.' Ha! A *policeman* trying to tell *me* about the mind. As if I need Cedar's Finest, fresh off another bang-up job, to lecture me on the—"

"Ted, I don't remember any of this. I've never been questioned by the police in my life."

Ted laughs. Scratches at the dark pink patch on his arm. I grimace at the sound. "Well, until recently," he says, "you didn't remember being kidnapped, either. And if I'm understanding you correctly, you still don't recall much of that." He pauses, a flicker of hope in his eyes. "Or am I wrong?"

"No," I say quickly. "Fine. I guess I don't remember. But Astrid Sullivan's memoir—I'm reading it, and—"

"You're reading her memoir?"

"Yes, and she said—"

"That is . . ." He stops. Seems to search for the right word. Ends up saying one he's already used: "noteworthy."

"Okay," I plunge ahead, "but listen, she writes about another girl who was with her in the basement. And I guess that's never been public until this book, but wouldn't the Cedar Police have heard about that—through the police department grapevine or whatever—and have connected that with what you and Mara told them about me?"

Ted's got his fingers on his chin. His eyes are moving back and forth, as if reading something. "You're expecting competency from the Cedar Police," he says. "That's why you're confused." His words are quiet. Dim. Lacking his attention even as he says them. Then he brightens. "So the memoir, has it jogged anything for you?"

"Not really. But I haven't read the whole thing. I only got to the part where she mentions the other girl, and then I stopped."

"You *stopped*? Why on earth would you stop?"

"Because it's a lot to take in! Because I . . . Do you even know that Astrid's missing again?"

"I did hear about that, yes," Ted replies. "And to be honest, I wondered how you'd—"

But I cut him off. "If I was in the basement with her . . ." I hear the *if*. Wince at it. "Then maybe there's something in the police report that can help. Maybe you're wrong and I did tell them something. Some seemingly insignificant detail or word that meant nothing to them at the time but might mean something to me now. And then I can help her, Ted. I can tell the police who to look for. Or *what* to look for, at least."

Ted shakes his head. "You're not understanding me. You were completely ineffectual during any inquiry at all. Which was particularly frustrating to me, because I could've used your answers!"

My mouth clamps shut for a second. "Used my answers for what?"

"What do you think? For research, obviously! It was so serendipitous—and yet so . . . infuriating. Here you were, clearly repressing something *because* of fear. But without your memories, whatever had happened to you was useless to my work. And as Mara so *loved* to point out, it seemed we were agitating you further by asking you about it. So I said fine, to hell with it then, and I went with her suggestion. I didn't try to seek your collaboration, because your mind wouldn't let you give it. I didn't bother following up with the police, because they couldn't be bothered in the first place. But now . . ."

He pushes his lips to the side, stares up and to the right. I know that look. He's getting an idea.

"If the memories are starting to come back," he says, "it might be only a matter of time before you remember everything. We could conduct some interviews now, like we couldn't back then." He taps his chin. "Yes . . . *Yes*. This is perfect actually. It could be wonderful, don't you think?"

I don't respond. I can't.

"You *want* to remember, Fern. Right?"

I watch his expression slip from pensive to eager. His lips part, as if looking at me makes him hungry. *Fascinating*, he said. *Serendipitous*, he said. *Noteworthy. Noteworthy.* Nausea whirls inside me. I've become so accustomed to this sickening feeling that I barely register it until it's climbed up my throat. I have to swallow hard to push it back down.

"You're . . ." I don't want to say it. I've never wanted to say it. But I know it's true. "Unhinged."

Ted's lips close. His eyes narrow. "Excuse me?"

"I mean, you have to be," I say. "It just isn't . . . *normal*, what you did. What you still want to do. I was"—I don't want to say this either—". . . *kidnapped*. I was kidnapped, Ted. And instead of breathing down the police's neck until they figured out who took me, or even *where I'd been*, you let it go. You were actually . . ." My voice is thick with a sob that's close to bursting. I swallow it down like the sick. "You were disappointed you couldn't study me."

"Of course I was disappointed! What do you expect? Fear is my life's work."

"And this was my *life*! Weren't you worried I had . . . psychological damage? Or *physical* damage? How do you know that whoever took me didn't hurt me? Didn't . . . do things to me."

"Give us *some* credit, Fern. We obviously checked you over."

"You're not doctors!"

"You didn't want to *see* a doctor!"

"I was twelve," I say. "I was *traumatized*. You don't let a traumatized child call the shots. You get her help. You try to find out what happened. You don't say, 'Well, if I can't study her, I might as well never speak of this again.' That isn't a normal thing for a parent to do!"

I'm gesticulating wildly. The stool wobbles beneath me. And now

Ted glares down at me from where he stands. Tall. I could jump up, try to meet his gaze, but it wouldn't matter. I'm a tiny thing. All bones and angles. *Small and fragile as a bird.* Like Astrid wrote about Lily. About me.

"There are worse things than silence," Ted says. His voice is quiet but coarse. The way it gets when he thinks about his father. "And anyway—" His gaze sharpens. "What would you know about normal? Mara and me, we're all you've had for parents. And you've never been one yourself."

I open my mouth to argue. But he's right.

All I've ever known for parents are him and Mara. And Kyla's, of course. And Eric's. But even after all my sit-down, table-set dinners with other people's families, which I participated in with the wonder of a person visiting a museum, I haven't known Kyla's and Eric's parents the way I've known my own—in that bone-deep, bone-aching way. Even when Ted and Mara are mysteries to me, their patterns and choices are profoundly familiar. It's why I'm so good at recognizing when a kid at school has nothing in his belly. It's why I know how to speak to the parents. How to keep them unguarded. How to convince them it's not their fault.

I haven't been a parent yet. But I'm going to be. Right now, the heat is flaring in this studio, because in nine months, there'll be a baby whose only option for a mother is me. A woman who wasn't raised to speak the language of normal.

My stomach roils. The baby is tiny. Can't be much larger than a seed. But still—it's rioting inside me. Wanting two parents, instead of just one, who will know enough to raise it right. To keep it safe.

"I have to go," I tell Ted.

"What?" he says as I head for the door. "We're nowhere close to done here."

The heat outside is thick. I wade through it to get to the house, then clomp through the door, up the stairs, into my room. I'm about to dive onto the bed, curl into myself—but there she is again. Astrid. Her book is on the floor now, right where it landed when I kicked it off the foot of the bed last night. When I pick it up, I open to the inside jacket of the back cover, stare at the face I should have remembered long before this.

That freckle again. Under her eyebrow. It means something to me, but whatever it is, it's still out of reach. My memories feel miles away—even with everything I've managed to recall: the man's outfit, Astrid's pleading, her voice in my dream. But if she wasn't asking me to save her, if both of us were stuck in that basement together—no, no *if* anymore; we *were*—then what was she pleading for?

I skim her bio on the back flap. She's a middle-school English teacher. We both spend our days in schools. We surround ourselves with children who need us to see them safely through their lives. I protect them with counseling and regulations, and I imagine she builds a home for them with words. Is this why I was drawn to social work in the first place? Because some part of me knew that deep inside me, so far down I couldn't even hear her calling out, was a girl who'd needed protection, but who'd been left alone instead?

"Is that the book?"

Ted's standing in the doorway, but I give him barely a glimpse.

"I can see you're upset," he says. "But I'm wondering—you said you've remembered a man. What did he look like? I think the Sullivan girl said she never saw his face, but do you remem—"

"Ted. Stop."

"Stop? Fern, this is important. Anything you remember could—"

"Could help the police find Astrid now. But that's not why you want to know this. Is it?"

I meet his eyes for a moment. A moment in which he looks frustrated and confused but not at all concerned.

"Well, of course we can pass this on to the police if you want," he says, "but I also think—now, I know I haven't talked much about my current project with you, but this revelation you've had, these memories—they'd fit in perfectly. Maybe, through a series of careful interviews, I could help you remember more. I was actually starting to get stuck last night, but this opens up a whole new window."

I drop my eyes from Ted's face. Look back at Astrid's bio. English teacher. Lives in Maine—*with her wife, Rita*.

Rita Diaz. I've seen her twice on the news. With her dark hair and dark eyes, her gaze both pained and hollow. Missing the same person I might be able to help. If only I can remember more.

I grab my purse off the nightstand. Nudge Ted's shoulder as I move past him out the room.

He calls after me as I hurry down the stairs. As I reach the front door. "Where are you going? When will you be back?"

Standard questions from a parent. But they're ones I've never heard.

Pushing open the screen, I refuse to satisfy him with an answer. It isn't his business that I'm heading to Maine. To see the woman who knows Astrid best. To see the place where she was kidnapped again.

eleven

As I drive past the woods, I see their abundant leaves, thick enough to obscure a child's way. I see their jutting branches, sharp enough to scrape. I see myself sprinting through them—a memory that crumbles at the edges.

Once I cross the town line, I pull over and pick up my phone. It turns out that Rita's Ridgeway, Maine, address is easy to find. Too easy, for Astrid's sake, even though I quickly discover that Astrid herself is unlisted. I punch the address into my GPS and all I can think is how the man who took her—took *us*—might have also read Astrid's memoir, also seen Rita's name. He might have done the same internet search as I just did. And with such a clear path back to Astrid, he might have felt an old desire twitch back to life.

Men who are never really done with you. Men who come back once you're sure you're finally free.

I try to picture him, beyond the outfit he wore. I try to remember where or when he might have taken me. As I walked home from Kyla's? As I sat alone on a curb in front of a store?

And did he first notice me in Foster? He must have, right? Because no matter what Ted's just told me, I was still in Foster when Astrid was taken. Maybe he spied me then and kept track of me somehow. Bided his time.

Did he seize me by the waist? Is that why I've been so sure he did that to Astrid? I try to remember the sensation of being snatched, the whoosh of panic, the pain in my gut where his arm would have dug. But there's nothing. And it ratchets up my heart—that emptiness where memories should be.

Dr. Lockwood says that when my anxiety is particularly overwhelming, I should concentrate on the task at hand, box up everything else. Right now, Ridgeway, Maine, is only an hour away, and my task is to get there. To turn on the radio, tune to some music I recognize, and pack away whatever happened to me. I close the lid on where I might have been taken. Seal up how Ted and Mara never came searching. How they didn't even know I was gone.

Somehow, I stay focused on the road for almost the entire hour, but as I pass a sign for Ridgeway, my phone rings. It interrupts the music, startles me into a swerve. I grip the wheel, course-correct, and see that it's Eric calling. I reach to answer it, then pause. I have only one task. And it isn't to open all these boxes, to unpack them truth by truth. It isn't to field Eric's questions, or listen to the fury in his voice. *Fucking Ted*, I can hear him saying.

He hardly ever swears, but for this, I know he would.

The ringing ends. The music surges back up. In a minute, there's the chime of my voice mail, and the GPS tells me that in point-three miles, I should turn left on Autumn Lane. I ache for Eric. For his kindness. His devotion. For how he reaches out, even as I keep getting further away. But I ignore the voice mail. I take the turn. Box up my guilt along with everything else.

Astrid's street is narrow and unpaved. Her house is cute—a yellow cottage with green shutters—but right now, it looks like a light that's been turned off. All the curtains are closed and the grass is brown and overgrown. I park along the edge of the lawn and don't allow myself to second-guess. My task is only this: to get to the front door.

When I knock, my fingers itch, and then my wrists, but I tighten my fist so I cannot scratch.

Inside, there's silence. I knock again. Harder this time. I hear a shuffling inside. Then there's a swish of curtains at the window, so quick I can't catch the person who flicked them open. Five heavy beats of quiet. And then a voice, muffled by the door: "Are you a reporter?"

"No."

"You don't look like police."

"I'm not."

"Amateur sleuth, then? I'm sorry, but it's not my job to tell you about my wife."

"No," I say, speaking straight at the door as if it's a person. "I . . . I think I . . ."

How do I explain this? I pause for so long that Rita attempts to finish my sentence.

"Know something about the case?" she provides. "You can call the tip line then. I've already had my hopes up with too many false leads."

"I'm sorry," I say. And I am. That sounds brutal. Like a cut that never scabs. But I'm not a false lead, I'm—"I'm Astrid's old neighbor," I say. "From Bleeker Street. We were friends growing up."

I didn't intend to lie. Not like I did to Father Murphy. But Rita's suspicion rattled me and I felt the words tumble out. Now I find it's a bit of comfort, actually—this distance from the truth.

"Sarah Yates?" Rita asks, and her voice sounds tentative.

I take a breath. Take a gamble. "Yes."

"Oh. Wow." There's a sliding sound, the click of a chain, a dead bolt unlocking. Then Rita opens the door, her hair piled on top of her head in a messy bun, dark flyaways framing her face. She squints at me.

"Sarah," she says. "What are you doing here?"

It feels like an accusation.

"I, um . . . Well—" But she cuts me off.

"Sorry," she says. "Astrid's always telling me I come off a little blunt. I'm just surprised you're here." She holds her hand out for me to shake. "It's nice to finally meet you."

Her grip is hard, almost aggressive, but when she lets go, she moves to the side, waves me into the house.

I step into an icy living room.

"Astrid's told me a lot about you," Rita says. "You're pretty much the only person from high school she actually likes. She was bummed you couldn't make it to the wedding."

She gestures toward a chair. "You can sit down if you want."

She plops down on a couch along the opposite wall and curls up her legs beneath her. The room is filled with the drone of an AC unit, but all I can focus on is how Rita's looking at me. Her eyes are a mix of wary and welcoming. Like I'm somewhere between a stranger and a friend.

Guilt stabs between my ribs. I have to confess my lie. But she looks almost comfortable: legs crossed, hands on a pillow she's pulled onto her lap, fingers playing with its fringe. And only a minute ago, she was so on edge I could feel the sharpness of her like a blade coming at me through the door.

"I can't believe you're here," she says. "Did you fly out, just to see if you could help?"

Help. Yes. That's what I'm here to do. I need answers from Rita. Answers that even Astrid's memoir, carefully crafted for public consumption, might not be able to give. And I'll get more answers, I think, by playing a woman she's familiar with.

"Yes, I . . . was visiting family," I improvise. "In New Hampshire. And I decided to come up here to see how you're doing. If I can help you at all. Help Astrid."

Rita chuckles dryly. "I wish. It's been almost two weeks and the police have nothing. I showed them her usual running route, right? But there was no 'visible disturbance' to mark where she might have been taken." She uses air quotes. Rolls her eyes. "And they can't try to ping a cell-phone tower, because she left her phone at home." She shakes her head. "I tell her all the time to take it with her, but she doesn't like the weight of it when she runs. You know how stubborn she is."

I nod. But only a little.

I glance around the room. There's a fireplace on one end, its mantel holding up a single copy of Astrid's book. A coffee table between us. A lone painting. And to the left of the couch where Rita sits, a hutch. The shelves are almost completely bare except for one photo in a frame: Rita and Astrid in wedding dresses, foreheads touching, arms wrapped around each other. Astrid has baby's breath looped through her hair, which flares out red and wild against her satin gown. She was safe that day. Safe and smiling—with absolutely no idea that she'd be hauled back into the nightmare we apparently both lived.

My heart kicks. My eyes dart from the photo, instead latching on to the painting behind the couch. It's of a ballerina stretching, her arms taut as she reaches toward her toes. I remember it from Rita's interview on the news.

"I love that painting," I say to break the silence. To stall until I figure out how to ask the questions that might fill my memory's gaps.

Rita glances behind her. "Thanks," she says. "I'm a dancer. Which I'm sure Astrid's told you."

"Right. Yeah."

Without any warning, a wave of nausea crests inside me. I put my hand to my mouth.

"Are you okay?" Rita asks.

I can't respond until it passes. I breathe through the spaces between my fingers. Wait for my stomach to settle. I picture the nausea like a mist rolling through me.

"Yes," I finally say, swallowing the last of it down. "Sorry. It's just that I'm pregnant."

I stiffen. It's the first time I've spoken those words out loud.

"Oh, wow," Rita says. "Congrats." But there's a wince in her eyes. She looks as if I've pinched her.

"Are *you* okay?" I ask.

Her lips twitch, an almost smile. "Yeah. No, yeah. That's great. Astrid's gonna be thrilled for you. We've been trying to get pregnant ourselves. But it's been a struggle. We've been through some unsuccessful rounds of IVF."

"Oh. I'm sorry to hear that."

She waves away my apology like it's smoke she's clearing from the air. "It's fine. It'll happen for us. We'll make sure of it. We can't wait to have a baby."

Her optimism feels strange to me—mostly because I don't understand how anyone could be excited about something so terrifying. Astrid knows how easy it is for a child to be dragged into darkness. So how would she wake each day without a litany of worries looping through her mind? *Children who walk away. Children who don't come back. Children who think they're just children—not prey.*

"So in terms of finding Astrid . . ." I say.

Rita looks surprised by the switch in subject, but this is why I'm here. To get information. To trigger memories. And I can't afford to waste more time when I have no idea how much Astrid has left.

"I've been thinking about Lily," I continue.

"Lily from the basement?" Rita says.

I nod. "I keep thinking how—if the police could find her . . . find Lily . . . then maybe she could tell them things that would help them locate Astrid. So I guess I'm wondering if Astrid's told you much about her."

"Well, yeah," Rita says, cocking her head to the side. Her eyes narrow at me. I can feel them zooming in. "She never told you?"

I shrug. Try to seem casual as I take another gamble. "She's not one to bring it up, you know? And I never wanted to ask her about it. I didn't want to make her relive something so horrible."

I hold my breath until she responds—"That makes sense," she says—and then I let it out. Slowly.

"But I have no idea where Lily is," she adds. "Supposedly, the police tried to find her, back in 2000. I'm not sure how long they looked, but I know they ran a composite sketch against the database of missing children. Nothing came up."

Of course it didn't. Because it couldn't. Because Lily's parents—*my* parents—never even reported her as missing; they only spoke to the police after I'd been returned. I rub my hand against an ache along my sternum. My heart is a fist clenching tighter and tighter.

"And then there was Astrid's therapist," Rita continues. "She made a statement to the police that she believed Lily was some sort of imaginary friend. She said it was a common coping mechanism for that type of trauma." She rolls her eyes. "As if Astrid would have an imaginary friend—at *fourteen*."

I scratch my wrist—long, deep strokes—and as I glance at my fingers, I remember a line from the memoir. *When he brought her down the stairs,* Astrid wrote about Lily, *she had ropes tied tightly around her wrists.*

My hand freezes. That's the reason for my itch. I'm sure of it. This whole time, I've been scratching because I remembered the ropes—only the memory was stored in my skin instead of my mind.

I need to know what else is inside me, what other disguises my memories wear.

"In the memoir . . ." I start. Rita's eyes brighten with eagerness.

"Did you read it?" she asks.

"Just the first few chapters," I say.

"Oh," Rita says. She looks disappointed. Picking the pillow up from her lap, she clutches it to her chest. Not like someone seeking comfort—but like someone holding a shield.

"I've been meaning to finish it," I say. "It's really well written, of course. But . . ."

I trail off. I can't, as Sarah, explain to her that my mind could only handle the memoir a bit at a time. That I threw the book across the room as soon as Lily appeared.

"It's fine," Rita says coolly. "I'm sure you're really busy."

I glance away. Down at the coffee table between us. It's empty too. Just like the hutch.

"Did she tell you how the memoir came to be?" Rita asks. When I look at her, her lips flick upward, but it's still not a smile.

"No," I say.

"Oh, well, it's kind of interesting. Astrid published a short story a couple years ago, and the editor from a small press here in Maine stumbled upon it. The editor recognized Astrid's name and saw that she could *write*. Like, really, truly write. So *he* actually approached *Astrid* with an offer to publish a memoir, in conjunction with the twentieth anniversary of her kidnapping."

The story has a practiced quality to it, like she's told it many times before, and something about it unsettles me.

"Weren't you worried," I ask, "that they were trying to capitalize on her trauma?"

Rita shrugs. "Yeah, well—they definitely were. But there's not much money in dancing. Or teaching. And we'd decided to start trying for a baby, but IVF was way more expensive than we realized." She shrugs again. "We needed the money. But—we're so stupid. Pretty much two seconds after Astrid signed the deal, one of our friends told us we probably could've taken the offer to bigger publishers—*New York City ones*—and used it as leverage for a larger advance."

She rubs her cheek, as if the regret is a painful, impacted tooth.

"There could have been a *bidding war*," she adds. Then she looks around the room. Its blank walls. Its bald surfaces. "We could have gotten out of this little house."

I look at my hands in my lap. Cross one leg over the other. Suddenly I can't stop picturing Astrid at her computer, her fingers paused over the keys, her forehead creased with a memory she isn't sure she wants to relive. Then I see Rita standing behind her. Bringing her a cup of tea. Massaging her shoulders. Whispering through the fog of chamomile steam that the money will be worth the words she has to bleed.

"Sales were only okay to start," she continues, and the image doesn't dissipate. It sharpens. Its colors deepen. "But then she went missing. Again."

And just like that, her voice changes. There's a hitch to it. A weighted sadness that has nothing to do with missed opportunities. I feel a burst of guilt, strong as nausea in my gut. This whole thing keeps messing with my mind. Making me look for villains everywhere.

"Now the book's doing great, but it doesn't even matter," Rita says. "All I care about is getting her back." She rakes her fingernails over the pillow. Slides over the tiny grooves in its fabric as if strumming a guitar.

A muscle quivers in her chin, but only for a moment. Then her jaw tightens. Her face becomes marble hard. "When Astrid comes home," she says, "we'll have to move away from here. We'll go to another country if we have to. Get away from *him.*"

"Him—the kidnapper?"

Her brows pinch together. "Who else?"

"Well, hopefully he'll be in jail," I say. "Then you won't have to worry about him at all."

She tilts her head back, exposes her throat to let out a punch of laughter. "In jail? They'd have to catch him first."

"They will."

"No, they won't. Because it's all gone exactly the same as last time. Taken while walking, taken while running. No witnesses, no trace; no witnesses, no trace. So he's going to return her, too. I know he will. But he'll do it when no one's looking, probably drop her off half a mile from here. She'll be blindfolded and sedated, and he'll be far away before she even wakes up. Exactly like before."

She looks at the pillow in her arms. "But at least she'll be back."

There's a delicate tremble to her voice. I imagine that the confidence she tries to project has all sorts of cracks in it. Maybe her own words are the only caulk that can fill them.

"What did he want with her?" I ask. "Twenty years ago. And what do you think he wants with her now?"

For the third time since I arrived, Rita rolls her eyes. It's a strange response to a question so chilling. "I think he's just a bully," she says. "I think this whole thing—then, now—is about power. Because he never hurt her. I mean, he did, of course. But he didn't rape her. Or torture her. He'd just look at her. And laugh at her. And the more she screamed at him, the more he laughed."

My skin prickles. My spine straightens. Because I've felt that before—somebody's laughter in the face of my terror. Am I remembering something? I stare straight ahead, try to will this feeling into a shape. But all I see is Cooper. His arm over my mouth as he holds me to the ground. The bees of his tattoo seeming to buzz against my tongue. His laughter spurting.

"That's terrible," I say, my voice thick. "But he must have wanted something. You don't keep a girl—two girls—in a basement because of a power trip. Right?"

Rita shrugs. "Maybe he planned to do something else, but he chickened out. I'm telling you, that laughter thing—whenever I picture him, I see an insecure, pathetic, power-guzzling boy. The kind who peaks in twelfth grade and never leaves town. The kind who used to grab my ass in the hallways and spread rumors about 'converting the lesbo' in high school. And even—okay, think about what he wore."

"The welder's mask?"

"All of it! The mask, the waders, the gloves. It's like something a kid would scrounge together in his dad's garage."

"So you think he was a kid? How would a kid overpower her like that?"

"I think he was young," Rita clarifies. "But he surprised and sedated her, so it wouldn't have taken much strength. And anyway, Astrid was pretty distracted when it happened. She'd just left her parents' party, and she was pissed."

"At the priest, you mean?"

"Yeah," Rita scoffs. "Fuck that guy."

Anger flares in her eyes. I can tell she wants to say more about Father Murphy, but we've already gone so far off course.

"What about Lily?" I ask. I know it's a non sequitur—and a question I've already tried. But I need to keep pushing. I need to see if Rita knows anything that can jolt my memories awake. "Did Astrid give you any details that could help the police trace her?"

Rita shakes her head. "I don't think so. For all we know, Lily's dead."

My heart stops for a second. "Dead?"

"She never came forward. If she was alive, why wouldn't she or her parents go to the police? And Jesus, the way things ended for her in the basement . . ." She shudders, and my skin goes cold. A flash freeze. How did things end for her—for me—in the basement? I lean forward—ready, but a little afraid, to ask. Except Rita's already speaking again.

"And if she *is* alive, I'm not sure I want to drag her into the investigation. Some reporter could find out, and then *all* the reporters would find out, and then she'd be all over the news." She takes a deep breath, lets it out. "And I couldn't live with myself if that happened."

"Why?" I ask, and Rita tilts her head, narrows her gaze. Like the answer is obvious. Like it's been waiting for me to see it all along.

"Because he'd probably come for her next."

twelve

Sometimes, anxiety turns my heart to a fist. Sends it punching against my ribs, trying to break out. Other times, it hardens me to stone. My heart doesn't beat at all. My blood doesn't run. My eyes can't blink. Dr. Lockwood says anxiety manifests in different ways at different times. *But no matter what it feels like,* she says, *your blood is always pumping.*

It's not, though. Right now, I know it's not.

It didn't even occur to me that I, too, might be in danger. Ever since Ted's confession in Mara's studio this morning, I've been trying so hard to compartmentalize. To consume the truth in the smallest, most manageable bites. But Rita's right. If the kidnapper is repeating his exact same patterns from twenty years ago, then soon he'll be coming after me.

Except—no—he wouldn't know how to find me. He only knew where Astrid was because she came back into the spotlight with her book.

So why does my body still feel like stone? Why hasn't my blood turned back to blood, my heart to a muscle instead of a rock?

What if he's here, right now, watching me through the cracks between curtains? I feel eyes on every inch of me. Ears attuned to everything I'll say.

"Are you okay?" Rita asks. "You look a little pale."

I'm stone, but I somehow crack a smile. Just a flick of the lips. But it's something. "I'm okay." My voice sounds like rocks scraping together. "It's morning sickness, I think."

Rita smirks. "Afternoon sickness, you mean?"

"I, um . . ." I clear my throat. "I've been queasy for days. Doesn't really matter what time it is."

"Mmm," Rita acknowledges. "That must be nice, though."

My face must show my confusion. "No, sorry," Rita says. "I didn't mean it's nice that you feel sick. That part sucks, I'm sure. I meant—it must be nice to have that constant reminder that there's a baby inside you."

She stands abruptly, making me jump. "I'll get you a snack," she says. "Maybe it'll settle your stomach."

A minute passes, there's clattering in the kitchen, and I'm alone in this empty room. But am I alone? Am I unwatched? The thought returns: *I might be next.* It adds itself to my already too-long list— *women on someone's radar, women who are next*—and my heart becomes a fist.

When Rita returns, she's carrying a plate and a chef's knife. "Here," she says, placing the plate on the coffee table. "The crackers should help with the nausea. And the cheese . . . Well. I like cheese. And maybe it'll . . . solidify things in there?"

She points to my stomach with the knife, and my eyes widen. I know she's just gesturing—doesn't mean it as threatening—but I cross my arms over my belly anyway.

Rita kneels in front of the coffee table, begins slicing up the cheese. I watch the blade as it glides through a block of cheddar.

"I feel like I should mention . . ." she begins, her voice slightly cooler than before, "I know that Astrid probably told you about"—the knife pauses—"the problems we were having." The cutting resumes. "But that wasn't anything, really. Just regular couple stuff."

She looks at me, and I can tell she's waiting for me to agree before she continues. "Of course," I say. "All couples . . . argue. From time to time."

"Right," she says. "Exactly. Because like I said, we're still trying for a family. That's the most important thing to Astrid. And to me. And we'll pick back up with it as soon as she comes home."

She takes a bite of her cracker. "Anyway," she says, "tell me something about Astrid."

I pause. My legs stiffen. "What do you mean?" I ask.

She grabs the knife and starts sliding it through the cheese again. "You must have some funny stories of her from your childhood. Especially from before."

"Before?"

Her gaze is penetrating. "Before she was . . . fourteen," she says. "I never got the chance to know that version of her. The version who wasn't . . ." She pauses, searches for the word. "Marked. By everything that happened to her. So tell me something about my wife, from when she was still a kid."

My mouth hangs open for a moment. It's a reasonable request—one that anyone might ask of their wife's childhood friend.

"Um . . ." I stall. I stare at the wedding photo on the hutch as if I could intuit something about Astrid through it alone. My heart thumps on and the room keeps filling with my silence. Then I notice it: even from across the room, I can see the freckle beneath the arch of Astrid's eyebrow. My heartbeat stutters. Then, like someone who's just crossed a finish line, it slows.

"She was always so good at calming me down," I say.

Rita chews a piece of cheese, then cuts another. She watches me instead of the knife. Waits for me to continue.

"I'd get really anxious. And . . . and I'd panic," I say. Rita stops chewing. Furrows her brow. "At school, I mean. Tests and stuff. And she'd point to the freckle under her eyebrow. She'd tell me to . . ."

Look at this.

The words are a whisper in my head. They're faceless and bodiless. A series of breathy sounds without a mouth. But still, they echo. As if someone's saying them from deep inside a well.

Look at this, I hear again. *Look at this freckle. Concentrate on only this. As long as you can see this dark little dot, everything's okay.*

I look at Rita. Her eyes are unchanged, watchful as before. But mine are stinging.

"She'd tell me—tell me to look at the freckle under her eyebrow." I stand up. Walk on shaky legs to the hutch and pick up the wedding photo. Point to the spot on Astrid's skin. "This one here. She'd tell me to stare at it—whenever I was upset, I think. And she'd say that if I could see it, I'd . . ."

"Know that everything was okay?" Rita offers.

"Yes," I breathe. "Does she say it to you, too?"

Rita shakes her head. "Not me," she says. "She used to do that for Lily."

The picture frame clatters against the shelf. I fumble to right it again. Then I scratch the side of my face. Attempt to look unfazed. But my pulse is quickening. Because it's true. It's true. The words I just heard—they're not some story I concocted. They're something I remembered.

I can see her now. She squats in front of me, red hair greasy and knotted. She puts a fingertip beneath her eyebrow. Taps it twice before speaking. *Keep your eyes on this*, she says. *He can't hurt you, okay? Nothing at all can hurt you as long as—*

"I'm not surprised she used the same trick on someone else," Rita says.

The memory dissolves like a dream. I can't see her in front of me anymore. Can't hear her either. It's only the memory of a memory now, and as it replays, it's as short as the first time. Stops in the exact same place. Right when Rita spoke.

I need to get out of here—now—while my mind is cracked open, while there's room for other moments to surface. I need to go, right away, to the place where I should have gone first.

"I'm sorry," I say, "but I have to get going."

"Already?" Rita asks. The knife stalls in midair. A beam of sunlight bounces off it, a flash of movement that briefly blinds. And now I have that feeling again—that someone's lurking outside, that I'm being watched. That by sitting in this house, I'm a sitting duck.

"Sorry," I say again. "I should've told you that I only had a few minutes when I got here. I'm—" My mind searches for excuses. "A friend of mine is expecting me. I was just stopping here on the way."

"A friend from high school?"

"No. Um. A friend from work."

Rita stands, the movement quick and fluid, evidence of her dancer's grace. But there's something catlike to it, too. Her limbs all lithe. Coiled with energy. As if, at any moment, she could pounce.

"But don't you live in LA?" she asks. "Or am I thinking of someone else?"

"Uh, no, I do," I say. "But she—my friend—moved out here. A couple years ago."

"To Ridgeway?" She takes a step forward. "We're a small town. What are the odds?"

I move toward the door. Put my hand on the knob. The metal is cold from the air conditioning. My hand is cold, too. "No, she lives about a half hour from here."

"Really? Where?"

"I don't . . . I don't remember the name of the town. I've got it stored in my GPS." I open the door. A burst of heat barges in. "Sorry, again, to run off like this. And thanks for speaking with me. And for the snack, too."

She stares at me, silent. Then, right as I turn, about to step through the doorway, she curls her fingers around my wrist.

"Wait," she says.

My heart kicks, but I don't know why. Rita isn't dangerous, even though she's trying so hard to project only strength. I'm sure, with Astrid gone, the truth is closer to this: she feels empty as her living room, her body like a hutch with nothing inside it. I bet the floor's grown creaky with her pacing. I bet she never sleeps at night.

"Let me give you my number," she says. "In case you want to stop by again while you're visiting family. This way, I'll know you're coming and won't assume you're somebody trying to tragedy-stalk."

"Yeah, sorry about that," I say.

"No, it's fine. It was good to talk to you. Even briefly. It's nice to have one of Astrid's friends in the house."

She looks at the hardwood beneath our feet. For the first time since I arrived, the extent of her sadness is palpable. It covers her whole face like a mask. This close, I can see that her eyelids are pink and bloated. That she's struggling to lift her eyes to meet my own.

"Kind of makes me feel like she's still here," she adds.

———

It's only a six-minute drive to my next destination, and this is my task now. Easy and mindless. Hands at ten and two on the steering wheel. Eyes on the tree-lined road.

I realized something, when Rita's request for an Astrid memory actually triggered one. These past couple days, I've been questioning other people in the hopes I'll remember something—but maybe what I really need is for someone to question me.

I think of Ted, of course. I know he'd love to get me into that chair in his office. But I need someone who's working for Astrid's sake. Not for his own.

As I drive to the Ridgeway police station, the new memory returns. Plays out on the faded pavement, flickering like an old filmstrip. In those few frames of it, Astrid's face is dirty. Her cheek is streaked with basement grime, and even though she's doing her best to calm me down, I know my heart is boxing. Because I was scared down there, in that basement we shared. I was panicked and petrified. And Astrid made her freckle into a beacon. A harmless, constant thing to pull me away from the edge of terror. To lull my pulse. Unclench my heart.

Right now, I have no beacon. I'm safe inside my car, but I still feel like I'm escaping from something. This is where Astrid was taken. Somewhere in this town, down the road from the house I've just left. It's possible—likely, in fact—that the kidnapper is keeping her someplace close. That his eyes are following me, even now, as I drive away. I scan from left to right, but all I see are woods, interrupted here and there with clapboard houses. Astrid could be in any one of them. She could be in none of them, too.

I shake my head, try to block out my thoughts. Listen only to the GPS as it leads me to the center of town.

When I arrive at the police station, I'm surprised to see how small it is. The brick one-story building looks more like an old schoolhouse than a place where cases are solved. Opening its door, I find an officer sitting at a desk a few feet in front of me. Behind him, there's an open room where a couple uniformed men and women talk on phones, their words slow and casual. Not urgent and sharp, as I'd imagine the search for a missing woman demands. The rest of the officers look at computer monitors, their chins like paperweights on their palms.

"Can I help you?" the man at the front desk asks. He's got a gold-plated name tag that identifies him as Lopez, and he's holding a pen over a crossword puzzle.

"Yes. Thanks." I sound wobbly, but I try again, this time with Social Worker Voice. "I'd like to speak to the detective in charge of Astrid Sullivan's case."

Lopez closes his eyes and inhales slowly. A strange reaction—one of annoyance, I think. I suppose the police must be bombarded with people hoping to learn about the case. But I look around the room again. Besides all the officers, I'm the only one here.

When Lopez opens his eyes, he scrutinizes me. "What is this regarding, specifically?"

Behind his head, I see a woman yawn. She stretches her arms out wide, like a cartoon character waking up.

Panic flutters in my stomach. There shouldn't be anyone in this room at all. Everyone should be out there, searching for Astrid. Knocking on doors. Scouring the forests for footsteps, for the slightest sign of dragging.

"I'm Lily," I say. Louder than I wanted. My throat tries to close around the confession, but I clear it and continue. "The girl who was kept with Astrid in the basement twenty years ago."

I expect all heads to turn my way. I expect them to set down their phones, snap their gazes toward me, and stand from their chairs. But no one moves at all. Instead, Lopez looks me up and down before rolling his eyes. Then he picks up a phone, punches in a number.

"Hey, Chief," he says after a few moments. "We've got another Lily."

thirteen

Chief Dixon's office is small. Just a desk crowded with folders and loose papers, a computer monitor and keyboard crammed into the corner. He sits on a black swivel chair, which creaks beneath his weight, and gestures for me to have a seat in the chair pointed toward his desk. I look at the framed photos on the wall: Dixon in uniform at a restaurant, shaking someone's hand; Dixon on the golf course, an arm around another man's shoulder; Dixon holding up a fish the size of a small canoe.

"Lily, is it?" he asks.

His expression looks nothing like it does in his photographs. There, his smile takes up half his face, his cheeks red with recent laughter. Here, his lips form a straight line, tight and pinched.

"No," I say. "I mean, yes—I am Lily. I was. But my real name is Fern Douglas. Fern Brierley at the time."

"Uh-huh," he says. "And why haven't you come forward until now?"

"I didn't know I was Lily until this morning."

"This morning?" He lets out a whistle. "That's quite a revelation."

He's mocking me. Isn't even bothering to hide it. But I answer him like I would a student who cops an attitude; I answer him as if he were serious. Right now, there's nothing more serious to me in the world.

"It was," I say. "But I wanted to come here to see how I can help. Or if—if you can help *me* . . . to remember."

"Remember?"

"Yeah, I . . ." I feel like I'm running out of breath, even though I've barely even started. "I repressed the memory of it. Of being in the basement with Astrid. But I've been getting these scraps. Of Astrid. Of a man in a welder's mask. So I know it's all in there, trapped inside me. And I thought that maybe you could . . . question me? And then I might remember more, or even . . ."

He puts a hand in the air, but I was about to stop anyway. I see on his face how crazy he thinks I sound. But he's wrong. I know very well how questions can uncover what you didn't know was inside you. One time, after Ted abandoned me at an unfamiliar grocery store, he asked if I'd been more afraid that I'd get lost trying to find my way home, or that something might happen to me in the absence of an adult. My answer surprised us both—him because it wasn't one of his options, and me because of the sudden, throbbing truth of it: *I was afraid it meant you don't love me.* Ted considered me for a moment, his chin jutting forward as his eyes roved my face. Then he gave his customary response—"noteworthy"—and clack-clack-clacked away.

"Listen," Dixon says. "Do you have any idea how many young women—and one young man, in fact—have come in here claiming to be Lily?"

My skin prickles. People are pretending to be me?

"Why would anyone do that?" I ask.

"That's a great question," Dixon replies. "Why *would* anyone do that?" Leaning forward, he clasps his hands together and rests them on his desk. "I'd encourage you to ask yourself if this is really the kind of thing you want to be associated with."

"But I *am* associated with it. I'm *her.* I'm Lily."

People who lie to the police. Women who aren't believed.

"My dad just told me this morning," I try, "that I went missing for a week, during the time of Astrid's kidnapping. And when I came home—when I was *returned*, like Astrid—I was freaking out about being in a basement with a red-haired girl."

"Do you have proof?" Dixon asks.

"No, I . . . no. Just the images I've had."

"Ah, yes, your . . . dream, was it? About Astrid?"

"And I remembered the welder's mask," I remind him.

"I see," he says. "But here's the problem, Ms. Douglas. The welder's mask is a detail available to the public in the memoir." He pulls the handle of a desk drawer, which squeals as it opens. He yanks out *Behind the Red Door*. Drops it with a thud between us.

"Okay," I say. "But—I had another memory too, a little while ago. Whenever I freaked out in the basement, Astrid would point to the freckle under her eyebrow and tell me to concentrate on that until I was calm. She said nothing could hurt me as long as I could still see the freckle. Did any of the other Lilys mention that?"

Dixon puts a finger to his chin. "Come to think of it, no. Nobody did mention that."

I let out a rush of air.

"But that's in the memoir too," he says.

Hope dissolves inside me. I look at the book on his desk. Why haven't I read it all by now? Why haven't I memorized it, cover to cover, to know my own story?

"I'm *her*," I say for the second time. "I swear, I . . . I just can't remember anything else. But I'm trying. The memories are coming back, and—maybe there's some detail that can crack the case."

Dixon sighs. "This supposed memory loss," he says. "That's awfully convenient, don't you think?"

"Convenient for *who*? I'm trying to help. That's what you want, isn't it? I've seen the tip line on the news."

He leans back in his chair. Stares at me.

"What are you doing to search for her?" I ask. "What have you found so far?"

"Surely you know I can't comment on that," he says.

My nails are needle-sharp against my palms. "I talked to Rita Diaz," I say. "Right before I came here. She said you've got nothing."

"Why did you go there first?" he asks. His eyes narrow in on mine, and it takes me a second to process his response.

"What?" I say.

"To Ms. Diaz's," he clarifies. "If you want to help us find Ms. Sullivan so badly, and if you're Lily, as you claim, why wouldn't you have come to us first?"

Because I was running from my father, I could say. Because I was running toward the one person who would feel as adrift as I do. I wanted to see Rita, I could say, to learn about the girl we're both missing. Even if we're missing her in completely different ways.

"It's complicated," I tell him. And I leave it at that.

"Of course," he says. "Our investigation is complicated too." He winks at me. Smiles on one side of his mouth. "So if you'll let us get back to it, Ms. Douglas . . ." He shifts in his chair, nods toward the door behind me.

"But I just got here," I say. "You haven't even taken my statement."

He shakes his head. "I don't think you want me to take your statement."

"Why not? Of course I do."

"If we have it on record," he says, speaking to me like he would a child, "that you made a statement which we then discover to be false—that wouldn't be good for you. That's a crime."

"But I'm not making this up."

"That's what the other Lilys have said."

"But I'm—"

"Listen," he snaps. "If you can give us some proof to corroborate your claim, then yes, I'll be happy to have you in for a formal interview. But until then, you're wasting police time and resources."

"How-how am I wasting it?" I stammer. "Nobody's doing anything out there."

Dixon watches me. Chuckles once and then falls silent. Dread pools in my stomach, and when the phone on his desk bleats out a ring, I flinch.

"Dixon," he answers, his lips rubbing against the mouthpiece. "Oh, already? Tell him I'll be right out." He hangs up, then puts his palms on his desk. Hoists himself up from his chair. "I'll see you out, Ms. Douglas. I'm heading that way myself."

I spring up to follow him. He opens the door, steps into the main room of the station, but I'm still trailing questions behind him: "That's it? Really? You don't want to ask me anything else?"

Glancing at the officers at their desks, I lock eyes with one in particular. He snickers, then nudges the woman beside him. She turns from her desk to look at me, too, and the two of them laugh.

I put my head down. Stare at the off-white tile beneath my feet as I walk. *Police who laugh instead of listen. Police who see victimizers instead of victims.*

We reach the hip-high wooden gate at the front of the station.

"Thank you for coming all this way," Dixon says. At first, I think he's talking to me, but then he adds, "Especially on such short notice."

I look up, but his broad back blocks my view of the person he's greeting.

"As I said on the phone," he continues, "I would have been happy to make the trip down to you, but this is very helpful, as I'm sure you can imagine."

"It's no problem at all, Chief," a man says. "It really wasn't that far."

His voice sounds familiar—accommodating and docile, but with an edge of condescension. I step aside to get a better look, and when I see him, my body tenses.

"What are you doing here?" I ask.

Father Murphy blinks at me in surprise. "Oh," he says. But he quickly recovers. "Hello. It's nice to see you again. I'm sorry, I don't recall your name."

Dixon looks back and forth between us. "You two know each other?"

"She stopped by St. Cecilia's yesterday," Father Murphy replies. "We had quite a lovely chat."

My forehead furrows. *Lovely* is not the word I would use to describe our "chat." But then again, he told me he had a "very good conversation" with Astrid the day she disappeared. The same conversation in which he called her sinful, warned her that "Hell is no place for a girl."

"Well," Dixon says, turning to me, "you've certainly been getting around." He opens the gate, gestures for me to pass through it. "Thanks for stopping by, Ms. Douglas."

"Wait," I say, stepping into the station's foyer, pushed forward by Dixon's bulky hand. Father Murphy passes me, fills the space I've left behind on the other side of the gate, and doesn't meet my eyes.

"Wait," I say again.

But the gate clicks closed, and Dixon waves Father Murphy down toward his office. "Right this way, Father." The sound of their shoes plodding over the floor beats in my ears like a pulse.

When they disappear behind his door, I look at Lopez. He's grinning at his crossword, his pen stalled in his hand.

"Why is Father Murphy here?" I ask. "Does he know something about who took Astrid?"

Lopez caps his pen and sets it down. Crosses his arms and glares at me. "Do I need to call security?" he asks.

"Aren't *you* security?" I fire back. The pulse in my neck is throbbing—with adrenaline or blood, I don't know. Either way, it's making me bolder than I am. "Isn't everyone in here supposed to be security?"

He shrugs. "You need to leave."

I look around the room, bounce from uniform to uniform, each of them staring at me in return. There's an open game of solitaire on one of the computers. Somebody's biting into a candy bar, caramel stretching between teeth and wrapper. A pen falls onto the floor, and nobody moves to pick it up. When laughter booms out from behind Dixon's door, I feel it rattle my bones.

I'm halfway back to Cedar, and my mind is stuck in the groove of all the things I have to do. Get the police to believe me. Find out why Murphy was there. Remember something else.

I squint at the road ahead, try to squeeze out memories like water from a rag, but all I see is the one I've recently recovered—and even that is mostly useless right now. It tells me that Astrid took care of me. Soothed my panic. Saved me from myself. But the freckle memory is too close-up. I can't see any details of the basement. Can't see the man, or his face behind the mask.

This is Ted's fault. And Mara's. If they'd just been like regular parents. If they'd seen my distress and called every doctor, every news station, until we had answers. If they'd taken me to the therapist the police suggested. Or even if Ted—I swallow at the thought—hadn't deemed me useless to his work, then maybe the memories wouldn't be so submerged. I could have reached them when they were still right under the surface. When they hadn't been lost to the muck of anxiety and time.

But I didn't have regular parents; I had the ones I have. Ones who returned to work as soon as they deemed me fine. Ones who let the case go cold. If they'd just kept up with the police. If they'd called them every day, relentless as parents should be. If they'd demanded a follow-up to the report they filed, then maybe— But I don't get to finish the thought.

I'm belting out commands to my phone, heart thumping out a single syllable: *proof, proof, proof.* When a woman picks up, I'm sure my heartbeat is so loud she can hear it through the phone.

"Ridgeway Police."

"Hi, this is Fern Douglas. I was there a little while ago. Can I speak to Chief Dixon?"

"He's in a meeting right now, but I can patch you through to his voice mail. One moment, plea—"

"No, wait! This is urgent. I need to speak to him right now. It's about the Astrid Sullivan case."

There's a pause. "We have a tip line for that. Would you like me to transfer you?"

"No, just—interrupt his meeting. Please. Tell him it's Fern Douglas. Tell him I have proof. He'll know what that means."

Another pause. This one lasts for so long I have to check that the call wasn't dropped. "One minute," the woman finally says.

But it's not one minute. It's four minutes and thirty-four seconds until Dixon picks up. I wait through each moment with my hands squeezing the steering wheel, my eyes flicking back and forth between the road and the screen.

"Ms. Douglas," he says when he answers, "this better be good."

"You asked if I have proof. And I do. I just didn't think of it—this day's been so crazy—but my father filed a police report. Back in 2000, soon after I was returned. I don't know the exact date of it, but it would have been right around the time Astrid was returned, too. Check with Cedar Police in New Hampshire. They'll have it."

Dixon clears his throat. "Your father filed a report," he says, his voice cool with suspicion, "*after* you came back. Not while you were allegedly missing."

"That's—he . . ." My stomach flips. "It's complicated," I tell him for the second time today. "But please—look into the report. You'll see I'm telling the truth."

"Uh-huh," he says. But then he sighs. "All right, let me get your information."

Relief rushes through me. "Thank you," I breathe.

"But Ms. Douglas?"

"Yeah?"

"Until you hear back from me," he says, "stay out of my investigation."

fourteen

When the woods swell into view, I feel the usual slosh of nausea. Branches lean over the road, obscure the late afternoon sky. The trees are so tightly packed that some of them look knotted together. Nature has kept them apart, though—and there's something hauntingly human in that. How the trees have tried, but failed, to make lives inside one another. How some might split, might fall, but the ones closest won't even flinch.

These woods are old. They've seen so much. They remember when Ted stopped the car, opened my door, and made me follow him, deeper and deeper into branches that scraped, leaves that loomed. They remember how loudly I screamed that day, listening to the story he told. That hungry couple. That pregnant wife. That husband with a blade. It was a story I believed simply because Ted was the one telling it—and the woods remember that too.

They probably even remember the man who took us. The man who, done with me in the basement, deposited me back on their grounds. They might have seen how, when I woke, I sprinted instinctively back home, desperate for a parent to protect me. They might have seen exactly how long I ran. How far. Might have guessed that, years later, the muscles in my legs would still be sore.

But like my memories, the trees have secrets. And they know how to keep them well.

Pulling up Ted's driveway, I see an SUV I don't recognize. I park behind it, study the Massachusetts plate, the green Zipcar logo on its bumper. My car ticks and settles, hot air swelling around me now that the engine is off. When a fist knocks on my window, I jump. Then I see who it is and I rip off my seat belt, burst out of the car.

"What are you doing here?" I practically squeal.

Eric engulfs me in his arms, and I close my eyes, breathe him in. His T-shirt, soft against my cheek, smells deeply, exquisitely, of home. "Didn't you get my voice mail?" he asks.

My eyes jerk open. It didn't even cross my mind to listen to the message he left while I drove to Rita's. It's only been a couple days since I left Boston, but I've been inexcusably out of touch to him. I don't deserve this hug I'm absorbing. The simple comfort of his embrace.

"I did," I say, my cheek still pressed to his chest. Arms looped around his waist. "But I forgot to listen. I'm sorry."

He rubs his hand up and down my back, makes no move to pull away. "It's okay," he says. "I was just a little worried, so I took the afternoon off to come up. That's all the voice mail said."

I take a step back. Look up into his eyes, which peer down at me with so much love that it almost hurts to see them. "*You* were worried?" I ask.

He shrugs. "You were already asleep when I called last night—which seemed strange, for you—and then no one answered this morning when I tried again." He drops his eyes to the ground. "I might have called more than a couple times. I guess I missed you, Bird."

A mosquito lands on his arm, and I swat it away before it can bite him. "I missed you, too."

Eric drags the toe of his shoe along the ground. Makes a letter *F*, for Fern. "Anyway," he says, "I had to make sure that Ted didn't have you hooked up to electrodes or something. Prodding at your brain for one of his Experiments."

I laugh. "That's not how Experiments work."

"Yeah," he says. "But you never know with that guy." He glances toward the front door. "He's been in a *mood* since I got here."

I bet he has. He's never seen me walk away from him before. Never heard me refuse a request. For a second, I feel a twinge of guilt like a stitch in my side. I picture him staring at the empty interview chair, at a loss for why I've left him.

But the ache quickly dissipates. Because I'm here, aren't I? I came back. Don't I always, always come back?

"What's he been doing?" I ask.

"A lot of grumbling and pacing: 'Your wife's been getting sick all over this house. Throwing up day and night like some kind of booze-hound.'"

I try to laugh at Eric's impression—over the years, he's perfected Ted's gravelly annoyance, the drama of his inflections—but I wish that Ted hadn't told him that. Because now I see the glint in Eric's eye. The hopeful smile budding at the corners of his mouth.

"So you've been sick?" he asks. "Anything I should know about?"

"It's my period," I blurt out.

The guilt comes gushing back. It's a tidal wave that could take us both down.

"I've got really bad cramps," I continue anyway. "You know how bad my period's been since I went off the pill."

His eyelids droop a little. His shoulders sag the slightest bit. "Oh," he says.

I want to make my husband happy, but now is not the time. He'll want to celebrate, spin me in circles—but my mind is spinning enough as it is. I'm dizzy from the day. Drowsy from revelations and dead ends. But looking at Eric, the disappointment clear as a wince on his face, I feel something else. Cruel. Selfish. A terrible vessel for all the love he's poured into me.

The screen door squeaks on its hinges. "Well, look who decided to come home," Ted says. He steps onto the porch, rests both hands on the railing, and the door whacks against the frame behind him.

"Wait," Eric says, looking back at me. "Where were you?"

Ted is staring at me. He'd love to know that too. "I'll tell you later," I say to my husband.

"Dr. Eric," Ted booms, speaking louder than the distance between us requires. "Would you mind taking out the trash for me? And not just the wastebasket in the kitchen. I noticed the most terrible odor as I walked by Fern's room. Seems like a woman's stagnant sick is something a husband should take care of."

Eric and I share a glance. *Unbelievable*, I can hear him thinking.

"You do *not* have to do that," I tell him. "I'll clean it up."

"No, that's all right," Eric says, already walking up the porch steps. "It's Ted's way of getting rid of me." He claps Ted on the back as he passes. "If you want to speak to her alone, that's all you need to say."

"Oh, I usually like to say more than I need to," Ted throws over his shoulder. "But thanks for the advice, Doc." He swivels his gaze back to me.

"Do you have to do that?" I ask.

He flashes a smile. "We're just having fun." Now his face goes slack. "Where did you run off to, Fern?"

I look up at him from my spot on the driveway. Standing on the porch, he appears like he's addressing me from a stage.

"I don't . . ." I start. "It doesn't matter, okay?"

"Oh, but it does matter. It matters very much to me."

"Yeah," I scoff. "I'm sure it does."

Ted tilts his head, regards me in a way I've never seen before. An expression so foreign on his face I don't know how to describe it. "Are you all right, Fern?"

The question surprises me. I try to think back to any time he's asked me that in the past, but I don't think he ever has. Not even when I gripped my stomach at the onset of appendicitis. Not even when I came home crying after enduring Cooper's torture.

"Why are you asking me that?"

"You've had quite a shock," he says. "And you ran off this morning before we had a chance to process it."

I cross my arms. Build a barrier across my chest. "I don't want to process it with you," I say. "If that's what you really wanted, you could have helped me process it back then. By following up with the police. By sending me to a doctor. Someone who actually knew what they were doing."

"But the police *didn't* know what they were doing, and you wouldn't . . ." He stops. Takes a moment to exhale. "I've already explained this. We did what we believed was best for you at the time. But now, if you're starting to remember, if you're trying to remember *more*, we should work together. I can help you with that. The source of your dissociative amnesia is fear—and who knows your fear better than me? Let me help you. Please."

There's concern in his voice. A thread of kindness, even. If I had my eyes closed, I might not know it was Ted who was speaking.

"I'm not interested in the kind of help you can give," I say. "I'm only interested in figuring out exactly what happened to me, so I can help the police find Astrid."

Ted shakes his head. *That's not what's important*, I expect he'll say.

But when he actually speaks, his voice is deeper than it's ever been. If I didn't know him better, I'd say he was choked up.

"You think I don't want that too?" he asks. "You think that, all these years, I haven't wanted you to figure out who did this to you? Do you really think me so . . . inhuman?"

I gape up at him. My heart is not a fist right now. My stomach does not whirl. It's warm. Buzzing a little. Like I've downed a shot. I'm about to respond when Eric pushes the door open and steps onto the porch, holding a black garbage bag in one hand, a book in the other. Ted glances at him, then throws out his arm like a bar in front of Eric's chest.

"Where do you think you're going with that?" he asks. His voice sounds normal again. Hard. Authoritative. Not pleading for anything.

"To the trash can?" Eric says. "You asked me to take out the garbage."

"Not that. The book." Ted grabs it out of Eric's hand.

"Oh. It was on top of the trash can in the kitchen. I assumed you meant to throw it away. It's one of Brennan's, so . . ."

"Throw it away? Are you mad? I was showing it its place."

"Showing it its . . . ?" Eric trails off and shakes his head. "Okay, sorry."

Ted mutters under his breath, rapid and incomprehensible, before spinning around to head into the house. When the door slaps closed behind him, Eric looks at me, waiting for me to explain.

"He does that," I say, "whenever a new Brennan book comes out. He puts all his old ones near the trash cans. 'Rubbish belongs with rubbish,' don't you know." I smile a little, shrug one shoulder. "There's one in the bathroom, too."

Eric gives an elaborate roll of his eyes, then winces. Puts his fingers to his temple. "I think I just strained a muscle," he says.

When we go inside, Ted's at the kitchen counter, flipping through the book Eric almost threw away: *The Desolation of Fear*.

"Ridiculous!" he bellows, to no one in particular. "Look at this, look at this." He opens one of Brennan's older books, *The Isolation of Terror*, and rummages around until he finds what he's looking for. "These passages are almost identical! He's plagiarizing himself!"

He snaps the older book shut without showing us the passages. "Yet somehow, this copy-and-paste disgrace is on the bestseller list, even though he continues to shackle himself with freshman psych ideas. No wonder he doesn't have a *true* following—just the drooling sheep who'll buy anything they see on TV. Trust me, at his bookstore events, where there are *real* people, it's always crickets."

That isn't true, of course. I've only attended one of his events, but it was clear that Brennan could captivate a crowd. The bookstore was strange, with murals of birds on every inch of empty wall space, and there was even a parrot in a cage, right near the podium where Brennan stood. The parrot kept picking out random snippets of Brennan's talk and interrupting him with a piercing voice. "Fear cycle!" he squawked, or "Echoes of trauma!" If it had been Ted up there, he would have gotten angry and flustered, but Brennan never once faltered. He made jokes out of it, made the audience grip their stomachs laughing, and when his talk was over, they leapt to their feet to applaud.

"And wait," Ted says. He marches toward the bathroom off the kitchen, returns with another of Brennan's books. "This one was published between the other two. And look!" He opens the cover, shoves the jacket copy toward our faces, too close for us to actually read it. "Same ideas! It's basically his Exam Experiment all over again!" he shouts.

He yanks the book back and whips to the title page. "Oh, but here we go. This is the best part. *This* is why I don't throw these books away, Dr. Eric. To prove what a fraud he really is. Here, look, read it."

Ted points the page toward Eric, who squints at the inscription scrawled across it. "*To my talented friend Ted—May these new ideas inspire you.*" Eric flicks his gaze back at Ted. "That's nice," he says.

"*Nice?*" Ted hisses. "The ideas aren't new at all! How could they be, when he insists on betraying his true self, his true impulses as a scientist, in favor of Cream of Wheat sound bites and antiseptic methods!"

"He called you talented," Eric offers.

"Oh please. Talent is for hobbies. And the audacity to think I'd even *want* him to sign it. But he did it, anyway, and gave it to me as some insipid thank-you gift when we let him stay with us—for two weeks, might I add, two weeks! He showed up with *three* suitcases and this book—wrapped in *gold paper*!"

He stares at the inscription like his eyes could burn it off the page.

"Brennan stayed with us for that long?" I ask.

Ted waves a hand in the air, swatting away the question. "It was during the New England leg of his book tour. And oh, if you think his publisher couldn't have put him up in hotels, think again. But he just loved to come back here and try to rub it in my face."

"I don't remember that," I say. "I remember—a few days, maybe."

The awkwardness of Brennan's forced friendliness, smiling at me over a bowl of cereal, asking me about my favorite subjects in school. The sizzling arguments between him and Ted that always ended with the two of them grinning so wide I thought their mouths would crack.

"Oh, trust me," Ted barks, "he was here. He'd travel *hours* sometimes, from some Boston or Connecticut event, and then he'd make a ruckus when he let himself in, just so we'd know he was back from his big fancy reading. There was one night where he had this *umbrella*, and . . ."

I lose track of what he's saying. His Brennan rants are always bloated with superfluous detail, cramped with complaints that no one else would see as an affront. My eyes land back on the inscription, blurring as Ted blathers. When they come back into focus, I register the date beneath Brennan's name.

"Wait," I say. I put my finger on the page, drag the book closer. Read it again to be sure. "This date—he was staying at our house then?"

Ted pinches his lips together, annoyed at being derailed from his favorite tirade. He squints at the handwriting above my finger. "That's the day he got here, I suppose."

"And he was here for two weeks?"

"He was always in and out, but it was a two-week span, so yes."

My eyes blur a second time, but now it has nothing to do with boredom. There's that swirl of nausea again. That balled-up, knocking heart.

"What's the matter?" Eric asks. He puts his hand on my back—to steady me, I think. Because, yes, I'm swaying. I feel that now. My body is a slow metronome.

I look at Eric, his eyes wide with worry. I look at Ted, his eyes squinty with suspicion. Ted knows what a realization looks like when it sweeps across my face. He wants to know what it is. Despite his appeal on the porch, he wants me back in that chair.

"Nothing," I say. "I'm—I'm starving. Let's go to The Diner, okay?"

Ted shrugs. "I wasn't really feeling a sandwich, but I guess I can—"

"No, Ted. Just me and Eric. Alone."

―――――

For the second day in a row, I've got a corned beef sandwich in front of me. Eric's got one, too, and he's just been Pegged. She gushed all over Eric, telling him how "Hollywood handsome" he looks without the beard he was growing the last time we came to Cedar. Rusty's here, too, sitting at the counter. He came over to shake Eric's hand as soon as we walked in. Two hard, fast pumps. "You're a good man," Rusty told him, "a good man," though Eric hadn't done or said anything yet to provoke his praise.

Now I'm staring at my sandwich, picking at the crust. It's a risk, taking a bite. I can already sense my stomach turning against it. But I've barely eaten today, and Eric will know that something's wrong if I ignore my favorite sandwich. I take a bite. Feel the meat squish between my teeth, chewier than usual. Is this what pregnancy does—drain a little love from the things I adore? Train my body to love the baby best?

Or maybe the baby is punishing me, for making it a secret instead of something to be celebrated. Maybe I deserve these surges in my stomach. Maybe they're the baby's roiling wrath.

Parents who get it wrong from the start. Parents who make their children wonder if they're loved.

"What is it?" Eric asks. He's on his third or fourth bite. There's mustard on his lip, and I reach across the table to wipe it.

"I lied to you before," I say.

"Oh yeah?" Eric puts his sandwich down. Rubs his hands together to dust off the crumbs.

"When you asked me," I say, "back at the house, what was wrong . . ."

I tell him everything. Not about the baby—and my belly burns at that—but about Astrid. About me. I tell him all I've learned the last couple days: details in the memoir, details I've remembered; Ted's studio confession, my own revelations; my visits with Father Murphy and Rita and the police.

As I speak, Eric's face is a kaleidoscope of expressions—surprise, anger, disbelief. He keeps trying to interrupt with questions, but I barrel ahead, afraid that if I don't finish, I'll never start again. But when I do finish, he's so silent that every sound in the room becomes magnified. The tap of a mug being set on the table. The clink of a fork against a plate.

"Are you sure?" Eric finally asks.

It's not the response I was expecting, and my face must give that away.

"No, what I mean is," he tries again, putting his hand over mine, "are you sure that Ted's not just messing with you? That making you think you were kidnapped isn't some Experiment to get you worked up and scared?"

I shake my head. "It's not. You've said it yourself—his Experiments are basically pranks. And this isn't that."

He rubs his thumb across my hand. A steady back and forth. "Are you sure?" he asks again. "Didn't he take you into the woods one time? Tell you some messed-up story about a guy who ate his unborn child? Couldn't this be another story he's telling you?"

I inhale deeply, exhale slowly. I will forgive him for this. For wanting to blame it all on Ted instead of hearing what I'm saying. In his mind, Ted is always the villain. Eric loves me so much, so well, that he can't understand why someone else wouldn't.

"But I've remembered things," I remind him. "And what Ted told me only corroborated those memories." I lean in closer, catch his thumb with my own. "This is real, Eric. I promise you."

He pushes his lips to the side, looks at his plate. His grip tightens on my hand.

"We have to go to the police," he says.

I sit back, straighten my spine against the booth. "I told you, I already tried that."

"Yeah, but—"

"I'll go back to them when they get the original police report. Chief Dixon said it might take a couple days, and until then, he's not going to believe me."

"Then you need to come home with me."

"Come home? I just got here. I have to . . . I still have to . . ."

Help Astrid, I should say. *Remember where we were kept*, I should say. But all I can picture is Ted. The way he looked at me on the porch, his expression something like tenderness. Something fatherly, I think. And maybe the thickness I heard in his voice was more of an apology than his lips could ever say.

"You have to be safe," Eric insists. "And if all this is true, then how do you know that the person who got Astrid isn't coming for you next?"

"I know. I thought of that earlier, but . . ." I pause. Remember what made me dizzy in Ted's kitchen. "Maybe I know who to look out for now."

"What do you mean?"

I slide my hand out from Eric's, let it fall to my lap, where it's free to scratch at my wrist. "That inscription Ted showed us," I start, "back from when Brennan stayed with us. It was dated June 23, 2000. The day before Astrid was kidnapped. And maybe that's why I don't remember him staying with us for so long. Because I was on vacation with the Kelleys until the day after Astrid was taken, and you heard Ted, Brennan was in and out—*a lot*. Because he would've been . . ."

Eric's brows squeeze together. "Would've been what?"

"What if . . . what if it was Brennan? What if he was the one who took Astrid? Took me."

Confusion warps his face. "You think Brennan Llewellyn, America's favorite pop psychologist, kidnapped you?"

"I don't know," I say. "Maybe. Isn't it too big a coincidence otherwise? That he just happened to be in New Hampshire when Astrid got taken?"

Eric's eyeing me carefully now. "But a lot of people were in New Hampshire, Fern." I hear the concern in the slow pace of his words. "A whole state full of them. And . . . why would Brennan do that?"

My wrist itches. Luckily, I haven't trimmed my nails in days.

"His books are about the intersection of fear and trauma," I say, "so maybe it was research."

"You think Brennan Llewellyn would kidnap someone for research? All Ted ever talks about is how sterile Brennan's methods are. Which we both know means they're legitimate."

"Okay," I concede. "But Ted also talks about how Brennan used to be much bolder with his work. That's why Ted thinks he's such a fraud now. Such a sellout. So maybe Brennan got tired of playing by the supposed rules—the same rules that he and Ted used to mock together. Maybe he reverted to his old ways, tried something similar to his woman-stalking experiment from grad school—"

"Wait. Woman-stalking experiment?"

"Yeah, he and Ted would follow these women home from the library, pretending to be stalkers or whatever."

Eric blinks at me. Shakes his head.

"So maybe it started as something like that," I continue, "only he took it too far and things spun out of control and he ended up not being able to use the research, because . . . you know, it would implicate him in a crime. A felony. But—but you heard Ted—Brennan's books have been regurgitating the same ideas, over and over. He must be desperate for new ways to spin it. And maybe now he's trying, again, to get new material—with Astrid."

"But, Bird," Eric says. "That doesn't make sense. It's still as much of a felony now as it was in 2000."

I scratch because I don't have the words to explain it yet. But something about this feels right. It fits.

Eric takes my silence for doubt. "You can't kidnap someone," he tries, "because you need research for a book. Who would publish something like that?"

I ignore Eric's rationalizations. A logical mind like his could never see the sense in this. You need a mind like mine.

"It would explain why I, of all people, was taken," I say. "Because Ted's always taking jabs at Brennan's career, even in person. So maybe Brennan was trying to—I don't know—to stick it to him or something, by taking his daughter, making Ted go crazy thinking I was missing. Only Ted *didn't* go crazy, as we know, because he barely noticed I was gone."

"Fern."

"Or maybe it was because he had easy access to me, staying at our house like he did. Think about it—I was put in the basement at the end of Astrid's second week. Brennan stayed with us for two weeks. Maybe he took me with him when he left. Maybe I even went without a fight because I didn't see him as a threat. Though, why he took *Astrid*, too—and first—I'm still not sure . . ."

"Fern."

"What?"

"You're spiraling."

I shake my head, but he nods, and it's like the two motions cancel each other out. Like neither of us is moving at all.

"You are," he says. "And it's even more of a reason to come back home. You could see Dr. Lockwood, talk this all out with her. She can help you, Bird. You've been—" He presses his lips together. Swallows. "You've been traumatized. And you've been carrying that trauma, without even knowing it, for a very long time." He crosses his arms, looks off to the side. "Fucking Ted."

I shake my head again, so hard that everything blurs. Dr. Lockwood isn't the answer this time. She never lets me trust the leaps my mind is able to make.

When you picture the man in the mask, I imagine her saying, *does he look like Brennan? Look at his body type, Fern, the way he carries himself—is it similar to the man you know?*

Brennan carries himself like he's always on the verge of being photographed. His chin is often tilted toward the ceiling. But the kidnapper—he's just a man, indistinct as anyone would be in a mask. There's nothing familiar about him at all.

Doesn't that tell you something then? Dr. Lockwood would press. Even in my head, her voice is gentle. *Looking back, wouldn't you be able to see if it were him? Or at least if it might be?*

Yes, and it might be. That's what I'm trying to say. It's just—with the mask and waders, it's so hard to know for sure.

So you can't be sure, then, that it is him.

I guess I can't. I guess it could be someone else. But there's no comfort in that thought. If it isn't Brennan, then there's no guarantee that the person who took Astrid will ever bring her back.

"I can't go home with you," I tell Eric.

He blows out a breath but doesn't look surprised. "You can't stay with Ted," he says. "He's been lying to you for decades. He made this so much worse than it had to be."

"Maybe. Or maybe he was right."

"To lie to you? How could you think that?"

"To let my brain keep protecting me," I clarify. "Clearly what Astrid and I experienced was horrible. So horrible that it would have hurt me more to remember it back then. But now . . . now it's starting to come back, and I can't *leave* while it is."

Eric bites his lip. Shakes his head.

"*This* is where it happened," I continue. "*This* is where I was taken." I look around the room, register the other customers for the first time in a while. "I mean, not here at The Diner," I add quietly. "Although you never know! If it wasn't Brennan, then for all I know, it could have been"—I gesture toward the counter, the old friend sipping coffee on one of its stools—"Rusty who took me!"

Despite everything, Eric chuckles, but it's a dry, reluctant sound.

"If I have any hope of recovering those memories," I say, "any hope of remembering something that can help find Astrid—it's going to happen here. Not in Boston. Not with Dr. Lockwood."

"But the police will—"

"The police haven't found anything."

A muscle jumps in Eric's jaw. "You're a victim, too, you know. It isn't your job to save her."

He's right, maybe. In the eyes of the law, at least. I'm not qualified to find a missing woman. My heart knocks me down so easily. It takes almost nothing to turn me to stone. But *look at this*, Astrid said, and she pointed to a freckle that, decades later, I still recognized, still felt a pull toward, even after I'd forgotten nearly everything else about her. It's possible that her freckle, that tiny speck of skin, had been enough to save me once. And it's possible that a single memory, a single salvaged detail, could be enough to save her, too.

I lean forward, take a bite of my sandwich, my stomach suddenly stronger. Finally, the corned beef tastes exactly like it always did. Like heaven. Like home.

"It *is* my job," I say after I swallow. "So I can't go back. I'm sorry. Not until Astrid's back too."

Excerpt from Chapter Four of
Behind the Red Door: A Memoir by Astrid Sullivan

He didn't drug her. He didn't chain her either. I don't think
she would have survived it. She was already too frightened
and fragile; she couldn't have handled another thing tether-
ing her to that barren, bare-bulbed place.

She had ropes on her wrists when he first brought her
down, but he took those off after only a few minutes. At
first, I thought it was a kindness. Despite ripping her from
her family, maybe he couldn't be so cruel as to tie up such a
tiny, trembling thing, or to drug someone whose body was
too small to safely absorb the dose. But in the end, I think
he removed the ropes only as a practicality. How else would
she eat the sandwiches he gave us or hold the can of sickly
sweet Sprite to her lips? How else would he keep her alive
just to torture her, like he'd tortured me, with the waiting
and the silence and the spotlighted red door?

She stared, unblinking, at her wrists, which were naked
now, except for the rings of red around them where the
ropes had chafed her skin. Meanwhile, he looked at my
ankle. I imagined him squinting as he registered that the
chain he'd hooked around me was the only one in that basement. It struck me then—not for the first time—that all
this seemed haphazard, unplanned. Here he was, dragging
another girl down into his dungeon, with no way to keep
her. It made me want to laugh in his face. It made me want
to roar. The only thing that kept me quiet was her. It seemed

that any noise, no matter how slight, would terrorize her even more. I didn't know, yet, that her fear was already so absolute, it had squeezed her voice right out of her throat. That the only time I'd hear her make a sound would be the very last time I saw her.

After a moment, the man seemed to give up on chaining the girl to the ground. He squatted in front of me, leaned in close, and hissed, "If you let her try to escape, I will kill her." I pulled back, more surprised that he'd spoken than by the threat itself. It was the most he'd said to me in a long time. But once again, his voice was muffled by the mask, and only a whisper at that. If I heard it again, I know I wouldn't know it.

———

I named her Lily.

Lily after Lilith, from Jewish folklore. In those stories, it is Lily, not Eve, who is the wife of Adam. And it is Lilith who leaves Adam when she refuses to bow down to him just for being a man. For this, she is classified as a demon.

We didn't learn about her in CCD, of course, but I looked her up while listening to my Lilith Fair CDs, and when I read her stories, I pictured her walking away from the Garden of Eden with both middle fingers piercing the air. Her exit was a blistering fuck-you. It said: a land that demands you suppress your desires is not a land worth living in.

I thought about Lilith a lot in the basement, even before Lily came. I wanted to believe that she was right. I wanted the idea of her to give me hope, the way she had whenever

I talked to Bridget late at night, when the phone was a sad substitute for hands and lips and breath. But Lilith had been wrong, hadn't she? Hadn't I left my own Garden—all that lush grass, those tablecloths that swayed in the breeze like the skirts of angels—and hadn't I ended up in hell?

It was Lily who turned things around for me. Lily who made me see the magic in Lilith again. Because I had walked away, yes, I had set certain things in motion—but what could this girl have done? She was so small, so innocent, and he'd taken her, too. Maybe it didn't matter, then, all the ways I'd made myself vulnerable. Maybe it only mattered that a man had seen that vulnerability and circled it like a vulture, instead of honoring vulnerability for what it is: a kind of bravery, a kind of strength.

I named her Lily because she needed a name. Because she wouldn't speak, not even to tell me who she was. I named her Lily as a reminder, to both of us, that we did not deserve our captivity. That it was men doing what men have done since the beginning of time, the beginning of women. Containing us. Chaining us. Like Father Murphy had tried to do that day at my party. So whenever I said Lily's name in that basement, it was like I was saying a prayer. To whom, I don't know. Not God, I don't think, who, after all, is another man.

I said her name often. When she folded into herself like a fetus, and all I wanted was to be the womb that kept her safe, "Lily," I said, "come here." When she cried instead of ate, her sobs the only sound she made, "Lily," I said, "it's not so bad; look, I'm eating it too." When her panic seemed to freeze her in place, "Lily," I said, "look at this, see this freckle under my eyebrow? As long as you can see it, everything's okay." When she started to climb the stairs, and I remembered the masked man's threat, "Lily," I said, "please, he's going to—" But I could not tell her what he was going to do. I could only reach out to her with pleading eyes and arms.

I broke her sandwiches into tiny bites, plopped them into her mouth that, eventually, opened for me like a bird's. I combed her hair with my fingers. I kept her from scratching at the faded rope marks on her wrists. I used my nails to slide the dirt out from underneath hers. I rubbed her back in gentle circles as she laid her head in my lap. I told her that the light at the top of the stairs was a sun shining just for us, that we were our own planet, that all that dirt and dust was ours to discover, not fear. When the man came down to bring food and soda and clothes, I kept her hidden behind me and I stared at him like Lilith would. Like a woman capable of walking away.

I invented games for us. I made a fort with a broom and a sheet and our mattress, and I called it our castle. Lily found a bag of marbles in a corner I couldn't reach, and I turned it into something that helped pass the hours, that distracted Lily with the satisfying *click-click* of the marbles hitting one another. I made up clapping games, like the ones I used to play in elementary school, only I made the words sillier, less sinister. (As girls, even our games were laced with threats: "Miss Mary Mack," who *never came back*; "CeeCee, My Playmate," with the *cellar* that becomes a *dungeon*. You're not supposed to think about the lyrics, but still, there they are, singing forth from little lips: *I'll scratch your eyes out and make you bleed to death*. No wonder girls aren't expected to grow up into women who love each other.)

The games kept Lily from crying, from staring, statue-still, into the distance, unable to move or blink. She still never spoke. She still never chanted along to my made-up songs as we slapped our palms together—but sometimes, she smiled, and in those days, that was all I cared about. Her smile gave me breath and purpose and life. How fulfilling it was to be the protector, I was learning, to be the one who had to stay strong. How beautiful it was to know I was needed, beyond the prayers and bent knees I could offer up to God.

fifteen

I'm huddled on my bed, reading Astrid's book, as Eric and Ted argue downstairs. I'm trying not to hear what they're saying, trying to focus on the words on these pages, but Eric isn't holding back.

"How could you be so irresponsible?" he yells. "Your twelve-year-old daughter tells you she's been imprisoned in a basement and you barely do anything about it? What if the person who took her had come back for her? Huh?"

"The police didn't think that was an issue," Ted fired back. "Are you implying, Dr. Eric, that you know better than the police?"

Ted wasn't home when we got back last night. He wasn't clacking in his office. Wasn't grumbling over Brennan in the kitchen. The house was a kind of quiet that made me uncomfortable. Made me itch. After a while, Eric and I squeezed into my twin bed together, struggled to share a sweaty night of sleep, and I don't know when Ted got back. The clunking fan muted the silence of his absence.

"It's not up to the police to care more about your daughter than you do," Eric says.

I turn the fan on now, even though it's mercifully cooler today. I can still hear their voices going back and forth, and though I can't make out the words anymore, their tones alone are distracting.

Like the ache I've been feeling in my ribs ever since their argument started.

I hold the book closer to my face, make it a shield.

Now, here it is, in permanent ink on the page. Here is the story of how Astrid renamed me—and why. When I read how I swallowed my own voice, suffering from a fear so much greater than Ted's Experiments or Cooper's attacks, I grip the book even harder. *The girl who saw everything*, Astrid called Lily in the prologue. *The girl who saw everything but never said a word.* Understanding swells in my lungs as I suck in a breath. She meant it literally. Not that I never came forward to tell someone what I'd seen—but that I never even spoke.

And Astrid didn't only rename me; she carried me through the darkness, too. *Look at this*, she said, pointing to her freckle, transforming it into a constant I could count on. Reading about it now, I shiver. It's a memory in this memoir I finally recognize.

So what else is there? What else?

As I learn about the ways she cared for me—how she combed my hair, cleaned me of dirt, broke my sandwich into bites—I feel another ache, deeper than the one in my ribs. It's like I miss her, even though these moments aren't familiar to me at all. It's like she was a temporary sister, and I've lived all these years never knowing what I lost.

But the ache isn't just gratitude. Isn't just love and admiration for a woman I don't even know. It's this agonizing, miraculous fact: Astrid protected me in that basement more than I'd ever been protected at home.

"She needed to be left alone! She didn't need some doctor poking at her." Ted's voice booms up the stairs, breaks through the fan's white noise. I close my eyes for a second. Then I turn the fan to a higher speed.

When I get to the passage about the games Astrid invented, I smile a little. But soon, the chapter is over, and instead of turning to the next one, something compels me to read those paragraphs again. There's a charge in the air. A prickle at the base of my spine. My eyes go back and forth, back and forth and—stop: this part right here, about the marbles. I pull the book closer. Hover over the words.

There's a tingle beneath my skin. Not an itch anymore, but a buzz. I read the sentence over and over, but it tells me nothing about what the game actually was. Still, there's something here. I try to hear the *click-click* Astrid mentioned, but I can only conjure the *clack* of Ted's typing instead.

Wincing, I close my eyes and try again and—yes. There it is. It's a sound like the Newton's Cradle in one of the science classrooms at school. The sound of small metal balls striking against each other. And—and what?

Click-click. Click-click. We slid them across the floor, I think.

Yes. I can picture it. Fingers flicking a marble. Waiting with held breath to hear if it will meet the target of another marble in a different part of the basement.

My lungs burn. I've been holding my breath now, too. Because the basement—I can see it.

In remembering the marbles, in watching them slide across the floor, I see where we were. I see how the light pooled at the bottom of the stairs but left all the corners in shadow. I see the bottom of the stairs themselves. Flaky gray paint. Loose nails. A step with one crooked side, making it trapezoidal. I try to see the door—the wound-red door—but I can't. I'm trying so hard, but I can't. I can't.

So how do I know this is real? How do I know I'm remembering, and not imagining? Not wishing more memories into place.

If only Astrid had said more about the game. If only she'd written what I think is true: it was like playing pool, only instead of balls, we had marbles. And instead of using cue sticks, we flicked them with our fingers. And instead of "eight ball, corner pocket," Astrid would say "third-farthest marble, one click."

Those details, if true, can confirm that my image of the basement is real. And if I can remember the basement, I might be on the verge of remembering something else.

My mind stumbles around until I think of Rita. Astrid might have told her about the game. I launch off my bed, burst into the hallway, pluck the landline off its base. Back in my room, I close the door and grab my cell. Pull up the number that Rita thrust upon me yesterday. Punch it into the phone.

"Rita, it's"—I panic for a moment, struggling to remember the name she called me yesterday—"Sarah. I'm so sorry to bother you, but I need to know—the marble game. What was that exactly?"

There's a long pause. "Who the hell is this?"

"It's Sarah," I say again. "I stopped by yesterday? You gave me your number, and—"

"Like hell this is Sarah."

"What—what do you mean?" I ask.

"After you left," she says, "I went on Facebook to try to friend you—but the Sarah Yates I found, who's from Foster and lives in LA, looks nothing like you. I shouldn't have assumed who you were—excuse me for being a little out of it lately—but you took advantage of me. So again: Who the hell are you?"

I look down at my hand. See it trembling. Now I look at Astrid's book, still splayed open to the chapter in which she christened me with a name she equated with strength.

"I'm Lily," I say.

"Oh, for fuck's sake. Not you, too. I can't believe I let you in my house."

I exhale, and my breath quivers. I'm losing her. Losing this chance.

"No, really, I am," I try. "I've only recently remembered, though, and I—"

"Bullshit. You said you didn't know anything about Lily."

"I know, but—"

"If you come near my house again, I'm calling the police."

"Please, I—"

But I don't get to finish. Even with the noise of the fan, I can hear she's already gone.

———

By the time Eric comes back to my room, I've steadied my breathing. Calmed my hands and heart. I try to smile as he enters, but it feels like a grimace.

Sitting beside me on the bed, he sighs. The mattress creaks beneath our weight.

"This isn't news or anything," he says, "but Ted's a piece of work."

"Did he say where he was last night?" I ask.

"Yup. At Wicker."

The name of the college is a pinch in my side. "Why?"

"He said he was rummaging through his office on campus, looking for some old files."

The pinch morphs into a jab. "His office? But he's retired. And he's *moving*."

Eric scoffs. "Apparently they've given him a couple months to pack everything up. You know—the same way he's so busy packing up his house."

I study the side of his face. Sarcasm is always strange on Eric. Like a shirt he's borrowed from somebody else. He's glaring at his shoes, squinting with a bitterness I only see when he speaks of Ted, but when he meets my gaze, his eyes become earnest again.

"Are you okay?" he asks. "You seem . . . shaken up."

I scratch my wrist. Scratch the ghost of ropes. "I remembered something. Or at least I think I did."

"Really? What?"

"This game we used to play. Astrid and me. It was like pool, only with marbles. And I think I remember what the basement looked like. I can see parts of it, anyway."

Eric's shoulders straighten. "That's great," he says. Then he scans the room, and when his eyes land on my bookshelf, he grabs an old notebook from the bottom, opens to a fresh page.

"Do you have something to write with?" he asks.

"Um, yeah. I think so." I reach for my purse on the floor, rummage through it until I pluck out a pen. Eric hands me the notebook.

"Can you draw the basement?" he asks. "What you remember, anyway?"

I stare at him for a few seconds, but he raises his eyebrows, gestures toward the page with a hurrying wave of his hand.

"Okay," I say, beginning to sketch. "But why?"

"You know Jim from the hospital?" he asks. I nod as I sketch the bottom of the stairs, careful to draw the last step as a trapezoid instead of a rectangle. "His wife's a P.I. I'm gonna ask her to look into all this. If the police won't believe you yet, fine, but we need *someone* to investigate."

I draw the perimeter of the basement as best as I can see it through the shadows of my memory, the shadows of that room. "Wow," I say. "Thank you."

"Of course, Bird," Eric says. "We need to figure this out. And Ted's no help. The way he talks, I just— I have a feeling there's something he's not telling us."

My hand freezes on the page. "What do you mean?"

"I don't know. It's like he's . . ." Eric pauses to choose his words. "Holding something back. Protecting someone maybe?"

My pulse flicks. "Who would he protect? He doesn't care about anyone enough for that."

When I say it, I mean acquaintances. People in Cedar. Friends, even—of which he has very few. But there's something about the sentence that sticks in my throat. It's like the sharp edge of a chip, scraping as it's swallowed.

"Unless you mean Brennan," I say quickly.

Eric scoffs. "I'm pretty sure Brennan would be the last person Ted would ever want to protect."

"Maybe not," I say. "They were friends once, you know. Back in grad school. Before Brennan supposedly sold out. Maybe Ted's been putting together the same pieces that I have. Maybe he thinks like I do—that Brennan might have done it, and he feels, like, an old impulse to look out for him or something."

Eric shakes his head. "I think that's a stretch, Bird. And I don't know, maybe he's being cagey because, deep down, he knows he did something terrible to you."

"What are you talking about?"

"How you were gone for an entire week, and they never even looked for you."

"They thought I was at Kyla's."

"Right," Eric says. "But they never checked. Which is completely insane behavior for a parent."

I open my mouth to find I can't speak. Can't formulate a defense of my father, other than the one that's buried so deep in my bones, it sinks into the marrow: Ted never learned the right way for a parent to behave.

Growing up, he had to lie to his teachers. It probably went something like this: *My cousin and I were roughhousing. He accidentally punched me.* Or this: *I wasn't watching where I was going. Walked straight into an open cabinet.* He probably didn't think anyone would believe him. His principal was friends with Saul Brierley. They probably saw Saul the way the rest of the town did, as a man who volunteered to rig the lights for the school musical every year. Who fixed his neighbor's fence, whether or not he was asked.

"So I guess what he's really doing is protecting himself," Eric says. "From looking too closely at how horribly—how *inexcusably*—he handled what happened to you."

Ted had a two-faced father, but he's nothing like Saul in that regard. What you see with Ted is what you get—his arrogance, his manic energy, his intolerance of distractions. Even during his Experiments, he always comes clean. He prides himself on that. So I can't see him holding anything back from us to try to make himself look better. He already thinks he looks great as he is.

I rub a hand over my knee. Try to wipe the sweat from my palm. Then I hand the notebook back to Eric. "Even if you think I'm wrong, can you still have Jim's wife look into Brennan?" I ask.

As I lay with my eyes open last night, I tried to remember how long it's been since I've seen Brennan in person. It's been decades, I think. Those weeks he stayed with us when I was twelve might have been the last time. And there has to be a reason he stopped stopping by.

Eric looks me in the eyes. His gaze is soft. Almost sad. "Sure, Bird," he says. Then he tears my sketch out of the notebook. "I should head out now. I've got a shift later today."

I drop my head onto his shoulder. Find the slope of bone where my forehead fits exactly right. "No," I moan.

He puts his arms around me. Envelops me almost completely. "You really won't come back with me?" he asks.

My heart thumps. "I can't."

"But—what are you gonna do here, all alone?"

"I'm not alone. Ted's here."

In the beat of silence that follows, Eric's breath rustles my hair. "You're not really gonna pack for him, are you?" he asks.

I try to shrug, but my shoulders can barely move in the tightness of his embrace. "I don't know."

"But, Bird . . ." Frustration simmers in his voice. "Think of everything he's done. Besides doing essentially nothing to find out what happened to you, he also kept it a secret for twenty years. And what if you hadn't started to remember? He might have never told you. How can you stay here and help him after all that?"

I pull away. Feel his arms slip off of me. "It's not about helping *him* anymore," I say. "It's about helping Astrid. I explained this last night."

Eric shakes his head. "I don't like this. Ted won't keep you safe."

"I'll keep myself safe."

Eric's eyes rove over my face, the way they do when he's trying to be careful with me. But there's no need to be careful. I'm not spiraling.

"Say what you want to say," I tell him.

He lets out his breath. I find myself holding mine. "He doesn't care about you."

Something jerks in my stomach. No—it kicks. I know the baby's too small for that. Doesn't even have legs yet. But I feel it all the same.

"Not the way a parent should," he adds.

I think of the witch from Forest Near. How Ted became her, initially, in the hopes that I would fear her. How fear was the language his father had taught him. But when I giggled that first time, when the way he shook me only made my laughter come harder, it was like he'd learned a new language. One both foreign and alluring. One his adult tongue has always found difficult to speak. I've only been back a few days, and he's Forest Neared me twice. That has to count for something.

"You're wrong," I say.

Eric puts his hand on my back, and for the first time ever, his touch causes discomfort.

"I know it's hard for you to see it," he says. "But it isn't good for you, being here with him. You went through a lot as a kid, and now you're going through this enormous revelation, and . . ."

He pauses. Stares at me. Still so careful.

"You're remembering something traumatic," he continues. "Which is difficult enough. You don't need to be reminded of all the additional trauma you endured by being Ted's daughter."

"Trauma?" I snap. "Who do you think you are—some second-rate Dr. Lockwood? Why don't you stick to pediatrics, okay?"

I gasp after I say it. Try to suck in the voice that sounds too much like Ted's. But it's too late. The hurt in Eric's eyes is palpable and instantaneous. Like a sheen of tears.

"I'm sorry," I say. I touch his cheek. Kiss the corners of his lips. "Eric, I'm so sorry."

He doesn't pull away from me, but his body is stiff. He's a statue, it seems. I've done that to him.

"It's okay," he says.

"It's not." I take his hand and squeeze it. I want to wring out the pain that's oozing through him right now. A slow, abundant poison.

"I don't know why I said that," I say. "I know you're only trying to help."

He nods but won't look at me. "I am," he says, "but I get it. You told me last night you needed to stay, and I shouldn't have pushed."

When his eyes finally meet mine, there's a wince in them. It's slight, but it makes me squeeze his hand again. And again and again.

"I know you haven't been feeling well, either," he continues. "So I'm sorry."

I shake my head. How could I have made this man, this incredible man—who sings Disney songs with the kids at the hospital, who endures all my panic with incomparable patience—think he needs to respond to my cruelty with an apology of his own?

"Is that any better, by the way?" he asks.

I'm rubbing my thumb over his hand, as if I could massage my poison from his veins. "Better?"

"Your period. The cramps."

There's another wince in his eyes as he says it. Even subtler this time. He doesn't want me to see. Doesn't want to burden me with his disappointment, the same way I didn't want to burden him with my anxiety over trying for a baby in the first place.

I could make him happy. I could remove that wince right now.

But I was right, wasn't I, to be so anxious? Haven't I just proven how easy it is to hurt someone you love?

And Astrid—didn't she show me what it takes to keep someone safe? How strong you have to be. How fearless and unflinching.

I am none of those things. Not yet. And I can't bring myself to let him down.

"Yeah," I say to Eric, managing a smile. "My period's lighter today. I'm feeling much better."

sixteen

Something terrible is about to happen to Lily. To me.

I've just started the next chapter in the memoir, and I'm afraid of reading it and not remembering.

I'm afraid of remembering, too.

I still have dreams about the last time I saw Lily. They're more like filmstrips, though—flickering, sepia-toned frames where she sees what she sees, screams the way she screams, and I can only watch and listen.

My hands shake as I hold the book, as my eyes drift farther into chapter five.

When he came down the stairs that day, everything was still normal. Or as normal as anything can be when you're a prisoner. He had a routine we came to expect, and at first, that day was no different. He brought down the food and the Sprite, set it all in the usual place, and then he reached for the waste bucket.

The waste bucket. I shiver as I read those words. She hasn't mentioned it much, but how awful that must have been. How degrading and inhuman.

That's when it happened—the moment that instigated Lily's violent removal from the basement.

Violent removal? My heart pounds as I recall what Rita said: "Jesus, the way things ended for her in the basement."

The handle of the bucket got caught. He always looped his arm beneath it and let it dangle from the crook of his elbow, but on that day, Lily's last, the handle snagged on the end of his glove.

She describes how he struggled with it, tried to unsnag it, but that only made it worse. And in all his fumbling, I saw something. Astrid doesn't know what. I don't know what. But she says I saw something and I flinched.

No, not just a flinch—her entire body jolted, as if she'd been zapped by a live wire.

But what was it? What would make me jolt like that?

Astrid has a theory.

She saw a feature of the man that I never did, something that revealed this alien-looking creature—no skin but the fabric of his clothes, no head but his welder's mask—to be an actual human being. Something that made clear that this man really was *a man, not just a monster from a nightmare.*

And then she screamed so loud I felt the sound of it vibrating in my ribs.

But I don't remember this moment. I can't remember what I would have seen. So maybe she's wrong. Maybe it was just my voice coming back to me. Maybe, after all those days of silence, the only way I could speak was through a scream.

Either way, the man reacted.

He snapped his head toward Lily so quickly that I thought the mask would spin.

Astrid was standing between us—me, the man. She looked back at him, then to me, and back again. Then, ankle still chained, she leaped toward me, arms outstretched to soothe me.

But he grabbed me by the waist—

An arm around her waist. An arm around her waist!

—*and he yanked me backward, tossed me aside.*

She says her hands were still reaching as she fell.

I landed on the mattress, which softened the impact, but Lily screamed harder then, as if she feared he'd intended to murder me. As if she thought I'd actually been killed.

He crossed the distance between us and he grabbed me, too. And Astrid says I did not stop the spurt of my voice.

He held her by the arm, with a grip tighter than any I've ever seen.

He shook me hard . . .

. . . like he thought he could shake off the scream.

Astrid struggled to get back up, but she couldn't stand in time. Not that it would have mattered.

He showed us then how strong and savage he was.

Rita said he was probably young, some teenage boy, but no. His muscles must have been honed. Lived in. Because Astrid says he pulled me by the hair, used it as a rope to haul me up the stairs . . .

. . . and she screamed louder then. Not with fear anymore, but pain. The sound of her agony was brighter than the bulb at the top of the stairs, which he pulled her toward, up and up and farther away.

But Astrid reached for me.

I yanked at the chain, stretched my ankle, my legs, my arms, as far as I could, but it wasn't far enough. The red door slammed. Her scream was on the other side.

And then it got smaller and smaller.

And then I could not hear it at all.

For a long time, I don't move. Not because my anxiety has turned me to stone, but because I'm waiting to remember this chapter. To recognize it, beyond the arm around her waist, as a scene I've actually lived.

I've closed the book. Don't want to see those pages again. If I memorize the details, I will compromise the memories. Won't know if they're real or implanted. If they ever come at all.

One thing I'm sure of now: the man who took us is dangerous. Capable of inflicting pain. He gripped my arm, pulled me by the hair, pushed Astrid to the ground. But it doesn't make sense. Why did he hurt me only to let me go? Why do I remember the way he grabbed her, but not the way he grabbed me? Why can't I remember the rest of this explosive moment, or what happened once he dragged me up the stairs?

I don't know what was on the other side of the red door. I don't know how long it was before he took me back home. I don't know if my arm had bruises, or if a clump of my hair came loose in his hand. I don't know if he blindfolded me, or if I was drugged and bound in the back of his car, or if—

I stop. I could continue this list forever; all I know is every essential thing I don't.

My fingers flex with frustration, and before I know it, I'm hurling the book across the room. It crashes against my dresser. Thuds onto the floor.

"Fern?"

Ted's voice is muffled through two sets of walls, but I hear the creak of his door, hear him say my name again as he gets close enough to knock.

"Come in."

When he opens my door, I'm cross-legged, elbows on my knees, forehead in the heels of my hands. I don't want to look at him, but he waits until I do.

His eyes are probing but not piercing. His gaze is surprisingly soft. Then he looks down, sees the book on the floor, crouches to pick it up.

"You've finished," he says.

I lean against the headboard. Tilt my head until it rests against the wall. "No," I say. "Just the part where I was"—what words did she use?—"violently removed from the basement."

Ted stares at the book, runs his hand along the cover as if it's a sacred text. "And you remembered something?" he asks. His voice is hopeful.

"No," I say. More grunt than word. "I mean, I think I remember the basement. I can't see the red door or anything, but I remember some of the room. Maybe. I don't know. But I *do* know I read this horrific scene where I was dragged up the stairs, and I don't remember that happening to me at all."

Ted nods. "When he pulled you by the hair."

I lift my head from the wall. "How do you know about that?"

"I read the book."

"When?"

"Last week. You could hardly walk through Rusty's without tripping over a copy."

"But why did you read it?"

"I should think that would be obvious," he says. "I've always wanted to know what happened. And seeing as I never got your account of it, I had to settle for somebody else's."

I narrow my eyes. "And you didn't feel the need to tell me this yesterday, when I mentioned the memoir?"

"I'm sure I would have," he says, "if you hadn't run off like you did."

He scratches at a patch of scaly skin on his neck. I scratch my wrist.

"Well," I say after a while. "What do you think? About what happened to me."

I'm careful as I look at him, one glance at a time. I don't want to see in his eyes how hungry he is for information. Don't want to see the twitch of his lips as they smile instead of frown.

"I think," he says, and he's completely unreadable, expressionless as a chalk outline, "that you should let me help you. You *need* me, Fern."

My lips part. The air feels cool as I sip it in. I've been waiting my whole life for him to realize this. For him to reverse the words he said to me on the phone last week: *I need you, Fern.* I came careening back to Cedar because I thought he was saying something new, that he was asking for a closeness between us—but the truth is, he's always needed me. For Experiments. For interviews. For a spellbound admirer. But now, here he is, finally admitting what a parent should always know, should constantly be driven by. That his child needs him, too.

Eric's voice jumps into my head: *He doesn't care about you—not the way a parent should.* I shove the sound of him away. Ted's never been a normal parent; it wouldn't be fair to hold him to the standards of others' affection. But now I'm watching Ted. He's looking at the book again, tracing the title with his finger, and my heart sinks.

There it is. That hunger. That vulgar, dripping desire.

"You should let me help you," he says again. But his voice is dreamy and distant. His eyes don't leave the book.

Something else Eric said: *I have a feeling there's something he's not telling us.* I picture Ted now, scouring the pages of Astrid's memoir. Was he really looking for answers to what happened to me in the basement? Or did he want something different from it? Like the satisfaction, maybe, of seeing his friemesis portrayed as a nemesis. An actual monster the whole world will hate.

I picture the man the way I remember him, dressed in his waders and mask and boots. He's about the same height as Brennan. Same build, too. Which is an average height. An average build. Indistinct enough to be anyone. But still.

"Ted," I say. "Do you know more than you're telling me? About my kidnapping."

His scoff comes quick. "I wish! But no, I told you—you were completely mute about it all. But now . . ." He places his palm on the top of the book, like it's a bible he's swearing on. "I can help you. I know you want to help the girl."

His eyes flick to the name on the cover. "Astrid Sullivan," he adds. "So let's do this together. I can interview you. I can help you remember."

Nausea snakes through my stomach, and I know it's not the baby this time. It's how he answered my question. *I wish.* And not with gentleness, either. Not with a plea for finding justice. It was an exclamation. The inflection he uses when he's buzzing with ideas.

Ted doesn't know anything more than he's already said—but he wants to. Desperately. He's probably got a fresh ribbon in his typewriter. Probably waiting for me to sit in that chair as he asks me questions he's been crafting for twenty years. He wants it so badly that he's willing to play kind, play soft, play the sort of father who puts his daughter first.

I'm desperate, too. But even without remembering the whole scene that Astrid described, I have other avenues to explore. And I have to try them, I have to exhaust every option before I subject myself to the discomfort of that chair, the pain of those spindles against my back.

"I don't need you to help me," I say, and I'm up off the bed, gathering my purse from the floor, my keys from the nightstand, pulling the book from his hands. "I'm going to help myself."

seventeen

Rusty's office hasn't changed. It's a tiny, windowless room. I used to come here after school to do homework, days when I needed internet access or a guaranteed snack. Days when I didn't want to return to an empty house—or a house that might as well have been. I can hear the buttons of Rusty's register, the *ding-click-slide* of the cash drawer. It's a soundtrack I'd forgotten, but one that used to bring comfort.

Now, that comfort is a distraction. It takes me back to the familiar safety of these walls. I keep expecting Rusty to open the door, thrust a box of Twinkies at me, and tell me to "Go nuts." But I'm not here for comfort. Not here to feel safe. I'm here to investigate my suspicions—and I need to get to work.

I start with Brennan. Scour his website. Briefly consider messaging him through the contact form. But this isn't the kind of thing you email, and if he's got Astrid, a message would only let him know I'm onto him. And then who knows what he'd do.

Men who grip arms. Men who pull hair. Men whose violence sits dormant inside them, waiting to explode.

What I need is an idea of where he is now. If he's bouncing from city to city on a book tour, then he probably isn't the man I'm looking for. But the Events page on his website says, "Come back soon for

The Desolation of Fear tour dates," and I find myself, in a last-ditch effort, tracking down the number for the literary agent listed in his bio. When I finally get her on the line, I listen to the lies tumble out of me: Brennan's a close family friend; my father is ill; I want to get in touch with him to let him know the situation; could you tell me how I can reach him please?

The agent isn't moved. "He's currently unavailable," she says curtly.

"Oh, because he's on a book tour? I tried to look up his events, but—"

"No," she cuts in. "He's just . . . unavailable."

There's something odd in the way she says it. Something bitter. Something that tells me there's more to this story.

"Who did you say this was?" she asks.

I hang up. Move to the next person on my list. I find the website for St. Cecilia's in Foster and dial the number for Father Murphy's office.

A woman picks up—ancient, by the sound of her. I ask to speak to the priest.

"He's not here," she says, and there's something familiar about the gruff tone of her voice. It nags at me, even as I respond.

"Oh, is he . . . doing Mass?" I ask.

"No," she says, already impatient. "Can I take a message?"

"Do you know why he was in Maine yesterday?" I blurt. "I saw him at the police station in Ridgeway."

She pauses for a long time. Then, finally: "He was helping with an investigation."

"Because he spoke to Astrid Sullivan right before she went missing?" I ask. "The first time, I mean?"

The more I've thought about it—Chief Dixon calling in Father Murphy—the more it's made sense. It's possible he saw something the day of the kidnapping that only now, decades later, seems significant. Of course the police can't let that stone go unturned. And neither can I.

The woman coughs, dry and rattling. "I know who you are," she says. "You're that lady from the other day. The one from Massachusetts."

I sit up straighter. It's the woman from the church parking lot. The one who knocked on my window, hissed *It's in God's hands now.* Said *What's done is done.*

"Father Murphy has done nothing wrong," she says.

"I—wasn't saying that he had. I just want to know what he told the police. It's a long story, but I'm looking for any—"

"I thought I told you to let this go," she snaps. "I don't know what you're expecting to find. Foster is a quiet place. A *good* place, filled with good people. But Astrid, she wasn't like the rest of us. She was a troublemaker. I had her as a student in CCD, and more often than not, she was brazenly defiant. She loved to bend the rules. Loved to laugh at them, too. So as far as I'm concerned—as far as we're *all* concerned—she brought this on herself. God, in his heavenly wisdom, knows what to do with disobedient children. So he brought in an outsider that day, and when Astrid chose to leave her parents' party, she became a temptation for that man. And the man was wicked, of course—but Astrid has wickedness in her, too."

For several seconds, I don't say anything. I can't even conjure some words to speak. I breathe shakily through the silence, and by the time I'm able to attempt a response, she's already hung up.

I drop my head into my hands. Rub my temples until they throb.

It's not the first time I've heard something like this. The news reporter in Foster said residents believe Astrid made herself a target. But this woman—she believes something even worse: that Astrid's kidnapping was a punishment from God. A punishment Astrid actually deserved—for being *defiant*, for being *disobedient*, for having *wickedness* inside her.

Astrid wrote nearly the same thing about herself in her memoir. Just this morning, I went back and read that passage so many times I have it memorized: *My throat became raw with screaming, but the discomfort was something I believed I deserved. I had made my promises to God. I had committed myself to his teachings and commandments. But I did not honor my mother and father. And he had seen fit to punish me.* My eyes watered when I read that. It reminded me so much of my students, the kids who blame themselves for the wounds someone else inflicts. Astrid was fourteen when she had these thoughts. Still very much a kid herself. But the woman on the phone—how could she think that too?

She brought this on herself, the woman said. *As far as I'm concerned. As far as we're* all *concerned.* She hit hard on that *all*, drawing out the vowel, and I wonder if she was referring to Father Murphy. If he, too, believes that what happened to Astrid was a righteous act of God.

And if he does, would he even take seriously his responsibility to the police? Would he scour his memories for every detail he might have previously overlooked? Or would he think, *It's in God's hands now*—just like that woman? *What's done is done.*

The trees blur by as I head back to Ted's. My breath comes out in huffs. I learned nothing at Rusty's, apart from what I already knew: it's up to me to find Astrid.

But these phone calls to literary agents, to churches with priests who have washed their hands of it all—I've only been wasting more time. While I sat at Rusty's desk, staring at the crumbs between the letters of his keyboard, Astrid was in a basement somewhere. Or a dim room. Or behind a red door.

If she's even still alive.

I tighten my grip on the steering wheel. I can feel the frantic ticking of my pulse, that wire connected to my heart. It's getting faster and faster, and if I don't figure this out soon, I'm going to explode.

I've read the chapters about Lily, I've spoken to everyone I can think of, but I'm no closer to remembering what will help me find Astrid.

I squint at the street ahead, as if I'll find those memories laid out on the road. And in a few more seconds, I see him. The drifter. He's in that dark outfit again—black on black on black, every inch of him covered.

Who would wear that in the summer?

Men who don't want to be seen.

Who would prowl these streets without a destination?

Monsters who search for prey.

My foot slams against the gas pedal, my car rockets ahead, and I skid to a stop at an angle in front of him—all before he has the chance to react. To scamper off into the woods like the cowards that monsters probably are.

It's the most reckless I've ever been, and he seems shocked by the near miss, his muscles stalled.

I roll down my window. "Who are you?" I shout.

There's another moment in which he doesn't move. The air is hot as I breathe it in. Then he takes a step toward me.

"Are you okay, ma'am?" he asks.

His voice is scratchy, as if he's gone too long without speaking. Without water. As if he's been living off cans of Sprite. His face is shadowed by the hood of his raincoat, but I can see some creases in his skin. He isn't young.

"Who are you?" I demand again, but this time, my voice is smaller.

It knows I'm not cut out for this. I can make calls at school, fill out paperwork, counsel a young student. But I'm not the person who confronts the danger. I assess it. I study it. And if things get really dicey, I call someone with more strength and authority than me.

The drifter puts his hand on my sideview mirror, and now I'm the one who's frozen. His chin moves as he speaks, but I hear the words on a delay.

"I'm nobody, ma'am," he says. "Just a guy."

Then he turns around, heads into the woods, and in all that dark clothing, he stalks away.

I make it back to Ted's somehow.

For a while, I sat on the road, breathing deeply, flexing my fingers and toes. A car came by and honked at me, but that didn't make me move. Only the thought that the drifter might return, might see me as someone who's asking to be hurt, made me turn the wheel and ease my foot onto the gas.

Now I'm back on the dirt driveway, coughing at the dust that swirls in the air. But I swallow my cough as soon as I hear a sound. It's a rustle of trees. A rummaging through the woods. Anyone else would think it's an animal, but I know it's not. It's too methodical. Too human. Could the drifter have sprinted through those branches, followed the track of my car somehow—or did he know all along that this was where I'd go?

It's almost dusk. The light isn't good. But when a figure steps out of the tree line and stumbles a little, his unsteady feet shooting him toward Mara's Break Room, I know him immediately.

"Cooper. What are you doing here?"

He straightens up, startled. "Brierley?"

"What are you doing?" I repeat.

"Exploring," he says. As he walks toward me, his fingers skim the side of Mara's studio. "I'm getting the lay of the land. Checking out the woods around my new property."

My brows knit together, but then I think of the boxes inside the studio. The packing I'm supposed to be doing. "You're buying Ted's house?" I ask.

He cocks his head. "You think I'd buy this place? No way. No potential. I'm talking about the cabin. Remember? I told you the other day I'm buying it."

That sagging porch. That shingleless roof. Those mold spores that looked like an infection.

"Right," I say.

"Technically it's not mine yet," Cooper says. "It'll take a while for all the nuts and bolts of the sale to go through, but I've been tooling around in it already. Cleaning it up so I can hit the ground running. I'm so fucking inspired. I might've gotten carried away with my exploring, though."

His words sound giddy, but his eyes seem wary. He's staring at the studio, his gaze so hard it's as if he sees right through the siding. "I must've taken a wrong turn," he says. "I didn't mean to end up here."

He pauses, flicks his eyes back toward me. Looks me up and down.

"You should be careful, actually," he adds. "It's easy to get lost in those woods."

My stomach whirls. I stiffen up. Remember running through those trees, gasping for breath as I burst into Mara's studio. The image is still so incomplete, but if I could stretch out its edges, widen the frame a bit, maybe I could glimpse enough to know the truth: what I saw when the man dragged me through the red door, how many miles he drove to return me to those woods. I clamp my eyes shut, as if complete darkness will coax the memories into the light.

"You okay?" Cooper asks.

I look at him, see him reach into his pocket, pull out a pack of cigarettes and lighter with one hand. He flips open the top of the pack, plucks one out with his teeth. Then he sets the flame against it and sucks.

"Eh, never mind," he says, "I already know you've got stuff going on." The cigarette bounces on his lip. "Ted hinted at it yesterday, when I saw him at Rusty's."

I stand up straighter. Rusty's? He told Eric he was at Wicker. Picking up a file. Dredging up notes that will keep him clacking away.

"What was he doing at Rusty's?" I ask.

"Ballet class," Cooper says. When I blink at him, he rolls his eyes. "Buying something, Brierley. Wow, Ted's right. You do need to lighten up."

"What do you mean? What did he say?"

Cooper shrugs. Takes another drag.

"Just that you're mad at him about something." He ashes onto the dirt. "You should give it up, though. Whatever it is—go easy on him, okay?"

Anger flickers in my chest. Hotter than the air.

"And why should I do that? You don't even know what it's about."

"No, I don't," Cooper admits, "but I know he's a good guy."

"Do you?" I mean to sound sarcastic, but the irony doesn't come through. Instead, I sound sincere. As if I really want to know.

"Hell yeah," Cooper says. "Ted's always been good to me, ever since I was a kid. Giving me jobs around your house, letting me fix stuff. That's probably why I'm so good at what I do now."

Cooper's definition of "kid" is very different from mine. He's talking about when he was twenty, twenty-one, back when Ted would hire him to fix a bent gutter or unclog a sink. Even though Ted knew how I felt about Cooper. Even though he could see I cowered in my room whenever he was there.

"You know, I've done some things I'm not proud of," Cooper adds. "Things I could've gotten in trouble for." He chuckles. "Like, a *lot* of trouble. But when Ted caught me one time, making a whole mess of something I had no business trying to do in the first place, he didn't turn me in. He's a good guy, like I said."

"Uh-huh," I mumble. I don't need to hear about Ted excusing things that are wrong.

"Uh-huh," Cooper echoes. "You should be grateful, you know. It's not easy being good."

He sucks on his cigarette. Breathes out a puff of gray. This time, he doesn't tilt his head to the side. The smoke erupts against my face.

"Well, sorry," I say. Then I cough, my throat stinging with nicotine. "But you're hardly the best judge of goodness."

I regret the comment instantly. Even more so when Cooper's voice turns sharp, when his eyes flash like embers.

"The hell is that supposed to mean?"

I shake my head. "Nothing. Sorry."

"Didn't sound like nothing."

He holds his cigarette limp at his side, exposing his tattoo. Those talon-sharp stingers. Those honeycomb holes in his skin. My jaw aches as my body remembers. The hairs on the back of my neck stick up.

"What're you staring at?" he asks.

I flick my eyes up, but it's too late. He knows.

He looks at his forearm. Flexes the muscle and cocks a grin.

"Still?" he asks.

Then he drops his cigarette. Stamps it out.

"Still what?"

His laughter is a growl. "You're still afraid of this?"

I don't get a chance to say no. Cooper leaps forward, grabs the back of my neck, holds his arm in front of my mouth. I try to jerk away, knees buckling, but his thumb pushes a pressure point below my ear, and he leans me backward, like he's dipping me in a dance.

"What are you so scared of? Huh?"

Boys who use their bodies as weapons.

I want to run. Want to scream. But my legs and throat aren't working. He's stronger than he was the last time he did this, and I'm suspended beneath him, stiff in the hand that grasps me, staring at the arm that's almost on my mouth. I watch him lower it, centimeter by centimeter, squeezing out the air that separates his skin from my lips. I open my mouth, even though I'm widening his target, and I try to squeak out a sound. Nothing comes, though. Not even breath.

"It's just a picture," he taunts. "What's so scary about a picture?"

His arm this close—it smells like it always did. Like sweat and dirt. Like my childhood.

Boys who never become men.

Finally, my voice surges back. I scream as loud as I can. And as soon as I do, he pulls his arm away. Yanks me upright.

"Jesus Christ," he says. He takes a step back. "What're you screaming for? You're an adult now. Grow up."

I'm shaking all over, my lungs are burning, but I still gasp out the words: "*Me* grow up?"

Cooper rubs his arm, as if he's wiping off my scream. "I was just having fun with you."

"*Fun*?" My heart bangs against my ribs.

"Look, I'll see you around," he says, turning away from me. He takes a flashlight from his pocket, clomps back toward the woods. Even in the coming darkness, I can see the prints of his boots in the dirt.

"You can't be so squeamish," he adds. "Not when there's things out there you should actually be afraid of."

As he speaks, he doesn't bother to look back. Doesn't see that my mouth hangs open. That I'm panting like an animal. That my hands are trembling so hard I can't even swat away the bugs.

All I can do is watch him go. All I can do is stand in the driveway, breathing in the dust his feet have kicked up.

eighteen

A strid reaches for me.

A man—masked, gloved, skin entirely covered—yanks her back. She clatters to the floor as if her body were ceramic. As if all she's made of are pieces meant to break.

But she doesn't break. She strains. She reaches.

Her face is so scrunched with the effort that the freckle under her eyebrow is difficult to see.

I'm getting farther from her. Dragged up. My legs are limp, thudding against each stair.

"I'm going to save you," she calls.

She opens her mouth again, but this time, it isn't her voice that pours out. It's a sound like a bell. A sound like—

The phone. Out in the hall. My eyes shoot open.

Now there's clacking. Ted's fingers punishing keys.

Even with the chaos of waking, I know the dream was a memory: chapter five re-created with color and sound. I saw the red of her hair, the green of her eyes, heard the bang of each stair against my calves. My pulse is still pounding from it, my breath coming in gasps. I should be relieved to have recovered so much at once, but it only reminds me how starkly our roles have reversed. Astrid's the one who needs saving now. I'm the one who's supposed to strain, be strong, keep fighting even when it hurts.

My body is hot, blanketed with sunlight, and my bedside lamp is on. I don't remember going to sleep last night. I only remember lying in the fetal position, thinking of Cooper's arm nearly between my teeth, how I only screamed instead of bit. I never even turned on the fan in the room, and now my skin is sticky with sweat. The phone stops ringing, Ted keeps clacking, and I turn to look at the time—then jolt up.

I've been sleeping for more than twelve hours, and while I dreamt of her face again and again, I've been wasting Astrid's time. I shower so fast the bathroom mirror doesn't have a chance to steam. It's only once I'm dressed again, slipping my wedding rings back on, that I remember I promised Eric I'd be better about checking in—and already, I fell asleep last night without thinking to call him at all.

When he answers the phone, I'm surprised to hear his voice.

"Hey," I say, "I was gonna leave a voice mail. I thought you'd be at work."

"I'm between patients," he says. "I tried calling you before, but no one answered."

"Oh, a little while ago?"

"No. A couple hours ago. Before my shift started."

I must have slept right through it. Must have dreamed so deeply of Astrid that not even my husband could reach me.

"I've been talking to Karen," Eric says.

"Who?"

"Jim's wife. The private investigator? I told you yesterday I was going to pick her brain. I asked her to look into Brennan, like you wanted, and—turns out, she was able to find his tour schedule from twenty years ago."

"Whoa," I say. "Already?"

"Yeah, I called her on my way back to Boston. And I know I should've run this by you first, but I kind of . . . hired her? In an official capacity? And I agreed to a higher fee for her to make it a priority." He pauses, listening to my silence. "Are you mad?"

"No," I say.

I'm grateful, actually, for how seriously he's taking this. I put my hand over my chest. It's warm from the shower, or warm from the sun, or warm from loving him so much.

"Good," he says. "It's expensive, but I think it's worth it, because the longer you're there, I . . ." There's a pinch in his voice, a clutch of worry and anger. "Anyway. Here's the thing. You mentioned how Brennan would have had easy access to you. But when would he have come across Astrid?"

I drop my hand to my side.

"Oh," I say. "I hadn't thought of that."

"Well, listen to this. Ted said Brennan was staying with you guys because of his book tour, right? So Karen looked into his event dates from 2000, and guess where he was on June 24."

My breath catches. Eric waits for me to respond, and when I don't, he fills the space I've left for him.

"A store called Books & Birds," he says. "In Foster, New Hampshire."

An electric jolt surges through me, and my mouth hangs open. Jaw slack. Tongue stuck. So many things strike me at once that it's hard to catalog them all. But Eric prompts me to speak—"Fern? Are you there?"—and for him, I try.

"The shops I saw there—in Foster—the other day—they all had names like that. Tom's Tackle. Cock-a-doodle Coffee. And I . . . oh my god."

"What? What is it?"

"I've been there," I say.

"To Books & Birds?"

"Yes, but—I was there, that day, I think. June 24."

"How do you know?"

"Because I . . . I've only seen Brennan do an event one time. And it was at this weird place, with bird murals, and a parrot. And . . . it had to be Books & Birds, right?"

"Hold on," Eric says. I hear him typing something, the sound of his keystrokes so different from Ted's. "Yep. This is from their website: 'Customers at Books & Birds can browse for their new favorite read alongside the store's cheerful mascot, Colton the cockatoo.'" He pauses. "But I don't get it. Why were you there? I can't imagine Ted sitting through one of Brennan's talks."

"I don't think Ted was there," I say. Because I'm realizing that I remember standing in the back of the store, watching the crowd laugh and nod and applaud, but what I don't remember is Ted beside me, scoffing and muttering, as he surely would have done. I close my eyes, try to scrounge up more of the memory. It would have been during my vacation with Kyla's family, but I don't remember Kyla being there either. And Kyla and I were never separated—except for during her haircut, when Cooper and I went to get her candy, and Cooper left me at a gas station because he saw some girl.

"Check to see if there's a gas station within walking distance of the store," I tell Eric, even though it doesn't really matter. The memory is taking shape.

It was daytime, the sun scorchingly bright, but I was still nervous to be left alone on a street I didn't know. I watched Cooper's car disappear around a corner, and I walked along the sidewalk, head down, arms tucked in tight, as strangers passed me by. I didn't know where I was supposed to go—Cooper didn't say anything about coming back to pick me up—and my lungs seemed to shrink, my breathing ragged. "Are you okay?" I think a woman asked me, and it was only when I saw a sign outside a store, Brennan's name in thick white chalk, that I knew I would be. I had made it safe inside somewhere. I had found a familiar face.

"Yep, there's a Mobil down the street," Eric says. "Why?"

"Kyla's brother left me at the gas station, while we were all on that vacation together, and I stumbled into the store during Brennan's talk."

I didn't speak to him, I remember now. When the talk was over and the crowd leapt to their feet, I didn't stick around to say hello. It would have been disloyal to Ted.

"I still don't get how it would happen, though," I say. "How do you go from giving a talk to abducting someone?" I pause. "Astrid lived on Bleeker Street, which was near where she was taken. Can you look up how close that is to Books & Birds?"

I hear more typing, then silence. A held-in breath. "It's close," Eric says.

I sit on the edge of my bed, rest my forehead in the palm of my hand. "So it fits," I say.

It's hot in my room, but I shiver anyway. It was only a couple days ago that we looked at Brennan's books in the kitchen. Ted was calling Brennan a sellout, a fraud, when he might be something so much worse than that. Maybe Brennan's books have even hinted at it, their titles filled with such ominous words—*terror, desolation, isolation.*

"Wait," I say.

"What is it?"

"Hold on."

I open my door quietly, tiptoe across the hall, sneak down the stairs. Brennan's books are still on the kitchen counter, and the one I'm looking for is second from the top. *The Terror of Isolation.* It's a title that's always pricked me, reminding me of the night that Ted and Mara didn't come home, the times Ted abandoned me at stores, the Saturday mornings I hoped he'd ignore his work to take me out to breakfast. Loneliness is a kind of terror. Sadness is too.

I open the book and skim the synopsis. Then, my throat tightening, I check the copyright date, look at the table of contents, and by the time I finish, my hands are shaking so much I can barely hold the phone.

"Eric," I whisper. "Brennan has a book called *The Terror of Isolation*. It's from a couple years after Astrid and I were . . ." I stop. Inhale. Keep going. "There are chapters on child abductions."

I hear Eric's breath against the phone. A whoosh of air, then a groan.

"Fuck," he says.

And Eric only swears for things like this—things so heavy no other words can hold them.

I'm climbing the stairs, two or three at a time, careful to avoid the steps that creak. When I'm back in my room, I close the door with a barely audible click.

"So I was right," I say. "What I told you at The Diner—when I first suspected Brennan. Astrid and I, we were—we were . . ."

"Research," he finishes for me, and hearing him say it—logical, steady Eric—my heart rattles so hard I think my ribs will crack.

He clears his throat. "It's crazy," he says. "Guess he's not playing by the rules anymore."

"Guess he really is a fraud," I manage.

"Yeah," Eric says. "Just not the kind Ted meant."

For a moment, neither of us speaks. Then I hear my voice tremble. "Does Karen know where Brennan is now? I talked to his literary agent yesterday, and all she would say is that he's unavailable."

"Karen talked to the agent, too," Eric says. "But it sounds like she was more forthcoming with Karen. She told her that Brennan demanded to delay his book tour this time around. Which is a big deal, I guess? Because you want to promote it right when it first comes out or something? Karen said the agent seemed annoyed about it."

I grip the bedpost. "She needs to find out where he is now," I say.

"Yeah, I've asked her to look into it."

"Okay. Thank you. But she has to do it quickly."

"I know," Eric says. "For Astrid's sake."

When he says her name, I feel that warmth in my chest again. He's on her side—on mine, too—and he's going to help me find her. We make a good team, Eric and I. We always have.

I look down at my stomach. Place my hand over my belly. "Eric, listen . . ."

I take a deep breath. But before I can exhale, the phone beeps in my ear. "Oh, hold on a sec. Call waiting. I'll get rid of them."

When I click over, I'm greeted by a gravelly voice.

"Ms. Douglas? This is Chief Dixon. I'm calling regarding the report you had me look into."

"Oh! Oh my god, thank you! Can you hang on a second?"

I switch back to Eric. "I've gotta go," I tell him. "It's Ridgeway Police—they have the report that Ted filed! I can tell them about Brennan, and maybe I can head up to Maine to help, I'll call you later, okay?"

I jab the button to click back over, apologize to Chief Dixon for making him wait.

"Yes, well," he says, "I called a while ago, and there was no voice mail or anything, so this is the second time I've reached out. But I wanted to tell you myself that this report of yours was not available."

My hand is on the doorknob, ready to rush out of the room as soon as the call is over. Now it slips to my side. "Not available?"

"That's right."

"But . . . why?" I step backward, slowly, away from the door. Ease myself onto the bed. "Is it because it's technically an unsolved case, so it's not public record?"

"No," Dixon says. "It's because it doesn't exist. No such report was ever filed."

My wrist blares with an itch. "That's . . . that's not possible," I say. "Are you sure?"

For a moment, the only sound is his breath—a long, impatient exhale. "I am absolutely positive," he says, "that there was no police report made by Ted Brierley in 2000. Now—"

"Wait. Can you check for it under Mara Brierley? I might have given you the wrong first name."

There's a slight pause, but I don't hear him typing or rustling through papers.

"If the surname is the same," he says, "it would have come up in our search. Now I made this call myself to make one thing clear: I followed up with this, I treated it as a potential lead—only to find you've wasted my time. If you try to interfere in this investigation again, appropriate action will be taken. Good-bye, Ms. Douglas."

I don't know if I respond to him. I only know I'm a hunk of stone on my bed, and the dial tone drones in my ear. It's such a stoic sound, so passive and indifferent. And I will sit here all day. I will listen to nothing but this.

But there's another sound too, stabbing its way in, cutting through the ceaseless monotone. *Clack. Clack-clack. Clack-clack-clack.*

I press the button to hang up, but I don't let go of the phone. It's stuck in my grip. Lodged in my palm. When I hear the sound again— *clack-clack-clack*—I find myself squeezing the plastic so hard I'm sure it will break.

Now I'm off my bed, swinging open my door, stomping down the hall. I burst into his office. But Ted keeps clacking.

As I wait for him to turn, I see myself as I once was, as I was a thousand times: a little girl, dressed in too-small clothes. She's got a blanket trailing behind her as she watches her father's back. His elbows jut to the sides as his fingers trot across the keys. The little girl breathes and waits and breathes. Then she coughs. Then she shifts her feet. She pinches herself, and when it doesn't hurt worse than her heart, she begins to wonder if she's dead—just a ghost now and nothing more—because in all that time, he doesn't turn around.

He never, ever turned.

"Hey!" I shout.

The phone launches out of my hand. It sails through the air and lands in the center of his back.

He hunches forward at the impact, swivels around in his chair. "What the . . . ?" he begins, but then he narrows his eyes. Examines my face. Something ripples through me, and for the first time, it isn't fear or nausea or anxiety. It's white-hot, scalding rage.

"The police would have followed up," I say.

"Excuse me?"

"Two girls missing from the same area? They wouldn't let that go."

"What? What are you talking about?"

"You never called the police, did you?" My voice sounds like somebody else's. "You never reported my kidnapping."

His gaze lingers on me a few seconds longer, and then he drops it. I can't see his eyes. I don't know if they're filled with remorse or confusion or if they wince like a misbehaving child who's just been caught.

But when he shifts them back up at me, I see they are none of these things. They're just eyes. Emotionless as lenses in a microscope. Not sorry at all.

"No," he says. "I didn't."

nineteen

His confirmation douses my rage. Because that's the thing with emotions that burn so hot. You can't sustain their heat for very long. Or, at least, I never could. My body was not built for rage. I am not the fire that gushes through a house, leaving it skeletal and charred. I am the small, quaking child who's crouched inside, watching the beams on the ceiling for the moment they begin to fall.

I knew it already, as soon as Dixon said the report was never filed, but hearing Ted admit it, I stumble backward. When my legs bump against the interview chair, I sit down. Never mind that I told him I wouldn't end up here. That the chair itself is as hard and uncomfortable as it ever was. I need something to catch me. A familiar place to land.

"Why?" I ask.

Ted blows out a breath. "Because the police would have only bungled the opportunity."

He says this as if it's answer enough, but when I don't respond, he grunts.

"Look," he says. "Contrary to what I told you before, I did study you in the weeks after your abduction. It's true that, at first, I was frustrated by your memory loss. But then—" He leans forward, rolls his chair a little closer. "I realized that your dissociative amnesia wasn't a setback; it was an opportunity. I could expand the scope of my research. Explore whether fear can be triggered even when the memory prompting it is gone. Explore what it takes to bring that memory back."

"Triggered," I say, my voice flat. "How?"

His eyes brighten. "I brought home newspapers with Astrid's face on them. Read them right in front of you, but you barely reacted. Sometimes you scratched your wrist"—he looks at my hand and smiles—"exactly like you're doing right now."

I didn't even know they were moving, but now my fingers stop.

"Noteworthy," he muses, and he scoots closer to his desk, types a few words onto a page that's nearly full.

"What else?" I ask.

For a moment, he looks reluctant to break his gaze from his typewriter. Then he stretches back in his chair, puts his hands behind his head. "You mentioned a basement," he says, "when you first came home. And that was all over the papers, too. So I'd come up with tasks that needed to be done in *our* basement, ask you to help me out with them." He shakes his head, disappointed. "It didn't work, though. You were always just eager to help. 'What should we do next, Ted?' you'd ask, and then I'd invent some other stupid thing for us to do. And you never showed any signs of fear at all. To the point where I almost wondered . . ."

His eyes slide away, sticking to the wall behind me, and the sentence ends right there.

"Wondered what?" I ask. "If I'd really been kidnapped?"

"Anyway," he says, ignoring the question, "any police investigation would have interfered with my research."

"But why? Why couldn't you do both? Why couldn't you call the police *and*"—I press my lips together before letting the rest come out—"study me?"

He snaps his attention back toward my face, incredulous. "Because they're incompetent! They wouldn't know how to interview you properly. They'd say things that would compromise the integrity of my research, and if anyone was going to get some real answers out of you, it had to be me. You're *my* daughter. It was *my* right!"

The room reels. I watch it spin for a second, and then I close my eyes, press my temples. I always knew that Ted would do anything for his work, but when I thought of that word—*anything*—I never truly meant *anything*. I certainly didn't mean prioritizing his research over taking the most basic step to help his daughter. What he did—it's more than I can rationalize. Or even begin to comprehend.

Unless.

Eric's theory from yesterday morning. That Ted might be holding something back. Protecting someone.

"Did Brennan Llewellyn do this to me?" I demand. "Did you find out somehow, and you . . . you decided to cover for him—and that's why you didn't go to the police?"

Ted laughs so hard it jostles me. "Brennan?" he barks. "You think *Brennan* would actually—no, no, no. Trust me, whoever it was, it was *not* Brennan Llewellyn."

He sounds sincere. I almost believe him. But then again, I believed he had really filed a report.

"Why did you lie to me about the police?" I ask.

His grin withers. He's contemplating something.

"I had to tell you I filed a report," he says after a few moments, "because I didn't want you figuring it out too soon."

"Figuring out what?"

"Why I called you here. If I told you the truth—that I'd been trying to study you back then—you would have put it all together."

I stare at him. "What are you talking about?"

"I couldn't believe my luck," he says, "when I heard that Astrid Sullivan was missing again. It was so fortuitous, this second disappearance. Of course I needed to get you back here. Needed to watch you for recovered memories. For heightened fear. Then I could pair all that research with the notes I took in 2000." His eyes gleam. "There could be a book! It could blow Brennan right out of the water!"

I try to shake my head, but my neck is slow to move. "I don't understand."

Ted sighs. Regards me like a child he's tired of tolerating. "I'm not moving to Florida, Fern. I only told you that so you'd agree to come home. So I could study you."

The words take a moment to sink in. But then I hear what he's saying, and my head drops into my hands. I taste my tears almost immediately. They rush down my cheeks. Splash onto my lips.

Of all his confessions and revelations, this is the one that breaks me. Because I was so stupid. Because I'm embarrassed. Because I should have already known. (*I need you*, he said to me on the phone—and how quickly I started packing. How easily I overlooked the fact that Ted is not a Florida man.) But most acutely, most achingly, my tears come hot and quick because a daughter shouldn't have to doubt her father or wonder what awful trick he has up his sleeve.

"How?" I ask from behind my hands. It's the only word I can manage.

"It was challenging," he says. "I couldn't appear to be watching you, of course. I had to be patient. Wait for *you* to come to *me*. And in the meantime, I've been crafting hypotheses. Revisiting my old notes. Studying that woman's mem—"

"No," I cut him off.

My stomach whirls. That roiling nausea. That reminder that there's someone growing inside me. I want to feel love toward this baby, but right now, I feel only my weakness. My anguish and fear. The child is clinging to me, sucking in nutrients that I alone can give, but what else is in my blood? What have I inherited from Ted?

"I'm not asking how you did this," I say. "I'm asking, how *could* you do this?"

"What? I can't hear you when you're covering your face like that."

I take a shaky breath, let my damp hands slip into my lap, and meet Ted's eyes. "I don't think you're a good man," I say. "I don't think you've been good for me at all."

My words are drowsy and slow, but his head rears back as if I've hissed at him. As if I'm a wild animal he doesn't know how to tame.

"I never hurt you," he says. That old, exhausted script. "I never laid a hand."

The room is stifling. The air too thick to breathe. But I nod. Try to take in oxygen anyway, through lungs that already burn.

"You're right," I agree. "You never pushed me or hit me or left me with bruises. But there are other kinds of wounds. And they hurt just as bad as the ones you can see."

I see the moment he swallows, his throat bobbing up and down. He seems surprised. And as I watch his eyes, how they glaze over a bit, it's as if I can see straight through to the wheels turning in his head. He's lost in thought. Realizing, maybe, that the abuse he suffered from his father is not the only kind of abuse there is. That maybe, in his way, he's spent my whole life inflicting another.

"But," he finally says, "you know—you know I love you. Right?"

My tears well up again. My lips separate. This is the first time he's ever said that to me.

I should be glad. Euphoric. I should be thinking of the way he used to praise me during interviews, like I was the piece of work he was proudest of. I should be remembering the witch from Forest Near, how I suspect he loved that game because it gave him an excuse to hold me. But mostly, I'm just sad. That it's taken him thirty-two years to tell me something so basic. That inquiring whether I know it to be true is a legitimate question to ask.

He scratches the side of his neck, the skin there scaly and red. And I hate that there's a part of me that wants to reach out, take his hand, tell him he's only harming himself more by touching the thing that hurts.

"I know you love me in your way," I say. My voice is weary and buckling. "But somebody kidnapped me. How could you not want to know who it was?"

"Haven't you been listening? That's my whole point. I want you to get to the bottom of those memories. See the man behind the mask. And actually, I've been thinking . . ." He glances at his typewriter. "You really don't remember anything about what he looked like?"

"He was covered from head to toe."

"Right. But he must have spoken. Or moved a certain way. Something you recognized. Did you know that ninety-nine percent of kidnapping victims know their abductor?"

I grip the sides of the chair. "I do know that," I say. "And I think it was Brennan, Ted."

"What? No. Stop it with that."

"He was in Foster the exact day that Astrid was kidnapped. He was staying with us around that time, too. He wrote about child abductions in one of his books. He—"

"It was *not* Brennan," he bellows.

"How can you be so sure?"

"Because Brennan is weak! And whoever did this—he's not weak!"

Ted fumbles with some papers on his desk, shuffles a pile to another spot, and picks up Astrid's book, which has been hiding underneath. He opens to a dog-eared page. Skims his finger along it. Taps the book when he finds what he's searching for.

"This man was strong," he says. "Clearly. And Brennan is not."

"How would you even know? You've never fought Brennan."

He scoffs. "Let's forget about that for a minute." He flips back a couple pages. His eyes shift from side to side as he reads. "It seems Astrid took care of you in the basement. Do you remember that at all?"

I shrug one shoulder. "Some things."

"Like what?"

"The thing she did with her freckle. The marble game."

"Ah, yes, the marble game. What was that exactly? She's vague about it."

I lean back farther in my chair. I am so tired. This room is so hot.

"We slid the marbles across the room. Picked one out that we tried to hit."

"Hmm," Ted says. "That's excellent. Really. You must be very close to remembering everything, Fern—to remember a detail as small as that."

"All I have are small details."

"That's good," he says. "You've been doing so great. What are some of the other details?"

I feel the spindles of the chair pushing against me. They fit into grooves in my back I didn't know were there.

"I remember Astrid reaching out to me."

Ted looks down at the book. Turns the page. "When he took you up the stairs, you mean?"

"I think so."

"You only think so?"

"No. Just—when I remembered that before . . ."

"Before?"

"From these dreams I always had. I thought she was reaching out for me to save her."

"And now?"

"I was wrong. She was reaching out to save *me*."

Ted pecks a few words into his typewriter. I hear each clack inside my skull.

"That's a noteworthy revelation," he says, swiveling back around. "You're remarkable, Fern."

I need to get out of this room. This airless office. This place where the ceiling slopes so close to my head it almost scrapes my hair.

But the chair. It's cradling me. Giving me a place to be steady—and I am so weary. So limp and useless.

"I'll want to go back to those dreams you mentioned," Ted says. "But first. In that moment you remember, of Astrid reaching for you . . . what are you feeling exactly?"

"I don't know."

"Yes you do. Come on, you're doing a great job. I'm so proud of your progress." I sit a little straighter. Warmth oozes through my body. "What do you feel when you think of Astrid reaching out, trying to save you?"

I picture it again. Her arms stretching farther than seems possible. The skin around her eyes crimped with desperation. The terror, deep inside me, that always sent me bolting up in bed.

"I'm scared," I say.

"Yes. Excellent. And why are you scared?"

"Because . . ." It's clearer now, like stepping back from a painting and seeing more than just brushstrokes. "Astrid is scared. And she never was before. She was always so strong."

Ted hesitates. "No, no, no. Let's try to pull the memory away from her, okay? Think of the memory as a toy train you can slide along a track. Put your finger on the back of the train, the back of that memory, and push it further from Astrid now. Can you do that?"

I stare at him. His pupils look cavernous.

"Good," he says. "Now, why are you scared? What's happened in the memory, right before he took you up the stairs?"

I shake my head. "I don't know."

"You do. The answer is inside you. You have to be willing to let it slip out." He gazes at the book, still open in his lap. "Astrid says you saw something. What did you see?"

Fresh tears prickle. "I don't remember."

"Memories are just stories, Fern. Tell me the story of what you saw in the basement."

I look down at my legs, and for a moment, I can almost see them as they once were. Too short to touch the floor. Dangling off the edge.

"I don't know," I say. My voice warbles.

"You do!" Ted insists. "You do. You just have to let yourself dwell in the discomfort of . . ." He stops. "Here. Let me read this to you. It's a passage from chapter five, the one describing your final day in captivity."

He lifts the book. Opens his mouth to begin reading.

"No." It's a small sound, more moan than protest.

"No?" he asks. "Why not?"

I dig my fingers into my legs. I dig instead of scratch.

"I don't want to hear that part. It's too—it's too much. And I have to . . ."

I was supposed to leave. Supposed to go somewhere. But the air is throbbing with heat. The ceiling is sinking.

"I think you need to hear it," Ted says. "Your resistance only proves that." He scoots closer. "I've read this passage a hundred times, and I believe that something important happened here. Something even

Astrid didn't know. I'm quite certain it's the key to everything. And if you can unlock this memory, you will open up a whole gulf of fear, the one that churned inside you all that time, and we will have so much work we can do together."

Together. I try to resist the pull of that word. Try to hear, instead, Dr. Lockwood's voice, how she'd define what's happening in this moment—because I know something's happening, something dark and hypnotic. But *together* still means something to me. He lied and he schemed and he never learned what love is meant to look like—but *together* is still a promise. *Together* is a chance.

"Will you do this with me?" Ted asks. Then he leans forward, touches my hand. I wrap my fingers around his before he can pull away. He doesn't try to, though. He holds my gaze with his eyes and holds my hand with his. His skin is dry. Papery. But it's my father's skin. My dad's.

"Will you listen to me read this, Fern? Please?"

Excerpt from Chapter Five of
Behind the Red Door: A Memoir **by Astrid Sullivan**

When he came down the stairs that day, everything was still normal. Or as normal as anything can be when you're a prisoner. He had a routine we came to expect, and at first, that day was no different. He brought down the food and the Sprite, set it all in the usual place, and then he reached for the waste bucket.

That's when it happened—the moment that instigated Lily's violent removal from the basement.

The handle of the bucket got caught. He always looped his arm beneath it and let it dangle from the crook of his elbow, but on that day, Lily's last, the handle snagged on the end of his glove. It became caught between the black rubber and the shirt he wore beneath, and the more he tried to shake it off, the tighter the handle clung.

I almost told Lily to run. He was distracted, his concentration pinpointed on fixing the handle and the glove. It was a problem so incongruently slapstick to our setting that it made me forget what he told me would happen if she tried to escape. Here he was—no longer a dangerous abductor, capable of killing a girl, but a man whose kidnapper costume had gotten caught on a bucket of shit.

I kept my gaze on Lily, who stared at the man as he fumbled, and suddenly she flinched. No, not just a flinch—her entire body jolted, as if she'd been zapped by a live wire.

I don't know what she saw. And it kills me that I've never

been able to ask her. But here's what I've always believed, the only answer that makes sense: she saw a feature of the man that I never did, something that revealed this alien-looking creature—no skin but the fabric of his clothes, no head but his welder's mask—to be an actual human being. Something that made clear that this man really *was* a man, not just a monster from a nightmare.

And then she screamed so loud I felt the sound of it vibrating in my ribs.

twenty

"Why'd you stop?"

I'm scratching my wrist, waiting for the rest of chapter five, where the man yanks Astrid back, pulls me by the hair, drags me out of the basement. I'm bracing myself for Astrid's desperation, the fear that burst from her body like another hand that tried to reach me. But Ted is silent now. Inspecting me.

"Because this is the climax of your fear," he says. "This is the moment that matters."

"But the stairs. Him grabbing me."

"No. It's this. What did you see?"

A bead of sweat hurries down my back. "I don't know. I'm not sure I saw anything. She seems— She sounds like she's just guessing."

Ted keeps his eyes on me, his chair pointed toward mine, but he raises the hand closest to his desk and types a word without ever breaking our stare. Six clacks.

"Say that she's not," he says. "Let's explore it at least. Go back to the moment you saw something."

"I can't. I don't remember that."

"You're not *letting* yourself remember it."

"That's not true," I argue. "I've been trying for days to remember everything."

Ted crosses his arms, glances at the ceiling. "Dissociative amnesia helps a person survive trauma," he says. He sounds so bored he could be reading from a textbook. "It allows the individual to move through life without being crippled by the memory of whatever they experienced." He leans forward, elbows on his legs. "But you don't need that anymore. You've already moved through life, and you've done so beautifully. You're all grown up, Fern, and I'm immensely proud of who you've become. Social worker and all."

I know I should feel his last sentence as a jab, another dismissal of the work I do, but I feel warm instead. And the warmth is softer, more soothing, than the heat pushing down on me from the ceiling. I could sink into the comfort of it. I could make a bed of this chair.

But I shift. Listen to the seat creak beneath my weight. Dr. Lockwood has warned me about this—hearing only the praise and missing the manipulation.

"Stop," I say.

"Think of your memory loss as a blindfold," he continues.

"Ted, please. Stop."

"All you have to do is choose to take it off."

I clench my jaw. "It's not that easy."

Ted sighs, rubs his face. Then he swivels away from me, toward the space to the side of his desk. A space I can't see.

"She says it got caught," he says, and when he spins back around, he's holding a black bucket.

My eyes stretch wide. "What are you doing?"

"I bought this yesterday," he explains, slapping it on its side, "to see if it could work as a trigger."

He reaches into the bucket, pulls out a pair of black gloves. My pulse kicks, but I watch, unblinking, as he slips them on, stretching them as far as they'll go, which is just over the cuffs of his rolled-up sleeves.

My heart pounds. My blood blares in my ears.

"Was it like this?" he asks. He stands, puts the handle of the bucket over his arm in a way that makes it catch against the end of his glove. "Fern, are you listening? Was this how it happened?"

"I don't know," I manage to say.

"Well, you have to try. Come on, watch. Maybe it was like this?"

He tugs on the handle, just enough so it pulls down his glove, making a gap between it and his shirt. Now there's a small strip of skin visible on his forearm, and I rake my nails against my wrist so hard I might be cutting myself.

"She said you saw a feature of him," he says. "What was it? And why did it *scare* you? Why was the sight of the arm, or whatever it might have been, even more frightening than the fact of being kidnapped itself? Why would you—" He stops. Shakes his head. "I'm sorry. I'm getting ahead of myself. Let's try to figure out what you saw first. Could it have been a freckle? Or a mole? Or . . . I don't know, what else could be distinctive about an arm?"

There's a final moment in which it doesn't occur to me. But then I suck in air so quickly it scalds my throat.

Ted straightens. "You're remembering."

I look from his exposed swatch of skin—its pigment unbroken, unaltered, unmarked—up to his eyes.

"Yes," I say. "I'm remembering."

I'm remembering an arm that terrified me more than anything else. An arm that was used as a weapon against me. An arm that always made me scream.

And it's only grown stronger after all these years, its muscles thickened and hardened by manual labor.

"I know where Astrid is," I gasp, and it's as if the invisible ropes tying me to this chair have broken loose. I leap up, run out of Ted's office, skid into my room to grab my keys off the bed, and dart down the stairs.

"Where are you going?" Ted calls after me. I can hear him even when I burst outside, even when the screen bangs shut behind me. "We're not done here, Fern! What is it? Where do you think she is?"

I've hardly put the car into park before I jump out of it, keys still dangling in the ignition.

Men who torment. Men who laugh.

The woods whisper, branches cast knife-sharp shadows, and my stomach churns—but I am going to fight through all of it, for her.

Men who were in Foster on June 24. Men whose time was unaccounted for.

Cooper's truck isn't parked in front of the cabin, so I shout her name as I try to barge through the front door. Only—the door won't open. I push with all my weight before considering the life inside me, whether it sloshes around as I slam us against this wood. Then I stop, beat my fists against the door instead, panting so hard it hurts. But for all its age and rot, the door doesn't budge.

Launching off the porch, I sprint around the side of the cabin, look for another entrance, scrape my nails against the siding as if I could claw my way inside. Around back, I find it—a screen door half off its hinges—and I crack it open just enough so I can squeeze through.

"Astrid!"

My voice bounces around the room, the echo so loud I can't hear if she responds. There are fallen beams, chunks of plaster. The walls tilt toward each other like all they want to do is give up and cave in. But I will not let them. I will hold this house up with my own two hands if I have to. And even still, I will pull her from its depths.

"Astrid!" I call again.

The floorboards groan beneath my feet—or are they Astrid's groans?

I propel myself forward and sidestep a jutting nail. There's a door, just off this room that I think was a kitchen, but when I rip it open, it's an empty closet. I try the next door a couple feet away, but there's only a cracked toilet. Half a porcelain sink.

Passing the bottom of the staircase that bisects the cabin, I enter another room. Moving through the space like I'm wading through wreckage, I dodge a couch without cushions, a paint-splattered saw-horse. As I round the corner of the wall that separates kitchen from living space, I find one more door, carved into the hollow beneath the rear of the staircase.

My breath hitches, but I yank it open and surge ahead, nearly tripping over what's on the landing inside.

A cooler. A toolbox.

A pair of black gloves.

For a moment, my body hardens. It wants so badly to be stone. But no. No. I kick the boxes and gloves aside and clomp down a set of stairs. "Astrid!" I shout, but I'm halfway down before I realize I'm heading into a dark, gaping pit. I look toward the open door at the top, search for a light switch, but there's only a fixture without a bulb, its pull chain dangling uselessly. I scramble back up the steps, root around in the toolbox until I find a thin flashlight. I flick it on, shake it to try to sharpen its weak beam, but when I pound down the stairs again, it's enough to show me that—my heart clamps shut—she isn't here.

I wave the light around. I have to be missing something. But all I see is a narrow window, so covered in grime the glass is opaque. There are layers of dust and dirt. Spiderwebs. A stack of lumber in the corner. There's no chain. No mattress. No Astrid. No person at all but me.

Does Cooper have her somewhere else? I skim the flashlight along the floor, as if I could find a map to Astrid in all its cracks.

What I find, instead, is familiarity.

I take a couple steps back. Then I crouch on the floor, imagine sliding a marble across the room, listening for its click in a corner we could barely even see. And yes—yes, it fits. So far, the basement matches the one I remembered. When I trace my eyes down the staircase in the center, I gasp. The bottom step—it has a crooked edge. It's shaped like a trapezoid.

This is where we were kept. I know it like I knew Astrid's face as soon as I saw it on the news.

I shudder as a chill climbs my spine.

I wasn't returned to the woods twenty years ago. I was in them the whole time.

My stomach quakes, but I swallow down the threat of bile. Whirling the flashlight around, I take in details that have been out of my grasp. The rough texture of the concrete walls. An alcove in one corner. I can even look up now, like I couldn't in my memories, and see the red door and—

The door isn't red. It's brown.

I creep up the stairs toward it, the boards shaky beneath my feet. Sitting down on the landing, I try to look closer at the paint. See if it's just an old, discolored red. Like blood that's long since dried.

Leaning in, I hold the beam of the flashlight steady, but the color doesn't change. It's cracked, nearly chipping, maybe even faded—but if anything, it's only a lighter shade of the dark brown it surely once was.

I press my forehead into the heels of my hands. Feel my heart pump hard but slow. I was wrong. This isn't it. But a second ago, I was so sure. So blissfully, terrifyingly sure. And Astrid isn't here. So she could be anywhere. Exactly the same as before.

I smack my hand against the door. Then I smack it again. And again and again, until my palm vibrates with pain. Only then do I look at my hands—how empty they are, how incapable of saving anyone—and see a fleck of color. I bend closer, shine the flashlight onto my palm. Stare at a chip of brown paint.

I look at the door. Focus on its cracks. Its little fissures that could easily flake off. I dig my nails into one of them, uncertain at first, but then I scratch and pull until the color splinters. When my fingers come away with a dime-sized layer, I see for sure that that's all this is: a layer. That beneath the brown paint is something else. I grab the flashlight, point it toward the door—and yes. Yes.

It's red.

Red like a firetruck. Like the cross on an ambulance. Red like an open wound.

It only takes a second for my heart to catch up. It pounds so loud I hear it like a fist knocking against the wood. But now I hear another sound too. Distant but approaching.

The crunch of tires. The rumble of an engine.

A beat of silence in which I hold my breath.

A car door slamming shut.

I act without thinking. Close the basement door. Turn off the flashlight. Curl into myself.

Seconds pulse by. Then hinges squeak. Footsteps thud.

"Hello?"

I'd know his voice anywhere.

He's come through the screen at the back, like I did, and he's tracing my steps toward the front of the cabin.

I've left my scent all over this place. I've always been so easy to catch.

"Brierley? Are you here?"

I pinch my lips together. Hold my hand over my nose and mouth.

"You shouldn't be," Cooper says. "I didn't want you to see this yet."

The whole cabin seems to shake with the weight of his steps. But then he pauses, and everything goes still.

"Are you up there?" he asks. "Hang on, I'm coming to get you."

When his footsteps thump again, they sound so close it's as if we're in this basement together. But then the ceiling rattles, dust sprinkles onto my head, and I realize he's above me now, climbing the stairs to the second floor—the one place I didn't check.

I breathe only once before making a break for it. I swing open the door and run toward the back of the cabin. I don't care about the noise I'm making. As I hurl myself through the screen, I know he's heard me, I know he's in pursuit. But I have a head start and I'm almost inside my car. I nearly burn myself on the scorching metal of his truck, pulled so close beside my driver's side, but I make it behind the wheel, turn the keys, and slam it into reverse.

That's when I see him rounding the corner of the cabin—when it's too late for him to snatch me up. I push the gas pedal to the floor, whoosh backward along the path that's barely visible through the trees. And all the while, I don't watch his face or his eyes, or even my rearview mirror. I stare at his tattoo, dangerous and disturbing as it's ever been, but becoming smaller and smaller as I back away.

When I whip my car onto the main road, I reach into my cupholder for my phone. It's not there, of course—I left Ted's house with only my keys—and anyway, it wouldn't work here. But I have to call the police. Have to tell them to look for Astrid on the second floor of the cabin.

I'm driving so fast I make it back to Ted's in less than two minutes. Then I spurt from the car, race into the house and up the stairs. I only stop when I see that the phone isn't on its base in the hall, and I remember that I threw it at Ted's back, seething with an anger I'd never indulged before.

Ted's office door is open, but he isn't inside. I search for the phone, but it's not on the floor where it must have landed. It's not on Ted's desk or chair. I pick up Astrid's book, let it clatter onto the floor. Pick up a pile of jacketless hardcovers and let them fall there too. Now I notice a sheet of paper that bulges on top of a stack, and as I pluck it up, I uncover the phone.

The paper is warm, as if its words have just been branded onto it. As if it's been ripped from the typewriter so fast it generated a spark. Or maybe it's the heat of this room, closing around me like before.

I turn on the phone. Press 9, then 1. Then a phrase on the paper hooks my eyes.

The subject is thirty-two years old, but she still behaves as an adolescent.

The subject. I've seen this kind of language before, whenever he would read back his notes to me as I sat in the interview chair. He was looking for praise, I think. Admiration. Adoration. But so was I.

She is unwilling to reconcile the truth of her memories with her greatest fear from childhood. She still requires the delusion of forgetting. But why?

The phone beeps twice, then returns to a dial tone. I let it drone for another moment before turning it off.

The subject, even when presented with a nearly exact reenactment of the Fear Climax, generates other hypotheses. She does not accept the answer even when it's staring her in the face. Perhaps the lack of skin disturbance in the exposed area was a factor in her avoidance. Perhaps the reenactment can be performed again, and this time, the glove will be dragged down farther, until it reveals a bit of rash.

A bit of rash? His psoriasis? But why would that—

My heart punches my sternum. I hear, instead of feel, myself moan. Then I drop the phone. Bring my hand to my mouth.

Perhaps only then will she remember what really happened.

There's a violent churning deep inside my gut. Because—because the handle snagged on the glove. And as the man worked to detach the metal from the fabric . . .

The reenactment will be tried again, as soon as the subject returns.

The glove was tugged down even more. And I saw it then—I see it now, scratching my wrist as the memory blazes back—a section of skin so red and raw, so hardened by scales, it could only belong to one man.

I screamed when I saw it.

I scream as I remember it now. I scream as I scratch and scratch and scratch.

It was Ted. The man. The kidnapper. The monster in the mask.

It was always my father.

"Damn it, Fern."

As soon as I hear his voice in the doorway, my throat closes. My scream snuffs out.

I whirl around to face him. He's leaning against the doorframe. The gloves are still on his hands. His eyes flick from my face to the paper I've been reading and back to my face again.

"I was hoping," he says, "you'd remember on your own."

twenty-one

I t was you?"

Even now, it comes out as a question.

Ted shakes his head. "The fact that you still have to ask that . . ."

He pulls at the glove on his right hand, finger by finger, until it slips off. When he drops it onto the floor, I stare at the patch of red on the back of his wrist. Red like a wound. Red like a door.

"We'll have to explore that," he says, "this delay in your understanding." He tugs the fingertips of the other glove. Discards that one, too. "But of course it was me. Of course it was. And really—it's mind-boggling that it took you *reading it in my notes* to see it."

He steps forward, plucks the paper from my hand, sets it down on the desk. Without something to hold on to, I'm dizzy. Untethered. My knees buckle and I fall into the chair behind me. Not the interview one this time. His.

Ted furrows his brow at me. Opens his mouth. Closes it. Turns his head to look at the interview chair, then shrugs and sits down. He has no wheels with which to swivel toward me, but he leans forward as far as he can. I see every scale on his skin.

"Maybe we should start there," he says. "Let's figure out why you didn't put it together. It made sense when you were younger. It's not uncommon for dissociative amnesia to occur so a child can maintain an attachment to a person on whom they're dependent. If a parent significantly frightens them, say, then the child's mind might simply push out the memory in order to protect itself. But you're not a child anymore. So it's noteworthy that your mind would continue to block you from seeing the most logical answer."

He opens his hand, begins ticking off his fingers. "You read the memoir. You and I have done countless Experiments together. I re-enacted the Fear Climax, and yet you still didn't recognize—or even suspect—that it was me." He lets his hand fall into his lap. "Where did you go just now? Who did you think it was?"

Somehow my mouth moves. Somehow it whispers: "Cooper."

"Cooper? He would have been a *kid* when this happened! I'd be offended if it weren't so laughable. You thought of a teenager before you thought of me. I don't . . ." He shakes his head again. "I think anyone else would have figured it out, Fern. A long time ago."

"But."

"But what?"

Now my voice pours out of me, but I can't even feel it on my tongue. "You've been lying. You told me you filed a report. That you had no idea who took me. How was I—"

"Uh-uh," Ted says. "I never said I had no idea who took you. I said I wanted you to figure out who did."

I stare at him. Unable to blink. "You wanted me to figure out it was you," I say, "because it was . . . an Experiment."

"Of course it was!" Ted beams at me.

Seconds pass, but his grin lingers. As if he's waiting for me, too, to break into a smile.

"How . . ." I start. "How could you do that to me?"

Ted waves off the question. "Oh, it had nothing to do with you.

Not at first, anyway. You came into it later, yes, but initially it was all about—"

"Astrid."

As I speak her name, I'm tugged toward another thought, one that's unraveling so quickly it's almost a blur. But then I hear him finish his sentence—"Brennan"—and I lose the thread completely.

"Brennan?" I ask. "You and Brennan . . . did it together? The kidnapping? The—"

"What? No, of course not."

"Then what are you saying?"

Ted throws his hands into the air. "You should have seen how smug he was!"

I wait for more, but he offers me nothing. "When?"

"That time he stayed with us. Those two insufferable weeks. It was right on the heels of his latest book deal, this time for some drivel about child abductions. And as he's standing there, going on and on about his ungodly contract, this abomination he's going to unleash onto the world, he has the audacity to criticize *my* work."

Ted scratches his neck so hard I almost check his nails for blood.

"It was right here in this room," he continues. "The unbelievable nerve of that man. He grabs a stack of notes off my desk, does this dramatic pause like he's gunning for an Oscar, and then he looks me right in the eyes and says, 'Ted, these games were fun when we were just kids in grad school, but if you ever want to be taken seriously, you're going to have to do some real work.'"

Ted waits for me to react, but my face is stone.

"Can you believe that? He's the one playing Connect the Dots with his research and he says *I'm* in the kiddie pool?" He shakes his head. "'I'm saying this as a friend,' he told me. That's how he framed it. And that was it. That's when I got the idea."

He shoots forward in his chair. "It didn't actually start as an Experiment, see. It started as a way to take Brennan down. To shatter that fraudulent foundation of his supposed success and watch him flail around in the rubble."

I stare at him. At this stranger who's as alien to me as he was when he was wearing the mask. "You're not making any sense," I say.

Ted chuffs out a breath. "He was writing a book about child abductions. So I staged one. I decided to take someone from Foster, where he was doing an event, so the police would connect it back to him once I planted some evidence."

My throat feels dry as cement. It scrapes as I speak. "You staged a . . . You mean you planned to frame Brennan?"

"I suppose that's one way of looking at it."

"But why?"

As Ted exhales, there's something besides impatience in the sound. Something fragile. Like the air is disappearing before it even leaves his mouth.

"I'm ashamed to admit this," he says, "but until that 'real work' comment, I'd actually held out hope that everything he'd done after grad school—all the diluted case studies and frivolous experiments— was just a way to gain a platform. And that once he had that, he'd introduce the world to *me* and *my* ideas, and then we'd resume our work—the *real* real work—together."

Ted leans back. Crosses his arms. "But then he said that to me. And I knew it was over." His eyes bore into mine. "Even now, I can't help but think back to the man Brennan used to be. You have no idea, that kind of betrayal, having someone abandon you in pursuit of their own glory."

My eyes water. My throat swells.

"And okay, I'll admit," Ted adds, "I didn't have it completely planned out. I was in a rage, I wasn't thinking clearly, I only wanted to see Brennan lose his sham of an empire. I wasn't sure *how* I was going to pin it on him, or what evidence I was going to use exactly, because I had to move quickly. His event was the next afternoon, and I was busy enough procuring the drugs from the chemistry lab and getting the cabin ready."

"The cabin in the woods," I mutter.

Ted smiles. "They used it in a movie once, you know. This was a few years later. I took you to see it, tried to trigger a response, and you were certainly petrified—but no memories surfaced. It was so . . . disappointing."

His eyes go distant.

"Anyway," he says. "Finding someone to take was simple. I just drove around Foster! And three streets from the bookstore, right around the time Brennan would be leaving it, I saw this girl with flaming red hair. Astrid, as you know—though I didn't have a clue who she was at the time. Just that she was all alone. Walking down the road." He laughs. "She never even saw me coming! And I figured, once I had her in the cabin, I would hammer out the rest of it—how to get the police to look at Brennan and all that. But then I saw the marvelous opportunity I'd created, and the plan had to change."

He stops, in the middle of the story, and from the glimmer in his eyes, I see that he's doing it on purpose. He wants me to ask the questions. To be the person in the interviewer's chair. His favorite part of his work was always when he revealed the Experiment. When he recalibrated our sense of reality. When he grinned and guffawed, giddy with his own brilliance. He's had to wait two decades for this moment, and he's relishing it now. He wants to make it last as long as it can.

"Changed how?" I ask—because he's taught me, so well, to make him happy.

"I was going about it all wrong! Brennan had pushed my buttons, and I'd gotten caught up in destroying him, but once it was just me and the girl, I saw things clearly. What I'd actually done was create a marvelous Experiment. A way to observe acute fear over a prolonged period of time. So instead of breaking Brennan, I decided I would beat him. Because in beating him, see, I would break him, too."

My hands tremble in my lap. "But what did you think you were going to do with your research? Write a book about terrorizing someone in a basement? Who would publish that? How did you think you'd even get someone to read it without calling the cops?"

"Oh, come on. These are your questions? Obviously, I wouldn't write it in a way that would implicate myself in the abduction. I'd frame it as information I gathered through interviews. Change the girl's name and claim I was keeping the victim anonymous. People love that kind of thing. A secret identity. A person in a mask."

"So why *me* then?" I blurt—because I am trying, so hard, not to picture the welder's mask. Not to imagine him opening the window in it and showing me his face.

Ted stretches out his legs. Crosses one ankle over the other. "I didn't *plan* to put you in the basement, but— Well, you read the memoir, you know she stopped eating. And clearly I wasn't out to kill her or anything, so I had to do *something*. I couldn't give up and return her either. Not when I'd already invested two weeks in studying her. So it was an act of desperation, really, bringing you down there with her. You were supposed to provide a bit of company, a bit of comfort. I assumed you'd be a calming and soothing presence to the girl. Only . . ."

He stops. Scratches. "You weren't calm at all. You were terrified."

"Because I'd been kidnapped."

"But I thought you would know that the danger wasn't real, that the man behind the mask was *me*. How could you not? We'd been doing Experiments together your entire life! And now here was someone scaring you so thoroughly you couldn't even speak, and yet you carried on as if you had no idea it was me. Really, Fern, it's almost insulting."

He shakes his head, apparently embarrassed by my ignorance. And on top of everything else, I'm embarrassed by it, too. Never mind that his Experiments relied on me *not* figuring it out. Never mind that he lived for his own confessions. I should have caught whiffs of the truth as soon as I started to remember, as soon as he leaned in, so hungry to know how much I recalled.

Thirty-two years as Ted's daughter, and I haven't learned anything at all.

"Anyway," he says, "once you were down there, the Sullivan girl was no longer so stubborn or withdrawn. It was like the act of taking care of someone"—he pauses, appears puzzled—"superseded all else. And soon, she ate because she wanted *you* to eat, drank because . . ."

His eyes fog over. "It was fascinating," he adds, his voice quieting. "I'd never seen such a thing."

In the silence that follows, I think of Saul Brierley. Ted's bruises and welts. His messy blueprint for parenting.

Clearing his throat, Ted continues, "Having you there turned out to be the perfect move. I could keep studying the other girl, I could note how her interest in your well-being muted her fear response, and in the end, I could interview you in ways I'd never be able to interview her. Imagine trying to conduct an interview from behind a mask?"

He laughs—three explosive bursts of sound—then quickly sobers.

"Except you screamed your head off the day you realized it was me, and even though I let you go, let you run on home, you wouldn't stop your hysterics. And then you just"—he lifts his hands and shoulders, an annoyed, exaggerated shrug—"forgot the whole thing."

As his eyes glaze, I see him remembering how I failed him.

"Which was fine," he adds. "It was . . . fine. I was disappointed at first, but as I told you earlier, your repression opened up possibilities for more compelling research. I didn't even care about the other girl anymore. I returned her a couple days later. That way, I could watch you around the clock."

Returned. It's the word the media has always used—*Astrid Sullivan was returned onto a curb, blindfolded and drugged, in her own neighborhood*—but it's only now that I hear how cold it is. Ted returned her. Like a shirt that didn't fit.

"But a lot of good that did," he scoffs. "You turned out to be useless. And that brilliant Experiment . . . it was all for nothing, in the end." He licks his lips. "Until now."

I still can't believe it. I'm trying to tread through this unbearable truth. Keep my head above its surface. But my body is exhausted, and I see that there isn't a bottom to the pool of Ted's cruelty and greed. All this time, I've been swimming in such toxic waters.

Ted indulges my silence for a moment. Then he stands. "Okay, get up," he says. "Now that you know everything, let's do this right. I'll ask the questions, you get in your chair."

When I don't budge, he grabs me by the arm—not hard exactly, but it brings me back to that basement. How, as I screamed, he hooked his fingers around my bicep, squeezed as if to wring the sound right out of me. I remember that now. Not as Astrid's words on the page, but as marks he left on my skin. I can feel them, all these years later, throbbing.

"Come on, Fern. We've wasted so much time already. Don't you want to be a good girl and help?"

It's the wrong word: *girl*. The wrong adjective: *good*. I do not want to be good—not Ted's kind, at least. Because when Ted says *good*, he means *pliant*. When Ted says *good*, he means *docile*.

He means *scared*.

"No," I say.

Ted grunts and drops my arm. Nudges the chair with his hip, sends its wheels skittering a few inches backward. Standing between me and the desk, he faces his typewriter, and as soon as his fingers move, I hear the first clack.

I refuse to hear a second.

"Stop it!" I scream. I jump from the chair and push him aside. I grab the typewriter and raise it over my head. I'm strong enough to hold it high as I stare at his bewildered face, and I'm strong enough to drop it. Hurl it onto the floor so hard that when it hits the wood, several keys break free.

We stare at the ruin. For a long while, neither of us moves.

A screech sounds from downstairs—the screen door opening. In a second, it thwacks shut, and a voice calls out to us. "Hello?"

"We're up here, Mara," Ted says, but his eyes are still on the broken machine at our feet.

Mara talks as she climbs the stairs, her words reaching us before we can see her. "Great job picking me up at the airport, Ted."

I had no idea she was getting home today, but it's just like Ted to know it and forget. Or know it and not care.

"I had to take a cab," she continues, "all the way from Logan! I gave the driver your credit card number. Tipped him real nice, too. And don't think that just because—"

She appears in the doorway, her face shadowed by a sunhat. "Fern," she says. Then she looks at the floor. "What's going on? What happened?"

"Ted happened," I say.

I'm about to explain it to her, to expose this impossible story, tell her the truth about the man we shared a house with for so many years. But she sighs before I can. Adjusts the strap of her cotton dress.

"So your Experiment worked?" she asks Ted. "Bringing her back here? Telling her you were moving?" She looks at me, her eyes wary. "You remember it all now?"

My mouth falls open. "You *knew*?"

Then my mind scrambles. Even after everything, even with the keys of Ted's typewriter scattered across the floor, I'm still desperate for a loophole. A place where this story veers off and I find my way out.

"But I . . . I talked to you," I say. "The day I drove here. I asked you if I knew Astrid Sullivan, and you acted like I was crazy!"

"Yes," Mara says. "That wasn't great of me, dear. But I knew Ted would have a fit if I interfered with the Experiment."

"So you sat back and let him *do* this? And back then—you let him *kidnap me*? Kidnap another girl? I can't—"

"Believe me, I never loved that," Mara cuts in. She puts her hand in the air, closes her eyes. "And it made it very difficult to love Ted. Why do you think we're not together anymore?"

For a moment, I only gape at her. Then I breathe in. Force myself to exhale. "Then why didn't you stop it?"

"I did. In my own way, at least. Afterward, when you didn't remember, Ted wanted to tell you everything, but—"

"That's true," Ted says. "You know me, I always reveal the Experiment."

Mara cuts a glance at him. "But I saw what he had done to you. And I couldn't let him put you through that again. I made him keep silent, in order to protect you."

The air pauses in my open mouth, going neither in nor out. "The time for protection," I say, "had come and gone. Why didn't you protect me when he *took* me?"

Mara sighs again, but this one is heavier than the other. "Ted said it was an important step in his work. He's always respected my needs as an artist, even when he didn't like it, so how could I interfere with what he needed to do? A person's work is their life, Fern. It's who they are."

My stomach tightens. I put my hand on my belly, low enough to cradle the life inside.

"But you were *parents*, too," I say. "Didn't that count for anything? Wasn't that as important as"—I swing my eyes toward Ted—"as beating Brennan, or"—turn back to Mara—"making art?"

"We never planned to have a child," Mara says. "But I ended up pregnant, and we decided to keep you anyway. You're alive today because we made that choice. So I think we did okay by you."

"*Okay* by me?" My pulse spasms in my neck. "You were . . . you are"—and I say it now, finally—"terrible parents. Terrible people! I could have *died* while you were neglecting me."

"Hey." Ted's voice is a single clap, and my head snaps toward him. "You can't begin to know what a terrible parent is. I never laid a hand on you. I never—"

"You dragged me up the stairs by my hair!"

That stops him for a second. But not nearly long enough.

"You were never in real danger," he says. "I wasn't going to kill you. But me—there were times I wasn't sure my father would stop. There was one night I actually hoped he would kill me. He cracked my ribs and punctured a lung. I couldn't even breathe. You want to talk about pain?"

"You dragged me up the stairs by my hair," I repeat, each word so slow it becomes its own sentence. "You tied me up with ropes. That wasn't an Experiment. It was abuse. And who knows what you did to Astrid! You probably—"

My breath catches, cuts off the thought before I can finish it.

"Oh my god," I say. And I can't believe I've gone this long without drawing the most obvious conclusion. Somehow, I'm still so slow, I still don't get it—and while I've been stammering and processing and throwing a typewriter around the room, she's been waiting for me to save her.

"Where is she?" I demand.

"Where's who, dear?" Mara asks.

"Astrid! He has her!" I point to Ted and he takes a step back from my finger.

"Whoa, wait a minute, I do not have that woman," he says.

"Of course you do! You took her to trigger me into remembering."

"No," Ted says. "I saw that she was missing again, and I called you back to see if her disappearance triggered anything. Just like I told you."

"You've told me nothing but lies!"

"Not this time," Mara says. "He's telling the truth." She narrows her eyes at him. "Or was there more to this Experiment than you told me, Ted?"

Ted laughs. "Of course there wasn't. Why would I need to take that woman?"

"I don't believe you," I say.

I will never believe him again.

Pushing past Mara in the doorway, I run down the hall, opening every door I pass—linen closet, bathroom—even though I know those won't be the ones she's behind. I rush down the stairs, round the corner, spring toward the basement and run down those stairs, too. Pulling the string on the lightbulb at the bottom, I look around, whip my head from side to side. There's the washer and dryer, stacks of old boxes—but Astrid isn't here.

When I race back up the stairs, Mara and Ted are waiting for me on the first floor. "Where is she?" I ask through my teeth.

"He doesn't have her," Mara says. "Trust me, Fern. I can't speak for Ted, but—whatever you might think of me, I'm not heartless. I wouldn't let him do that to her again."

"You just said his work comes first! And he thinks that Astrid is part of his work."

Mara shakes her head. "Listen to me. I saw her only once while she was here, the day he returned her. She was unconscious in his trunk, all curled up, and she was—she was so pretty, dear. Like a piece of art. But she was fragile, too. I saw how easily he might have broken her. And that's what she was, lying in his car like that. This beautiful, broken thing."

Her eyes shine. She clears her throat. "And I told him," she continues, "that he was never to do something like that again. Not even for the sake of his work. He promised me that he wouldn't, and I thought the promise would be enough, but sometimes I would think of her—that beautiful, broken thing—and . . . well. You know how things are between me and Ted now."

I stare at her without seeing. I don't care why she and Ted broke up. I care about something else she said. *Beautiful, broken thing.* The phrase resonates, like a string plucked in my mind. But I can't remember where I've heard it before.

Then I realize: I haven't. It's just similar to another of Mara's phrases—Exquisite Fragments. The title of the project that brought her some success. Named for beautiful, broken things of a different kind.

I picture her Break Room, the pieces of pottery glued to the floor, a mosaic of pain that Mara stepped across, week after week, in bare and blistered feet, just to glue more of it down. I picture myself, a few days earlier, trying to open the door as we packed her studio. I twisted the knob but nothing happened. Ted told me it was locked.

"Mara, give me your keys," I say.

She blinks at me, and I hold out my palm.

"Now!" I shout.

She walks to the front door. Picks up one of her bags. After digging around for a moment, she extracts a set of keys.

I hurry past her, plucking them from her fingers. Ted follows close behind me. "What's this about?" he asks.

I ready the key while I jog toward the studio. It's the blue one. I know that much about my mother—the color she painted the key to the room where she spent so much of my life.

The studio is boiling when I burst inside, and I pray he's left her something—a fan, a cooler of ice, water instead of Sprite.

"Fern, what are you doing?"

I feel them both at my back as I insert the key into the lock. I expect it to stick as I turn it, one more obstacle before I find her, but it moves easily, and I hear a click.

I think only this as I open the door: Astrid is not a beautiful, broken thing. Beautiful, yes, but not broken. She held her own against Ted in ways I never could. She's the kind of strong I'm going to teach myself to be. The kind of strong my child deserves. And she is not—

Here.

She isn't here.

The floor is sharp as it ever was. All these shattered, jagged pieces. But there's no woman crouched among them. No face turning to mine after all this time. No eyes widening as she recognizes the girl I was in the person I am now.

She isn't here to see that I came back for her. That my mind tried to bury her, but I dug through everything, even the packed soil of my own fear, to find her.

I slump to the floor. Lay my cheek against a fragment that jabs against bone.

Women who disappear. Women who can't be found.

"I don't have her, Fern," Ted says.

And the fragment is wet now. And I'm just another piece that Mara can glue down.

twenty-two

Now I know why the woods have always haunted me. It was my body's way of remembering what my mind could not. As I pass them, my stomach whirls once again—but is the nausea from fear, or knowledge? For someone like me, is there any difference between the two?

I grabbed my phone from my room and left my parents. Ted and Mara stood in the open doorway of the studio, and I felt their eyes on me—curious, but not too concerned—as I got behind the wheel. Seems like half this trip to Cedar has been me speeding down the driveway. I wonder when my leaving will stick. Even this time, I'll have to return for my things.

But first, I have to help Astrid. The trees are rushing by, and as soon as I get a signal on my phone, I'm going to call the police. Ted has her—I know he does; who else could it possibly be?—and the cops will have to take him in, question him until he breaks. It probably won't take much. He is crazy enough—and I mean that word, *crazy*, even though I work in a field where we do not use it lightly—to want to boast about his Experiment, if only allowed an audience.

The woods darken this road on an otherwise sunny day, and my phone still says No Service. Maybe I should have used the landline.

But then I would have had to stay longer, and I don't believe I can ever share space with them again.

I press harder on the gas, and in a couple minutes, the trees thin out. When I pass some houses and a gas station, I know I've made it. I'm about to command my Bluetooth to call 911, but then I think of someone who needs to hear from me first.

"Call Rita," I say. She answers on the second ring.

"Rita, this is Fern, please don't hang up."

"This is *who*?"

"Fern Doug—oh. We met the other day. You thought I was Sarah, but don't hang up—please—I know who has Astrid and I'm gonna call the police. I just want you to know it's gonna be okay. We're going to find her."

I wait through her stunned silence. "What?" she finally says.

"I know who took her twenty years ago. And I know he has her now, too, but I don't know where. I'm about to call the police, I just thought you should know, first, that everything's gonna be all right."

"No," Rita says, and her voice is thick and warbling. "Please, you can't call the police."

I squint at the road ahead. "Why not?"

"Because. I can't . . . Just. Don't do that. Please. Come here immediately, and whatever you do, don't call them. Things will be so much worse for Astrid if you do."

My heart ticks faster. "What are you talking about?"

"I can't say it, they could—"

There's a pause. It stretches on for a few seconds, and my chest throbs. "Rita, what's going on?"

"You have to trust me," she says. "Can you come here? Right now? Please."

"Yes," I say, and I'm already jabbing at my GPS, pulling up a previous destination. "Yes, I'm on my way."

The front door opens before I'm out of my car. Rita pokes her head out, scans up and down the street, then waves me inside. She's rattled, her eyes skittering back and forth like an animal looking for predators. I rush past her, into the house, and hear the door shut behind me. The dead bolt clicks like the cocking of a gun.

When I turn toward her, I almost jump. Her panic is gone, as if she wiped it off her face as soon as she closed the door. Now there's a cool hardness to her features, and a flicker at the corner of her lips.

"I wish you'd left it alone," she says. She takes a step toward me. "But here we are, and I guess we have no choice."

Her voice is icy. It sounds the way a blade looks when it flashes silver in the light.

As Rita moves closer to me, away from the door, my phone rings in my back pocket.

"Don't answer that," she snaps, and her tone freezes me in place.

I know it's Eric calling. I left him a voice mail on my way up, told him I was heading to Astrid's and I'd try him again when I left. But there's no way he'd wait around for me to call him back. He loves me, he's worried about me, and at least he knows where I was headed.

Women who disappear.

"I have something to show you," Rita says, and she's so close to me I can smell her. Her skin has a flowery sourness. Like perfume sprayed over sweat.

She stretches out her arm. She's going to grab me. But when I close my eyes, I don't feel her grip. Instead I hear something behind me, and I turn, and step back, and watch as Rita pushes the hutch that holds only a wedding photo. She slides the furniture away so that it blocks the entrance to the stairwell, the kitchen, any other way out.

Women who disappear.

When she steps aside, I look at the section of wall she's exposed.

There's a door in it. Just a few feet high. Not far beneath the ballerina painting.

"Okay," Rita says, and she knocks twice on the wall.

The door pops open, and I see only darkness. And then I see red. Hair like flames in a child's drawing. Hair so bright I wonder if it's fire.

The hair moves, and now there's a forehead, a face. Now there's an entire body coming out of this hole in the wall. It's a woman, standing, stretching her limbs, turning her face to the light. I notice her eyes first—green like oak leaves—and then her smattering of freckles. The one that's darker than the rest, beneath her brow.

"Astrid," I whisper.

Her eyes study me. They squint a little, even as they fill with tears. "Oh my god," she says. "Lily."

She crosses the room in only three strides. Gathers me into an embrace. Holds me so tightly I can barely breathe. And suddenly it isn't fear that freezes me. It's shock. Even my mind feels stalled. I can't process what I'm seeing, what this means. I can only listen to her voice, nearly the same one I heard in my dreams.

"Rita said you claimed to be Lily," she says, "but I didn't want to believe it, you're not the first who— Oh my god, I can't believe you're alive."

She steps back, holds her arms out straight as she continues to clutch my shoulders. "You're alive," she says again.

She stares at me like I'm a miracle. But she's the one who looks holy. Her cheeks are glowing; her hair falls in perfect, angelic curls. My eyes shift up and down to take her in. She's wearing white shorts, a billowy white blouse—both of which are pristine. No dirt. No rips or tears. No signs that she's been struggling at all.

"You," I say, but the word trembles. "You were here? The whole time?"

Even as I ask it, I know it's an echo of a question I've asked before. To a man who stood outside his house all night. Watching me panic. Letting me think he was hurt or dead.

"The whole time!" Astrid confirms.

I register the blast of the AC on my skin. The whole house shakes with it. Or maybe just me.

"That's—" I start. But I don't have the word, yet, to describe what I'm realizing she's done. She faked her disappearance. She wasn't missing this time at all.

I stare at her freckle, but it doesn't soothe me right now. Instead, it makes my stomach slosh, my mouth taste sour. I try to take a step away from her, but her grip on me is strong.

"I'm sorry if I'm gawking at you," she says. "I'm just so thrilled to see you. Here, have a seat. You look a little shaken up."

She leads me to the couch, where she sits us down. Hooks one arm around me and uses the other to smooth my hair. Separating her fingers, she makes them into a comb, and I remember this feeling. The sensation of being cared for. I close my eyes for a moment. Almost lose myself to the tingle on my scalp. But then I look at Astrid—this not-missing woman—and her fingers feel like bugs.

Rita sits in the chair I occupied last time. The chair from which I stared at the ballerina painting that's behind me now. And that entire time, not far beneath that painting—there was a door. There was a woman behind it.

"I'm sure this is shocking to you," Rita says.

Astrid nods beside me. Her eyes stick to the side of my face like leeches.

"But you have to understand," Rita continues. "We've been trying to have a baby for so long."

"I have some fertility issues," Astrid chimes in. "And poor Rita—I know this has been hard for her, but I *have* to be the one who carries our baby. When I came out to my parents, one of the first things they said—right after all the Catholic tears about my 'sinful lifestyle'—was: 'Now you'll never have a child.' As if I'm defective because I'm gay. Or less of a woman somehow. They're dead now, but . . ." She shrugs. "I'm still trying to prove them wrong."

"Yes," Rita says. "She is." Her voice is tight. "So we've gone through several rounds of IVF, and . . ." She closes her eyes. Shakes her head. "We burned through the advance for Astrid's book so quickly, and sales were only okay to start—not even close to what everyone was expecting, given Astrid's name."

She leans forward. Elbows on her knees. Eyes latched to mine. "We had to do something. We needed to jump-start sales so that royalties could kick in. Because—you heard her—Astrid's hell-bent on carrying our baby. And we won't be able to afford another round of IVF without the extra money."

"So," Astrid says, "we staged my disappearance. We thought it might generate more interest in the book. And we were right." She presses closer to me, even as I try to inch away. She hisses in my ear, "It's *number five* now."

But she said *staged*—the same word Ted used to describe what he did. Acid simmers in my stomach. It crawls up my esophagus until I can taste it on my tongue.

"And it hasn't been so bad," Astrid says. "Whenever the police or reporters come over, I hide in the storage space under the staircase." She removes her hand from my hair to gesture toward the tiny open door. "No one's ever even suspected."

"It's true," Rita says. "I mean, you were sitting five feet away from her the other day and you had no idea."

"It's not like I love being in an enclosed space," Astrid says. "I'm a little claustrophobic. You are, too, I'm sure. But it's roomier than it looks from the outside. And I don't know, I've got pillows and a book and a flashlight, and . . . it's kind of like a fort in there." She stops. Looks haunted for a second. "Remember when I made us a fort in the basement?"

I shake my head, even though it already feels like it's spinning. "I . . ." My throat grates as I speak. "I repressed a lot of what happened."

Astrid puts her fingers under my chin. Pulls my head to the side so I have no choice but to look her straight in her eyes. "You don't remember?" She seems almost wounded. As if our time in the basement was worth holding on to.

"Some things," I manage. "Your freckle. The marbles."

Astrid replies with a solemn nod. "You were so scared. All the time. And hell, I was, too, but . . . it was clear you needed me to be strong for you." She flashes a quick smile that looks like it hurts. "So I was." Her face goes slack. "That man was a coward, anyway. Some asshole who got lost on the way to a costume party."

I jolt at the mention of Ted. Then I blurt it out: "I know who he was. I know who took us."

Her eyes grow big. Her brow pulls her freckle up. "Rita said you said that." She swallows. "Who is he?"

I hold off for as long as I can, glancing between Astrid and Rita, both of whom are leaning closer to me—Rita in her chair, Astrid beside me, safe, not missing, her breath a little shaky as it breaks against my cheek.

"My father," I finally say.

And then I tell the rest of it, too. Who he is. What he wants. How he's willing, I know now, to do absolutely anything for the admiration he believes he deserves. Tears sting my eyes as I speak, as I recognize the horror in the story I'm telling. As I remember again and again that it isn't a story at all. It's the truth. It's my life.

"I'm going to tell the police," I assure them when I'm done. Though maybe I'm assuring myself. On the way here, I was desperate to call them because I figured Ted still had Astrid. But now that I know he doesn't, I feel a twinge in my stomach, picturing him limp and alone behind bars.

How could you do this to me? I can hear him asking.

But that's my question. To him. And it's one I will probably be wondering until the day I die.

"It doesn't matter that he's my dad," I say. "He deserves to go to prison."

Rita and Astrid are mirror images of each other: mouths slightly open, brows furrowed with horror as they try to understand. And when they speak, they mirror each other as well.

"No!" they both say.

"What?"

"No," Rita repeats. "You can't go to the police."

I gape at her. "Why not?"

She said the same thing on the phone, but sitting here with Astrid, who was not a victim this time, but certainly once was, I can't understand why they wouldn't leap at the chance to put the man—the monster—my father—behind bars.

"It'll ruin our reentry plan," Rita says.

"Reentry plan?"

"We're gonna re-create the way Astrid was returned twenty years ago. She's gonna be found in town, blindfolded and sedated. She's not gonna know anything about her abductor, of course, just that he was wearing the same thing as last time, and that he kept her in a basement again."

I flick my eyes back and forth between the two of them. "But—"

"Please," Astrid says. "Please don't report your father."

She wipes the tears off my face, closes her eyes, and presses her forehead to mine. Her skin nearly singes me, but I let her do it.

"God, I can't believe he did that to you," she says. "I'm— I don't even know what to say. It's so horrifying. And disgusting. It doesn't even seem real to me. He's always been this faceless person. This guy that . . . might come back for me someday. God, I've spent most of my life in therapy, I've paid for state-of-the-art alarm systems even when I could barely afford rent. But all this time, he was your . . ."

She trails off, and I know it's because she's still trying to understand.

"It doesn't even seem like something a parent could do," she adds.

Now she pulls away a couple inches, but locks her eyes onto mine. They're so green, they look fake. Like some fairy-tale potion. Or poison.

"You and I," she says, "we've both gone through so much. But this is a way for me to have the life I want. If you call the police, our plan will fall apart. They'll know I wasn't taken by the same man as last time. I mean . . . maybe it could be a copycat, but . . ."

She looks at Rita, who shakes her head.

"No," Astrid says. "It would still invite too many questions. And people are already starting to doubt me. I know what they're saying out there, now that they've all read the book. I've seen the stories online, reporting from Foster no less. They're skeptical. They think I might have brought this on myself somehow. Like the first time."

"You didn't bring it on yourself," Rita says. Her words sound flat. Like she's said them many times before. "You were a kid. You know that."

Astrid nods. "I do. But I really thought I had," she says to me, "when

I was in the basement. And I've certainly had moments in the years since, really dark moments where I—" She cuts herself off. Shakes her head. "The bottom line is—we need everyone to believe that the person who took me now is the same one who took me before. The same one who was totally untraceable. If people have reason to doubt that— if the *police* have reason to doubt that—then we, Rita and I, we could go to prison." She takes my hand. Squeezes it twice. "All we're trying to do is be parents."

Her pleas sink inside me. Heavy as an anchor. *All we're trying to do is be parents.* I can almost hear the exact same sentence coming from Ted's mouth, with just a few amendments. *All I'm trying to do is work.*

"Say you won't tell," Astrid begs. "Say you'll be the same sweet girl you always were in the basement. Say we can trust you. We can, Lily— right?"

I flinch. At the name that isn't mine. The description that doesn't fit. *Sweet girl*, she said, and Ted's voice bellows in my head: *Don't you want to be a good girl and help?*

"My name isn't Lily," I seethe. "It's Fern."

There's a surge of adrenaline inside me. A deep swell of anger— something I haven't fully felt until this moment. I've been numbed by the news, stunned by finding Astrid in the last place I'd expect. I've been buried beneath the day's pileup of discoveries—but I can feel myself breaking through.

"And that's not—" I start. "Wanting to be parents—that's not a good enough reason for what you've done."

I stand up. Look down at them both, at their surprised faces that seemed to assume I would just shut up.

"This is illegal," I go on. "It's *fraud.* And don't you . . . do you even care that people are worried about you? That *I've* been sick to death with worry for you? I've done everything to find you. Gone through every possibility. God, I-I even went to your church in Foster! I talked to your priest!"

"Father Murphy?" Rita jumps in. "He's *not* her priest. He's the reason she walked away that day. He's why she was taken in the first place."

"She was taken because my father is a narcissist."

The term flies out of my mouth. No forethought. No warning. But as soon as I hear it, hissing in the air, I know it's true. It's the name for people like Ted—not just a label that means selfish and arrogant, but shorthand for a personality disorder. For someone with a dangerous way of viewing himself and those around him.

"I'm offering you the opportunity to see justice served," I tell Astrid, "for the both of us. So how can you want me to lie? How can you even take such a risk with all this? Just to have a child? You know what the world is like. What can happen. I mean . . ."

I hear my voice softening. It crumbles at the edges. Caves in at the center.

"Aren't you terrified?" I ask. "To bring a child into a world like this?"

Astrid's eyes drill into mine. After a moment, she reaches forward to take my hand. She's tugging, just a little, trying to coax me back down onto the couch. I keep my feet firm.

"The world *is* terrifying," she says. Then she cocks her head to the side. "But don't you think it's beautiful, too? I mean, look at us—we're together. After all these years. We *survived*."

I stare at the freckle. Even now, it's hypnotic. I feel my anger blunting. The sharpness inside me becoming so dull.

"I refuse to be held captive by anything ever again," Astrid says. "Whether it's by a man. Or society. Or my fears of what *could* happen."

She strokes my hand. Her freckle is small but dark. A perfect, unending circle.

"Because fuck fear," she adds. "I'd rather live."

I breathe in slowly. Feel the air pass between my lips like a drink I need to survive.

Could it really be that simple? Just ignore the fear and live? Even if—

"Even if the life you're living is all because of a lie?"

Astrid smiles. Clasps her hand around my wrist.

"I don't think of it as a lie," she says, glancing at Rita. "I think of it as a means to a beautiful end."

I look at her hand. Her grip is gentle. But it's a grip nonetheless. Might as well be a rope.

"That's exactly something my father would say," I tell her. Then I snatch my hand away. "My whole life, he's justified every bad behavior by saying it's in service of his work. Even when it broke my family apart. Even when it broke my heart."

Astrid shakes her head. "There's a huge difference between lying to bring a child into the world and kidnapping someone for . . . for revenge, or for research, or whatever it was. What we're doing—it's not hurting anyone!"

"It's hurting me," I say.

And isn't that enough?

I take a few steps backward, mumbling that I have to go, but I stop when Rita stands and puts her hand on my back.

"Wait," she says, and Astrid stands too. "You're not going to tell the police, are you?"

I stare at Astrid, whose eyes widen as she stares back. For a moment, I see the girl who reached for me, who tried so desperately to save me from the man who dragged me up the stairs.

My throat swells. Becomes hard.

The things Ted did to her. To us. He almost ruined us both. But she's right about one thing. We're here now. Standing together. Two women who survived the same man. Two women trying, each in our own way, to be parents.

We know, better than anyone, that children need protection—and I trust that we will mother them with our eyes wide open.

So do I owe her this, my silence? Is that how I make amends for the terrible things my father did, even if they aren't my amends to make?

"I don't know what I'm going to do," I tell her, and as I head toward the door, Astrid wraps her hand around my arm, tries to pull me back.

I turn my head to look at her, but do not turn my body.

"But we just found each other," she says. "I've thought of you so much, every day, for twenty years. You can't go. Please—say you'll call. Say you'll come back soon."

I see it again in her eyes. The pleading. The girl I saw in dreams. In fragments of memory. I'd love to spend time with that girl again. I'd love to thank her for showing me how strong I want to be. But that girl is a woman now. And she should have known so much better.

I put my hand on hers and watch as her expression blossoms with hope. Her freckle seems to stare at me. A tiny, other eye. Now I pull her fingers off my arm, hold them as tenderly as you would a friend's, and I tell her what I know to be true.

"I'm never coming back here again."

twenty-three

I'm never coming back to Cedar, either.

Ted doesn't believe me when I tell him that. As I gather my things, he smirks in the doorway of my childhood room. "You'll be back," he says.

"I won't," I promise him. Promise myself, too. Because even now, there is a part of me that wants to hug him good-bye. Wants to manufacture a closeness between us. I guess it's hard to stop craving something you've wanted for so long. I guess it's a kind of addiction—grasping for love in the dark.

"Don't you think we should talk first?" he asks.

I slip my toothbrush into my bag, then close my eyes. My back is to him. He can't see how hope, how longing—those old, unreliable drugs—crease my lids as I squeeze them shut.

"About what?" I ask.

I give him this chance. He could say the right thing. Prove himself to be human. And then maybe, for a few more minutes, I'd stay.

"About your memories," he says. "I have so many questions."

Tears rush to the backs of my eyelids. I give myself a moment. Then two. Three. I don't dare open my eyes until the tears have receded. Because now I know for sure: to offer him anything of myself—even my anger, my despair, all the questions of my own that will disturb me forever—is to give him more than he deserves. So I walk away. Hear him follow me down the stairs and out the door. Hear Mara shuffle after us, too.

Soon the two of them are in my rearview mirror, the sun sinking into the trees behind them. At the last second, before I drive on and lose them completely, I see Ted wave.

I have to grip the steering wheel, knuckles white, to keep myself from lifting my hand in return.

Eric knows I'm coming home. I called him on my way back from Astrid's, and he picked up on the first ring. When he realized the magnitude of all I had to tell him, he canceled the rest of his appointments, and we talked until I was close enough to the woods to lose our connection. Eric wanted to call the police immediately, but I asked him to wait. To give me a day, at least, to keep on processing, to figure out which secrets are worth keeping, which people I owe something to. Now, feeling that same old surge of nausea as I drive by the woods, I'm remembering what I already forgot, my realization from a few minutes ago: I don't owe anything to any of those people. I will have to repeat that to myself until it sticks.

As I near the path to the cabin, my instinct is to look away. But instead I turn, and I drive through the trees, swallowing down the bile that crawls up my throat. Cooper's truck is still out front, like I hoped it would be. He's dropping bags of trash into the bed of it, and it's good he's already outside. Now I won't have to enter the cabin to find him. Won't need to step a single foot inside that haunted house.

"Hey," he says when I get out of the car, but it sounds more like a question than a greeting.

I waste no time. I want to get home to Eric.

"It was really messed up, what you did to me yesterday, attacking me like that. It's always been messed up, *especially* when I was a kid. It's never *once* been fun, as you said. Got it?"

He doesn't blink as he looks at me, but after a moment, he nods. "Yeah," he says.

"The reason I was here before?" I continue. "Running away from you like that? It's because I thought you'd kidnapped Astrid Sullivan." He cocks an eyebrow, lets out a baffled chuckle, but I barrel forward. "You told me at The Diner that you're a completely different person now, but you're not, you're still the same. You're—"

"An asshole," Cooper says.

I close my mouth. Open it again. "What?"

He shakes his head. "I swear, I've done so much work on myself over the years." He gazes off into the trees. "Everyone's got their shit to deal with, you know? And the way I acted yesterday? That shit's mine. And I *am* different now, I'm so much better at controlling my impulses, so sometimes I try to act like . . . like the person I used to be never existed. But the past doesn't just go away, you know? It's always there, isn't it?"

I don't answer him. But for my own sake, I'm hoping like hell that he's wrong.

"Anyway," he says, "I'm sorry, okay? About yesterday. And the way I used to treat you. I know I said at The Diner that it's not worth apologizing for, but that was just me trying to ignore the past again. So I'm sorry, Brierley. Really. I felt like shit about it all last night."

The apology stuns me. It's the first one I've heard all day—and it didn't come from Ted, or from Astrid, but from Cooper, of all people. The same man who, days ago, repulsed me with his words at The Diner, still speaking like a twenty-year-old even at forty. But maybe— somehow—he's the most grown-up of all the people who have hurt me.

"Thank you," I say.

I'm about to leave, but my eyes linger on the cabin. I wonder if, soon, the police will be combing through it, looking for evidence of the horrors that happened within its walls. A part of me almost feels guilty that Cooper will lose his project. I can picture the yellow tape now, cordoning off the dilapidated house, labeling it what it was: a crime scene.

As I'm walking back to my car, Cooper calls out to me.

"Hey, Brierley." I turn around. "I solved the mystery, you know. About the drifter."

My chest tightens, remembering his dark clothes. "Oh yeah?"

"Yeah. Turns out he *is* homeless. He's been sleeping in the cabin at night. Which is so dangerous, but . . ." He shrugs. "He gets restless. And bored. So he walks all day. He used to be a cross-country coach, before things turned bad for him."

"And his clothing?" I ask. "The black coat in all this heat?"

Cooper shrugs again. "I don't know. Maybe it's all he's got, and he's afraid of leaving it behind." He reaches for a cigarette tucked behind his ear, pulls out a lighter from his pocket. "Or maybe he runs cold. Either way, I think I'm gonna give him this place once I fix it up. He's a pretty good dude. Really shy. But good."

"You'd give up the money you could get from flipping it?" I ask. The thought seems so strange—a generosity I didn't know him to be capable of.

He puts the cigarette between his lips. Lights it and inhales.

"It's not about the money," he says. I can almost see his words in the smoke he breathes. "It's about strengthening a home from the inside out. Making something beautiful out of everything that's ruined."

It's dark when I get back to Boston, but inside our loft, it's light. Eric springs off the couch as soon as I open the door. Every lamp we own is on.

When he folds me into his arms, I allow myself to let go of everything I've been keeping in. It's a deluge. A hiccupping flood. His shirt is wet from my tears. My cheek is wet from his shirt. He leads me to the couch, and I continue to cry. He holds me as I do.

I cry about Ted. About Astrid. About losing them both on the very same day. And I cry for myself. For the lonely girl I used to be. Who never got the love she wanted. The love she deserved. Not from Ted, anyway.

"I'm sorry, Bird," Eric whispers. "I'm so sorry."

On the third time he says this, I break away to look at him. He gazes back at me, and our hands collide as we lift them to wipe away my tears. He's an excellent husband. An excellent man. I've never doubted that. Not once since the night I met him. The night he cleaned up the puke in a complete stranger's hair.

What a gift it is, to be certain that he loves me. It's a marvel, really. It's a miracle.

"Before we talk about Ted," I say, "I need to tell you something."

I practiced this speech the whole way back from Cedar, but my voice still quakes.

"I want to make you happy," I continue.

"You do make me happy. I love you, Bird."

"No, I know, it's just—growing up, all I wanted to do was make Ted happy. Because when I made him happy, he paid attention to me. But that was . . ." I pluck a tissue from the box on the coffee table. Soak up the tears under my eyes. "I know that was all a part of his manipulation. But it was a hard habit to break—conceding to him, silencing my needs and concerns. Which explains some things about how I've acted with you, I think."

Eric's forehead wrinkles. "Are you saying I'm not attentive enough?"

"No," I'm quick to say. "No, not at all. What I'm saying is . . ." I take a deep breath. "I wasn't ready to start trying for a baby. I was too nervous. Too anxious. I would have liked more time."

Eric's eyes go wide. "I didn't know that. Bird, if I pressured you at all, then I'm—"

"You didn't. And that's the thing—you didn't know because I never told you. Because I was afraid that if I didn't give you what you wanted, then you'd . . ."

"Then I'd what?"

"I don't know. Realize you'd made some big mistake in marrying me, I guess. Realize you wanted to be . . . elsewhere."

He actually laughs. But it's a sweet sound. It's kind.

"That would never happen," he says.

I nod. Look down at the tissue balled in my hand. "I'm sorry I didn't tell you."

"It's okay," he says. "You're telling me now. And we can wait until you're ready. Of course we can."

I meet his eyes again. I don't know if he can see the wince in mine. "Well, that's the thing," I begin. "I lied to you at Ted's. I didn't have my period."

His eyes narrow with confusion, and I rush ahead so I can say it myself before he understands it on his own.

"I'm pregnant. And I didn't know how to deal with that yet, which is why I didn't tell you. I was so scared, because so much can happen to a child. It's such a huge responsibility to keep someone safe, and that's why I was so nervous to start trying in the first place. But I think—I think I can do it. I think I'm stronger than I've given myself credit for. I mean, I'll be paranoid and anxious all the time—that won't change, I'm sure. But I want this baby. I want to have a family. I want to give this child everything I never had growing up. Which is just love, really. And attention. And protection."

His face hasn't moved since I started. His lips are parted a little and I can hear the breath slipping through them. I prepare myself for the possibility of his anger. I lied to him, after all, and you shouldn't lie to the people you love.

"I'm sorry I—" I start. But he cuts me off.

"You're pregnant?"

And there's hope in his voice, not anger. The hope is tentative, though.

"Yes," I say.

He smiles for a moment, his face as bright as the room, but then he stops. Grows serious. "And you're okay with that?"

"I'm terrified," I say. Because I will not lie to my husband again. "But yes. I'm okay with it. I'm actually—"

I don't get to finish my sentence. Eric is up off the couch, pulling me into his arms, laughing as he kisses my forehead, my face, my lips. He has one hand on my cheek, the other cupping the back of my neck. He's an excellent husband. An excellent man. He'll make an excellent father, too. I've been worried about almost everything, but I've never been worried about that.

I try to smile as Eric kisses me, but even in this moment of my husband's uncensored joy, I can't help but think of Ted. Or not Ted, exactly, but everything he's taught me. How the world is full of monsters who pretend to be men. How love is both a right and a responsibility. And most importantly, this: I could never do to my child what my parents did to me. If nothing else, my list of anxiety triggers, my memories I'll work with Dr. Lockwood to keep uncovering, will only help me protect my family from all that is unsafe.

But still. Still.

"I'm terrified," I admit to Eric again.

He looks at me, his eyes shining. Then he nods, suddenly solemn. "Me too," he says.

When he places his hand on my belly, we look down at it together. It's still flat. Still unrecognizable as the stomach of a pregnant woman. But even now, as we gaze at where that baby will be, my body is making space for the life inside me.

We look back at each other, and at the same moment, we laugh. It feels so good after crying, after learning these things I can never unknow. But it feels timid, too. Like uncertainty. Like hope. And now, the laughter surges up and up until it overwhelms me. Until it feels everything and nothing like fear.

acknowledgments

First, I'd like to thank you, the reader. You have brought this story to life simply by investing your time in it. There are so many books in the world, and such limited hours in which to read them, so I am honored that you have taken a chance on mine. I hope you found it worth your time. I hope it made you feel something.

In a similar vein, I'd like to thank all the booksellers, librarians, bookstagrammers, bloggers, and others who work in service of connecting readers with books. Your passion and generosity provide so much joy to authors, and I hope you know that we see you as nothing less than a gift.

Thank you to Sharon Pelletier, my exceptional agent, who calmly handles all my publishing-related anxiety and has guided me into the career I've always dreamed of having. Her enthusiasm for this story, as well as her expert feedback and advice, was exactly the push I needed to believe in it myself.

I am beyond grateful to have had the opportunity to work with my superstar editor, Kaitlin Olson, on another book. She continually pushes me to dig deeper, write better, and deliver a more impactful and nuanced story. Thank you, as well, to the rest of the Atria team, especially Megan Rudloff and Isabel DaSilva.

I have been blown away by the support I've received from my former and current students, and I can't articulate how much it means to me when they buy my books, attend my events, or help spread the word in any number of quiet or exuberant ways. For the past twelve years, I have had the immense privilege of working with young people who continually inspire and challenge me as both a writer and teacher. The opportunity to share this journey with them has been one of the most rewarding aspects of my career. Thank you, with all of my heart.

One of the best parts of being an author is making connections with other writers—and for those I've made within the DA19 group, I am eternally grateful. Over the past couple years, we've become a family of anxiety-ridden, roller-coaster-riding authors, and it's been an honor to get to know these kind and generous people, read their excellent books, and celebrate their many successes. Special thanks to Andrea Bartz, Sarah Blake, Kate Hope Day, Julie Langsdorf, and Angie Kim.

Thank you, as always, to my friends and family, especially my parents, to whom this book is dedicated. With my first book, they transformed into a surprise PR team, talking the novel up to absolute strangers, passing out *The Winter Sister* business cards to waiters and waitresses, my dad's customers, people they met on vacation, always with the same start to their pitch: "Do you like to read?" I have no doubt that they will lovingly badger unsuspecting people about this book as well, and for that I am very thankful and only slightly appalled.

Finally, thank you to my husband, Marc, who by turns acts as my reader, editor, event photographer, and cheerleader. But above all that, he is my best friend and a complete gem. He didn't necessarily sign up for the emotional chaos that comes with being married to a published author, but he has handled it the way he handles everything—with kindness, a rational mind, and unparalleled humor.

Oh, and thank you to my golden retriever, Maisy, who tries very hard to be a supportive writing assistant but usually just sleeps on the job.

about the author

Megan Collins is the author of *The Winter Sister*. She holds an MFA in creative writing from Boston University and is a creative writing teacher at an arts high school. She is also the managing editor of *3Elements Literary Review*. Megan is a Pushcart Prize and Best of the Net nominee and has been published in many literary journals, including *Off the Coast, Spillway, Tinderbox Poetry Journal*, and *Rattle*. She lives in Connecticut.

Turn the page

for an exclusive excerpt

from Megan Collins's latest novel,

The Family Plot

one

My parents named me Dahlia, after the Black Dahlia—that actress whose body was cleaved in half, left in grass as sharp as scalpels, a permanent smile sliced onto her face—and when I first learned her story at four years old, I assumed a knife would one day carve me up. My namesake was part of me, my future doomed by her violent death. That meant my oldest brother, Charlie, who had escaped the Lindbergh baby's fate by living past age two, would still be abducted someday. My sister, Tate, would follow in her own namesake's footsteps, become a movie star, then become a body in a pool of blood. And my twin brother, Andy, named for Lizzie Borden's father—I was sure his head was destined for the ax.

It didn't take me long to shed that belief, to understand that our names were just one of the many ways we honored victims of murder. But even after I stopped expecting us all to be killed, Andy insisted our family was "unnatural," that the way we were raised wasn't right.

I still don't know where he got that idea; back then, the life we lived in our drafty, secluded mansion was the only kind of life we knew.

Now, I'm standing in front of it, the home he ran away from on our sixteenth birthday—two years before we were scheduled to get our inheritance ("Leaving Money," as Charlie called it), and three before I left myself, having waited there, certain my twin would return, for as long as I could. I used to sit at the bottom of the stairs, gaze pinned to the door, hoping he'd walk through it again, tell me all my missing him was for nothing.

I was the only one who missed him. Mom read his note—*The only way out is to never come back*—and swallowed hard. "Your brother's chosen his own path," she said, swiping at her tears as if that was the end of it. Dad stomped around the house for a while, grumbling about the hunting trip Andy had skipped out on. "He's a coward, that twin of yours," Dad told me, as if Andy belonged to me alone. And then there was Charlie and Tate, who were visiting when we found the note. They'd come all this way for our sixteenth birthday, but they left without helping me look for him, Charlie claiming he had an audition, Tate trailing after him like always. Which left just me, alone in my anguish for years after that, lighting the candles with Mom and Dad, saying the Honoring prayer that I've since learned they created themselves.

Dad died the other day. That's why I've come back. And I'm hoping this will be the thing that brings Andy back, too. Maybe he's already inside, listening for my footsteps. Maybe I can stop my internet searches. Every week, I look for my brother on Facebook and Twitter and Instagram. Greta, who runs the café beneath my tiny apartment, has taught me all the tricks on social media, but still, my searches come back each time with nothing.

Today, I took the long way up from the ferry, watching the rocky shore recede below me as I climbed higher toward the center of Blackburn Island, where our house looms stony and colorless in front of the woods. For minutes now, I've been staring at those skeletal trees, remembering how Andy used to whack at them, how he'd pick up his ax whenever something flared inside him—and how almost anything could set him off: Dad quizzing him about hunting rifles; Mom teaching us about Ted Bundy's victims; Tate sketching her namesake, Sharon. For all the hours Andy and I spent locked to each other's hips—hiding in the credenza to jump out at Mom; distracting our groundskeeper with leaf pile forts—I never understood why he'd spring out of the house sometimes and pick up the ax that leaned against the shed. And when he told me, over and over, that our family was unnatural, that we needed the outside world, needed to trust people beyond each other, I didn't understand that, either.

The November wind is icy on the back of my neck, pushing me closer to the front door. Dead leaves skitter around my feet as if welcoming me home.

It's been seven years since I last stepped foot on this porch, even though when I left at nineteen, I didn't go far. My apartment on the mainland is a quarter mile from the ferry, easy access should Andy ever return, but when I first moved there, Greta acted like I was from a distant, mythical place. *I can't believe you grew up on Blackburn Island,* she said. *I'm obsessed with the Blackburn Killer. I have every article that's ever mentioned him, and I spend hours a day on message boards, discussing all the theories. Oh my god, did you know any of the victims?*

I could recite their names in my sleep. Not just the victims of our island's serial killer, who murdered seven women over two decades and was never caught, but the ones from quiet neighborhoods, the ones on city streets. We honored them each year on the anniversaries of their deaths. We uttered their names as we stood in a circle, lighting one another's slim white candles. Then we whispered the prayer—*we can't restore your life, but we strive to restore your memory with this breath*—before blowing out the flames. When I told Greta I didn't know the victims personally, but that they were part of our Honoring calendar, her forehead wrinkled with confusion, and I wondered for the first time if Andy had been right, that there was something unnatural about us.

But is he here now, sitting on the stairs, watching the door from inside as I force myself to turn its knob and finally push it open?

I blink until my eyes adjust. The light outside was dazzling and real, but in here it's dimmer than dusk. The foyer, I see now, is vacant and cavernous; the staircase holds nobody up. The chandelier sways a little, as if something has nudged it, and I have to focus on breathing until the pang of being wrong subsides.

"Look who finally showed up. Tate and I have been here since yesterday."

I turn toward Charlie's voice. Through the wide archway to the right, I see him sitting in the living room, in curtained, lampless dark. I can just make out the glass of amber liquid in his hand. He sips it now, barely ten a.m., before he stands and approaches, burgundy-sweatered and lanky as ever.

"What, you're not a hugger?" he asks with a wink.

He embraces me before I can answer. When he lets go, he takes my bag off my shoulder and slings it over his own, the weight of it tipping him farther than his typical sideways slouch.

"You look good, Dolls," he says. "What's it been—nine years?"

I blink at him like he's another dark room I have to get used to. How can he not know it's been ten years, four months, and three days since we last saw each other? It's easy to remember. You just take the time it's been since we last saw Andy and subtract one day. I suppose, though, that Charlie's tried to see me before now. He's sent me texts over the years, inviting me to his shows—the off-Broadway ones and the *really* off-Broadway ones—but I've never gone. I knew I wouldn't be able to stomach it, watching him pretend to be somebody else. To me, he'll always be the man who read Andy's note—*The only way out is to never come back*—and returned right away to New York. Greta likes to remind me that Charlie was twenty-six at the time, someone with a life already separate from us, but what she doesn't get is that when I talk about Charlie, or Tate, or my parents, I'm not looking for perspective; I'm looking for her to agree that all of them failed my twin.

Now, I tell Charlie exactly how long it's been, and he eyes me strangely before sipping his drink again.

"Where's everyone else?" I ask.

"Tate's playing dutiful daughter to the grieving widow upstairs. And Dad—well, he's in the morgue still, waiting for his Honoring tomorrow."

I skip past the image of our father, cold in a drawer somewhere. "Is that really what we're calling it?" I ask. "An Honoring?"

Charlie's mouth tilts in amusement. "What else would we call it?"

I shrug. "Dad wasn't murdered. It doesn't seem like the Honoring rules would apply."

"Well." He leans in conspiratorially, bourbon on his breath. "The way I hear it, Dad's heart was a real bastard about it. Took him out in two seconds flat. Pushed him facedown in his venison stew." He demonstrates by pitching his head toward the mouth of his glass. "Mom had to wipe the meat off his cheeks before the paramedics came. It's poetic, really. Dad hunted so many deer in his lifetime, and in the end, he died on top of one. Seems almost . . . intentional, doesn't it? Like his heart knew what he'd been up to and murdered him for it."

He's smirking. And his words are wobbly. Tate's warned me about this, through her frequent emails I rarely return. She's said that Charlie's a disturbing drunk.

"That's quite a welcome," I tell him. "Thanks."

He shrugs like it's no problem. Like it isn't appalling, describing our father's death that way. But I don't feel it like the kick in the gut I know

I should. I didn't feel much of anything when I learned of Dad's heart attack. Just sort of an: *Oh. Okay.* I was at the café, looking for traces of Andy in Detroit (I've been working my way through all the major cities again), and Greta overheard me on the phone. She brought me hot chocolate with extra whipped cream and said she was *so, so sorry, god, that's awful, Dahlia.* But actually, the news of Dad's death was, to me, just news. An inevitable update on the time line of my life.

I get why Charlie's acting out, why he's smirky and buzzed. It's a front, I'm sure, for the pain roiling inside him. Charlie actually knew Dad, in ways that I—and I suspect Tate—never did. Dad paid attention to Charlie the same way he paid attention to Andy. All those shooting lessons over the years, those whispered conversations while scoping the woods for the flick of a tail. *I don't know what to do with girls,* Dad confessed once, when I asked why it was only boys who got to go on hunting trips. It's not that I wanted to hunt; I just hated the idea of Andy experiencing something without me. But hearing Dad admit that was a relief. I didn't know what to do with him, either, this man with few words and fewer smiles; with no involvement in our education, not even to watch the murder documentaries Mom showed us; with nothing more than nods of acknowledgment whenever he passed me, as if I were an employee like our groundskeeper, Fritz. I got permission, then, to love Dad less. To not even worry about loving him at all. Which was fine with me. It left more space for Andy.

"Come on," Charlie says. He sets his glass on the credenza, gestures with his chin toward the staircase. "Mom's been waiting for you."

As I follow him up, I glance behind me, still always checking for Andy.

"Don't be rude, Dahlia, say hi to Grandma and Grandpa," Charlie says, throwing me another smirk over his shoulder. And that's fine, if he needs to make this all a joke, but the photos of Mom's parents that line the staircase wall are anything but funny. I know the faces in those frames aren't ghosts—ghosts don't have weddings, don't smoke cigarettes, don't kiss with smiling lips—but they started this, didn't they? Our haunted childhoods. Our haunted lives. And maybe this is what Andy meant when he said our family was unnatural. Because Mom crowded our walls with her murdered parents.

It is unusual, our origin story: Mom moved here at twenty-one, to her family's summer house, immediately after home invaders killed her parents at their Connecticut estate; she married Daniel Lighthouse, an orphan himself, who—for someone who didn't *know what to do with girls*—captivated Mom right away; and Dad indulged her eccentricities, encouraged them even, and did not protest as she turned the mansion into something like a mausoleum.

Before we reach the top of the stairs, I hear footsteps on the landing, and then a gasp. It's Tate, pushing Charlie to the side, rushing to meet me.

"Dahlia!" she says. "What the hell? You're all grown up!"

She laughs like I'm playing a joke on her, like I'll unzip my skin and emerge as the girl I was the last time she saw me. Then she pulls me into a hug so fierce I almost lose my footing.

"Careful, Tate," Charlie says. "Let's not kill our sister, shall we? Mom hardly has any room left in her shrine." He smiles at our grandparents on the wall, as if they're in on the joke.

It's weird, though—these hugs they've both given me, as if we Lighthouse children were a happy foursome of siblings, not divided into pairs by the difference in our ages, by the fact that Andy and I could read each other's minds, and that Tate just worshiped Charlie. She ignores him now, stepping back to examine me again, and she's as striking as ever, wavy blond hair piled on top of her head, wayward curls framing her face. She's wearing a turquoise sweater over a pair of magenta jeans, and she's the first bright thing I've seen since entering this house. That's part of her "brand" now, brightness. When she photographs herself with her dioramas on Instagram, she's always in pink or aqua or yellow. It's contradictory to her depictions of the Blackburn Killer's crime scenes—the dark rocky shores, the obsidian water, those dead women, who, even in their miniature ice-blue dresses, look like shadows flung upon the rocks—but it works somehow.

I wonder if Andy is one of Tate's fifty-seven thousand followers. I wonder if he ever scrolls through the feed of @die_orama, feeling exposed by our sister's art.

The *New York Post* profiled her last year, and Greta taped those pages to the café wall, insisting I was related to "true-crime royalty." When I read the article, I held my breath, unsure how much Tate had shared with the *Post* about our way of life. Greta's the only one I've told about the possibly "unnatural" things from our childhood, details she's both devoured and savored: the library in the back hall, which we dubbed "the victim room," its bookshelves crowded with newspapers reporting on murders; Mom's homeschooling curriculum that required us to write our own "murder reports," in which we presented our theories of unsolved cases in neat five-paragraph essays. (This detail is Greta's favorite; *You were just like me*, she says, *a citizen detective!* At first, I thought she invented that term, until she told me about the network of people online who lose hours each day investigating cases.)

The article didn't mention murder reports, but Tate explained that she felt a kinship with the Blackburn Killer's victims, given that he'd been active on the island while she lived there. More than that, she believed that by re-creating the bodies, right down to the rope marks on the women's necks, the B branded on their ankles, she was returning the focus to the seven people whose lives were cut short, instead of the intrigue of "whatever sick fuck" did the cutting.

In her Instagram posts, Tate never writes how we grew up honoring those seven women on the anniversaries of their deaths, accumulating dates as the years went by, as the killer kept strangling, kept branding, kept dressing his victims in identical ice-blue gowns, and dumping their bodies in shallow water. But whenever I see Tate's dioramas—those intricate, lifelike, bite-size crime scenes—I can't help but feel like she's sharing family secrets.

"You're *so* grown up," Tate tells me again. She turns so she appears in profile and tilts her chin up. "And what about me? How do I look? How's"—she pauses to give a mock grimace—"thirty-five treating me?"

"You look great," I say. But she knows that. In the selfies she posts between dioramas, her followers shower her with praise: *Girl, you're gorgeous; I'd kill for your hair.* They love her style, her dioramas, her captions about each victim—and they love Blackburn, too. The *Post* profile, which quoted people who'd learned of Blackburn through @die_orama, explained that Tate has essentially transformed it into a tourist destination, that the shores where all those women were found are now a draw, not a deterrent. "It's exhilarating," one person said, "standing on land where a real serial killer dumped his bodies."

It's been a decade since the Blackburn Killer last struck, but people on the island still dead bolt their doors—a precaution we never needed. It seemed that no one, not even a serial killer, wanted to slip inside our house. "Murder Mansion," the islanders called it.

"Dahlia. You came."

It's Mom at the top of the stairs this time.

"Of course I came," I say.

She's dressed the same as always—sweats and slippers—but she's paler than I've ever seen her, skin like a crumpled piece of paper some-one's tried to smooth back out.

Mom wraps me in her arms, leaning down to rest her chin on my shoulder. "I'm so glad you're here," she says on a sigh.

Charlie, above us, fidgets with the strap of my bag. "Yes, what a lovely family reunion," he says. "Right where everyone hoped it would take place: on the stairs."

Tate smacks his arm. Mom exhales into my neck, breath heavy with loss. As she hugs me tighter, I feel how potently she's missing Dad. She was like a moth with him, drawn to a light I could never see. When he entered a room, her eyes flew to his face; when he recounted a recent hunting trip, she leaned forward, fluttery with anticipation. He didn't have to say much—usually didn't—and maybe it's because he said so little that she hung on every word, grateful and stunned that he'd spoken to her at all.

"I'm sorry," I say to her.

"About what?" she asks.

"Global warming?" Charlie can't help but quip. "The wage gap? All your fault, Dolls."

Tate smacks him again.

"About Dad," I say.

Mom pulls back to put her hands on either side of my face. Her eyes are puffy and red, cupped by dark pouches. "Don't be sorry about Dad, he didn't suffer at all. It was a quick, natural death. Shocking, and horrible, but the best there is in the end." She strokes my cheek. "Now, if you're going to be sorry about anything . . ."

"Oh, Mom, not again," Tate says.

"What?" I ask.

"She's been guilt-tripping us," Charlie says.

"No." Mom shakes her head. "No guilt trip."

"She's mad," he continues, "that we've stayed away for so long."

"I'm not mad," Mom insists. "I've just missed you, that's all."

Tate puts her arm around Mom's shoulder. "Do I or do I not call you three times a week?" she asks. "And do I or do I not send you all the treats you can only get in Manhattan? You said you loved those chocolates from Moretti's."

"I did love those chocolates," Mom agrees. "I just love you all more."

"Aw. That's sweet," Charlie says, but there's something tart in his tone. "But like we told you yesterday, which I'm sure Dahlia would agree with—" He looks at me meaningfully, urging me to mimic his nod. "We've had to make our way. And that requires distance. Time. I've been gone as long as I lived here, and I'm *still* adjusting to the world."

Mom swivels to face Charlie, her jaw quivering. "I always meant," she says, "to prepare you for that. For the outside world. That's what everything was for."

She extends her arm toward a photo on the wall, one where her parents laugh at some party, each with a cigarette between their fingers, and she caresses the frame slowly. It's a haunted gesture, as if she's trying to touch the past, trying to save her parents from their future.

"What Charlie means," Tate says, cutting him a glance, "is just— There's so much life out there, you know? I had no idea how much! The world is huge with it."

Mom's fingers drop from the frame. Her shoulders slump.

"And in a way," Tate adds, squeezing Mom closer, "I appreciate it more, I think, because of everything you taught us. Don't you agree, Dahlia?"

Tate's eyes lock onto mine, and they're so blue, so hypnotic, that I find myself nodding. But then I remember Mom's response to Andy's runaway note—*Your brother's chosen his own path*—and I don't know why I'm bothering to comfort her. She's never cared before if we stayed away, and I still haven't forgiven her for that, for giving Andy up so easily.

The fact is, we all had our reasons for never coming back. Charlie claimed he needed to stay close to the city, be ready at the drop of a hat for whatever new role might open up. And because Charlie didn't return to Blackburn, Tate didn't either. *Codependent*, Greta tsked when I told her how they've lived together in the same Manhattan walk-up ever since they both got their inheritance. And me, I lasted only three years in the house without Andy, done with dodging the shadows that piled up like dust bunnies in every corner. But what about him? He left without telling me why, without even saying goodbye, and I've had to live all these years in the not knowing, which is a lonely, comfortless place.

I know he was troubled by things I wasn't. I know he took his ax to the trees in the woods—not to cut them down, but to wound them, scar them, to make them carry something on their bark he couldn't hold inside him anymore. I know his emotions ran hot and hard; he was quick to anger, frustration. But what was it that made him run? I don't believe—I've never believed—that our "unnatural" life was enough of a reason. I haven't forgiven our family for letting him go, and I haven't forgiven him, either, for going.

"I'm just glad you're here now," Mom says to us. "The circumstances are dreadful, of course, but I'm happy to have all my children back home."

All?

Did she really just say all?

"Did you—"

But I'm cut off by a shout bursting through the back door.

"Mrs. Lighthouse! Mrs. Lighthouse!"

The urgency in Fritz's voice prickles the hair on the back of my neck.

He's limps into the foyer, quick as a man nearing eighty can. His right leg—the bad one—drags a little, and his long, milky hair is streaked with dirt.

Mom rushes down the stairs to meet him. "What is it?" she asks.

Charlie, Tate, and I clomp down as well, and when Fritz spots me, he does a double take. "You came," he says, breathy from running, from shouting.

"Of course I came," I say, for the second time. "What's going on?"

"It's . . . Outside, I . . ."

He trails off, prompting Charlie to roll his eyes. "What is it? Is everything o-*kay*?" And I remember this now—how Charlie used to speak to Fritz as if he were dumb.

"No. N-n-no," Fritz stammers, his focus still on Mom. "I was in the woods out back, digging up Mr. Lighthouse's plot, and—"

"We're burying him *here*?" Charlie asks Mom.

"Of course. They'll transport him when we're ready."

"But— Isn't that a bit . . . ghoulish?" Charlie asks. And it's a strange question, given our lives.

Mom's shoulders roll back as if he's offended her. "Not at all. That's where my parents are buried. It's the family plot. We put in stones for your father and me."

"Um, guys?" Tate says. She gestures to Fritz, whose eyes are wide, seemingly all pupil.

"I don't know what . . ." our groundskeeper starts. "Or-or *how*, but somebody's already . . ."

"Already what? Spit it out!" Charlie booms, plucking his bourbon off the credenza.

Fritz swallows then, throat bobbing in his neck like all those actors in the crime scene reenactments we saw, their fear looking hard and bulbous inside them. It makes me swallow, too, makes me rub at the hair still rising on the back of my neck. But when Fritz speaks again, his voice doesn't waver.

"Somebody's already buried in Mr. Lighthouse's plot. And I think—" Fritz shifts his gaze to me. "I think it's Andy."

Discover more
CHILLING SUSPENSE
from MEGAN COLLINS

Available wherever books are sold or at
SimonandSchuster.com